THE REFUGEES
A Tale Of Two Continents

by

A. Conan Doyle

Double 9
BOOKS

THE REFUGEES
A Tale Of Two Continents
by A. Conan Doyle

ISBN: 978-93-58012-28-6

Published by

DOUBLE 9 BOOKS

2/13-B, Ansari Road
Daryaganj, New Delhi – 110002
info@double9books.com
www.double9books.com
Tel. 011-40042856

ABOUT THE AUTHOR

Doyle is also known as Sir Arthur Conan Doyle" or "Conan Doyle", suggesting that "Conan" is the part of the title of his compound name. He got baptized in St Mary's Cathedral, Edinburgh. After baptism, he got the name "Arthur Ignatius Conan" and "Doyle" as his last name. Many other names like Michael Conan were regarded as his godfather. The indexes of the British Library and the Library of Congress treat "Doyle" alone as his last name.

Doyle was born on 22 May 1859 at 11 Picardy Place, Edinburgh, Scotland. His father, Charles Altamont Doyle, settled in England, of Irish Catholic plummet, and his mother, Mary (née Foley), was Irish Catholic. His parents got married in 1855. In 1864, the family dissipated due to Charles' developing liquor addiction, and the children were briefly housed across Edinburgh. Arthur stayed with Mary Burton, the aunt of a companion, at Liberton Bank House on Gilmer ton Road and continued studying at Newington Academy.

Sir Arthur Ignatius Conan was a British essayist and doctor. He was the man behind the creation of the famous fictional detective, Sherlock Holmes in 1887 for 'A Study in Scarlet'. He had written four books and 56 brief tales about Holmes and Dr. Watson. The Sherlock Holmes stories are achievements in the field of thriller fiction.Doyle was a famous essayist. Other than Holmes stories, his works include fantasy and sci-fi anecdotes about Professor Challenger and hilarious tales about the Napoleonic fighter Brigadier Gerard, as well as plays.

CONTENTS

PART I.
IN THE OLD WORLD.

CHAPTER I.
THE MAN FROM AMERICA.

It was the sort of window which was common in Paris about the end of the seventeenth century. It was high, mullioned, with a broad transom across the centre, and above the middle of the transom a tiny coat of arms—three caltrops gules upon a field argent—let into the diamond-paned glass. Outside there projected a stout iron rod, from which hung a gilded miniature of a bale of wool which swung and squeaked with every puff of wind. Beyond that again were the houses of the other side, high, narrow, and prim, slashed with diagonal wood-work in front, and topped with a bristle of sharp gables and corner turrets. Between were the cobble-stones of the Rue St. Martin and the clatter of innumerable feet.

Inside, the window was furnished with a broad bancal of brown stamped Spanish leather, where the family might recline and have an eye from behind the curtains on all that was going forward in the busy world beneath them. Two of them sat there now, a man and a woman, but their backs were turned to the spectacle, and their faces to the large and richly furnished room. From time to time they stole a glance at each other, and their eyes told that they needed no other sight to make them happy.

Nor was it to be wondered at, for they were a well-favoured pair. She was very young, twenty at the most, with a face which was pale, indeed, and yet of a brilliant pallor, which was so clear and fresh, and carried with it such a suggestion of purity and innocence, that one would not wish its maiden grace to be marred by an intrusion of colour. Her features were delicate and sweet, and her blue-black hair and long dark eyelashes formed a piquant contrast to her dreamy gray eyes and her ivory skin. In her whole expression there was something quiet and subdued, which was accentuated by her simple dress of black taffeta, and by the little jet brooch and bracelet which were her sole ornaments. Such was Adele Catinat, the only daughter of the famous Huguenot cloth-merchant.

But if her dress was sombre, it was atoned for by the magnificence of her companion. He was a man who might have been ten years her senior, with a keen soldier face, small well-marked features, a carefully trimmed black moustache, and a dark hazel eye which might harden to command a man, or soften to supplicate a woman, and be successful at either. His coat was of sky-blue, slashed across with silver braidings, and with broad silver shoulder-straps on either side. A vest of white calamanca peeped out from beneath it, and knee-breeches of the same disappeared into high polished boots with gilt spurs upon the heels. A silver-hilted rapier and a plumed cap lying upon a settle beside him completed a costume which was a badge of honour to the wearer, for any Frenchman would have recognised it as being that of an officer in the famous Blue Guard of Louis the Fourteenth. A trim, dashing soldier he looked, with his curling black hair and well-poised head. Such he had proved himself before now in the field, too, until the name of Amory de Catinat had become conspicuous among the thousands of the valiant lesser *noblesse* who had flocked into the service of the king.

They were first cousins, these two, and there was just sufficient resemblance in the clear-cut features to recall the relationship. De Catinat was sprung from a noble Huguenot family, but having lost his parents early he had joined the army, and had worked his way without influence and against all odds to his present position. His father's younger brother, however, finding every path to fortune barred to him through the persecution to which men of his faith were already subjected, had dropped the "de" which implied his noble descent, and he had taken to trade in the city of Paris, with such success that he was now one of the richest and most prominent citizens of the town. It was under his roof that the guardsman now sat, and it was his only daughter whose white hand he held in his own.

"Tell me, Adele," said he, "why do you look troubled?"

"I am not troubled, Amory,"

"Come, there is just one little line between those curving brows. Ah, I can read you, you see, as a shepherd reads the sky."

"It is nothing, Amory, but—"

"But what?"

"You leave me this evening."

"But only to return to-morrow."

"And must you really, really go to-night?"

"It would be as much as my commission is worth to be absent. Why, I am on duty to-morrow morning outside the king's bedroom! After chapel-time Major de Brissac will take my place, and then I am free once more."

"Ah, Amory, when you talk of the king and the court and the grand ladies, you fill me with wonder."

"And why with wonder?"

"To think that you who live amid such splendour should stoop to the humble room of a mercer."

"Ah, but what does the room contain?"

"There is the greatest wonder of all. That you who pass your days amid such people, so beautiful, so witty, should think me worthy of your love, me, who am such a quiet little mouse, all alone in this great house, so shy and so backward! It is wonderful!"

"Every man has his own taste," said her cousin, stroking the tiny hand. "It is with women as with flowers. Some may prefer the great brilliant sunflower, or the rose, which is so bright and large that it must ever catch the eye. But give me the little violet which hides among the mosses, and yet is so sweet to look upon, and sheds its fragrance round it. But still that line upon your brow, dearest."

"I was wishing that father would return."

"And why? Are you so lonely, then?"

Her pale face lit up with a quick smile. "I shall not be lonely until to-night. But I am always uneasy when he is away. One hears so much now of the persecution of our poor brethren."

"Tut! my uncle can defy them."

"He has gone to the provost of the Mercer Guild about this notice of the quartering of the dragoons."

"Ah, you have not told me of that."

"Here it is." She rose and took up a slip of blue paper with a red seal dangling from it which lay upon the table. His strong, black brows knitted together as he glanced at it.

"Take notice," it ran, "that you, Theophile Catinat, cloth-mercer of the Rue St. Martin, are hereby required to give shelter and rations to twenty men of the Languedoc Blue Dragoons under Captain Dalbert, until such time as you receive a further notice. [Signed] De Beaupre (Commissioner of the King)."

De Catinat knew well how this method of annoying Huguenots had been practised all over France, but he had flattered himself that his own position at court would have insured his kinsman from such an outrage. He threw the paper down with an exclamation of anger.

"When do they come?"

"Father said to-night."

"Then they shall not be here long. To-morrow I shall have an order to remove them. But the sun has sunk behind St. Martin's Church, and I should already be upon my way."

"No, no; you must not go yet."

"I would that I could give you into your father's charge first, for I fear to leave you alone when these troopers may come. And yet no excuse will avail me if I am not at Versailles. But see, a horseman has stopped before the door. He is not in uniform. Perhaps he is a messenger from your father."

The girl ran eagerly to the window, and peered out, with her hand resting upon her cousin's silver-corded shoulder.

"Ah!" she cried, "I had forgotten. It is the man from America. Father said that he would come to-day."

"The man from America!" repeated the soldier, in a tone of surprise, and they both craned their necks from the window. The horseman, a sturdy, broad-shouldered young man, clean-shaven and crop-haired, turned his long, swarthy face and his bold features in their direction as he ran his eyes over the front of the house. He had a soft-brimmed gray hat of a shape which was strange to Parisian eyes, but his sombre clothes and high boots were such as any citizen might have worn. Yet his general appearance was so unusual that a group of townsfolk had already assembled round him, staring with open mouth at his horse and himself. A battered gun with an extremely long barrel was fastened by the stock to his stirrup, while the muzzle stuck up into the air behind him. At each holster was a large dangling black bag, and a gaily coloured red-slashed blanket was rolled up at the back of his saddle. His horse, a strong-limbed dapple-gray, all shiny with sweat above, and all caked with mud beneath, bent its fore knees as it stood, as though it were overspent. The rider, however, having satisfied himself as to the house, sprang lightly out of his saddle, and disengaging his gun, his blanket, and his bags, pushed his way unconcernedly through the gaping crowd and knocked loudly at the door.

"Who is he, then?" asked De Catinat. "A Canadian? I am almost one myself. I had as many friends on one side of the sea as on the other. Perchance I know him. There are not so many white faces yonder, and in two years there was scarce one from the Saguenay to Nipissing that I had not seen."

"Nay, he is from the English provinces, Amory. But he speaks our tongue. His mother was of our blood."

"And his name?"

"Is Amos—Amos—ah, those names! Yes, Green, that was it—Amos Green. His father and mine have done much trade together, and now his son, who, as I understand, has lived ever in the woods, is sent here to see something of men and cities. Ah, my God! what can have happened now?"

A sudden chorus of screams and cries had broken out from the passage beneath, with the shouting of a man and the sound of rushing steps. In an instant De Catinat was half-way down the stairs, and was staring in amazement at the scene in the hall beneath.

Two maids stood, screaming at the pitch of their lungs, at either side. In the centre the aged man-servant Pierre, a stern old Calvinist, whose dignity had never before been shaken, was spinning round, waving his arms, and roaring so that he might have been heard at the Louvre. Attached to the gray worsted stocking which covered his fleshless calf was a fluffy black hairy ball, with one little red eye glancing up, and the gleam of two white teeth where it held its grip. At the shrieks, the young stranger, who had gone out to his horse, came rushing back, and plucking the creature off, he slapped it twice across the snout, and plunged it head-foremost back into the leather bag from which it had emerged.

"It is nothing," said he, speaking in excellent French; "it is only a bear."

"Ah, my God!" cried Pierre, wiping the drops from his brow. "Ah, it has aged me five years! I was at the door, bowing to monsieur, and in a moment it had me from behind."

"It was my fault for leaving the bag loose. The creature was but pupped the day we left New York, six weeks come Tuesday. Do I speak with my father's friend, Monsieur Catinat?"

"No, monsieur," said the guardsman, from the staircase. "My uncle is out, but I am Captain de Catinat, at your service, and here is Mademoiselle Catinat, who is your hostess."

The stranger ascended the stair, and paid his greetings to them both with the air of a man who was as shy as a wild deer, and yet who had steeled himself to carry a thing through. He walked with them to the sitting-room, and then in an instant was gone again, and they heard his feet thudding upon the stairs. Presently he was back, with a lovely glossy skin in his hands. "The bear is for your father, mademoiselle," said he. "This little skin I have brought from America for you. It is but a trifle, and yet it may serve to make a pair of mocassins or a pouch."

Adele gave a cry of delight as her hands sank into the depths of its softness. She might well admire it, for no king in the world could have had a finer skin. "Ah, it is beautiful, monsieur," she cried; "and what creature is it? and where did it come from?"

"It is a black fox. I shot it myself last fall up near the Iroquois villages at Lake Oneida."

She pressed it to her cheek, her white face showing up like marble against its absolute blackness. "I am sorry my father is not here to welcome you, monsieur," she said; "but I do so very heartily in his place. Your room is above. Pierre will show you to it, if you wish."

"My room? For what?"

"Why, monsieur, to sleep in!"

"And must I sleep in a room?"

De Catinat laughed at the gloomy face of the American.

"You shall not sleep there if you do not wish," said he.

The other brightened at once and stepped across to the further window, which looked down upon the court-yard. "Ah," he cried. "There is a beech-tree there, mademoiselle, and if I might take my blanket out yonder, I should like it better than any room. In winter, indeed, one must do it, but in summer I am smothered with a ceiling pressing down upon me."

"You are not from a town then?" said De Catinat.

"My father lives in New York—two doors from the house of Peter Stuyvesant, of whom you must have heard. He is a very hardy man, and he can do it, but I—even a few days of Albany or of Schenectady are enough for me. My life has been in the woods."

"I am sure my father would wish you to sleep where you like and to do what you like, as long as it makes you happy."

"I thank you, mademoiselle. Then I shall take my things out there, and I shall groom my horse."

"Nay, there is Pierre."

"I am used to doing it myself."

"Then I will come with you," said De Catinat, "for I would have a word with you. Until to-morrow, then, Adele, farewell!"

"Until to-morrow, Amory."

The two young men passed downstairs together, and the guardsman followed the American out into the yard.

"You have had a long journey," he said.

"Yes; from Rouen."

"Are you tired?"

"No; I am seldom tired."

"Remain with the lady, then, until her father comes back."

"Why do you say that?"

"Because I have to go, and she might need a protector."

The stranger said nothing, but he nodded, and throwing off his black coat, set to work vigorously rubbing down his travel-stained horse.

CHAPTER II.
A MONARCH IN DESHABILLE.

It was the morning after the guardsman had returned to his duties. Eight o'clock had struck on the great clock of Versailles, and it was almost time for the monarch to rise. Through all the long corridors and frescoed passages of the monster palace there was a subdued hum and rustle, with a low muffled stir of preparation, for the rising of the king was a great state function in which many had a part to play. A servant with a steaming silver saucer hurried past, bearing it to Monsieur de St. Quentin, the state barber. Others, with clothes thrown over their arms, bustled down the passage which led to the ante-chamber. The knot of guardsmen in their gorgeous blue and silver coats straightened themselves up and brought their halberds to attention, while the young officer, who had been looking wistfully out of the window at some courtiers who were laughing and chatting on the terraces, turned sharply upon his heel, and strode over to the white and gold door of the royal bedroom.

He had hardly taken his stand there before the handle was very gently turned from within, the door revolved noiselessly upon its hinges, and a man slid silently through the aperture, closing it again behind him.

"Hush!" said he, with his finger to his thin, precise lips, while his whole clean-shaven face and high-arched brows were an entreaty and a warning. "The king still sleeps."

The words were whispered from one to another among the group who had assembled outside the door. The speaker, who was Monsieur Bontems, head *valet de Chambre*, gave a sign to the officer of the guard, and led him into the window alcove from which he had lately come.

"Good-morning, Captain de Catinat," said he, with a mixture of familiarity and respect in his manner.

"Good-morning, Bontems. How has the king slept?"

"Admirably."

"But it is his time."

"Hardly."

"You will not rouse him yet?"

"In seven and a half minutes." The valet pulled out the little round watch which gave the law to the man who *was* the law to twenty millions of people.

"Who commands at the main guard?"

"Major de Brissac."

"And you will be here?"

"For four hours I attend the king."

"Very good. He gave me some instructions for the officer of the guard, when he was alone last night after the *petit coucher*. He bade me to say that Monsieur de Vivonne was not to be admitted to the *grand lever*. You are to tell him so."

"I shall do so."

"Then, should a note come from *her*—you understand me, the new one—"

"Madame de Maintenon?"

"Precisely. But it is more discreet not to mention names. Should she send a note, you will take it and deliver it quietly when the king gives you an opportunity."

"It shall be done."

"But if the other should come, as is possible enough—the other, you understand me, the former—"

"Madame de Montespan."

"Ah, that soldierly tongue of yours, captain! Should she come, I say, you will gently bar her way, with courteous words, you understand, but on no account is she to be permitted to enter the royal room."

"Very good, Bontems."

"And now we have but three minutes."

He strode through the rapidly increasing group of people in the corridor with an air of proud humility as befitted a man who, if he was a valet, was at least the king of valets, by being the valet of the king. Close by the door stood a line of footmen, resplendent in their powdered wigs, red plush coats, and silver shoulder knots.

"Is the officer of the oven here?" asked Bontems.

"Yes, sir," replied a functionary who bore in front of him an enamelled tray heaped with pine shavings.

"The opener of the shutters?"

"Here, sir."

"The remover of the taper?"

"Here, sir."

"Be ready for the word." He turned the handle once more, and slipped into the darkened room.

It was a large square apartment, with two high windows upon the further side, curtained across with priceless velvet hangings. Through the chinks the morning sun shot a few little gleams, which widened as they crossed the room to break in bright blurs of light upon the primrose-tinted wall. A large arm-chair stood by the side of the burnt-out fire, shadowed over by the huge marble mantel-piece, the back of which was carried up twining and curving into a thousand arabesque and armorial devices until it blended with the richly painted ceiling. In one corner a narrow couch with a rug thrown across it showed where the faithful Bontems had spent the night.

In the very centre of the chamber there stood a large four-post bed, with curtains of Gobelin tapestry looped back from the pillow. A square of polished rails surrounded it, leaving a space some five feet in width all round between the enclosure and the bedside. Within this enclosure, or *ruelle*, stood a small round table, covered over with a white napkin, upon which lay a silver platter and an enamelled cup, the one containing a little Frontiniac wine and water, the other bearing three slices of the breast of a chicken, in case the king should hunger during the night.

As Bontems passed noiselessly across the room, his feet sinking into the moss-like carpet, there was the heavy close smell of sleep in the air, and he could near the long thin breathing of the sleeper. He passed through the opening in the rails, and stood, watch in hand, waiting for the exact instant when the iron routine of the court demanded that the monarch should be roused. Beneath him, from under the costly green coverlet of Oriental silk, half buried in the fluffy Valenciennes lace which edged the pillow, there protruded a round black bristle of close-cropped hair, with the profile of a curving nose and petulant lip outlined against the white background. The valet snapped his watch, and bent over the sleeper.

"I have the honour to inform your Majesty that it is half-past eight," said he.

"Ah!" The king slowly opened his large dark-brown eyes, made the sign of the cross, and kissed a little dark reliquary which he drew from under his night-dress. Then he sat up in bed, and blinked about him with the air of a man who is collecting his thoughts.

"Did you give my orders to the officer of the guard, Bontems?" he asked.

"Yes, sire."

"Who is on duty?"

"Major de Brissac at the main guard, and Captain de Catinat in the corridor."

"De Catinat! Ah, the young man who stopped my horse at Fontainebleau. I remember him. You may give the signal, Bontems."

The chief valet walked swiftly across to the door and threw it open. In rushed the officer of the ovens and the four red-coated, white-wigged footmen, ready-handed, silent-footed, each intent upon his own duties. The one seized upon Bontem's rug and couch, and in an instant had whipped them off into an ante-chamber, another had carried away the *en cas* meal and the silver taper-stand; while a third drew back the great curtains of stamped velvet and let a flood of light into the apartment. Then, as the flames were already flickering among the pine shavings in the fireplace, the officer of the ovens placed two round logs crosswise above them, for the morning air was chilly, and withdrew with his fellow-servants.

They were hardly gone before a more august group entered the bed-chamber. Two walked together in front, the one a youth little over twenty years of age, middle-sized, inclining to stoutness, with a slow, pompous bearing, a well-turned leg, and a face which was comely enough in a mask-like fashion, but which was devoid of any shadow of expression, except perhaps of an occasional lurking gleam of mischievous humour. He was richly clad in plum-coloured velvet, with a broad band of blue silk; across his breast, and the glittering edge of the order of St. Louis protruding from under it. His companion was a man of forty, swarthy, dignified, and solemn, in a plain but rich dress of black silk, with slashes of gold at the neck and sleeves. As the pair faced the king there was sufficient resemblance between the three faces to show that they were of one blood, and to enable a stranger to guess that the older was Monsieur, the younger brother of the king, while the other was Louis the Dauphin, his only legitimate child, and heir to a throne to which in the strange workings of Providence neither he nor his sons were destined to ascend.

Strong as was the likeness between the three faces, each with the curving Bourbon nose, the large full eye, and the thick Hapsburg under-lip, their common heritage from Anne of Austria, there was still a vast difference of temperament and character stamped upon their features. The king was now in his six-and-fortieth year, and the cropped black head was already thinning a little on the top, and shading away to gray over the temples. He still, however, retained much of the beauty of his youth, tempered by the dignity and sternness which increased with his years. His dark eyes were full of expression, and his clear-cut features were the delight of the sculptor and the painter. His firm and yet sensitive mouth and his thick, well-arched brows gave an air of authority and power to his face, while the more subdued expression which was habitual to his brother marked the man whose whole life had been spent in one long exercise of deference and self-effacement. The dauphin, on the other hand, with a more regular face than his father, had none of that quick play of feature when excited, or that kingly serenity when composed, which had made a shrewd observer say that Louis, if he were not the greatest monarch that ever lived, was at least the best fitted to act the part.

Behind the king's son and the king's brother there entered a little group of notables and of officials whom duty had called to this daily ceremony. There was the grand master of the robes, the first lord of the bed-chamber, the Duc du Maine, a pale youth clad in black velvet, limping heavily with his left leg, and his little brother, the young Comte de Toulouse, both of them the illegitimate sons of Madame de Montespan and the king. Behind them, again, was the first valet of the wardrobe, followed by Fagon, the first physician, Telier, the head surgeon, and three pages in scarlet and gold who bore the royal clothes. Such were the partakers in the family entry, the highest honour which the court of France could aspire to.

Bontems had poured on the king's hands a few drops of spirits of wine, catching them again in a silver dish; and the first lord of the bedchamber had presented the bowl of holy water with which he made the sign of the cross, muttering to himself the short office of the Holy Ghost. Then, with a nod to his brother and a short word of greeting to the dauphin and to the Due du Maine, he swung his legs over the side of the bed and sat in his long silken night-dress, his little white feet dangling from beneath it—a perilous position for any man to assume, were it not that he had so heart-felt a sense of his own dignity that he could not realise that under any circumstances it might be compromised in the eyes of others. So he sat, the master of France, yet the slave to every puff of wind, for a wandering draught had set him shivering and shaking. Monsieur de St. Quentin, the noble barber, flung a purple dressing-gown over the royal shoulders, and placed a long many-curled court wig upon his head, while Bontems drew on his red stockings and laid before him his slippers of embroidered velvet. The monarch thrust his feet into them, tied his dressing-gown, and passed out to the fireplace, where he settled himself down in his easy-chair, holding out his thin delicate hands towards the blazing logs, while the others stood round in a semicircle, waiting for the *grand lever* which was to follow.

"How is this, messieurs?" the king asked suddenly, glancing round him with a petulant face. "I am conscious of a smell of scent. Surely none of you would venture to bring perfume into the presence, knowing, as you must all do, how offensive it is to me."

The little group glanced from one to the other with protestations of innocence. The faithful Bontems, however, with his stealthy step, had passed along behind them, and had detected the offender.

"My lord of Toulouse, the smell comes from you," he said.

The Comte de Toulouse, a little ruddy-cheeked lad, flushed up at the detection.

"If you please, sire, it is possible that Mademoiselle de Grammont may have wet my coat with her casting-bottle when we all played together at Marly yesterday," he stammered. "I had not observed it, but if it offends your Majesty—"

"Take it away! take it away!" cried the king. "Pah! it chokes and stifles me! Open the lower casement, Bontems. No; never heed, now that he is gone. Monsieur de St. Quentin, is not this our shaving morning?"

"Yes, sire; all is ready."

"Then why not proceed? It is three minutes after the accustomed time. To work, sir; and you, Bontems, give word for the *grand lever*."

It was obvious that the king was not in a very good humour that morning. He darted little quick questioning glances at his brother and at his sons, but whatever complaint or sarcasm may have trembled upon his lips, was effectually stifled by De St. Quentin's ministrations. With the nonchalance born of long custom, the official covered the royal chin with soap, drew the razor swiftly round it, and sponged over the surface with spirits of wine. A nobleman then helped to draw on the king's black velvet *haut-de-chausses*, a second assisted in arranging them, while a third drew the night-gown over the shoulders, and handed the royal shirt, which had been warming before the fire. His diamond-buckled shoes, his gaiters, and his scarlet inner vest were successively fastened by noble courtiers, each keenly jealous of his own privilege, and over the vest was placed the blue ribbon with the cross of the Holy Ghost in diamonds, and that of St. Louis tied with red. To one to whom the sight was new, it might have seemed strange to see the little man, listless, passive, with his eyes fixed thoughtfully on the burning logs, while this group of men, each with a historic name, bustled round him, adding a touch here and a touch there, like a knot of children with a favourite doll. The black undercoat was drawn on, the cravat of rich lace adjusted, the loose overcoat secured, two handkerchiefs of costly point carried forward upon an enamelled saucer, and thrust by separate officials into each side pocket, the silver and ebony cane laid to hand, and the monarch was ready for the labours of the day.

During the half-hour or so which had been occupied in this manner there had been a constant opening and closing of the chamber door, and a muttering of names from the captain of the guard to the attendant in charge, and from the attendant in charge to the first gentleman of the chamber, ending always in the admission of some new visitor. Each as he entered bowed profoundly three times, as a salute to majesty, and then attached himself to his own little clique or coterie, to gossip in a low voice over the news, the weather, and the plans of the day. Gradually the numbers increased, until by the time the king's frugal first breakfast of bread and twice watered wine had been carried in, the large square chamber was quite filled with a throng of men many of whom had helped to make the epoch the most illustrious of French history. Here, close by the king, was the harsh but energetic Louvois, all-powerful now since the death of his rival Colbert, discussing a question of military organisation with two officers, the one a tall and stately soldier, the other a strange little figure, undersized and misshapen, but bearing the insignia of a marshal of France, and owning a name which was of evil omen over the Dutch frontier, for Luxembourg was looked upon already as the successor of Conde, even as his companion Vauban was of Turenne. Beside them, a small white-haired clerical with a kindly face, Pere la Chaise, confessor to the king, was whispering his views upon Jansenism to the portly Bossuet, the eloquent Bishop of Meaux, and to the tall thin young Abbe de Fenelon, who listened with a clouded brow, for it was suspected that his own opinions were tainted with the heresy in question. There, too, was Le Brun, the painter, discussing art in a small circle which contained his fellow-workers Verrio and Laguerre, the architects Blondel and Le Notre, and sculptors Girardon, Puget, Desjardins, and Coysevox, whose works had done so much to beautify the new palace of the king. Close to the door, Racine, with his handsome face wreathed in smiles, was chatting with the poet Boileau and the architect Mansard, the three laughing and jesting with the freedom which was natural to the favourite servants of the king, the only subjects who might walk unannounced and without ceremony into and out of his chamber.

"What is amiss with him this morning?" asked Boileau in a whisper, nodding his head in the direction of the royal group. "I fear that his sleep has not improved his temper."

"He becomes harder and harder to amuse," said Racine, shaking his head. "I am to be at Madame De Maintenon's room at three to see whether a page or two of the *Phedre* may not work a change."

"My friend," said the architect, "do you not think that madame herself might be a better consoler than your *Phedre*?"

"Madame is a wonderful woman. She has brains, she has heart, she has tact—she is admirable."

"And yet she has one gift too many."

"And that is?"

"Age."

"Pooh! What matter her years when she can carry them like thirty? What an eye! What an arm! And besides, my friends, he is not himself a boy any longer."

"Ah, but that is another thing."

"A man's age is an incident, a woman's a calamity."

"Very true. But a young man consults his eye, and an older man his ear. Over forty, it is the clever tongue which wins; under it, the pretty face."

"Ah, you rascal! Then you have made up your mind that five-and-forty years with tact will hold the field against nine-and-thirty with beauty. Well, when your lady has won, she will doubtless remember who were the first to pay court to her."

"But I think that you are wrong, Racine."

"Well, we shall see."

"And if you are wrong—"

"Well, what then?"

"Then it may be a little serious for you."

"And why?"

"The Marquise de Montespan has a memory."

"Her influence may soon be nothing more."

"Do not rely too much upon it, my friend. When the Fontanges came up from Provence, with her blue eyes and her copper hair, it was in every man's mouth that Montespan had had her day. Yet Fontanges is six feet under a church crypt, and the marquise spent two hours with the king last week. She has won once, and may again."

"Ah, but this is a very different rival. This is no slip of a country girl, but the cleverest woman in France."

"Pshaw, Racine, you know our good master well, or you should, for you seem to have been at his elbow since the days of the Fronde. Is he a man, think you, to be amused forever by sermons, or to spend his days at the feet of a lady of that age, watching her at her tapestry-work, and fondling her poodle, when all the fairest faces and brightest eyes of France are as thick in his *salons* as the tulips in a Dutch flower-bed? No, no, it will be the Montespan, or if not she, some younger beauty."

"My dear Boileau, I say again that her sun is setting. Have you not heard the news?"

"Not a word."

"Her brother, Monsieur de Vivonne, has been refused the *entre*."

"Impossible!"

"But it is a fact."

"And when?"

"This very morning."

"From whom had you it?"

"From De Catinat, the captain of the guard. He had his orders to bar the way to him."

"Ha! then the king does indeed mean mischief. That is why his brow is so cloudy this morning, then. By my faith, if the marquise has the spirit with which folk credit her, he may find that it was easier to win her than to slight her."

"Ay; the Mortemarts are no easy race to handle."

"Well, heaven send him a safe way out of it! But who is this gentleman? His face is somewhat grimmer than those to which the court is accustomed. Ha! the king catches sight of him, and Louvois beckons to him to advance. By my faith, he is one who would be more at his ease in a tent than under a painted ceiling."

The stranger who had attracted Racine's attention was a tall thin man, with a high aquiline nose, stern fierce gray eyes, peeping out from under tufted brows, and a countenance so lined and marked by age, care, and stress of weather that it stood out amid the prim courtier faces which surrounded it as an old hawk might in a cage of birds of gay plumage. He was clad in a sombre-coloured suit which had become usual at court since the king had put aside frivolity and Fontanges, but the sword which hung from his waist was no fancy rapier, but a good brass-hilted blade in a stained leather-sheath, which showed every sign of having seen hard service. He had been standing near the door, his black-feathered beaver in his hand, glancing with a half-amused, half-disdainful expression at the groups of gossips around him, but at the sign from the minister of war he began to elbow his way forward, pushing aside in no very ceremonious fashion all who barred his passage.

Louis possessed in a high degree the royal faculty of recognition. "It is years since I have seen him, but I remember his face well," said he, turning to his minister. "It is the Comte de Frontenac, is it not?"

"Yes, sire," answered Louvois; "it is indeed Louis de Buade, Comte de Frontenac, and formerly governor of Canada."

"We are glad to see you once more at our *lever*," said the monarch, as the old nobleman stooped his head, and kissed the white hand which was extended to him. "I hope that the cold of Canada has not chilled the warmth of your loyalty."

"Only death itself, sire, would be cold enough for that."

"Then I trust that it may remain to us for many long years. We would thank you for the care and pains which you have spent upon our province, and if we have recalled you, it is chiefly that we would fain hear from your own lips how all things go there. And first, as the affairs of God take precedence of those of France, how does the conversion of the heathen prosper?"

"We cannot complain, sire. The good fathers, both Jesuits and Recollets, have done their best, though indeed they are both rather ready to abandon the affairs of the next world in order to meddle with those of this."

"What say you to that, father?" asked Louis, glancing, with a twinkle of the eyes, at his Jesuit confessor.

"I say, sire, that when the affairs of this world have a bearing upon those of the next, it is indeed the duty of a good priest, as of every other good Catholic, to guide them right."

"That is very true, sire," said De Frontenac, with an angry flush upon his swarthy cheek; "but as long as your Majesty did me the honour to intrust those affairs no my own guidance, I would brook no interference in the performance of my duties, whether the meddler were clad in coat or cassock."

"Enough, sir, enough!" said Louis sharply. "I had asked you about the missions."

"They prosper, sire. There are Iroquois at the Sault and the mountain, Hurons at Lorette, and Algonquins along the whole river *cotes* from Tadousac in the East to Sault la Marie, and even the great plains of the Dakotas, who have all taken the cross as their token. Marquette has passed down the river of the West to preach among the Illinois, and Jesuits have carried the Gospel to the warriors of the Long House in their wigwams at Onondaga."

"I may add, your Majesty," said Pere la Chaise, "that in leaving the truth there, they have too often left their lives with it."

"Yes, sire, it is very true," cried De Frontenac cordially. "Your Majesty has many brave men within your domains, but none braver than these. They have come back up the Richelieu River from the Iroquois villages with their nails gone, their fingers torn out, a cinder where their eye should be, and the scars of the pine splinters as thick upon their bodies as the *fleurs-de-lis* on yonder curtain. Yet, with a month of nursing from the good Ursulines, they have used their remaining eye to guide them back to the Indian country once more, where even the dogs have been frightened at their haggled faces and twisted limbs."

"And you have suffered this?" cried Louis hotly. "You allow these infamous assassins to live?"

"I have asked for troops, sire."

"And I have sent some."

"One regiment."

"The Carignan-Saliere. I have no better in my service.

"But more is needed, sire."

"There are the Canadians themselves. Have you not a militia? Could you not raise force enough to punish these rascally murderers of God's priests? I had always understood that you were a soldier."

De Frontenac's eyes flashed, and a quick answer seemed for an instant to tremble upon his lips, but with an effort the fiery old man restrained himself. "Your Majesty will learn best whether I am a soldier or not," said he, "by asking those who have seen me at Seneffe, Mulhausen, Salzbach, and half a score of other places where I had the honour of upholding your Majesty's cause."

"Your services have not been forgotten."

"It is just because I am a soldier and have seen something of war that I know how hard it is to penetrate into a country much larger than the Lowlands, all thick with forest and bog, with a savage lurking behind every tree, who, if he has not learned to step in time or to form line, can at least bring down the running caribou at two hundred paces, and travel three leagues to your one. And then when you have at last reached their villages, and burned their empty wigwams and a few acres of maize fields, what the better are you then? You can but travel back again to your own land with a cloud of unseen men lurking behind you, and a scalp-yell for every straggler. You are a soldier yourself, sire. I ask you if such a war is an easy task for a handful of soldiers, with a few *censitaires* straight from the plough, and a troop of *coureurs-de-bois* whose hearts are all the time are with their traps and their beaver-skins."

"No, no; I am sorry if I spoke too hastily," said Louis. "We shall look into the matter at our council."

"Then it warms my heart to hear you say so," cried the old governor. "There will be joy down the long St. Lawrence, in white hearts and in red, when it is known that their great father over the waters has turned his mind towards them."

"And yet you must not look for too much, for Canada has been a heavy cost to us, and we have many calls in Europe."

"Ah, sire, I would that you could see that great land. When your Majesty has won a campaign over here, what may come of it? Glory, a few miles of land Luxembourg, Strassburg, one more city in the kingdom; but over there, with a tenth of the cost and a hundredth part of the force, there is a world ready to your hand. It is so vast, sire, so rich, so beautiful! Where are there such hills, such forests, such rivers? And it is all for us if we will but take it. Who is there to stand in our way? A few nations of scattered Indians and a thin strip of English farmers and fishermen. Turn your thoughts there, sire, and in a few years you would be able to stand upon your citadel at Quebec, and to say there is one great empire here from the snows of the North to the warm Southern Gulf, and from the waves of the ocean to the great plains beyond Marquette's river, and the name of this empire is France, and her king is Louis, and her flag is the *fleurs-de-lis*."

Louis's cheek had flushed at this ambitious picture, and he had leaned forward in his chair, with flashing eyes, but he sank back again as the governor concluded.

"On my word, count," said he, "you have caught something of this gift of Indian eloquence of which we have heard. But about these English folk. They are Huguenots, are they not?"

"For the most part. Especially in the North."

"Then it might be a service to Holy Church to send them packing. They have a city there, I am told. New—New—How do they call it?"

"New York, sire. They took it from the Dutch."

"Ah, New York. And have I not heard of another? Bos—Bos—"

"Boston, sire."

"That is the name. The harbours might be of service to us. Tell me, now, Frontenac," lowering his voice so that his words might be audible only to the count, Louvois, and the royal circle, "what force would you need to clear these people out? One regiment, two regiments, and perhaps a frigate or two?"

But the ex-governor shook his grizzled head. "You do not know them, sire," said he. "They are stern folk, these. We in Canada, with all your gracious help, have found it hard to hold our own. Yet these men have had no help, but only hindrance, with cold and disease, and barren lands, and Indian wars, but they have thriven and multiplied until the woods thin away in front of them like ice in the sun, and their church bells are heard where but yesterday the wolves were howling. They are peaceful folk, and slow to war, but when they have set their hands to it, though they may be slack to begin, they are slacker still to cease. To put New England into your Majesty's hands, I would ask fifteen thousand of your best troops and twenty ships of the line."

Louis sprang impatiently from his chair, and caught up his cane. "I wish," said he, "that you would imitate these people who seem to you to be so formidable, in their excellent habit of doing things for themselves. The matter may stand until our council. Reverend father, it has struck the hour of chapel, and all else may wait until we have paid out duties to heaven." Taking a missal from the hands of an attendant, he walked as fast as his very high heels would permit him, towards the door, the court forming a lane through which he might pass, and then closing up behind to follow him in order of precedence.

CHAPTER III.
THE HOLDING OF THE DOOR.

Whilst Louis had been affording his court that which he had openly stated to be the highest of human pleasures—the sight of the royal face—the young officer of the guard outside had been very busy passing on the titles of the numerous applicants for admission, and exchanging usually a smile or a few words of greeting with them, for his frank, handsome face was a well-known one at the court. With his merry eyes and his brisk bearing, he looked like a man who was on good terms with Fortune. Indeed, he had good cause to be so, for she had used him well. Three years ago he had been an unknown subaltern bush-fighting with Algonquins and Iroquois in the wilds of Canada. An exchange had brought him back to France and into the regiment of Picardy, but the lucky chance of having seized the bridle of the king's horse one winter's day in Fontainebleau when the creature was plunging within a few yards of a deep gravel-pit had done for him what ten campaigns might have failed to accomplish. Now as a trusted officer of the king's guard, young, gallant, and popular, his lot was indeed an enviable one. And yet, with the strange perversity of human nature, he was already surfeited with the dull if magnificent routine of the king's household, and looked back with regret to the rougher and freer days of his early service. Even there at the royal door his mind had turned away from the frescoed passage and the groups of courtiers to the wild ravines and foaming rivers of the West, when suddenly his eyes lit upon a face which he had last seen among those very scenes.

"Ah, Monsieur de Frontenac!" he cried. "You cannot have forgotten me."

"What! De Catinat! Ah, it is a joy indeed to see a face from over the water! But there is a long step between a subaltern in the Carignan and a captain in the guards. You have risen rapidly."

"Yes; and yet I may be none the happier for it. There are times when I would give it all to be dancing down the Lachine Rapids in a birch canoe, or to see the red and the yellow on those hill-sides once more at the fall of the leaf."

"Ay," sighed De Frontenac. "You know that my fortunes have sunk as yours have risen. I have been recalled, and De la Barre is in my place. But there will be a storm there which such a man as he can never stand against. With the Iroquois all dancing the scalp-dance, and Dongan behind them in New York to whoop them on, they will need me, and they will find me waiting when they send. I will see the king now, and try if I cannot rouse him to play the great monarch there as well as here. Had I but his power in my hands, I should change the world's history."

"Hush! No treason to the captain of the guard," cried De Catinat, laughing, while the stern old soldier strode past him into the king's presence.

A gentleman very richly dressed in black and silver had come up during this short conversation, and advanced, as the door opened, with the assured air of a man whose rights are beyond dispute. Captain de Catinat, however, took a quick step forward, and barred him off from the door.

"I am very sorry, Monsieur de Vivonne," said he, "but you are forbidden the presence."

"Forbidden the presence! I? You are mad!" He stepped back with gray face and staring eyes, one shaking hand half raised in protest,

"I assure you that it is his order."

"But it is incredible. It is a mistake."

"Very possibly."

"Then you will let me past."

"My orders leave me no discretion."

"If I could have one word with the king."

"Unfortunately, monsieur, it is impossible."

"Only one word."

"It really does not rest with me, monsieur."

The angry nobleman stamped his foot, and stared at the door as though he had some thoughts of forcing a passage. Then turning on his heel, he hastened away down the corridor with the air of a man who has come to a decision.

"There, now," grumbled De Catinat to himself, as he pulled at his thick dark moustache, "he is off to make some fresh mischief. I'll have his sister here presently, as like as not, and a pleasant little choice between breaking my orders and making an enemy of her for life. I'd rather hold Fort Richelieu against the Iroquois than the king's door against an angry woman. By my faith, here *is* a lady, as I feared! Ah, Heaven be praised! it is a friend, and not a foe. Good-morning, Mademoiselle Nanon."

"Good-morning, Captain de Catinat."

The new-comer was a tall, graceful brunette, her fresh face and sparkling black eyes the brighter in contrast with her plain dress.

"I am on guard, you see. I cannot talk with you."

"I cannot remember having asked monsieur to talk with me."

"Ah, but you must not pout in that pretty way, or else I cannot help talking to you," whispered the captain. "What is this in your hand, then?"

"A note from Madame de Maintenon to the king. You will hand it to him, will you not?"

"Certainly, mademoiselle. And how is Madame, your mistress?"

"Oh, her director has been with her all the morning, and his talk is very, very good; but it is also very, very sad. We are not very cheerful when Monsieur Godet has been to see us. But I forget monsieur is a Huguenot, and knows nothing of directors."

"Oh, but I do not trouble about such differences. I let the Sorbonne and Geneva fight it out between them. Yet a man must stand by his family, you know."

"Ah! if Monsieur could talk to Madame de Maintenon a little! She would convert him."

"I would rather talk to Mademoiselle Nanon, but if—"

"Oh!" There was an exclamation, a whisk of dark skirts, and the soubrette had disappeared down a side passage.

Along the broad, lighted corridor was gliding a very stately and beautiful lady, tall, graceful, and exceedingly haughty. She was richly clad in a bodice of gold-coloured camlet and a skirt of gray silk trimmed with gold and silver lace. A handkerchief of priceless Genoa point half hid and half revealed her beautiful throat, and was fastened in front by a cluster of pearls, while a rope of the same, each one worth a bourgeois' income, was coiled in and out through her luxuriant hair. The lady was past her first youth, it is true, but the magnificent curves of her queenly figure, the purity of her complexion, the brightness of her deep-lashed blue eyes and the clear regularity of her features enabled her still to claim to be the most handsome as well as the most sharp-tongued woman in the court of France. So beautiful was her bearing, the carriage of her dainty head upon her proud white neck, and the sweep of her stately walk, that the young officer's fears were overpowered in his admiration, and he found it hard, as he raised his hand in salute, to retain the firm countenance which his duties demanded.

"Ah, it is Captain de Catinat," said Madame de Montespan, with a smile which was more embarrassing to him than any frown could have been.

"Your humble servant, marquise."

"I am fortunate in finding a friend here, for there has been some ridiculous mistake this morning."

"I am concerned to hear it."

"It was about my brother, Monsieur de Vivonne. It is almost too laughable to mention, but he was actually refused admission to the *lever*."

"It was my misfortune to have to refuse him, madame."

"You, Captain de Catinat? And by what right?" She had drawn up her superb figure, and her large blue eyes were blazing with indignant astonishment.

"The king's order, madame."

"The king! Is it likely that the king would cast a public slight upon my family? From whom had you this preposterous order?"

"Direct from the king through Bontems."

"Absurd! Do you think that the king would venture to exclude a Mortemart through the mouth of a valet? You have been dreaming, captain."

"I trust that it may prove so, madame."

"But such dreams are not very fortunate to the dreamer. Go, tell the king that I am here, and would have a word with him."

"Impossible, madame."

"And why?"

"I have been forbidden to carry a message."

"To carry any message?"

"Any from you, madame."

"Come, captain, you improve. It only needed this insult to make the thing complete. You may carry a message to the king from any adventuress, from any decayed governess" —she laughed shrilly at her description of her rival— "but none from Francoise de Mortemart, Marquise de Montespan?"

"Such are my orders, madame. It pains me deeply to be compelled to carry them out."

"You may spare your protestations, captain. You may yet find that you have every reason to be deeply pained. For the last time, do you refuse to carry my message to the king?"

"I must, madame."

"Then I carry it myself."

She sprang forward at the door, but he slipped in front of her with outstretched arms.

"For God's sake, consider yourself, madame!" he entreated. "Other eyes are upon you."

"Pah! Canaille!" She glanced at the knot of Switzers, whose sergeant had drawn them off a few paces, and who stood open-eyed, staring at the scene.

"I tell you that I *will* see the king."

"No lady has ever been at the morning *lever*."

"Then I shall be the first."

"You will ruin me if you pass."

"And none the less, I shall do so."

The matter looked serious. De Catinat was a man of resource, but for once he was at his wits' end. Madame de Montespan's resolution, as it was called in her presence, or effrontery, as it was termed behind her back, was proverbial. If she attempted to force her way, would he venture to use violence upon one who only yesterday had held the fortunes of the whole court in the hollow of her hand, and who, with her beauty, her wit, and her energy, might very well be in the same position to-morrow? If she passed him, then his future was ruined with the king, who never brooked the smallest deviation from his orders. On the other hand, if he thrust her back, he did that which could never be forgiven, and which would entail some deadly vengeance should she return to power. It was an unpleasant dilemma. But a happy thought flashed into his mind at the very moment when she, with clenched hand and flashing eyes, was on the point of making a fresh attempt to pass him.

"If madame would deign to wait," said he soothingly, "the king will be on his way to the chapel in an instant."

"It is not yet time."

"I think the hour has just gone."

"And why should I wait, like a lackey?"

"It is but a moment, madame."

"No, I shall not wait." She took a step forward towards the door.

But the guardsman's quick ear had caught the sound of moving feet from within, and he knew that he was master of the situation.

"I will take Madame's message," said he.

"Ah, you have recovered your senses! Go, tell the king that I wish to speak with him."

He must gain a little time yet. "Shall I say it through the lord in waiting?"

"No; yourself."

"Publicly?"

"No, no; for his private ear."

"Shall I give a reason for your request?"

"Oh, you madden me! Say what I have told you, and at once."

But the young officer's dilemma was happily over.

At that instant the double doors were swung open, and Louis appeared in the opening, strutting forwards on his high-heeled shoes, his stick tapping, his broad skirts flapping, and his courtiers spreading out behind him. He stopped as he came out, and turned to the captain of the guard.

"You have a note for me?"

"Yes, sire."

The monarch slipped it into the pocket of his scarlet undervest, and was advancing once more when his eyes fell upon Madame de Montespan standing very stiff and erect in the middle of the passage. A dark flush of anger shot to his brow, and he walked swiftly past her without a word; but she turned and kept pace with him down the corridor.

"I had not expected this honour, madame," said he.

"Nor had I expected this insult, sire."

"An insult, madame? You forget yourself."

"No; it is you who have forgotten me, sire."

"You intrude upon me."

"I wished to hear my fate from your own lips," she whispered. "I can bear to be struck myself, sire, even by him who has my heart. But it is hard to hear that one's brother has been wounded through the mouths of valets and Huguenot soldiers for no fault of his, save that his sister has loved too fondly."

"It is no time to speak of such things."

"When can I see you, then, sire?"

"In your chamber."

"At what hour?"

"At four."

"Then I shall trouble your Majesty no further." She swept him one of the graceful courtesies for which she was famous, and turned away down a side passage with triumph shining in her eyes. Her beauty and her spirit had never failed her yet, and now that she had the monarch's promise of an interview she never doubted that she could do as she had done before, and win back the heart of the man, however much against the conscience of the king.

CHAPTER IV.
THE FATHER OF HIS PEOPLE.

Louis had walked on to his devotions in no very charitable frame of mind, as was easily to be seen from his clouded brow and compressed lips. He knew his late favourite well, her impulsiveness, her audacity, her lack of all restraint when thwarted or opposed. She was capable of making a hideous scandal, of turning against him that bitter tongue which had so often made him laugh at the expense of others, perhaps even of making some public exposure which would leave him the butt and gossip of Europe. He shuddered at the thought. At all costs such a catastrophe must be averted. And yet how could he cut the tie which bound them? He had broken other such bonds as these; but the gentle La Valliere had shrunk into a convent at the very first glance which had told her of waning love. That was true affection. But this woman would struggle hard, fight to the bitter end, before she would quit the position which was so dear to her. She spoke of her wrongs. What were her wrongs? In his intense selfishness, nurtured by the eternal flattery which was the very air he breathed, he could not see that the fifteen years of her life which he had absorbed, or the loss of the husband whom he had supplanted, gave her any claim upon him. In his view he had raised her to the highest position which a subject could occupy. Now he was weary of her, and it was her duty to retire with resignation, nay, even with gratitude for past favours. She should have a pension, and the children should be cared for. What could a reasonable woman ask for more?

And then his motives for discarding her were so excellent. He turned them over in his mind as he knelt listening to the Archbishop of Paris reciting the Mass, and the more he thought, the more he approved. His conception of the deity was as a larger Louis, and of heaven as a more gorgeous Versailles. If he exacted obedience from his twenty millions, then he must show it also to this one who had a right to demand it of him. On the whole, his conscience acquitted him. But in this one matter he had been lax. From the first coming of his gentle and forgiving young wife from Spain, he had never once permitted her to be without a rival. Now that she was dead, the matter was no better.

One favourite had succeeded another, and if De Montespan had held her own so long, it was rather from her audacity than from his affection. But now Father La Chaise and Bossuet were ever reminding him that he had topped the summit of his life, and was already upon that downward path which leads to the grave. His wild outburst over the unhappy Fontanges had represented the last flicker of his passions. The time had come for gravity and for calm, neither of which was to be expected in the company of Madame de Montespan.

But he had found out where they were to be enjoyed. From the day when De Montespan had introduced the stately and silent widow as a governess for his children, he had found a never-failing and ever-increasing pleasure in her society. In the early days of her coming he had sat for hours in the rooms of his favourite, watching the tact and sweetness of temper with which her dependent controlled the mutinous spirits of the petulant young Duc du Maine and the mischievous little Comte de Toulouse. He had been there nominally for the purpose of superintending the teaching, but he had confined himself to admiring the teacher. And then in time he too had been drawn into the attraction of that strong sweet nature, and had found himself consulting her upon points of conduct, and acting upon her advice with a docility which he had never shown before to minister or mistress. For a time he had thought that her piety and her talk of principle might be a mere mask, for he was accustomed to hypocrisy all round him. It was surely unlikely that a woman who was still beautiful, with as bright an eye and as graceful a figure as any in his court, could, after a life spent in the gayest circles, preserve the spirit of a nun. But on this point he was soon undeceived, for when his own language had become warmer than that of friendship, he had been met by an iciness of manner and a brevity of speech which had shown him that there was one woman at least in his dominions who had a higher respect for herself than for him. And perhaps it was better so. The placid pleasures of friendship were very soothing after the storms of passion. To sit in her room every afternoon, to listen to talk which was not tainted with flattery, and to hear opinions which were not framed to please his ear, were the occupations now of his happiest hours. And then her influence over him was all so good! She spoke of his kingly duties, of his example to his subjects, of his preparation for the World beyond, and of the need for an effort to snap the guilty ties which he had formed. She was as good as a confessor—a confessor with a lovely face and a perfect arm.

And now he knew that the time had come when he must choose between her and De Montespan. Their influences were antagonistic. They could not continue together. He stood between virtue and vice, and he must choose. Vice was very attractive too, very comely, very witty, and holding him by that chain of custom which is so hard to shake off. There were hours when his nature swayed strongly over to that side, and when he was tempted to fall back into his old life. But Bossuet and Pere la Chaise were ever at his elbows to whisper encouragement, and, above all, there was Madame de Maintenon to remind him of what was due to his position and to his six-and-forty years. Now at last he had braced himself for a supreme effort. There was no safety for him while his old favourite was at court. He knew himself too well to have any faith in a lasting change so long as she was there ever waiting for his moment of weakness. She must be persuaded to leave Versailles, if without a scandal it could be done. He would be firm when he met her in the afternoon, and make her understand once for all that her reign was forever over.

Such were the thoughts which ran through the king's head as he bent over the rich crimson cushion which topped his *prie-dieu* of carved oak. He knelt in his own enclosure to the right of the altar, with his guards and his immediate household around him, while the court, ladies and cavaliers, filled the chapel. Piety was a fashion now, like dark overcoats and lace cravats, and no courtier was so worldly-minded as not to have had a touch of grace since the king had taken to religion. Yet they looked very bored, these soldiers and seigneurs, yawning and blinking over the missals, while some who seemed more intent upon their devotions were really dipping into the latest romance of Scudery or Calpernedi, cunningly bound up in a sombre cover. The ladies, indeed, were more devout, and were determined that all should see it, for each had lit a tiny taper, which she held in front of her on the plea of lighting up her missal, but really that her face might be visible to the king, and inform him that hers was a kindred spirit. A few there may have been, here and there, whose prayers rose from their hearts, and who were there of their own free will; but the policy of Louis had changed his noblemen into courtiers and his men of the world into hypocrites, until the whole court was like one gigantic mirror which reflected his own likeness a hundredfold.

It was the habit of Louis, as he walked back from the chapel, to receive petitions or to listen to any tales of wrong which his subjects might bring to him. His way, as he returned to his rooms, lay partly across an open space, and here it was that the suppliants were wont to assemble. On this particular morning there were but two or three—a Parisian, who conceived himself injured by the provost of his guild, a peasant whose cow had been torn by a huntsman's dog, and a farmer who had had hard usage from his feudal lord. A few questions and then a hurried order to his secretary disposed of each case, for if Louis was a tyrant himself, he had at least the merit that he insisted upon being the only one within his kingdom. He was about to resume his way again, when an elderly man, clad in the garb of a respectable citizen, and with a strong deep-lined face which marked him as a man of character, darted forward, and threw himself down upon one knee in front of the monarch.

"Justice, sire, justice!" he cried.

"What is this, then?" asked Louis. "Who are you, and what is it that you want?"

"I am a citizen of Paris, and I have been cruelly wronged."

"You seem a very worthy person. If you have indeed been wronged you shall have redress. What have you to complain of?"

"Twenty of the Blue Dragoons of Languedoc are quartered in my house, with Captain Dalbert at their head. They have devoured my food, stolen my property, and beaten my servants, yet the magistrates will give me no redress.'

"On my life, justice seems to be administered in a strange fashion in our city of Paris!" exclaimed the king wrathfully.

"It is indeed a shameful case," said Bossuet.

"And yet there may be a very good reason for it," suggested Pere la Chaise. "I would suggest that your Majesty should ask this man his name, his business, and why it was that the dragoons were quartered upon him."

"You hear the reverend father's question."

"My name, sire, is Catinat, by trade I am a merchant in cloth, and I am treated in this fashion because I am of the Reformed Church."

"I thought as much!" cried the confessor.

"That alters matters," said Bossuet.

The king shook his head and his brow darkened. "You have only yourself to thank, then. The remedy is in your hands."

"And how, sire?"

"By embracing the only true faith."

"I am already a member of it, sire."

The king stamped his foot angrily. "I can see that you are a very insolent heretic," said he. "There is but one Church in France, and that is my Church. If you are outside that, you cannot look to me for aid."

"My creed is that of my father, sire, and of my grandfather."

"If they have sinned it is no reason why you should. My own grandfather erred also before his eyes were opened."

"But he nobly atoned for his error," murmured the Jesuit.

"Then you will not help me, sire?"

"You must first help yourself."

The old Huguenot stood up with a gesture of despair, while the king continued on his way, the two ecclesiastics, on either side of him, murmuring their approval into his ears.

"You have done nobly, sire."

"You are truly the first son of the Church."

"You are the worthy successor of St. Louis."

But the king bore the face of a man who was not absolutely satisfied with his own action.

"You do not think, then, that these people have too hard a measure?" said he.

"Too hard? Nay, your Majesty errs on the side of mercy."

"I hear that they are leaving my kingdom in great numbers."

"And surely it is better so, sire; for what blessing can come upon a country which has such stubborn infidels within its boundaries?"

"Those who are traitors to God can scarce be loyal to the king," remarked Bossuet. "Your Majesty's power would be greater if there were no temple, as they call their dens of heresy, within your dominions."

"My grandfather promised them protection. They are shielded, as you well know, by the edict which be gave at Nantes."

"But it lies with your Majesty to undo the mischief that has been done."

"And how?"

"By recalling the edict."

"And driving into the open arms of my enemies two millions of my best artisans and of my bravest servants. No, no, father, I have, I trust, every zeal for Mother-Church, but there is some truth in what De Frontenac said this morning of the evil which comes from mixing the affairs of this world with those of the next. How say you, Louvois?"

"With all respect to the Church, sire, I would say that the devil has given these men such cunning of hand and of brain that they are the best workers and traders in your Majesty's kingdom. I know not how the state coffers are to be filled if such tax-payers go from among us. Already many have left the country and taken their trades with them. If all were to go, it would be worse for us than a lost campaign."

"But," remarked Bossuet, "if it were once known that the king's will had been expressed, your Majesty may rest assured that even the worst of his subjects bear him such love that they would hasten to come within the pale of Holy Church. As long as the edict stands, it seems to them that the king is lukewarm, and that they may abide in their error."

The king shook his head. "They have always been stubborn folk," said he.

"Perhaps," remarked Louvois, glancing maliciously at Bossuet, "were the bishops of France to make an offering to the state of the treasures of their sees, we might then do without these Huguenot taxes."

"All that the Church has is at the king's service," answered Bossuet curtly.

"The kingdom is mine and all that is in it," remarked Louis, as they entered the *Grand Salon*, in which the court assembled after chapel, "yet I trust that it may be long before I have to claim the wealth of the Church."

"We trust so, sire," echoed the ecclesiastics.

"But we may reserve such topics for our council-chamber. Where is Mansard? I must see his plans for the new wing at Marly." He crossed to a side table, and was buried in an instant in his favourite pursuit, inspecting the gigantic plans of the great architect, and inquiring eagerly as to the progress of the work.

"I think," said Pere la Chaise, drawing Bossuet aside, "that your Grace has made some impression upon the king's mind."

"With your powerful assistance, father."

"Oh, you may rest assured that I shall lose no opportunity of pushing on the good work."

"If you take it in hand, it is done."

"But there is another who has more weight than I."

"The favourite, De Montespan?"

"No, no; her day is gone. It is Madame de Maintenon."

"I hear that she is very devout."

"Very. But she has no love for my Order. She is a Sulpitian. Yet we may all work to one end. Now if you were to speak to her, your Grace."

"With all my heart."

"Show her how good a service it would be could she bring about the banishment of the Huguenots."

"I shall do so."

"And offer her in return that we will promote—" he bent forward and whispered into the prelate's ear.

"What! He would not do it!"

"And why? The queen is dead."

"The widow of the poet Scarron!"

"She is of good birth. Her grandfather and his were dear friends."

"It is impossible."

"But I know his heart, and I say it is possible."

"You certainly know his heart, father, if any can. But such a thought had never entered my head."

"Then let it enter and remain there. If she will serve the Church, the Church will serve her. But the king beckons, and I must go."

The thin dark figure hastened off through the throng of courtiers, and the great Bishop of Meaux remained standing with his chin upon his breast, sunk in reflection.

By this time all the court was assembled in the *Grand Salon*, and the huge room was gay from end to end with the silks, the velvets, and the brocades of the ladies, the glitter of jewels, the flirt of painted fans, and the sweep of plume or aigrette. The grays, blacks, and browns of the men's coats toned down the mass of colour, for all must be dark when the king was dark, and only the blues of the officers' uniforms, and the pearl and gray of the musketeers of the guard, remained to call back those early days of the reign when the men had vied with the women in the costliness and brilliancy of their wardrobes. And if dresses had changed, manners had done so even more. The old levity and the old passions lay doubtless very near the surface, but grave faces and serious talk were the fashion of the hour. It was no longer the lucky *coup* at the lansquenet table, the last comedy of Moliere, or the new opera of Lully about which they gossiped, but it was on the evils of Jansenism, on the expulsion of Arnauld from the Sorbonne, on the insolence of Pascal, or on the comparative merits of two such popular preachers as Bourdaloue and Massilon. So, under a radiant ceiling and over a many-coloured floor, surrounded by immortal paintings, set thickly in gold and ornament, there moved these nobles and ladies of France, all moulding themselves upon the one little dark figure in their midst, who was himself so far from being his own master that he hung balanced even now between two rival women, who were playing a game in which the future of France and his own destiny were the stakes.

CHAPTER V.
CHILDREN OF BELIAL.

The elderly Huguenot had stood silent after his repulse by the king, with his eyes cast moodily downwards, and a face in which doubt, sorrow, and anger contended for the mastery. He was a very large, gaunt man, raw-boned and haggard, with a wide forehead, a large, fleshy nose, and a powerful chin. He wore neither wig nor powder, but Nature had put her own silvering upon his thick grizzled locks, and the thousand puckers which clustered round the edges of his eyes, or drew at the corners of his mouth, gave a set gravity to his face which needed no device of the barber to increase it. Yet in spite of his mature years, the swift anger with which he had sprung up when the king refused his plaint, and the keen fiery glance which he had shot at the royal court as they filed past him with many a scornful smile and whispered gibe at his expense, all showed that he had still preserved something of the strength and of the spirit of his youth. He was dressed as became his rank, plainly and yet well, in a sad-coloured brown kersey coat with silver-plated buttons, knee-breeches of the same, and white woollen stockings, ending in broad-toed black leather shoes cut across with a great steel buckle. In one hand he carried his low felt hat, trimmed with gold edging, and in the other a little cylinder of paper containing a recital of his wrongs, which he had hoped to leave in the hands of the king's secretary.

His doubts as to what his next step should be were soon resolved for him in a very summary fashion. These were days when, if the Huguenot was not absolutely forbidden in France, he was at least looked upon as a man who existed upon sufferance, and who was unshielded by the laws which protected his Catholic fellow-subjects. For twenty years the stringency of the persecution had increased until there was no weapon which bigotry could employ, short of absolute expulsion, which had not been turned against him. He was impeded in his business, elbowed out of all public employment, his house filled with troops, his children encouraged to rebel against him, and all redress refused him for the insults and assaults to which he was subjected. Every rascal who wished to gratify his personal spite, or to gain favour with his bigoted superiors, might do his worst upon him without fear of the law. Yet, in spite of all, these men clung to the land which disowned them, and, full of the love for their native soil which lies so deep in a Frenchman's heart, preferred insult and contumely at home to the welcome which would await them beyond the seas. Already, however, the shadow of those days was falling upon them when the choice should no longer be theirs.

Two of the king's big blue-coated guardsmen were on duty at that side of the palace, and had been witnesses to his unsuccessful appeal. Now they tramped across together to where he was standing, and broke brutally into the current of his thoughts.

"Now, Hymn-books," said one gruffly, "get off again about your business."

"You're not a very pretty ornament to the king's pathway," cried the other, with a hideous oath. "Who are you, to turn up your nose at the king's religion, curse you?"

The old Huguenot shot a glance of anger and contempt at them, and was turning to go, when one of them thrust at his ribs with the butt end of his halberd.

"Take that, you dog!" he cried. "Would you dare to look like that at the king's guard?"

"Children of Belial," cried the old man, with his hand pressed to his side, "were I twenty years younger you would not have dared to use me so."

"Ha! you would still spit your venom, would you? That is enough, Andre! He has threatened the king's guard. Let us seize him and drag him to the guard-room."

The two soldiers dropped their halberds and rushed upon the old man, but, tall and strong as they were, they found it no easy matter to secure him. With his long sinewy arms and his wiry frame, he shook himself clear of them again and again, and it was only when his breath had failed him that the two, torn and panting, were able to twist round his wrists, and so secure him. They had hardly won their pitiful victory, however, before a stern voice and a sword flashing before their eyes, compelled them to release their prisoner once more.

It was Captain de Catinat, who, his morning duties over, had strolled out on to the terrace, and had come upon this sudden scene of outrage. At the sight of the old man's face he gave a violent start, and drawing his sword, had rushed forward with such fury that the two guardsmen not only dropped their victim, but, staggering back from the threatening sword-point, one of them slipped and the other rolled over him, a revolving mass of blue coat and white kersey.

"Villains!" roared De Catinat. "What is the meaning of this?"

The two had stumbled on to their feet again, very shamefaced and ruffled.

"If you please, captain," said one, saluting, "this is a Huguenot who abused the royal guard."

"His petition had been rejected by the king, captain, and yet he refused to go."

De Catinat was white with fury. "And so, when a French citizen has come to have a word with the great master of his country, he must be harassed by two Swiss dogs like you?" he cried. "By my faith, we shall soon see about that!"

He drew a little silver whistle from his pocket, and at the shrill summons an old sergeant and half a dozen soldiers came running from the guard-room.

"Your names?" asked the captain sternly.

"Andre Meunier."

"And yours?"

"Nicholas Klopper."

"Sergeant, you will arrest these men, Meunier and Klopper."

"Certainly, captain," said the sergeant, a dark grizzled old soldier of Conde and Turenne.

"See that they are tried to-day."

"And on what charge, captain?"

"For assaulting an aged and respected citizen who had come on business to the king."

"He was a Huguenot on his own confession," cried the culprits together.

"Hum!" The sergeant pulled doubtfully at his long moustache. "Shall we put the charge in that form, captain? Just as the captain pleases." He gave a little shrug of his epauletted shoulders to signify his doubt whether any good could arise from it.

"No," said De Catinat, with a sudden happy thought. "I charge them with laying their halberds down while on duty, and with having their uniforms dirty and disarranged."

"That is better," answered the sergeant, with the freedom of a privileged veteran. "Thunder of God, but you have disgraced the guards! An hour on the wooden horse with a musket at either foot may teach you that halberds were made for a soldier's hand, and not for the king's grass-plot. Seize them! Attention! Right half turn! March!"

And away went the little clump of guardsmen with the sergeant in the rear.

The Huguenot had stood in the background, grave and composed, without any sign of exultation, during this sudden reversal of fortune; but when the soldiers were gone, he and the young officer turned warmly upon each other.

"Amory, I had not hoped to see you!"

"Nor I you, uncle. What, in the name of wonder, brings you to Versailles?"

"My wrongs, Amory. The hand of the wicked is heavy upon us, and whom can we turn to save only the king?"

The young officer shook his head. "The king is at heart a good man," said he. "But he can only see the world through the glasses which are held before him. You have nothing to hope from him."

"He spurned me from his presence."

"Did he ask your name?"

"He did, and I gave it."

The young guardsman whistled. "Let us walk to the gate," said he. "By my faith, if my kinsmen are to come and bandy arguments with the king, it may not be long before my company finds itself without its captain."

"The king would not couple us together. But indeed, nephew, it is strange to me how you can live in this house of Baal and yet bow down to no false gods."

"I keep my belief in my own heart."

The older man shook his head gravely.

"Your ways lie along a very narrow path," said he, "with temptation and danger ever at your feet. It is hard for you to walk with the Lord, Amory, and yet go hand in hand with the persecutors of His people."

"Tut, uncle!" said the young man impatiently. "I am a soldier of the king's, and I am willing to let the black gown and the white surplice settle these matters between them. Let me live in honour and die in my duty, and I am content to wait to know the rest."

"Content, too, to live in palaces, and eat from fine linen," said the Huguenot bitterly, "when the hands of the wicked are heavy upon your kinsfolk, and there is a breaking of phials, and a pouring forth of tribulation, and a wailing and a weeping throughout the land."

"What is amiss, then?" asked the young soldier, who was somewhat mystified by the scriptural language in use among the French Calvinists of the day.

"Twenty men of Moab have been quartered upon me, with one Dalbert, their captain, who has long been a scourge to Israel."

"Captain Claude Dalbert, of the Languedoc Dragoons? I have already some small score to settle with him."

"Ay, and the scattered remnant has also a score against this murderous dog and self-seeking Ziphite."

"What has he done, then?"

"His men are over my house like moths in a cloth bale. No place is free from them. He sits in the room which should be mine, his great boots on my Spanish leather chairs, his pipe in his mouth, his wine-pot at his elbow, and his talk a hissing and an abomination. He has beaten old Pierre of the warehouse."

"Ha!"

"And thrust me into the cellar."

"Ha!"

"Because I have dragged him back when in his drunken love he would have thrown his arms about your cousin Adele."

"Oh!" The young man's colour had been rising and his brows knitted at each successive charge, but at this last his anger boiled over, and he hurried forward with fury in his face, dragging his elderly companion by the elbow. They had been passing through one of those winding paths, bordered by high hedges, which thinned away every here and there to give a glimpse of some prowling faun or weary nymph who slumbered in marble amid the foliage. The few courtiers who met them gazed with surprise at so ill-assorted a pair of companions. But the young soldier was too full of his own plans to waste a thought upon their speculations. Still hurrying on, he followed a crescent path which led past a dozen stone dolphins shooting water out of their mouths over a group of Tritons, and so through an avenue of great trees which looked as if they had grown there for centuries, and yet had in truth been carried over that very year by incredible labour from St. Germain and Fontainebleau. Beyond this point a small gate led out of the grounds, and it was through it that the two passed, the elder man puffing and panting with this unusual haste.

"How did you come, uncle?"

"In a caleche."

"Where is it?"

"That is it, beyond the auberge."

"Come, let us make for it."

"And you, Amory, are you coming?"

"My faith, it is time that I came, from what you tell me. There is room for a man with a sword at his side in this establishment of yours."

"But what would you do?"

"I would have a word with this Captain Dalbert."

"Then I have wronged you, nephew, when I said even now that you were not whole-hearted towards Israel."

"I know not about Israel," cried De Catinat impatiently. "I only know that if my Adele chose to worship the thunder like an Abenaqui squaw, or turned her innocent prayers to the Mitche Manitou, I should like to set eyes upon the man who would dare to lay a hand upon her. Ha, here comes our caleche! Whip up, driver, and five livres to you if you pass the gate of the Invalides within the hour."

It was no light matter to drive fast in an age of springless carriages and deeply rutted roads, but the driver lashed at his two rough unclipped horses, and the caleche jolted and clattered upon its way. As they sped on, with the road-side trees dancing past the narrow windows, and the white dust streaming behind them, the guardsman drummed his fingers upon his knees, and fidgeted in his seat with impatience, shooting an occasional question across at his grim companion.

"When was all this, then?"

"It was yesterday night."

"And where is Adele now?"

"She is at home."

"And this Dalbert?"

"Oh, he is there also!"

"What! you have left her in his power while you came away to Versailles?"

"She is locked in her room."

"Pah! what is a lock?" The young man raved with his hands in the air at the thought of his own impotence.

"And Pierre is there?"

"He is useless."

"And Amos Green."

"Ah, that is better. He is a man, by the look of him."

"His mother was one of our own folk from Staten Island, near Manhattan. She was one of those scattered lambs who fled early before the wolves, when first it was seen that the king's hand waxed heavy upon Israel. He speaks French, and yet he is neither French to the eye, nor are his ways like our ways."

"He has chosen an evil time for his visit."

"Some wise purpose may lie hid in it."

"And you have left him in the house?"

"Yes; he was sat with this Dalbert, smoking with him, and telling him strange tales."

"What guard could he be? He is a stranger in a strange land. You did ill to leave Adele thus, uncle."

"She is in God's hands, Amory."

"I trust so. Oh, I am on fire to be there!"

He thrust his head through the cloud of dust which rose from the wheels, and craned his neck to look upon the long curving river and broad-spread city, which was already visible before them, half hid by a thin blue haze, through which shot the double tower of Notre Dame, with the high spire of St. Jacques and a forest of other steeples and minarets, the monuments of eight hundred years of devotion. Soon, as the road curved down to the river-bank, the city wall grew nearer and nearer, until they had passed the southern gate, and were rattling over the stony causeway, leaving the broad Luxembourg upon their right, and Colbert's last work, the Invalides, upon their left. A sharp turn brought them on to the river quays, and crossing over the Pont Neuf, they skirted the stately Louvre, and plunged into the labyrinth of narrow but important streets which extended to the northward. The young officer had his head still thrust out of the window, but his view was obscured by a broad gilded carriage which lumbered heavily along in front of them. As the road broadened, however, it swerved to one side, and he was able to catch a glimpse of the house to which they were making.

It was surrounded on every side by an immense crowd.

CHAPTER VI.
A HOUSE OF STRIFE.

The house of the Huguenot merchant was a tall, narrow building standing at the corner of the Rue St. Martin and the Rue de Biron. It was four stories in height, grim and grave like its owner, with high peaked roof, long diamond-paned windows, a frame-work of black wood, with gray plaster filling the interstices, and five stone steps which led up to the narrow and sombre door. The upper story was but a warehouse in which the trader kept his stock, but the second and third were furnished with balconies edged with stout wooden balustrades. As the uncle and the nephew sprang out of the caleche, they found themselves upon the outskirts of a dense crowd of people, who were swaying and tossing with excitement, their chins all thrown forwards and their gaze directed upwards. Following their eyes, the young officer saw a sight which left him standing bereft of every sensation save amazement.

From the upper balcony there was hanging head downwards a man clad in the bright blue coat and white breeches of one of the king's dragoons. His hat and wig had dropped off, and his close-cropped head swung slowly backwards and forwards a good fifty feet above the pavement. His face was turned towards the street, and was of a deadly whiteness, while his eyes were screwed up as though he dared not open them upon the horror which faced them. His voice, however, resounded over the whole place until the air was filled with his screams for mercy.

Above him, at the corner of the balcony, there stood a young man who leaned with a bent back over the balustrades, and who held the dangling dragoon by either ankle. His face, however, was not directed towards his victim, but was half turned over his shoulder to confront a group of soldiers who were clustering at the long, open window which led out into the balcony. His head, as he glanced at them, was poised with a proud air of defiance, while they surged and oscillated in the opening, uncertain whether to rush on or to retire.

Suddenly the crowd gave a groan of excitement. The young man had released his grip upon one of the ankles, and the dragoon hung now by one only, his other leg flapping helplessly in the air. He grabbed aimlessly with his hands at the wall and the wood-work behind him, still yelling at the pitch of his lungs.

"Pull me up, son of the devil, pull me up!" he screamed. "Would you murder me, then? Help, good people, help!"

"Do you want to come up, captain?" said the strong clear voice of the young man above him, speaking excellent French, but in an accent which fell strangely upon the ears of the crowd beneath.

"Yes, sacred name of God, yes!"

"Order off your men, then."

"Away, you dolts, you imbeciles! Do you wish to see me dashed to pieces? Away, I say! Off with you!"

"That is better," said the youth, when the soldiers had vanished from the window. He gave a tug at the dragoon's leg as he spoke, which jerked him up so far that he could twist round and catch hold of the lower edge of the balcony. "How do you find yourself now?" he asked.

"Hold me, for heaven's sake, hold me!"

"I have you quite secure."

"Then pull me up!"

"Not so fast, captain. You can talk very well where you are."

"Let me up, sir, let me up!"

"All in good time. I fear that it is inconvenient to you to talk with your heels in the air."

"Ah, you would murder me!"

"On the contrary, I am going to pull you up."

"Heaven bless you!"

"But only on conditions."

"Oh, they are granted! I am slipping!"

"You will leave this house—you and your men. You will not trouble this old man or this young girl any further. Do you promise?"

"Oh yes; we shall go."

"Word of honour?"

"Certainly. Only pull me up!"

"Not so fast. It may be easier to talk to you like this. I do not know how the laws are over here. Maybe this sort of thing is not permitted. You will promise me that I shall have no trouble over the matter."

"None, none. Only pull me up!"

"Very good. Come along!"

He dragged at the dragoon's leg while the other gripped his way up the balustrade until, amid a buzz of congratulation from the crowd, he tumbled all in a heap over the rail on to the balcony, where he lay for a few moments as he had fallen. Then staggering to his feet, without a glance at his opponent, he rushed, with a bellow of rage, through the open window.

While this little drama had been enacted overhead, the young guardsman had shaken off his first stupor of amazement, and had pushed his way through the crowd with such vigour that he and his companion had nearly reached the bottom of the steps. The uniform of the king's guard was in itself a passport anywhere, and the face of old Catinat was so well known in the district that everyone drew back to clear a path for him towards his house. The door was flung open for them, and an old servant stood wringing his hands in the dark passage.

"Oh, master! Oh, master!" he cried.

"Such doings, such infamy! They will murder him!"

"Whom, then?"

"This brave monsieur from America. Oh, my God, hark to them now!"

As he spoke, a clatter and shouting which had burst out again upstairs ended suddenly in a tremendous crash, with volleys of oaths and a prolonged bumping and smashing, which shook the old house to its foundations. The soldier and the Huguenot rushed swiftly up the first flight of stairs, and were about to ascend the second one, from the head of which the uproar seemed to proceed, when a great eight-day clock came hurtling down, springing four steps at a time, and ending with a leap across the landing and a crash against the wall, which left it a shattered heap of metal wheels and wooden splinters. An instant afterwards four men, so locked together that they formed but one rolling bundle, came thudding down amid a *debris* of splintered stair-rails, and writhed and struggled upon the landing, staggering up, falling down, and all breathing together like the wind in a chimney. So twisted and twined were they that it was hard to pick one from the other, save that the innermost was clad in black Flemish cloth, while the three who clung to him were soldiers of the king. Yet so strong and vigorous was the man whom they tried to hold that as often as he could find his feet he dragged them after him from end to end of the passage, as a boar might pull the curs which had fastened on to his haunches. An officer, who had rushed down at the heels of the brawlers, thrust his hands in to catch the civilian by the throat, but he whipped them back again with an oath as the man's strong white teeth met in his left thumb. Clapping the wound to his mouth, he flashed out his sword and was about to drive it through the body of his unarmed opponent, when De Catinat sprang forward and caught him by the wrist.

"You villain, Dalbert!" he cried.

The sudden appearance of one of the king's own bodyguard had a magic effect upon the brawlers. Dalbert sprang back, with his thumb still in his mouth, and his sword drooping, scowling darkly at the new-comer. His long sallow face was distorted with anger, and his small black eyes blazed with passion and with the hell-fire light of unsatisfied vengeance. His troopers had released their victim, and stood panting in a line, while the young man leaned against the wall, brushing the dust from his black coat, and looking from his rescuer to his antagonists.

"I had a little account to settle with you before, Dalbert," said De Catinat, unsheathing his rapier.

"I am on the king's errand," snarled the other.

"No doubt. On guard, sir!"

"I am here on duty, I tell you!"

"Very good. Your sword, sir!"

"I have no quarrel with you."

"No?" De Catinat stepped forward and struck him across the face with his open hand. "It seems to me that you have one now," said he.

"Hell and furies!" screamed the captain. "To your arms, men! *Hola*, there, from above! Cut down this fellow, and seize your prisoner! *Hola*! In the king's name!"

At his call a dozen more troopers came hurrying down the stairs, while the three upon the landing advanced upon their former antagonist. He slipped by them, however, and caught out of the old merchant's hand the thick oak stick which he carried.

"I am with you, sir," said he, taking his place beside the guardsman.

"Call off your canaille, and fight me like a gentleman," cried De Catinat.

"A gentleman! Hark to the bourgeois Huguenot, whose family peddles cloth!"

"You coward! I will write liar on you with my sword-point!"

He sprang forward, and sent in a thrust which might have found its way to Dalbert's heart had the heavy sabre of a dragoon not descended from the side and shorn his more delicate weapon short off close to the hilt. With a shout of triumph, his enemy sprang furiously upon him with his rapier shortened, but was met by a sharp blow from the cudgel of the young stranger which sent his weapon tinkling on to the ground. A trooper, however, on the stair had pulled out a pistol, and clapping it within a foot of the guardsman's head, was about to settle the combat, once and forever, when a little old gentleman, who had quietly ascended from the street, and who had been looking on with an amused and interested smile at this fiery sequence of events, took a sudden step forward, and ordered all parties to drop their weapons with a voice so decided, so stern, and so full of authority, that the sabre points all clinked down together upon the parquet flooring as though it were a part of their daily drill.

"Upon my word, gentlemen, upon my word!" said he, looking sternly from one to the other. He was a very small, dapper man, as thin as a herring, with projecting teeth and a huge drooping many-curled wig, which cut off the line of his skinny neck and the slope of his narrow shoulders. His dress was a long overcoat of mouse-coloured velvet slashed with gold, beneath which were high leather boots, which, with his little gold-laced, three-cornered hat, gave a military tinge to his appearance. In his gait and bearing he had a dainty strut and backward cock of the head, which, taken with his sharp black eyes, his high thin features, and his assured manner, would impress a stranger with the feeling that this was a man of power. And, indeed, in France or out of it there were few to whom this man's name was not familiar, for in all France the only figure which loomed up as large as that of the king was this very little gentleman who stood now, with gold snuff-box in one hand, and deep-laced handkerchief in the other, upon the landing of the Huguenot's house. For who was there who did not know the last of the great French nobles, the bravest of French captains, the beloved Conde, victor of Recroy and hero of the Fronde? At the sight of his pinched, sallow face the dragoons and their leader had stood staring, while De Catinat raised the stump of his sword in a salute.

"Heh, heh!" cried the old soldier, peering at him.

"You were with me on the Rhine—heh? I know your face, captain. But the household was with Turenne."

"I was in the regiment of Picardy, your Highness. De Catinat is my name."

"Yes, yes. But you, sir, who the devil are you?"

"Captain Dalbert, your Highness, of the Languedoc Blue Dragoons."

"Heh! I was passing in my carriage, and I saw you standing on your head in the air. The young man let you up on conditions, as I understood."

"He swore he would go from the house," cried the young stranger. "Yet when I had let him up, he set his men upon me, and we all came downstairs together."

"My faith, you seem to have left little behind you," said Conde, smiling, as he glanced at the litter which was strewed all over the floor. "And so you broke your parole, Captain Dalbert?"

"I could not hold treaty with a Huguenot and an enemy of the king," said the dragoon sulkily.

"You could hold treaty, it appears, but not keep it. And why did you let him go, sir, when you had him at such a vantage?"

"I believed his promise."

"You must be of a trusting nature."

"I have been used to deal with Indians."

"Heh! And you think an Indian's word is better than that of an officer in the king's dragoons?"

"I did not think so an hour ago."

"Hem!" Conde took a large pinch of snuff, and brushed the wandering grains from his velvet coat with his handkerchief of point.

"You are very strong, monsieur," said he, glancing keenly at the broad shoulders and arching chest of the young stranger. "You are from Canada, I presume?"

"I have been there, sir. But I am from New York."

Conde shook his head. "An island?"

"No, sir; a town."

"In what province?"

"The province of New York."

"The chief town, then?"

"Nay; Albany is the chief town."

"And how came you to speak French?"

"My mother was of French blood."

"And how long have you been in Paris?"

"A day."

"Heh! And you already begin to throw your mother's country-folk out of windows!"

"He was annoying a young maid, sir, and I asked him to stop, whereon he whipped out his sword, and would have slain me had I not closed with him, upon which he called upon his fellows to aid him. To keep them off, I swore that I would drop him over if they moved a step. Yet when I let him go, they set upon me again, and I know not what the end might have been had this gentleman not stood my friend."

"Hem! You did very well. You are young, but you have resource."

"I was reared in the woods, sir."

"If there are many of your kidney, you may give my friend De Frontenac some work ere he found this empire of which he talks. But how is this, Captain Dalbert? What have you to say?"

"The king's orders, your Highness."

"Heh! Did he order you to molest the girl? I have never yet heard that his Majesty erred by being too *harsh* with a woman." He gave a little dry chuckle in his throat, and took another pinch of snuff.

"The orders are, your Highness, to use every means which may drive these people into the true Church."

"On my word, you look a very fine apostle and a pretty champion for a holy cause," said Conde, glancing sardonically out of his twinkling black eyes at the brutal face of the dragoon. "Take your men out of this, sir, and never venture to set your foot again across this threshold."

"But the king's command, your Highness."

"I will tell the king when I see him that I left soldiers and that I find brigands. Not a word, sir! Away! You take your shame with you, and you leave your honour behind." He had turned in an instant from the sneering, strutting old beau to the fierce soldier with set face and eye of fire. Dalbert shrank back from his baleful gaze, and muttering an order to his men, they filed off down the stair with clattering feet and clank of sabres.

"Your Highness," said the old Huguenot, coming forward and throwing open one of the doors which led from the landing, "you have indeed been a saviour of Israel and a stumbling-block to the froward this day. Will you not deign to rest under my roof, and even to take a cup of wine ere you go onwards?"

Conde raised his thick eyebrows at the scriptural fashion of the merchant's speech, but he bowed courteously to the invitation, and entered the chamber, looking around him in surprise and admiration at its magnificence. With its panelling of dark shining oak, its polished floor, its stately marble chimney-piece, and its beautifully moulded ceiling, it was indeed a room which might have graced a palace.

"My carriage waits below," said he, "and I must not delay longer. It is not often that I leave my castle of Chantilly to come to Paris, and it was a fortunate chance which made me pass in time to be of service to honest men. When a house hangs out such a sign as an officer of dragoons with his heels in the air, it is hard to drive past without a question. But I fear that as long as you are a Huguenot, there will be no peace for you in France, monsieur."

"The law is indeed heavy upon us."

"And will be heavier if what I hear from court is correct. I wonder that you do not fly the country."

"My business and my duty lie here."

"Well, every man knows his own affairs best. Would it not be wise to bend to the storm, heh?"

The Huguenot gave a gesture of horror.

"Well, well, I meant no harm. And where is this fair maid who has been the cause of the broil?"

"Where is Adele, Pierre?" asked the merchant of the old servant, who had carried in the silver tray with a squat flask and tinted Venetian glasses.

"I locked her in my room, master."

"And where is she now?"

"I am here, father." The young girl sprang into the room, and threw her arms round the old merchant's neck. "Oh, I trust these wicked men have not hurt you, love!"

"No, no, dear child; none of us have been hurt, thanks to his Highness the Prince of Conde here."

Adele raised her eyes, and quickly drooped them again before the keen questioning gaze of the old soldier. "May God reward your Highness!" she stammered. In her confusion the blood rushed to her face, which was perfect in feature and expression. With her sweet delicate contour, her large gray eyes, and the sweep of the lustrous hair, setting off with its rich tint the little shell-like ears and the alabaster whiteness of the neck and throat, even Conde, who had seen all the beauties of three courts and of sixty years defile before him, stood staring in admiration at the Huguenot maiden.

"Heh! On my word, mademoiselle, you make me wish that I could wipe forty years from my account." He bowed, and sighed in the fashion that was in vogue when Buckingham came to the wooing of Anne of Austria, and the dynasty of cardinals was at its height.

"France could ill spare those forty years, your Highness."

"Heh, heh! So quick of tongue too? Your daughter has a courtly wit, monsieur."

"God forbid, your Highness! She is as pure and good—"

"Nay, that is but a sorry compliment to the court. Surely, mademoiselle, you would love to go out into the great world, to hear sweet music, see all that is lovely, and wear all that is costly, rather than look out ever upon the Rue St. Martin, and bide in this great dark house until the roses wither upon your cheeks."

"Where my father is, I am happy at his side," said she, putting her two hands upon his sleeve. "I ask nothing more than I have got."

"And I think it best that you go up to your room again," said the old merchant shortly, for the prince, in spite of his age, bore an evil name among women. He had come close to her as he spoke, and had even placed one yellow hand upon her shrinking arm, while his little dark eyes twinkled with an ominous light.

"Tut, tut!" said he, as she hastened to obey. "You need not fear for your little dove. This hawk, at least, is far past the stoop, however tempting the quarry. But indeed, I can see that she is as good as she is fair, and one could not say more than that if she were from heaven direct. My carriage waits, gentlemen, and I wish you all a very good day!" He inclined his be-wigged head, and strutted off in his dainty, dandified fashion. From the window De Catinat could see him slip into the same gilded chariot which had stood in his way as he drove from Versailles.

"By my faith," said he, turning to the young American, "we all owe thanks to the prince, but it seems to me, sir, that we are your debtors even more. You have risked your life for my cousin, and but for your cudgel, Dalbert would have had his blade through me when he had me at a vantage. Your hand, sir! These are things which a man cannot forget."

"Ay, you may well thank him, Amory," broke in the old Huguenot, who had returned after escorting his illustrious guest to the carriage. "He has been raised up as a champion for the afflicted, and as a helper for those who are in need. An old man's blessing upon you, Amos Green, for my own son could not have done for me more than you, a stranger."

But their young visitor appeared to be more embarrassed by their thanks than by any of his preceding adventures. The blood flushed to his weather-tanned, clear-cut face, as smooth as that of a boy, and yet marked by a firmness of lip and a shrewdness in the keen blue eyes which spoke of a strong and self-reliant nature.

"I have a mother and two sisters over the water," said he diffidently.

"And you honour women for their sake?"

"We always honour women over there. Perhaps it is that we have so few. Over in these old countries you have not learned what it is to be without them. I have been away up the lakes for furs, living for months on end the life of a savage among the wigwams of the Sacs and the Foxes, foul livers and foul talkers, ever squatting like toads around their fires. Then when I have come back to Albany where my folk then dwelt, and have heard my sisters play upon the spinet and sing, and my mother talk to us of the France of her younger days and of her childhood, and of all that they had suffered for what they thought was right, then I have felt what a good woman is, and how, like the sunshine, she draws out of one's soul all that is purest and best."

"Indeed, the ladies should be very much obliged to monsieur, who is as eloquent as he is brave," said Adele Catinat, who, standing in the open door, had listened to the latter part of his remarks.

He had forgotten himself for the instant, and had spoken freely and with energy. At the sight of the girl, however, he coloured up again, and cast down his eyes.

"Much of my life has been spent in the woods," said he, "and one speaks so little there that one comes to forget how to do it. It was for this that my father wished me to stay some time in France, for he would not have me grow up a mere trapper and trader."

"And how long do you stop in Paris?" asked the guardsman.

"Until Ephraim Savage comes for me."

"And who is he?"

"The master of the *Golden Rod*."

"And that is your ship?"

"My father's ship. She has been to Bristol, is now at Rouen, and then must go to Bristol again. When she comes back once more, Ephraim comes to Paris for me, and it will be time for me to go."

"And how like you Paris?"

The young man smiled. "They told me ere I came that it was a very lively place, and truly from the little that I have seen this morning, I think that it is the liveliest place that I have seen."

"By my faith," said De Catinat, "you came down those stairs in a very lively fashion, four of you together with a Dutch clock as an *avant-courier*, and a whole train of wood-work at your heels. And you have not seen the city yet?"

"Only as I journeyed through it yester-evening on my way to this house. It is a wondrous place, but I was pent in for lack of air as I passed through it. New York is a great city. There are said to be as many as three thousand folk living there, and they say that they could send out four hundred fighting-men, though I can scarce bring myself to believe it. Yet from all parts of the city one may see something of God's handiwork—the trees, the green of the grass, and the shine of the sun upon the bay and the rivers. But here it is stone and wood, and wood and stone, look where you will. In truth, you must be very hardy people to keep your health in such a place."

"And to us it is you who seem so hardy, with your life in the forest and on the river," cried the young girl. "And then the wonder that you can find your path through those great wildernesses, where there is naught to guide you."

"Well, there again! I marvel how you can find your way among these thousands of houses. For myself, I trust that it will be a clear night to-night."

"And why?"

"That I may see the stars."

"But you will find no change in them."

"That is it. If I can but see the stars, it will be easy for me to know how to walk when I would find this house again. In the daytime I can carry a knife and notch the door-posts as I pass, for it might be hard to pick up one's trail again, with so many folk ever passing over it."

De Catinat burst out laughing again. "By my faith, you will find Paris livelier than ever," said he, "if you blaze your way through on the door-posts as you would on the trees of a forest. But perchance it would be as well that you should have a guide at first; so, if you have two horses ready in your stables, uncle, our friend and I might shortly ride back to Versailles together, for I have a spell of guard again before many hours are over. Then for some days he might bide with me there, if he will share a soldier's quarters, and so see more than the Rue St. Martin can offer. How would that suit you, Monsieur Green?"

"I should be right glad to come out with you, if we may leave all here in safety."

"Oh, fear not for that," said the Huguenot. "The order of the Prince of Conde will be as a shield and a buckler to us for many a day. I will order Pierre to saddle the horses."

"And I must use the little time I have," said the guardsman, as he turned away to where Adele waited for him in the window.

CHAPTER VII.
THE NEW WORLD AND THE OLD.

The young American was soon ready for the expedition, but De Catinat lingered until the last possible minute. When at last he was able to tear himself away, he adjusted his cravat, brushed his brilliant coat, and looked very critically over the sombre suit of his companion.

"Where got you those?" he asked.

"In New York, ere I left."

"Hem! There is naught amiss with the cloth, and indeed the sombre colour is the mode, but the cut is strange to our eyes."

"I only know that I wish that I had my fringed hunting tunic and leggings on once more."

"This hat, now. We do not wear our brims flat like that. See if I cannot mend it." He took the beaver, and looping up one side of the brim, he fastened it with a golden brooch taken from his own shirt front. "There is a martial cock," said he, laughing, "and would do credit to the King's Own Musketeers. The black broad-cloth and silk hose will pass, but why have you not a sword at your side?"

"I carry a gun when I ride out."

"*Mon Dieu*, you will be laid by the heels as a bandit!"

"I have a knife, too."

"Worse and worse! Well, we must dispense with the sword, and with the gun too, I pray! Let me re-tie your cravat. So! Now if you are in the mood for a ten-mile gallop, I am at your service."

They were indeed a singular contrast as they walked their horses together through the narrow and crowded causeways of the Parisian streets. De Catinat, who was the older by five years, with his delicate small-featured face, his sharply trimmed moustache, his small but well-set and dainty figure, and his brilliant dress, looked the very type of the great nation to which he belonged.

His companion, however, large-limbed and strong, turning his bold and yet thoughtful face from side to side, and eagerly taking in all the strange, new life amidst which he found himself, was also a type, unfinished, it is true, but bidding fair to be the higher of the two. His close yellow hair, blue eyes, and heavy build showed that it was the blood of his father, rather than that of his mother, which ran in his veins; and even the sombre coat and swordless belt, if less pleasing to the eye, were true badges of a race which found its fiercest battles and its most glorious victories in bending nature to its will upon the seas and in the waste places of the earth.

"What is yonder great building?" he asked, as they emerged into a broader square.

"It is the Louvre, one of the palaces of the king."

"And is he there?"

"Nay; he lives at Versailles."

"What! Fancy that a man should have two such houses!"

"Two! He has many more—St. Germain, Marly, Fontainebleau, Clugny."

"But to what end? A man can but live at one at a time."

"Nay; he can now come or go as the fancy takes him."

"It is a wondrous building. I have seen the Seminary of St. Sulpice at Montreal, and thought that it was the greatest of all houses, and yet what is it beside this?"

"You have been to Montreal, then? You remember the fort?"

"Yes, and the Hotel Dieu, and the wooden houses in a row, and eastward the great mill with the wall; but what do you know of Montreal?"

"I have soldiered there, and at Quebec, too. Why, my friend, you are not the only man of the woods in Paris, for I give you my word that I have worn the caribou mocassins, the leather jacket, and the fur cap with the eagle feather for six months at a stretch, and I care not how soon I do it again,"

Amos Green's eyes shone with delight at finding that his companion and he had so much in common, and he plunged into a series of questions which lasted until they had crossed the river and reached the south-westerly gate of the city. By the moat and walls long lines of men were busy at their drill.

"Who are those, then?" he asked, gazing at them with curiosity.

"They are some of the king's soldiers."

"But why so many of them? Do they await some enemy?"

"Nay; we are at peace with all the world. Worse luck!"

"At peace. Why then all these men?"

"That they may be ready."

The young man shook his head in bewilderment. "They might be as ready in their own homes surely. In our country every man has his musket in his chimney corner, and is ready enough, yet he does not waste his time when all is at peace."

"Our king is very great, and he has many enemies."

"And who made the enemies?"

"Why, the king, to be sure."

"Then would it not be better to be without him?"

The guardsman shrugged his epaulettes in despair. "We shall both wind up in the Bastille or Vincennes at this rate," said he. "You must know that it is in serving the country that he has made these enemies. It is but five years since he made a peace at Nimeguen, by which he tore away sixteen fortresses from the Spanish Lowlands. Then, also, he had laid his hands upon Strassburg and upon Luxembourg, and has chastised the Genoans, so that there are many who would fall upon him if they thought that he was weak."

"And why has he done all this?"

"Because he is a great king, and for the glory of France."

The stranger pondered over this answer for some time as they rode on between the high, thin poplars, which threw bars across the sunlit road.

"There was a great man in Schenectady once," said he at last. "They are simple folk up yonder, and they all had great trust in each other. But after this man came among them they began to miss—one a beaver-skin and one a bag of ginseng, and one a belt of wampum, until at last old Pete Hendricks lost his chestnut three-year-old. Then there was a search and a fuss until they found all that had been lost in the stable of the new-comer, so we took him, I and some others, and we hung him up on a tree, without ever thinking what a great man he had been."

De Catinat shot an angry glance at his companion. "Your parable, my friend, is scarce polite," said he. "If you and I are to travel in peace you must keep a closer guard upon your tongue."

"I would not give you offence, and it may be that I am wrong," answered the American, "but I speak as the matter seems to me, and it is the right of a free man to do that."

De Catinat's frown relaxed as the other turned his earnest blue eyes upon him. "By my soul, where would the court be if every man did that?" said he. "But what in the name of heaven is amiss now?"

His companion had hurled himself off his horse, and was stooping low over the ground, with his eyes bent upon the dust. Then, with quick, noiseless steps, he zigzagged along the road, ran swiftly across a grassy bank, and stood peering at the gap of a fence, with his nostrils dilated, his eyes shining, and his whole face aglow with eagerness.

"The fellow's brain is gone," muttered De Catinat, as he caught at the bridle of the riderless horse. "The sight of Paris has shaken his wits. What in the name of the devil ails you, that you should stand glaring there?"

"A deer has passed," whispered the other, pointing down at the grass. "Its trail lies along there and into the wood. It could not have been long ago, and there is no slur to the track, so that it was not going fast. Had we but fetched my gun, we might have followed it, and brought the old man back a side of venison."

"For God's sake get on your horse again!" cried De Catinat distractedly. "I fear that some evil will come upon you ere I get you safe to the Rue St. Martin again!"

"And what is wrong now?" asked Amos Green, swinging himself into the saddle.

"Why, man, these woods are the king's preserves and you speak as coolly of slaying his deer as though you were on the shores of Michigan!"

"Preserves! They are tame deer!" An expression of deep disgust passed over his face, and spurring his horse, he galloped onwards at such a pace that De Catinat, after vainly endeavouring to keep up, had to shriek to him to stop.

"It is not usual in this country to ride so madly along the roads," he panted.

"It is a very strange country," cried the stranger, in perplexity. "Maybe it would be easier for me to remember what *is* allowed. It was but this morning that I took my gun to shoot a pigeon that was flying over the roofs in yonder street, and old Pierre caught my arm with a face as though it were the minister that I was aiming at. And then there is that old man—why, they will not even let him say his prayers."

De Catinat laughed. "You will come to know our ways soon," said he. "This is a crowded land, and if all men rode and shot as they listed, much harm would come from it. But let us talk rather of your own country. You have lived much in the woods from what you tell me."

"I was but ten when first I journeyed with my uncle to Sault la Marie, where the three great lakes meet, to trade with the Chippewas and the tribes of the west."

"I know not what La Salle or De Frontenac would have said to that. The trade in those parts belongs to France."

"We were taken prisoners, and so it was that I came to see Montreal and afterwards Quebec. In the end we were sent back because they did not know what they could do with us."

"It was a good journey for a first."

"And ever since I have been trading—first, on the Kennebec with the Abenaquis, in the great forests of Maine, and with the Micmac fish-eaters over the Penobscot. Then later with the Iroquois, as far west as the country of the Senecas. At Albany and Schenectady we stored our pelts, and so on to New York, where my father shipped them over the sea."

"But he could ill spare you surely?"

"Very ill. But as he was rich, he thought it best that I should learn some things that are not to be found in the woods. And so he sent me in the *Golden Rod*, under the care of Ephraim Savage."

"Who is also of New York?"

"Nay; he is the first man that ever was born at Boston."

"I cannot remember the names of all these villages."

"And yet there may come a day when their names shall be as well known as that of Paris."

De Catinat laughed heartily. "The woods may have given you much, but not the gift of prophecy, my friend. Well, my heart is often over the water even as yours is, and I would ask nothing better than to see the palisades of Point Levi again, even if all the Five Nations were raving upon the other side of them. But now, if you will look there in the gap of the trees, you will see the king's new palace."

The two young men pulled up their horses, and looked down at the wide-spreading building in all the beauty of its dazzling whiteness, and at the lovely grounds, dotted with fountain and with statue, and barred with hedge and with walk, stretching away to the dense woods which clustered round them. It amused De Catinat to watch the swift play of wonder and admiration which flashed over his companion's features.

"Well, what do you think of it?" he asked at last.

"I think that God's best work is in America, and man's in Europe."

"Ay, and in all Europe there is no such palace as that, even as there is no such king as he who dwells within it."

"Can I see him, think you?"

"Who, the king? No, no; I fear that you are scarce made for a court."

"Nay, I should show him all honour."

"How, then? What greeting would you give him?"

"I would shake him respectfully by the hand, and ask as to his health and that of his family."

"On my word, I think that such a greeting might please him more than the bent knee and the rounded back, and yet, I think, my son of the woods, that it were best not to lead you into paths where you would be lost, as would any of the courtiers if you dropped them in the gorge of the Saguenay. But *hola!* what comes here? It looks like one of the carriages of the court."

A white cloud of dust, which had rolled towards them down the road, was now so near that the glint of gilding and the red coat of the coachman could be seen breaking out through it. As the two cavaliers reined their horses aside to leave the roadway clear, the coach rumbled heavily past them, drawn by two dapple grays, and the Horsemen caught a glimpse, as it passed, of a beautiful but haughty face which looked out at them. An instant afterwards a sharp cry had caused the driver to pull up his horses, and a white hand beckoned to them through the carriage window.

"It is Madame de Montespan, the proudest woman in France," whispered De Catinat. "She would speak with us, so do as I do."

He touched his horse with the spur, gave a *gambade* which took him across to the carriage, and then, sweeping off his hat, he bowed to his horse's neck; a salute in which he was imitated, though in a somewhat ungainly fashion, by his companion.

"Ha, captain!" said the lady, with no very pleasant face, "we meet again."

"Fortune has ever been good to me, madame."

"It was not so this morning."

"You say truly. It gave me a hateful duty to perform."

"And you performed it in a hateful fashion."

"Nay, madame, what could I do more?"

The lady sneered, and her beautiful face turned as bitter as it could upon occasion.

"You thought that I had no more power with the king. You thought that my day was past. No doubt it seemed to you that you might reap favour with the new by being the first to cast a slight upon the old."

"But, madame—"

"You may spare your protestations. I am one who judges by deeds and not by words. Did you, then, think that my charm had so faded, that any beauty which I ever have had is so withered?"

"Nay, madame, I were blind to think that."

"Blind as a noontide owl," said Amos Green with emphasis.

Madame de Montespan arched her eyebrows and glanced at her singular admirer. "Your friend at least speaks that which he really feels," said she. "At four o'clock to-day we shall see whether others are of the same mind; and if they are, then it may be ill for those who mistook what was but a passing shadow for a lasting cloud." She cast another vindictive glance at the young guardsman, and rattled on once more upon her way.

"Come on!" cried De Catinat curtly, for his companion was staring open-mouthed after the carriage. "Have you never seen a woman before?"

"Never such a one as that."

"Never one with so railing a tongue, I dare swear," said De Catinat.

"Never one with so lovely a face. And yet there is a lovely face at the Rue St. Martin also."

"You seem to have a nice taste in beauty, for all your woodland training."

"Yes, for I have been cut away from women so much that when I stand before one I feel that she is something tender and sweet and holy."

"You may find dames at the court who are both tender and sweet, but you will look long, my friend, before you find the holy one. This one would ruin me if she can, and only because I have done what it was my duty to do. To keep oneself in this court is like coming down the La Chine Rapids where there is a rock to right, and a rock to left, and another perchance in front, and if you so much as graze one, where are you and your birch canoe? But our rocks are women, and in our canoe we bear all our worldly fortunes. Now here is another who would sway me over to her side, and indeed I think it may prove to be the better side too."

They had passed through the gateway of the palace, and the broad sweeping drive lay in front of them, dotted with carriages and horsemen. On the gravel walks were many gaily dressed ladies, who strolled among the flower-beds or watched the fountains with the sunlight glinting upon their high water sprays. One of these, who had kept her eyes turned upon the gate, came hastening forward the instant that De Catinat appeared. It was Mademoiselle Nanon, the *confidante* of Madame de Maintenon.

"I am so pleased to see you, captain," she cried, "and I have waited so patiently. Madame would speak with you. The king comes to her at three, and we have but twenty minutes. I heard that you had gone to Paris, and so I stationed myself here. Madame has something which she would ask you."

"Then I will come at once. Ah, De Brissac, it is well met!"

A tall, burly officer was passing in the same uniform which De Catinat wore. He turned at once, and came smiling towards his comrade.

"Ah, Amory, you have covered a league or two from the dust on your coat!"

"We are fresh from Paris. But I am called on business. This is my friend, Monsieur Amos Green. I leave him in your hands, for he is a stranger from America, and would fain see all that you can show. He stays with me at my quarters. And my horse, too, De Brissac. You can give it to the groom."

Throwing the bridle to his brother officer, and pressing the hand of Amos Green, De Catinat sprang from his horse, and followed at the top of his speed in the direction which the young lady had already taken.

CHAPTER VIII.
THE RISING SUN.

The rooms which were inhabited by the lady who had already taken so marked a position at the court of France were as humble as were her fortunes at the time when they were allotted to her, but with that rare tact and self-restraint which were the leading features in her remarkable character, she had made no change in her living with the increase of her prosperity, and forbore from provoking envy and jealousy by any display of wealth or of power. In a side wing of the palace, far from the central *salons*, and only to be reached by long corridors and stairs, were the two or three small chambers upon which the eyes, first of the court, then of France, and finally of the world, were destined to be turned. In such rooms had the destitute widow of the poet Scarron been housed when she had first been brought to court by Madame de Montespan as the governess of the royal children, and in such rooms she still dwelt, now that she had added to her maiden Francoise d'Aubigny the title of Marquise de Maintenon, with the pension and estate which the king's favour had awarded her. Here it was that every day the king would lounge, finding in the conversation of a clever and virtuous woman a charm and a pleasure which none of the professed wits of his sparkling court had ever been able to give to him, and here, too, the more sagacious of the courtiers were beginning to understand, was the point, formerly to be found in the magnificent *salons* of De Montespan, whence flowed those impulses and tendencies which were so eagerly studied, and so keenly followed up by all who wished to keep the favour of the king. It was a simple creed, that of the court. Were the king pious, then let all turn to their missals and their rosaries. Were he rakish, then who so rakish as his devoted followers? But woe to the man who was rakish when he should be praying, or who pulled a long face when the king wore a laughing one! And thus it was that keen eyes were ever fixed upon him, and upon every influence that came near him, so that the wary courtier, watching the first subtle signs of a coming change, might so order his conduct as to seem to lead rather than to follow.

The young guardsman had scarce ever exchanged a word with this powerful lady, for it was her taste to isolate herself, and to appear with the court only at the hours of devotion. It was therefore with some feelings both of nervousness and of curiosity that he followed his guide down the gorgeous corridors, where art and wealth had been strewn with so lavish a hand. The lady paused in front of the chamber door, and turned to her companion.

"Madame wishes to speak to you of what occurred this morning," said she. "I should advise you to say nothing to madame about your creed, for it is the only thing upon which her heart can be hard." She raised her finger to emphasise the warning, and tapping at the door, she pushed it open. "I have brought Captain de Catinat, madame," said she.

"Then let the captain step in." The voice was firm, and yet sweetly musical.

Obeying the command, De Catinat found himself in a room which was no larger and but little better furnished than that which was allotted to his own use. Yet, though simple, everything in the chamber was scrupulously neat and clean, betraying the dainty taste of a refined woman. The stamped-leather furniture, the La Savonniere carpet, the pictures of sacred subjects, exquisite from an artist's point of view, the plain but tasteful curtains, all left an impression half religious and half feminine but wholly soothing. Indeed, the soft light, the high white statue of the Virgin in a canopied niche, with a perfumed red lamp burning before it, and the wooden *prie-dieu* with the red-edged prayer-book upon the top of it, made the apartment look more like a private chapel than a fair lady's boudoir.

On each side of the empty fireplace was a little green-covered arm-chair, the one for madame and the other reserved for the use of the king. A small three-legged stool between them was heaped with her work-basket and her tapestry. On the chair which was furthest from the door, with her back turned to the light, madame was sitting as the young officer entered. It was her favourite position, and yet there were few women of her years who had so little reason to fear the sun, for a healthy life and active habits had left her with a clear skin and delicate bloom which any young beauty of the court might have envied. Her figure was graceful and queenly, her gestures and pose full of a natural dignity, and her voice, as he had already remarked, most sweet and melodious. Her face was handsome rather than beautiful, set in a statuesque classical mould, with broad white forehead, firm, delicately sensitive mouth, and a pair of large serene gray eyes, earnest and placid in repose, but capable of reflecting the whole play of her soul, from the merry gleam of humour to the quick flash of righteous anger. An elevating serenity was, however, the leading expression of her features, and in that she presented the strongest contrast to her rival, whose beautiful face was ever swept by the emotion of the moment, and who gleamed one hour and shadowed over the next like a corn-field in the wind. In wit and quickness of tongue it is true that De Montespan had the advantage, but the strong common-sense and the deeper nature of the elder woman might prove in the end to be the better weapon. De Catinat, at the moment, without having time to notice details, was simply conscious that he was in the presence of a very handsome woman, and that her large pensive eyes were fixed critically upon him, and seemed to be reading his thoughts as they had never been read before.

"I think that I have already seen you, sir, have I not?"

"Yes, madame, I have once or twice had the honour of attending upon you though it may not have been my good fortune to address you."

"My life is so quiet and retired that I fear that much of what is best and worthiest at the court is unknown to me. It is the curse of such places that evil flaunts itself before the eye and cannot be overlooked, while the good retires in its modesty, so that at times we scarce dare hope that it is there. You have served, monsieur?"

"Yes, madame. In the Lowlands, on the Rhine, and in Canada."

"In Canada! Ah! What nobler ambition could woman have than to be a member of that sweet sisterhood which was founded by the holy Marie de l'Incarnation and the sainted Jeanne le Ber at Montreal? It was but the other day that I had an account of them from Father Godet des Marais. What joy to be one of such a body, and to turn from the blessed work of converting the heathen to the even more precious task of nursing back health and strength into those of God's warriors who have been struck down in the fight with Satan!"

It was strange to De Catinat, who knew well the sordid and dreadful existence led by these same sisters, threatened ever with misery, hunger, and the scalping-knife, to hear this lady at whose feet lay all the good things of this earth speaking enviously of their lot.

"They are very good women," said he shortly, remembering Mademoiselle Nanon's warning, and fearing to trench upon the dangerous subject.

"And doubtless you have had the privilege also of seeing the holy Bishop Laval?"

"Yes, madame, I have seen Bishop Laval."

"And I trust that the Sulpitians still hold their own against the Jesuits?"

"I have heard, madame, that the Jesuits are the stronger at Quebec, and the others at Montreal."

"And who is your own director, monsieur?"

De Catinat felt that the worst had come upon him. "I have none, madame."

"Ah, it is too common to dispense with a director, and yet I know not how I could guide my steps in the difficult path which I tread if it were not for mine. Who is your confessor, then?"

"I have none. I am of the Reformed Church, madame."

The lady gave a gesture of horror, and a sudden hardening showed itself in mouth and eye. "What, in the court itself," she cried, "and in the neighbourhood of the king's own person!"

De Catinat was lax enough in matters of faith, and held his creed rather as a family tradition than from any strong conviction, but it hurt his self-esteem to see himself regarded as though he had confessed to something that was loathsome and unclean. "You will find, madame," said he sternly, "that members of my faith have not only stood around the throne of France, but have even seated themselves upon it."

"God has for His own all-wise purposes permitted it, and none should know it better than I, whose grandsire, Theodore d'Aubigny, did so much to place a crown upon the head of the great Henry. But Henry's eyes were opened ere his end came, and I pray—oh, from my heart I pray—that yours may be also."

She rose, and throwing herself down upon the *prie-dieu* sunk her face in her hands for some few minutes, during which the object of her devotions stood in some perplexity in the middle of the room, hardly knowing whether such an attention should be regarded as an insult or as a favour. A tap at the door brought the lady back to this world again, and her devoted attendant answered her summons to enter.

"The king is in the Hall of Victories, madame," said she. "He will be here in five minutes."

"Very well. Stand outside, and let me know when he comes. Now, sir," she continued, when they were alone once more, "you gave a note of mine to the king this morning?"

"I did, madame."

"And, as I understand, Madame de Montespan was refused admittance to the *grand lever*?"

"She was, madame."

"But she waited for the king in the passage?"

"She did."

"And wrung from him a promise that he would see her to-day?"

"Yes, madame."

"I would not have you tell me that which it may seem to you a breach of your duty to tell. But I am fighting now against a terrible foe, and for a great stake. Do you understand me?"

De Catinat bowed.

"Then what do I mean?"

"I presume that what madame means is that she is fighting for the king's favour with the lady you mentioned."

"As heaven is my judge, I have no thought of myself. I am fighting with the devil for the king's soul."

"'Tis the same thing, madame."

The lady smiled. "If the king's body were in peril, I could call on the aid of his faithful guards, and not less so now, surely, when so much more is at stake. Tell me, then, at what hour was the king to meet the marquise in her room?"

"At four, madame."

"I thank you. You have done me a service, and I shall not forget it."

"The king comes, madame," said Mademoiselle Nanon, again protruding her head.

"Then you must go, captain. Pass through the other room, and so into the outer passage. And take this. It is Bossuet's statement of the Catholic faith. It has softened the hearts of others, and may yours. Now, adieu!"

De Catinat passed out through another door, and as he did so he glanced back. The lady had her back to him, and her hand was raised to the mantel-piece. At the instant that he looked she moved her neck, and he could see what she was doing. She was pushing back the long hand of the clock.

CHAPTER IX.
LE ROI S'AMUSE.

Captain de Catinat had hardly vanished through the one door before the other was thrown open by Mademoiselle Nanon, and the king entered the room. Madame de Maintenon rose with a pleasant smile and curtsied deeply, but there was no answering light upon her visitor's face, and he threw himself down upon the vacant arm-chair with a pouting lip and a frown upon his forehead.

"Nay, now this is a very bad compliment," she cried, with the gaiety which she could assume whenever it was necessary to draw the king from his blacker humours. "My poor little dark room has already cast a shadow over you."

"Nay; it is Father la Chaise and the Bishop of Meaux who have been after me all day like two hounds on a stag, with talk of my duty and my position and my sins, with judgment and hell-fire ever at the end of their exhortations."

"And what would they have your Majesty do?"

"Break the promise which I made when I came upon the throne, and which my grandfather made before me. They wish me to recall the Edict of Nantes, and drive the Huguenots from the kingdom."

"Oh, but your Majesty must not trouble your mind about such matters."

"You would not have me do it, madame?"

"Not if it is to be a grief to your Majesty."

"You have, perchance, some soft feeling for the religion of your youth?"

"Nay, sire; I have nothing but hatred for heresy."

"And yet you would not have them thrust out?"

"Bethink you, sire, that the Almighty can Himself incline their hearts to better things if He is so minded, even as mine was inclined. May you not leave it in His hands?"

"On my word," said Louis, brightening, "it is well put. I shall see if Father la Chaise can find an answer to that. It is hard to be threatened with eternal flames because one will not ruin one's kingdom. Eternal torment! I have seen the face of a man who had been in the Bastille, for fifteen years. It was like a dreadful book, with a scar or a wrinkle to mark every hour of that death in life. But Eternity!" He shuddered, and his eyes were filled with the horror of his thought. The higher motives had but little power over his soul, as those about him had long discovered, but he was ever ready to wince at the image of the terrors to come.

"Why should you think of such things, sire?" said the lady, in her rich, soothing voice. "What have you to fear, you who have been the first son of the Church?"

"You think that I am safe, then?"

"Surely, sire."

"But I have erred, and erred deeply. You have yourself said as much."

"But that is all over, sire. Who is there who is without stain? You have turned away from temptation. Surely, then, you have earned your forgiveness."

"I would that the queen were living once more. She would find me a better man."

"I would that she were, sire."

"And she should know that it was to you that she owed the change. Oh, Francoise, you are surely my guardian angel, who has taken bodily form! How can I thank you for what you have done for me?" He leaned forward and took her hand, but at the touch a sudden fire sprang into his eyes, and he would have passed his other arm round her had she not risen hurriedly to avoid the embrace.

"Sire!" said she, with a rigid face and one finger upraised.

"You are right, you are right, Francoise. Sit down, and I will control myself. Still at the same tapestry, then! My workers at the Gobelins must look to their laurels." He raised one border of the glossy roll, while she, having reseated herself, though not without a quick questioning glance at her companion, took the other end into her lap and continued her work.

"Yes, sire. It is a hunting scene in your forests at Fontainebleau. A stag of ten tines, you see, and the hounds in full cry, and a gallant band of cavaliers and ladies. Has your Majesty ridden to-day?"

"No. How is it, Francoise, that you have such a heart of ice?"

"I would it were so, sire. Perhaps you have hawked, then?"

"No. But surely no man's love has ever stirred you! And yet you have been a wife."

"A nurse, sire, but never a wife. See the lady in the park! It is surely mademoiselle. I did not know that she had come up from Choisy."

But the king was not to be distracted from his subject.

"You did not love this Scarron, then?" he persisted. "He was old, I have heard, and as lame as some of his verses."

"Do not speak lightly of him, sire. I was grateful to him; I honoured him; I liked him."

"But you did not love him."

"Why should you seek to read the secrets of a woman's heart?"

"You did not love him, Francoise?"

"At least I did my duty towards him."

"Has that nun's heart never yet been touched by love then?"

"Sire, do not question me."

"Has it never—"

"Spare me, sire, I beg of you!"

"But I must ask, for my own peace hangs upon your answer."

"Your words pain me to the soul."

"Have you never, Francoise, felt in your heart some little flicker of the love which glows in mine?" He rose with his hands outstretched, a pleading monarch, but she, with half-turned bead, still shrank away from him.

"Be assured of one thing, sire," said she, "that even if I loved you as no woman ever loved a man yet, I should rather spring from that window on to the stone terraces beneath than ever by word or sign confess as much to you."

"And why, Francoise?"

"Because, sire, it is my highest hope upon earth that I have been chosen to lift up your mind towards loftier things—that mind the greatness and nobility of which none know more than I."

"And is my love so base, then?"

"You have wasted too much of your life and of your thoughts upon woman's love. And now, sire, the years steal on and the day is coming when even you will be called upon to give an account of your actions, and of the innermost thoughts of your heart. I would see you spend the time that is left to you, sire, in building up the Church, in showing a noble example to your subjects, and in repairing any evil which that example may have done in the past."

The king sank back into his chair with a groan. "Forever the same," said he. "Why, you are worse than Father la Chaise and Bossuet."

"Nay, nay," said she gaily, with the quick tact in which she never failed. "I have wearied you, when you have stooped to honour my little room with your presence. That is indeed ingratitude, and it were a just punishment if you were to leave me in solitude to-morrow, and so cut off all the light of my day. But tell me, sire, how go the works at Marly? I am all on fire to know whether the great fountain will work."

"Yes, the fountain plays well, but Mansard has thrown the right wing too far back. I have made him a good architect, but I have still much to teach him. I showed him his fault on the plan this morning, and he promised to amend it."

"And what will the change cost, sire?"

"Some millions of livres, but then the view will be much improved from the south side. I have taken in another mile of ground in that direction, for there were a number of poor folk living there, and their hovels were far from pretty."

"And why have you not ridden to-day, sire?"

"Pah! it brings me no pleasure. There was a time when my blood was stirred by the blare of the horn and the rush of the hoofs, but now it is all wearisome to me."

"And hawking too?"

"Yes; I shall hawk no more."

"But, sire, you must have amusement."

"What is so dull as an amusement which has ceased to amuse? I know not how it is. When I was but a lad, and my mother and I were driven from place to place, with the Fronde at war with us and Paris in revolt, with our throne and even our lives in danger, all life seemed to be so bright, so new, and so full of interest. Now that there is no shadow, and that my voice is the first in France, as France's is in Europe, all is dull and lacking in flavour. What use is it to have all pleasure before me, when it turns to wormwood when it is tasted?"

"True pleasure, sire, lies rather in the inward life, the serene mind, the easy conscience. And then, as we grow older, is it not natural that our minds should take a graver bent? We might well reproach ourselves if it were not so, for it would show that we had not learned the lesson of life."

"It may be so, and yet it is sad and weary when nothing amuses. But who is there?"

"It is my companion knocking. What is it, mademoiselle?"

"Monsieur Corneille, to read to the king," said the young lady, opening the door.

"Ah, yes, sire; I know how foolish is a woman's tongue, and so I have brought a wiser one than mine here to charm you. Monsieur Racine was to have come, but I hear that he has had a fall from his horse, and he sends his friend in his place. Shall I admit him?"

"Oh, as you like, madame, as you like," said the king listlessly. At a sign from Mademoiselle Nanon a little peaky man with a shrewd petulant face, and long gray hair falling back over his shoulders, entered the room. He bowed profoundly three times, and then seated himself nervously on the very edge of the stool, from which the lady had removed her work-basket. She smiled and nodded to encourage the poet, while the monarch leaned back in his chair with an air of resignation.

"Shall it be a comedy, or a tragedy, or a burlesque pastoral?" Corneille asked timidly.

"Not the burlesque pastoral," said the king with decision. "Such things may be played, but cannot be read, since they are for the eye rather than the ear."

The poet bowed his acquiescence.

"And not the tragedy, monsieur," said Madame de Maintenon, glancing up from her tapestry. "The king has enough that is serious in his graver hours, and so I trust that you will use your talent to amuse him."

"Ay, let it be a comedy," said Louis; "I have not had a good laugh since poor Moliere passed away."

"Ah, your Majesty has indeed a fine taste," cried the courtier poet. "Had you condescended to turn your own attention to poetry, where should we all have been then?"

Louis smiled, for no flattery was too gross to please him.

"Even as you have taught our generals war and our builders art, so you would have set your poor singers a loftier strain. But Mars would hardly deign to share the humbler laurels of Apollo."

"I have sometimes thought that I had some such power," answered the king complacently; "though amid my toils and the burdens of state I have had, as you say, little time for the softer arts."

"But you have encouraged others to do what you could so well have done yourself, sire. You have brought out poets as the sun brings out flowers. How many have we not seen—Moliere, Boileau, Racine, one greater than the other? And the others, too, the smaller ones—Scarron, so scurrilous and yet so witty—Oh, holy Virgin! what have I said?"

Madame had laid down her tapestry, and was staring in intense indignation at the poet, who writhed on his stool under the stern rebuke of those cold gray eyes.

"I think, Monsieur Corneille, that you had better go on with your reading," said the king dryly.

"Assuredly, sire. Shall I read my play about Darius?"

"And who was Darius?" asked the king, whose education had been so neglected by the crafty policy of Cardinal Mazarin that he was ignorant of everything save what had come under his own personal observation.

"Darius was King of Persia, sire."

"And where is Persia?"

"It is a kingdom of Asia."

"Is Darius still king there?"

"Nay, sire; he fought against Alexander the Great."

"Ah, I have heard of Alexander. He was a famous king and general, was he not?"

"Like your Majesty, he both ruled wisely and led his armies victoriously."

"And was King of Persia, you say?"

"No, sire; of Macedonia. It was Darius who was King of Persia."

The king frowned, for the slightest correction was offensive to him.

"You do not seem very clear about the matter, and I confess that it does not interest me deeply," said he. "Pray turn to something else."

"There is my *Pretended Astrologer*."

"Yes, that will do."

Corneille commenced to read his comedy, while Madame de Maintenon's white and delicate fingers picked among the many-coloured silks which she was weaving into her tapestry. From time to time she glanced across, first at the clock and then at the king, who was leaning back, with his lace handkerchief thrown over his face. It was twenty minutes to four now, but she knew that she had put it back half an hour, and that the true time was ten minutes past.

"Tut! tut!" cried the king suddenly. "There is something amiss there. The second last line has a limp in it, surely." It was one of his foibles to pose as a critic, and the wise poet would fall in with his corrections, however unreasonable they might be.

"Which line, sire? It is indeed an advantage to have one's faults made clear."

"Read the passage again."

"Et si, quand je lui dis le secret de mon ame,
Avec moins de rigueur elle eut traite ma flamme,
Dans ma fayon de vivre, et suivant mon humeur,
Une autre eut bientot le present de mon coeur."

"Yes, the third line has a foot too many. Do you not remark it, madame?"

"No; but I fear that I should make a poor critic."

"Your Majesty is perfectly right," said Corneille unblushingly. "I shall mark the passage, and see that it is corrected."

"I thought that it was wrong. If I do not write myself, you can see that I have at least got the correct ear. A false quantity jars upon me. It is the same in music. Although I know little of the matter, I can tell a discord where Lully himself would miss it. I have often shown him errors of the sort in his operas, and I have always convinced him that I was right."

"I can readily believe it, your Majesty." Corneille had picked up his book again, and was about to resume his reading when there came a sharp tap at the door.

"It is his Highness the minister, Monsieur de Louvois," said Mademoiselle Nanon.

"Admit him," answered Louis. "Monsieur Corneille, I am obliged to you for what you have read, and I regret that an affair of state will now interrupt your comedy. Some other day perhaps I may have the pleasure of hearing the rest of it." He smiled in the gracious fashion which made all who came within his personal influence forget his faults and remember him only as the impersonation of dignity and of courtesy.

The poet, with his book under his arm, slipped out, while the famous minister, tall, heavily wigged, eagle-nosed, and commanding, came bowing into the little room. His manner was that of exaggerated politeness, but his haughty face marked only too plainly his contempt for such a chamber and for the lady who dwelt there. She was well aware of the feeling with which he regarded her, but her perfect self-command prevented her from ever by word or look returning his dislike.

"My apartments are indeed honoured to-day," said she, rising with outstretched hand. "Can monsieur condescend to a stool, since I have no fitter seat to offer you in this little doll's house? But perhaps I am in the way, if you wish to talk of state affairs to the king. I can easily withdraw into my boudoir."

"No, no, nothing of the kind, madame," cried Louis. "It is my wish that you should remain here. What is it, Louvois?"

"A messenger arrived from England with despatches, your Majesty," answered the minister, his ponderous figure balanced upon the three-legged stool. "There is very ill feeling there, and there is some talk of a rising. The letter from Lord Sunderland wished to know whether, in case the Dutch took the side of the malcontents, the king might look to France for help. Of course, knowing your Majesty's mind, I answered unhesitatingly that he might."

"You did what?"

"I answered, sire, that he might."

King Louis flushed with anger, and he caught up the tongs from the grate with a motion as though he would have struck his minister with them. Madame sprang from her chair, and laid her hand upon his arm with a soothing gesture. He threw down the tongs again, but his eyes still flashed with passion as he turned them upon Louvois.

"How dared you?" he cried.

"But, sire—"

"How dared you, I say? What! You venture to answer such a message without consulting me! How often am I to tell you that I am the state— I alone; that all is to come from me; and that I am answerable to God only? What are you? My instrument! my tool! And you venture to act without my authority!"

"I thought that I knew your wishes, sire," stammered Louvois, whose haughty manner had quite deserted him, and whose face was as white as the ruffles of his shirt.

"You are not there to think about my wishes, sir. You are there to consult them and to obey them. Why is it that I have turned away from my old nobility, and have committed the affairs of my kingdom to men whose names have never been heard of in the history of France, such men as Colbert and yourself? I have been blamed for it. There was the Duc de St. Simon, who said, the last time that he was at the court, that it was a bourgeois government. So it is. But I wished it to be so, because I knew that the nobles have a way of thinking for themselves, and I ask for no thought but mine in the governing of France. But if my bourgeois are to receive messages and give answers to embassies, then indeed I am to be pitied. I have marked you of late, Louvois. You have grown beyond your station. You take too much upon yourself. See to it that I have not again to complain to you upon this matter."

The humiliated minister sat as one crushed, with his chin sunk upon his breast. The king muttered and frowned for a few minutes, but the cloud cleared gradually from his face, for his fits of anger were usually as short as they were fierce and sudden.

"You will detain that messenger, Louvois," he said at last, in a calm voice.

"Yes, sire."

"And we shall see at the council meeting to-morrow that a fitting reply be sent to Lord Sunderland. It would be best perhaps not to be too free with our promises in the matter. These English have ever been a thorn in our sides. If we could leave them among their own fogs with such a quarrel as would keep them busy for a few years, then indeed we might crush this Dutch prince at our leisure. Their last civil war lasted ten years, and their next may do as much. We could carry our frontier to the Rhine long ere that. Eh, Louvois?"

"Your armies are ready, sire, on the day that you give the word."

"But war is a costly business. I do not wish to have to sell the court plate, as we did the other day. How are the public funds?"

"We are not very rich, sire. But there is one way in which money may very readily be gained. There was some talk this morning about the Huguenots, and whether they should dwell any longer in this Catholic kingdom. Now, if they are driven out, and if their property were taken by the state, then indeed your Majesty would at once become the richest monarch in Christendom."

"But you were against it this morning, Louvois?"

"I had not had time to think of it, sire."

"You mean that Father la Chaise and the bishop had not had time to get at you," said Louis sharply. "Ah, Louvois, I have not lived with a court round me all these years without learning how things are done. It is a word to him, and so on to another, and so to a third, and so to the king. When my good fathers of the Church have set themselves to bring anything to pass, I see traces of them at every turn, as one traces a mole by the dirt which it has thrown up. But I will not be moved against my own reason to do wrong to those who, however mistaken they may be, are still the subjects whom God has given me."

"I would not have you do so, sire," cried Louvois in confusion. The king's accusation had been so true that he had been unable at the moment even to protest.

"I know but one person," continued Louis, glancing across at Madame de Maintenon, "who has no ambitions, who desires neither wealth nor preferment, and who can therefore never be bribed to sacrifice my interests. That is why I value that person's opinion so highly." He smiled at the lady as he spoke, while his minister cast a glance at her which showed the jealousy which ate into his soul.

"It was my duty to point this out to you, sire, not as a suggestion, but as a possibility," said he, rising. "I fear that I have already taken up too much of your Majesty's time, and I shall now withdraw." Bowing slightly to the lady, and profoundly to the monarch, he walked from the room.

"Louvois grows intolerable," said the king. "I know not where his insolence will end. Were it not that he is an excellent servant, I should have sent him from the court before this. He has his own opinions upon everything. It was but the other day that he would have it that I was wrong when I said that one of the windows in the Trianon was smaller than any of the others. It was the same size, said he. I brought Le Metre with his measures, and of course the window was, as I had said, too small. But I see by your clock that it is four o'clock. I must go."

"My clock, sire, is half an hour slow."

"Half an hour!" The king looked dismayed for an instant, and then began to laugh. "Nay, in that case," said he, "I had best remain where I am, for it is too late to go, and I can say with a clear conscience that it was the clock's fault rather than mine."

"I trust that it was nothing of very great importance, sire," said the lady, with a look of demure triumph in her eyes.

"By no means."

"No state affair?"

"No, no; it was only that it was the hour at which I had intended to rebuke the conduct of a presumptuous person. But perhaps it is better as it is. My absence will in itself convey my message, and in such a sort that I trust I may never see that person's face more at my court. But, ah, what is this?"

The door had been flung open, and Madame de Montespan, beautiful and furious, was standing before them.

CHAPTER X.
AN ECLIPSE AT VERSAILLES.

Madame de Maintenon was a woman who was always full of self-restraint and of cool resource. She had risen in an instant, with an air as if she had at last seen the welcome guest for whom she had pined in vain. With a frank smile of greeting, she advanced with outstretched hand.

"This is indeed a pleasure," said she.

But Madame de Montespan was very angry, so angry that she was evidently making strong efforts to keep herself within control, and to avoid breaking into a furious outburst. Her face was very pale, her lips compressed, and her blue eyes had the set stare and the cold glitter of a furious woman. So for an instant they faced each other, the one frowning, the other smiling, two of the most beautiful and queenly women in France. Then De Montespan, disregarding her rival's outstretched hand, turned towards the king, who had been looking at her with a darkening face.

"I fear that I intrude, sire."

"Your entrance, madame, is certainly somewhat abrupt."

"I must crave pardon if it is so. Since this lady has been the governess of my children I have been in the habit of coming into her room unannounced."

"As far as I am concerned, you are most welcome to do so," said her rival, with perfect composure.

"I confess that I had not even thought it necessary to ask your permission, madame," the other answered coldly.

"Then you shall certainly do so in the future, madame," said the king sternly. "It is my express order to you that every possible respect is to be shown in every way to this lady."

"Oh, to *this* lady!" with a wave of her hand in her direction. "Your Majesty's commands are of course our laws. But I must remember that it *is* this lady, for sometimes one may get confused as to which name it is that your Majesty has picked out for honour. To-day it is De Maintenon; yesterday it was Fontanges; to-morrow—Ah, well, who can say who it may be to-morrow?"

She was superb in her pride and her fearlessness as she stood, with her sparkling blue eyes and her heaving bosom, looking down upon her royal lover. Angry as he was, his gaze lost something of its sternness as it rested upon her round full throat and the delicate lines of her shapely shoulders. There was something very becoming in her passion, in the defiant pose of her dainty head, and the magnificent scorn with which she glanced at her rival.

"There is nothing to be gained, madame, by being insolent," said he.

"Nor is it my custom, sire."

"And yet I find your words so."

"Truth is always mistaken for insolence, sire, at the court of France."

"We have had enough of this."

"A very little truth is enough."

"You forget yourself, madame. I beg that you will leave the room."

"I must first remind your Majesty that I was so far honoured as to have an appointment this afternoon. At four o'clock I had your royal promise that you would come to me. I cannot doubt that your Majesty will keep that promise in spite of the fascinations which you may find here."

"I should have come, madame, but the clock, as you may observe, is half an hour slow, and the time had passed before I was aware of it."

I beg, sire, that you will not let that distress you. I am returning to my chamber, and five o'clock will suit me as well as four."

"I thank you, madame, but I have not found this interview so pleasant that I should seek another."

"Then your Majesty will not come?"

"I should prefer not."

"In spite of your promise!"

"Madame!"

"You will break your word!"

"Silence, madame; this is intolerable."

"It is indeed intolerable!" cried the angry lady, throwing all discretion to the winds. "Oh, I am not afraid of you, sire. I have loved you, but I have never feared you. I leave you here. I leave you with your conscience and your— your lady confessor. But one word of truth you shall hear before I go. You have been false to your wife, and you have been false to your mistress, but it is only now that I find that you can be false also to your word." She swept him an indignant courtesy, and glided, with head erect, out of the room.

The king sprang from his chair as if he had been stung. Accustomed as he was to his gentle little wife, and the even gentler La Valliere, such language as this had never before intruded itself upon the royal ears. It was like a physical blow to him. He felt stunned, humiliated, bewildered, by so unwonted a sensation. What odour was this which mingled for the first time with the incense amid which he lived? And then his whole soul rose up in anger at her, at the woman who had dared to raise her voice against him. That she should be jealous of and insult another woman, that was excusable. It was, in fact, an indirect compliment to himself. But that she should turn upon him, as if they were merely man and woman, instead of monarch and subject, that was too much. He gave an inarticulate cry of rage, and rushed to the door.

"Sire!" Madame de Maintenon, who had watched keenly the swift play of his emotions over his expressive face, took two quick steps forward, and laid her hand upon his arm.

"I will go after her."

"And why, sire?"

To forbid her the court."

"But, sire—"

"You heard her! It is infamous! I shall go."

"But, sire, could you not write?"

"No, no; I shall see her." He pulled open the door.

"Oh, sire, be firm, then!" It was with an anxious face that she watched him start off, walking rapidly, with angry gestures, down the corridor. Then she turned back, and dropping upon her knees on the *prie-dieu*, bowed her head in prayer for the king, for herself, and for France.

De Catinat, the guardsman, had employed himself in showing his young friend from over the water all the wonders of the great palace, which the other had examined keenly, and had criticised or admired with an independence of judgment and a native correctness of taste natural to a man whose life had been spent in freedom amid the noblest works of nature. Grand as were the mighty fountains and the artificial cascades, they had no overwhelming effect on one who had travelled up from Erie to Ontario, and had seen the Niagara River hurl itself over its precipice, nor were the long level swards so very large to eyes which had rested upon the great plains of the Dakotas. The building itself, however, its extent, its height, and the beauty of its stone, filled him with astonishment.

"I must bring Ephraim Savage here," he kept repeating. "He Would never believe else that there was one house in the world which would weigh more than all Boston and New York put together."

De Catinat had arranged that the American should remain with his friend Major de Brissac, as the time had come round for his own second turn of guard. He had hardly stationed himself in the corridor when he was astonished to see the King, without escort or attendants, walking swiftly down the passage. His delicate face was disfigured with anger, and his mouth was set grimly, like that of a man who had taken a momentous resolution.

"Officer of the guard," said he shortly.

"Yes, sire."

"What! You again, Captain de Catinat? You have not been on duty since morning?"

"No, sire. It is my second guard."

"Very good. I wish your assistance."

"I am at your command, sire."

"Is there a subaltern here?"

"Lieutenant de la Tremouille is at the side guard."

"Very well. You will place him in command."

"Yes, sire."

"You will yourself go to Monsieur de Vivonne. You know his apartments?"

"Yes, sire."

"If he is not there, you must go and seek him. Wherever he is, you must find him within the hour."

"Yes, sire."

"You will give him an order from me. At six o'clock he is to be in his carriage at the east gate of the palace. His sister, Madame de Montespan, will await him there, and he is charged by me to drive her to the Chateau of Petit Bourg. You will tell him that he is answerable to me for her arrival there."

"Yes, sire." De Catinat raised his sword in salute, and started upon his mission.

The king passed on down the corridor, and opened a door which led him into a magnificent ante-room, all one blaze of mirrors and gold, furnished to a marvel with the most delicate ebony and silver suite, on a deep red carpet of Aleppo, as soft and yielding as the moss of a forest. In keeping with the furniture was the sole occupant of this stately chamber—a little negro boy in a livery of velvet picked out with silver tinsel, who stood as motionless as a small swart statuette against the door which faced that through which the king entered.

"Is your mistress there?"

"She has just returned, sire."

"I wish to see her."

"Pardon, sire, but she—"

"Is everyone to thwart me to-day?" snarled the king, and taking the little page by his velvet collar, he hurled him to the other side of the room. Then, without knocking, he opened the door, and passed on into the lady's boudoir.

It was a large and lofty room, very different to that from which he had just come. Three long windows from ceiling to floor took up one side, and through the delicate pink-tinted blinds the evening sun cast a subdued and dainty light. Great gold candelabra glittered between the mirrors upon the wall, and Le Brun had expended all his wealth of colouring upon the ceiling, where Louis himself, in the character of Jove, hurled down his thunder-bolts upon a writhing heap of Dutch and Palatine Titans. Pink was the prevailing tone in tapestry, carpet, and furniture, so that the whole room seemed to shine with the sweet tints of the inner side of a shell, and when lit up, as it was then, formed such a chamber as some fairy hero might have built up for his princess. At the further side, prone upon an ottoman, her face buried in the cushion, her beautiful white arms thrown over it, the rich coils of her brown hair hanging in disorder across the long curve of her ivory neck, lay, like a drooping flower, the woman whom he had come to discard.

At the sound of the closing door she had glanced up, and then, at the sight of the king, she sprang to her feet and ran towards him, her hands out, her blue eyes bedimmed with tears, her whole beautiful figure softening into womanliness and humility.

"Ah, sire," she cried, with a pretty little sunburst of joy through her tears, "then I have wronged you! I have wronged you cruelly! You have kept your promise. You were but trying my faith! Oh, how could I have said such words to you—how could I pain that noble heart! But you have come after me to tell me that you have forgiven me!" She put her arms forward with the trusting air of a pretty child who claims an embrace as her due, but the king stepped swiftly back from her, and warned her away from him with an angry gesture.

"All is over forever between us," he cried harshly. "Your brother will await you at the east gate at six o'clock, and it is my command that you wait there until you receive my further orders."

She staggered back as if he had struck her.

"Leave you!" she cried.

"You must leave the court."

"The court! Ay, willingly, this instant! But you! Ah, sire, you ask what is impossible."

"I do not ask, madame; I order. Since you have learned to abuse your position, your presence has become intolerable. The united kings of Europe have never dared to speak to me as you have spoken to-day. You have insulted me in my own palace—me, Louis, the king. Such things are not done twice, madame. Your insolence has carried you too far this time. You thought that because I was forbearing, I was therefore weak. It appeared to you that if you only humoured me one moment, you might treat me as if I were your equal the next, for that this poor puppet of a king could always be bent this way or that. You see your mistake now. At six o'clock you leave Versailles forever." His eyes flashed, and his small upright figure seemed to swell in the violence of his indignation, while she leaned away from him, one hand across her eyes and one thrown forward, as if to screen her from that angry gaze.

"Oh, I have been wicked!" she cried. "I know it, I know it!"

"I am glad, madame, that you have the grace to acknowledge it."

"How could I speak to you so! How could I! Oh, that some blight may come upon this unhappy tongue! I, who have had nothing but good from you! I to insult you, who are the author of all my happiness! Oh, sire, forgive me, forgive me! for pity's sake forgive me!"

Louis was by nature a kind-hearted man. His feelings were touched, and his pride also was flattered by the abasement of this beautiful and haughty woman. His other favourites had been amiable to all, but this one was so proud, so unyielding, until she felt his master-hand. His face softened somewhat in its expression as he glanced at her, but he shook his head, and his voice was as firm as ever as he answered.

"It is useless, madame," said he. "I have thought this matter over for a long time, and your madness to-day has only hurried what must in any case have taken place. You must leave the palace."

"I will leave the palace. Say only that you forgive me. Oh, sire, I cannot bear your anger. It crushes me down. I am not strong enough. It is not banishment, it is death to which you sentence me. Think of our long years of love, sire, and say that you forgive me. I have given up all for your sake—husband, honour, everything. Oh, will you not give your anger up for mine? My God, he weeps! Oh, I am saved, I am saved!"

"No, no, madame," cried the king, dashing his hand across his eyes. "You see the weakness of the man, but you shall also see the firmness of the king. As to your insults to-day, I forgive them freely, if that will make you more happy in your retirement. But I owe a duty to my subjects also, and that duty is to set them an example. We have thought too little of such things. But a time has come when it is necessary to review our past life, and to prepare for that which is to come."

"Ah, sire, you pain me. You are not yet in the prime of your years, and you speak as though old age were upon you. In a score of years from now it may be time for folk to say that age has made a change in your life."

The king winced. "Who says so?" he cried angrily.

"Oh, sire, it slipped from me unawares. Think no more of it. Nobody says so. Nobody."

"You are hiding something from me. Who is it who says this?"

"Oh, do not ask me, sire."

"You said that it was reported that I had changed my life not through religion, but through stress of years. Who said so?"

"Oh, sire, it was but foolish court gossip, all unworthy of your attention. It was but the empty common talk of cavaliers who had nothing else to say to gain a smile from their ladies."

"The common talk?" Louis flushed crimson.

"Have I, then, grown so aged? You have known me for nearly twenty years. Do you see such changes in me?"

"To me, sire, you are as pleasing and as gracious as when you first won the heart of Mademoiselle Tonnay-Charente."

The king smiled as he looked at the beautiful woman before him.

"In very truth," said he, "I can say that there has been no such great change in Mademoiselle Tonnay-Charente either. But still it is best that we should part, Francoise."

"If it will add aught to your happiness, sire, I shall go through it, be it to my death."

"Now that is the proper spirit."

"You have but to name the place, sire—Petit Bourg, Chargny, or my own convent of St. Joseph in the Faubourg St. Germain. What matter where the flower withers, when once the sun has forever turned from it? At least, the past is my own, and I shall live in the remembrance of the days when none had come between us, and when your sweet love was all my own. Be happy, sire, be happy, and think no more of what I said about the foolish gossip of the court. Your life lies in the future. Mine is in the past. Adieu, dear sire, adieu!" She threw forward her hands, her eyes dimmed over, and she would have fallen had Louis not sprung forward and caught her in his arms. Her beautiful head drooped upon his shoulder, her breath was warm upon his cheek, and the subtle scent of her hair was in his nostrils. His arm, as he held her, rose and fell with her bosom, and he felt her heart, beneath his hand, fluttering like a caged bird. Her broad white throat was thrown back, her eyes almost closed, her lips just parted enough to show the line of pearly teeth, her beautiful face not three inches from his own. And then suddenly the eyelids quivered, and the great blue eyes looked up at him, lovingly, appealingly, half deprecating, half challenging, her whole soul in a glance. Did he move? or was it she? Who could tell? But their lips had met in a long kiss, and then in another, and plans and resolutions were streaming away from Louis like autumn leaves in the west wind.

"Then I am not to go? You would not have the heart to send me away, would you?"

"No, no; but you must not annoy me, Francoise."

"I had rather die than cause you an instant of grief. Oh, sire, I have seen so little of you lately! And I love you so! It has maddened me. And then that dreadful woman—"

"Who, then?"

"Oh, I must not speak against her. I will be civil for your sake even to her, the widow of old Scarron."

"Yes, yes, you must be civil. I cannot have any unpleasantness."

"But you will stay with me, sire?" Her supple arms coiled themselves round his neck. Then she held him for an instant at arm's length to feast her eyes upon his face, and then drew him once more towards her. "You will not leave me, dear sire. It is so long since you have been here."

The sweet face, the pink glow in the room, the hush of the evening, all seemed to join in their sensuous influence. Louis sank down upon the settee.

"I will stay," said he.

"And that carriage, dear sire, at the east door?"

"I have been very harsh with you, Francoise. You will forgive me. Have you paper and pencil, that I may countermand the order?"

"They are here, sire, upon the side table. I have also a note which, if I may leave you for an instant, I will write in the anteroom."

She swept out with triumph in her eyes. It had been a terrible fight, but all the greater the credit of her victory. She took a little pink slip of paper from an inlaid desk, and dashed off a few words upon it. They were: "Should Madame de Maintenon have any message for his Majesty, he will be for the next few hours in the room of Madame de Montespan." This she addressed to her rival, and it was sent on the spot, together with the king's order, by the hands of the little black page.

CHAPTER XI.
THE SUN REAPPEARS.

For nearly a week the king was constant to his new humour. The routine of his life remained unchanged, save that it was the room of the frail beauty, rather than of Madame de Maintenon, which attracted him in the afternoon. And in sympathy with this sudden relapse into his old life, his coats lost something of their sombre hue, and fawn-colour, buff-colour, and lilac began to replace the blacks and the blues. A little gold lace budded out upon his hats also and at the trimmings of his pockets, while for three days on end his *prie-dieu* at the royal chapel had been unoccupied. His walk was brisker, and he gave a youthful flourish to his cane as a defiance to those who had seen in his reformation the first symptoms of age. Madame had known her man well when she threw out that artful insinuation.

And as the king brightened, so all the great court brightened too. The *salons* began to resume their former splendour, and gay coats and glittering embroidery which had lain in drawers for years were seen once more in the halls of the palace. In the chapel, Bourdaloue preached in vain to empty benches, but a ballet in the grounds was attended by the whole court, and received with a frenzy of enthusiasm. The Montespan ante-room was crowded every morning with men and women who had some suit to be urged, while her rival's chambers were as deserted as they had been before the king first turned a gracious look upon her. Faces which had been long banished the court began to reappear in the corridors and gardens unchecked and unrebuked, while the black cassock of the Jesuit and the purple soutane of the bishop were less frequent colours in the royal circle.

But the Church party, who, if they were the champions of bigotry, were also those of virtue, were never seriously alarmed at this relapse. The grave eyes of priest or of prelate followed Louis in his escapade as wary huntsmen might watch a young deer which gambols about in the meadow under the impression that it is masterless, when every gap and path is netted, and it is in truth as much in their hands as though it were lying bound before them. They knew how short a time it would be before some ache, some pain, some chance word, would bring his mortality home to him again, and envelop him once more in those superstitious terrors which took the place of religion in his mind. They waited, therefore, and they silently planned how the prodigal might best be dealt with on his return.

To this end it was that his confessor, Pere la Chaise, and Bossuet, the great Bishop of Meaux, waited one morning upon Madame de Maintenon in her chamber. With a globe beside her, she was endeavouring to teach geography to the lame Due du Maine and the mischievous little Comte de Toulouse, who had enough of their father's disposition to make them averse to learning, and of their mother's to cause them to hate any discipline or restraint. Her wonderful tact, however, and her unwearying patience had won the love and confidence even of these little perverse princes, and it was one of Madame de Montespan's most bitter griefs that not only her royal lover, but even her own children, turned away from the brilliancy and riches of her salon to pass their time in the modest apartment of her rival.

Madame de Maintenon dismissed her two pupils, and received the ecclesiastics with the mixture of affection and respect which was due to those who were not only personal friends, but great lights of the Gallican Church. She had suffered the minister Louvois to sit upon a stool in her presence, but the two chairs were allotted to the priests now, and she insisted upon reserving the humbler seat for herself. The last few days had cast a pallor over her face which spiritualised and refined the features, but she wore unimpaired the expression of sweet serenity which was habitual to her.

"I see, my dear daughter, that you have sorrowed," said Bossuet, glancing at her with a kindly and yet searching eye.

"I have indeed, your Grace. All last night I spent in prayer that this trial may pass away from us."

"And yet you have no need for fear, madame—none, I assure you. Others may think that your influence has ceased; but we, who know the king's heart, we think otherwise. A few days may pass, a few weeks at the most, and once more it will be upon your rising fortunes that every eye in France will turn."

The lady's brow clouded, and she glanced at the prelate as though his speech were not altogether to her taste. "I trust that pride does not lead me astray," she said. "But if I can read my own soul aright, there is no thought of myself in the grief which now tears my heart. What is power to me? What do I desire? A little room, leisure for my devotions, a pittance to save me from want—what more can I ask for? Why, then, should I covet power? If I am sore at heart, it is not for any poor loss which I have sustained. I think no more of it than of the snapping of one of the threads on yonder tapestry frame. It is for the king I grieve—for the noble heart, the kindly soul, which might rise so high, and which is dragged so low, like a royal eagle with some foul weight which ever hampers its flight. It is for him and for France that my days are spent in sorrow and my nights upon my knees."

"For all that, my daughter, you are ambitious."

It was the Jesuit who had spoken. His voice was clear and cold, and his piercing gray eyes seemed to read into the depths of her soul.

"You may be right, father. God guard me from self-esteem. And yet I do not think that I am. The king, in his goodness, has offered me titles— I have refused them; money—I have returned it. He has deigned to ask my advice in matters of state, and I have withheld it. Where, then, is my ambition?"

"In your heart, my daughter. But it is not a sinful ambition. It is not an ambition of this world. Would you not love to turn the king towards good?"

"I would give my life for it."

"And there is your ambition. Ah, can I not read your noble soul? Would you not love to see the Church reign pure and serene over all this realm—to see the poor housed, the needy helped, the wicked turned from their ways, and the king ever the leader in all that is noble and good? Would you not love that, my daughter?"

Her cheeks had flushed, and her eyes shone as she looked at the gray face of the Jesuit, and saw the picture which his words had conjured up before her. "Ah, that would be joy indeed!" she cried.

"And greater joy still to know, not from the mouths of the people, but from the voice of your own heart in the privacy of your chamber, that you had been the cause of it, that your influence had brought this blessing upon the king and upon the country."

"I would die to do it."

"We wish you to do what may be harder. We wish you to live to do it."

"Ah!" She glanced from one to the other with questioning eyes.

"My daughter," said Bossuet solemnly, leaning forward, with his broad white hand outstretched and his purple pastoral ring sparkling in the sunlight, "it is time for plain speaking. It is in the interests of the Church that we do it. None hear, and none shall ever hear, what passes between us now. Regard us, if you will, as two confessors, with whom your secret is inviolable. I call it a secret, and yet it is none to us, for it is our mission to read the human heart. You love the king."

"Your Grace!" She started, and a warm blush, mantling up in her pale cheeks, deepened and spread until it tinted her white forehead and her queenly neck.

"You love the king."

"Your Grace—father!" She turned in confusion from one to the other.

"There is no shame in loving, my daughter. The shame lies only in yielding to love. I say again that you love the king."

"At least I have never told him so," she faltered.

"And will you never?"

"May heaven wither my tongue first!"

"But consider, my daughter. Such love in a soul like yours is heaven's gift, and sent for some wise purpose. This human love is too often but a noxious weed which blights the soil it grows in, but here it is a gracious flower, all fragrant with humility and virtue."

"Alas! I have tried to tear it from my heart."

"Nay; rather hold it firmly rooted there. Did the king but meet with some tenderness from you, some sign that his own affection met with an answer from your heart, it might be that this ambition which you profess would be secured, and that Louis, strengthened by the intimate companionship of your noble nature, might live in the spirit as well as in the forms of the Church. All this might spring from the love which you hide away as though it bore the brand of shame."

The lady half rose, glancing from the prelate to the priest with eyes which had a lurking horror in their depths.

"Can I have understood you!" she gasped. "What meaning lies behind these words? You cannot counsel me to—"

The Jesuit had risen, and his spare figure towered above her.

"My daughter, we give no counsel which is unworthy of our office. We speak for the interests of Holy Church, and those interests demand that you should marry the king."

"Marry the king!" The little room swam round her. "Marry the king!"

"There lies the best hope for the future. We see in you a second Jeanne d'Arc, who will save both France and France's king."

Madame sat silent for a few moments. Her face had regained its composure, and her eyes were bent vacantly upon her tapestry frame as she turned over in her mind all that was involved in the suggestion.

"But surely—surely this could never be," she said at last, "Why should we plan that which can never come to pass?"

"And why?"

"What King of France has married a subject? See how every princess of Europe stretches out her hand to him. The Queen of France must be of queenly blood, even as the last was."

"All this may be overcome."

"And then there are the reasons of state. If the king marry, it should be to form a powerful alliance, to cement a friendship with a neighbour nation, or to gain some province which may be the bride's dowry. What is my dowry? A widow's pension and a work-box." She laughed bitterly, and yet glanced eagerly at her companions, as one who wished to be confuted.

"Your dowry, my daughter, would be those gifts of body and of mind with which heaven has endowed you. The king has money enough, and the king has provinces enough. As to the state, how can the state be better served than by the assurance that the king will be saved in future from such sights as are to be seen in this palace to-day?"

"Oh, if it could be so! But think, father, think of those about him— the dauphin, monsieur his brother, his ministers. You know how little this would please them, and how easy it is for them to sway his mind. No, no; it is a dream, father, and it can never be."

The faces of the two ecclesiastics, who had dismissed her other objections with a smile and a wave, clouded over at this, as though she had at last touched upon the real obstacle.

"My daughter," said the Jesuit gravely, "that is a matter which you may leave to the Church. It may be that we, too, have some power over the king's mind, and that we may lead him in the right path, even though those of his own blood would fain have it otherwise. The future only can show with whom the power lies. But you? Love and duty both draw you one way now, and the Church may count upon you."

"To my last breath, father."

"And you upon the Church. It will serve you, if you in turn will but serve it."

"What higher wish could I have?"

"You will be our daughter, our queen, our champion, and you will heal the wounds of the suffering Church."

"Ah! if I could!"

"But you can. While there is heresy within the land there can be no peace or rest for the faithful. It is the speck of mould which will in time, if it be not pared off, corrupt the whole fruit."

"What would you have, then, father?"

"The Huguenots must go. They must be driven forth. The goats must be divided from the sheep. The king is already in two minds. Louvois is our friend now. If you are with us, then all will be well."

"But, father, think how many there are!"

"The more reason that they should be dealt with."

"And think, too, of their sufferings should they be driven forth."

"Their cure lies in their own hands."

"That is true. And yet my heart softens for them."

Pere la Chaise and the bishop shook their heads. Nature had made them both kind and charitable men, but the heart turns to flint when the blessing of religion is changed to the curse of sect.

"You would befriend God's enemies then?"

"No, no; not if they are indeed so."

"Can you doubt it? Is it possible that your heart still turns towards the heresy of your youth?"

"No, father; but it is not in nature to forget that my father and my grandfather—"

"Nay, they have answered for their own sins. Is it possible that the Church has been mistaken in you? Do you then refuse the first favour which she asks of you? You would accept her aid, and yet you would give none in return."

Madame de Maintenon rose with the air of one who has made her resolution. "You are wiser than I," said she, "and to you have been committed the interests of the Church. I will do what you advise."

"You promise it?"

"I do."

Her two visitors threw up their hands together. "It is a blessed day," they cried, "and generations yet unborn will learn to deem it so."

She sat half stunned by the prospect which was opening out in front of her. Ambitious she had, as the Jesuit had surmised, always been— ambitious for the power which would enable her to leave the world better than she found it. And this ambition she had already to some extent been able to satisfy, for more than once she had swayed both king and kingdom. But to marry the king—to marry the man for whom she would gladly lay down her life, whom in the depths of her heart she loved in as pure and as noble a fashion as woman ever yet loved man—that was indeed a thing above her utmost hopes. She knew her own mind, and she knew his. Once his wife, she could hold him to good, and keep every evil influence away from him. She was sure of it. She should be no weak Maria Theresa, but rather, as the priest had said, a new Jeanne d'Arc, come to lead France and France's king into better ways. And if, to gain this aim, she had to harden her heart against the Huguenots, at least the fault, if there were one, lay with those who made this condition rather than with herself. The king's wife! The heart of the woman and the soul of the enthusiast both leaped at the thought.

But close at the heels of her joy there came a sudden revulsion to doubt and despondency. Was not all this fine prospect a mere day-dream? and how could these men be so sure that they held the king in the hollow of their hand? The Jesuit read the fears which dulled the sparkle of her eyes, and answered her thoughts before she had time to put them into words.

"The Church redeems its pledges swiftly," said he. "And you, my daughter, you must be as prompt when your own turn comes."

"I have promised, father."

"Then it is for us to perform. You will remain in your room all evening."

"Yes, father."

"The king already hesitates. I spoke with him this morning, and his mind was full of blackness and despair. His better self turns in disgust from his sins, and it is now when the first hot fit of repentance is just coming upon him that he may best be moulded to our ends. I have to see and speak with him once more, and I go from your room to his. And when I have spoken, he will come from his room to yours, or I have studied his heart for twenty years in vain. We leave you now, and you will not see us, but you will see the effects of what we do, and you will remember your pledge to us." They bowed low to her both together, and left her to her thoughts.

An hour passed, and then a second one, as she sat in her *fauteuil*, her tapestry before her, but her hands listless upon her lap, waiting for her fate. Her life's future was now being settled for her, and she was powerless to turn it in one way or the other. Daylight turned to the pearly light of evening, and that again to dusk, but she still sat waiting in the shadow. Sometimes as a step passed in the corridor she would glance expectantly towards the door, and the light of welcome would spring up in her gray eyes, only to die away again into disappointment. At last, however, there came a quick sharp tread, crisp and authoritative, which brought her to her feet with flushed cheeks and her heart beating wildly. The door opened, and she saw outlined against the gray light of the outer passage the erect and graceful figure of the king.

"Sire! One instant, and mademoiselle will light the lamp."

"Do not call her." He entered and closed the door behind him. "Francoise, the dusk is welcome to me, because it screens me from the reproaches which must lie in your glance, even if your tongue be too kindly to speak them."

"Reproaches, sire! God forbid that I should utter them!"

"When I last left you, Francoise, it was with a good resolution in my mind. I tried to carry it out, and I failed—I failed. I remember that you warned me. Fool that I was not to follow your advice!"

"We are all weak and mortal, sire. Who has not fallen? Nay, sire, it goes to my heart to see you thus."

He was standing by the fireplace, his face buried in his hands, and she could tell by the catch of his breath that he was weeping. All the pity of her woman's nature went out to that silent and repenting figure dimly seen in the failing light. She put out her hand with a gesture of sympathy, and it rested for an instant upon his velvet sleeve. The next he had clasped it between his own, and she made no effort to release it.

"I cannot do without you, Francoise," he cried. "I am the loneliest man in all this world, like one who lives on a great mountain-peak, with none to bear him company. Who have I for a friend? Whom can I rely upon? Some are for the Church; some are for their families; most are for themselves. But who of them all is single-minded? You are my better self, Francoise; you are my guardian angel. What the good father says is true, and the nearer I am to you the further am I from all that is evil. Tell me, Francoise, do you love me?"

"I have loved you for years, sire." Her voice was low but clear—the voice of a woman to whom coquetry was abhorrent.

"I had hoped it, Francoise, and yet it thrills me to hear you say it. I know that wealth and title have no attraction for you, and that your heart turns rather towards the convent than the palace. Yet I ask you to remain in the palace, and to reign there. Will you be my wife, Francoise?"

And so the moment had in very truth come. She paused for an instant, only an instant, before taking this last great step; but even that was too long for the patience of the king.

"Will you not, Francoise?" he cried, with a ring of fear in his voice.

"May God make me worthy of such an honour, sire!" said she. "And here I swear that if heaven double my life, every hour shall be spent in the one endeavour to make you a happier man!"

She had knelt down, and the king, still holding her hand, knelt down beside her.

"And I swear too," he cried, "that if my days also are doubled, you will now and forever be the one and only woman for me."

And so their double oath was taken, an oath which was to be tested in the future, for each did live almost double their years, and yet neither broke the promise made hand in hand on that evening in the shadow-girt chamber.

CHAPTER XII.
THE KING RECEIVES.

It may have been that Mademoiselle Nanon, the faithful *confidante* of Madame de Maintenon, had learned something of this interview, or it may be that Pere la Chaise, with the shrewdness for which his Order is famous, had come to the conclusion that publicity was the best means of holding the king to his present intention; but whatever the source, it was known all over the court next day that the old favourite was again in disgrace, and that there was talk of a marriage between the king and the governess of his children. It was whispered at the *petit lever*, confirmed at the *grand entree*, and was common gossip by the time that the king had returned from chapel. Back into wardrobe and drawer went the flaring silks and the feathered hats, and out once more came the sombre coat and the matronly dress. Scudery and Calpernedi gave place to the missal and St. Thomas a Kempis, while Bourdaloue, after preaching for a week to empty benches, found his chapel packed to the last seat with weary gentlemen and taper-bearing ladies. By midday there was none in the court who had not heard the tidings, save only Madame de Montespan, who, alarmed by her lover's absence, had remained in haughty seclusion in her room, and knew nothing of what had passed. Many there were who would have loved to carry her the tidings; but the king's changes had been frequent of late, and who would dare to make a mortal enemy of one who might, ere many weeks were past, have the lives and fortunes of the whole court in the hollow of her hand?

Louis, in his innate selfishness, had been so accustomed to regard every event entirely from the side of how it would affect himself, that it had never struck him that his long-suffering family, who had always yielded to him the absolute obedience which he claimed as his right, would venture to offer any opposition to his new resolution. He was surprised, therefore, when his brother demanded a private interview that afternoon, and entered his presence without the complaisant smile and humble air with which he was wont to appear before him.

Monsieur was a curious travesty of his elder brother. He was shorter, but he wore enormously high boot-heels, which brought him to a fair stature. In figure he had none of that grace which marked the king, nor had he the elegant hand and foot which had been the delight of sculptors. He was fat, waddled somewhat in his walk, and wore an enormous black wig, which rolled down in rows and rows of curls over his shoulders. His face was longer and darker than the king's, and his nose more prominent, though he shared with his brother the large brown eyes which each had inherited from Anne of Austria. He had none of the simple and yet stately taste which marked the dress of the monarch, but his clothes were all tagged over with fluttering ribbons, which rustled behind him as he walked, and clustered so thickly over his feet as to conceal them from view. Crosses, stars, jewels, and insignia were scattered broadcast over his person, and the broad blue ribbon of the Order of the Holy Ghost was slashed across his coat, and was gathered at the end into a great bow, which formed the incongruous support of a diamond-hilted sword. Such was the figure which rolled towards the king, bearing in his right hand his many-feathered beaver, and appearing in his person, as he was in his mind, an absurd burlesque of the monarch.

"Why, monsieur, you seem less gay than usual to-day," said the king, with a smile. "Your dress, indeed, is bright, but your brow is clouded. I trust that all is well with Madame and with the Duc de Chartres?"

"Yes, sire, they are well; but they are sad like myself, and from the same cause."

"Indeed! and why?"

"Have I ever failed in my duty as your younger brother, sire?"

"Never, Philippe, never!" said the king, laying his hand affectionately upon the other's shoulder. "You have set an excellent example to my subjects."

"Then why set a slight upon me?"

"Philippe!"

"Yes, sire, I say it is a slight. We are of royal blood, and our wives are of royal blood also. You married the Princess of Spain; I married the Princess of Bavaria. It was a condescension, but still I did it. My first wife was the Princess of England. How can we admit into a house which has formed such alliances as these a woman who is the widow of a hunchback singer, a mere lampooner, a man whose name is a byword through Europe?"

The king had stared in amazement at his brother, but his anger now overcame his astonishment.

"Upon my word!" he cried; "upon my word! I have said just now that you have been an excellent brother, but I fear that I spoke a little prematurely. And so you take upon yourself to object to the lady whom I select as my wife!"

"I do, sire."

"And by what right?"

"By the right of the family honour, sire, which is as much mine as yours."

"Man," cried the king furiously, "have you not yet learned that within this kingdom I am the fountain of honour, and that whomsoever I may honour becomes by that very fact honourable? Were I to take a cinder-wench out of the Rue Poissonniere, I could at my will raise her up until the highest in France would be proud to bow down before her. Do you not know this?"

"No, I do not," cried his brother, with all the obstinacy of a weak man who has at last been driven to bay. "I look upon it as a slight upon me and a slight upon my wife."

"Your wife! I have every respect for Charlotte Elizabeth of Bavaria, but how is she superior to one whose grandfather was the dear friend and comrade in arms of Henry the Great? Enough! I will not condescend to argue such a matter with you! Begone, and do not return to my presence until you have learned not to interfere in my affairs."

"For all that, my wife shall not know her!" snarled monsieur; and then, as his brother took a fiery step or two towards him, he turned and scuttled out of the room as fast as his awkward gait and high heels would allow him.

But the king was to have no quiet that day. If Madame de Maintenon's friends had rallied to her yesterday, her enemies were active to-day. Monsieur had hardly disappeared before there rushed into the room a youth who bore upon his rich attire every sign of having just arrived from a dusty journey. He was pale-faced and auburn-haired, with features which would have been strikingly like the king's if it were not that his nose had been disfigured in his youth. The king's face had lighted up at the sight of him, but it darkened again as he hurried forward and threw himself down at his feet.

"Oh, sire," he cried, "spare us this grief—spare us this humiliation! I implore you to pause before you do what will bring dishonour upon yourself and upon us!"

The king started back from him, and paced angrily up and down the room.

"This is intolerable!" he cried. "It was bad from my brother, but worse from my son. You are in a conspiracy with him, Louis. Monsieur has told you to act this part."

The dauphin rose to his feet and looked steadfastly at his angry father.

"I have not seen my uncle," he said. "I was at Meudon when I heard this news—this dreadful news—and I sprang upon my horse, sire, and galloped over to implore you to think again before you drag our royal house so low."

"You are insolent, Louis."

"I do not mean to be so, sire. But consider, sire, that my mother was a queen, and that it would be strange indeed if for a step-mother I had a—"

The king raised his hand with a gesture of authority which checked the word upon his lips.

"Silence!" he cried, "or you may say that which would for ever set a gulf between us. Am I to be treated worse than my humblest subject, who is allowed to follow his own bent in his private affairs?"

"This is not your own private affair, sire; all that you do reflects upon your family. The great deeds of your reign have given a new glory to the name of Bourbon. Oh, do not mar it now, sire! I implore it of you upon my bended knees!"

"You talk like a fool!" cried his father roughly. "I propose to marry a virtuous and charming lady of one of the oldest noble families of France, and you talk as if I were doing something degrading and unheard of. What is your objection to this lady?"

"That she is the daughter of a man whose vices were well known, that her brother is of the worst repute, that she has led the life of an adventuress, is the widow of a deformed scribbler, and that she occupies a menial position in the palace."

The king had stamped with his foot upon the carpet more than once during this frank address, but his anger blazed into a fury at its conclusion.

"Do you dare," he cried, with flashing eyes, "to call the charge of my children a menial position? I say that there is no higher in the kingdom. Go back to Meudon, sir, this instant, and never dare to open your mouth again on the subject. Away, I say! When, in God's good time, you are king of this country, you may claim your own way, but until then do not venture to cross the plans of one who is both your parent and your monarch."

The young man bowed low, and walked with dignity from the chamber; but he turned with his hand upon the door.

"The Abbe Fenelon came with me, sire. Is it your pleasure to see him?"

"Away! away!" cried the king furiously, still striding up and down the room with angry face and flashing eyes. The dauphin left the cabinet, and was instantly succeeded by a tall thin priest, some forty years of age, strikingly handsome, with a pale refined face, large well-marked features, and the easy deferential bearing of one who has had a long training in courts. The king turned sharply upon him, and looked hard at him with a distrustful eye.

"Good-day, Abbe Fenelon," said he. "May I ask what the object of this interview is?"

"You have had the condescension, sire, on more than one occasion, to ask my humble advice, and even to express yourself afterwards as being pleased that you had acted upon it."

"Well? Well? Well?" growled the monarch.

"If rumour says truly, sire, you are now at a crisis when a word of impartial counsel might be of value to you. Need I say that it would—"

"Tut! tut! Why all these words?" cried the king. "You have been sent here by others to try and influence me against Madame de Maintenon."

"Sire, I have had nothing but kindness from that lady. I esteem and honour her more than any lady in France."

"In that case, abbe, you will, I am sure, be glad to hear that I am about to marry her. Good-day, abbe. I regret that I have not longer time to devote to this very interesting conversation."

"But, sire—"

"When my mind is in doubt, abbe, I value your advice very highly. On this occasion my mind is happily *not* in doubt. I have the honour to wish you a very good-day."

The king's first hot anger had died away by now, and had left behind it a cold, bitter spirit which was even more formidable to his antagonists. The abbe, glib of tongue and fertile of resource as he was, felt himself to be silenced and overmatched. He walked backwards, with three long bows, as was the custom of the court, and departed.

But the king had little breathing space. His assailants knew that with persistence they had bent his will before, and they trusted that they might do so again. It was Louvois, the minister, now who entered the room, with his majestic port, his lofty bearing, his huge wig, and his aristocratic face, which, however, showed some signs of trepidation as it met the baleful eye of the king.

"Well, Louvois, what now?" he asked impatiently. "Has some new state matter arisen?"

"There is but one new state matter which has arisen, sire, but it is of such importance as to banish all others from our mind."

"What then?"

"Your marriage, sire."

"You disapprove of it?"

"Oh, sire, can I help it?"

"Out of my room, sir! Am I to be tormented to death by your importunities? What! You dare to linger when I order you to go!" The king advanced angrily upon the minister, but Louvois suddenly flashed out his rapier. Louis sprang back with alarm and amazement upon his face, but it was the hilt and not the point which was presented to him.

"Pass it through my heart, sire!" the minister cried, falling upon his knees, his whole great frame in a quiver with emotion. "I will not live to see your glory fade!"

"Great heaven!" shrieked Louis, throwing the sword down upon the ground, and raising his hands to his temples, "I believe that this is a conspiracy to drive me mad. Was ever a man so tormented in his life? This will be a private marriage, man, and it will not affect the state in the least degree. Do you hear me? Have you understood me? What more do you want?"

Louvois gathered himself up, and shot his rapier back into its sheath.

"Your Majesty is determined?" he asked.

"Absolutely."

"Then I say no more. I have done my duty." He bowed his head as one in deep dejection when he departed, but in truth his heart was lightened within him, for he had the king's assurance that the woman whom he hated would, even though his wife, not sit on the throne of the Queens of France.

These repeated attacks, if they had not shaken the king's resolution, had at least irritated and exasperated him to the utmost. Such a blast of opposition was a new thing to a man whose will had been the one law of the land. It left him ruffled and disturbed, and without regretting his resolution, he still, with unreasoning petulance, felt inclined to visit the inconvenience to which he had been put upon those whose advice he had followed. He wore accordingly no very cordial face when the usher in attendance admitted the venerable figure of Father la Chaise, his confessor.

"I wish you all happiness, sire," said the Jesuit, "and I congratulate you from my heart that you have taken the great step which must lead to content both in this world and the next."

"I have had neither happiness nor contentment yet, father," answered the king peevishly. "I have never been so pestered in my life. The whole court has been on its knees to me to entreat me to change my intention."

The Jesuit looked at him anxiously out of his keen gray eyes.

"Fortunately, your Majesty is a man of strong will," said he, "and not to be so easily swayed as they think."

"No, no, I did not give an inch. But still, it must be confessed that it is very unpleasant to have so many against one. I think that most men would have been shaken."

"Now is the time to stand firm, sire; Satan rages to see you passing out of his power, and he stirs up all his friends and sends all his emissaries to endeavour to detain you."

But the king was not in a humour to be easily consoled.

"Upon my word, father," said he, "you do not seem to have much respect for my family. My brother and my son, with the Abbe Fenelon and the Minister of War, are the emissaries to whom you allude."

"Then there is the more credit to your Majesty for having resisted them. You have done nobly, sire. You have earned the praise and blessing of Holy Church."

"I trust that what I have done is right, father," said the king gravely. "I should be glad to see you again later in the evening, but at present I desire a little leisure for solitary thought."

Father la Chaise left the cabinet with a deep distrust of the king's intentions. It was obvious that the powerful appeals which had been made to him had shaken if they had failed to alter his resolution. What would be the result if more were made? And more would be made; that was as certain as that darkness follows light. Some master-card must be played now which would bring the matter to a crisis at once, for every day of delay was in favour of their opponents. To hesitate was to lose. All must be staked upon one final throw.

The Bishop of Meaux was waiting in the ante-room, and Father la Chaise in a few brief words let him see the danger of the situation and the means by which they should meet it. Together they sought Madame de Maintenon in her room. She had discarded the sombre widow's dress which she had chosen since her first coming to court, and wore now, as more in keeping with her lofty prospects, a rich yet simple costume of white satin with bows of silver serge. A single diamond sparkled in the thick coils of her dark tresses. The change had taken years from a face and figure which had always looked much younger than her age, and as the two plotters looked upon her perfect complexion, her regular features, so calm and yet so full of refinement, and the exquisite grace of her figure and bearing, they could not but feel that if they failed in their ends, it was not for want of having a perfect tool at their command.

She had risen at their entrance, and her expression showed that she had read upon their faces something of the anxiety which filled their minds.

"You have evil news!" she cried.

"No, no, my daughter." It was the bishop who spoke. "But we must be on our guard against our enemies, who would turn the king away from you if they could."

Her face shone at the mention of her lover.

"Ah, you do not know!" she cried. "He has made a vow. I would trust him as I would trust myself. I know that he will be true."

But the Jesuit's intellect was arrayed against the intuition of the woman.

"Our opponents are many and strong," said he shaking his head. "Even if the king remain firm, he will be annoyed at every turn, so that he will feel his life is darker instead of lighter, save, of course, madame, for that brightness which you cannot fail to bring with you. We must bring the matter to an end."

"And how, father?"

"The marriage must be at once!"

"At once!"

"Yes. This very night, if possible."

"Oh, father, you ask too much. The king would never consent to such a proposal."

"It is he that will propose it."

"And why?"

"Because we shall force him to. It is only thus that all the opposition can be stopped. When it is done, the court will accept it. Until it is done, they will resist it."

"What would you have me do, then, father?"

"Resign the king."

"Resign him!" She turned as pale as a lily, and looked at him in bewilderment.

"It is the best course, madame."

"Ah, father, I might have done it last month, last week, even yesterday morning. But now—oh, it would break my heart!"

"Fear not, madame. We advise you for the best. Go to the king now, at once. Say to him that you have heard that he has been subjected to much annoyance upon your account, that you cannot bear to think that you should be a cause of dissension in his own family, and therefore you will release him from his promise, and will withdraw yourself from the court forever."

"Go now? At once?"

"Yes, without loss of an instant."

She cast a light mantle about her shoulders.

"I follow your advice," she said. "I believe that you are wiser than I. But, oh, if he should take me at my word!"

"He will not take you at your word."

"It is a terrible risk."

"But such an end as this cannot be gained without risks. Go, my child, and may heaven's blessing go with you!"

CHAPTER XIII.
THE KING HAS IDEAS.

The king had remained alone in his cabinet, wrapped in somewhat gloomy thoughts, and pondering over the means by which he might carry out his purpose and yet smooth away the opposition which seemed to be so strenuous and so universal. Suddenly there came a gentle tap at the door, and there was the woman who was in his thoughts, standing in the twilight before him. He sprang to his feet and held out his hands with a smile which would have reassured her had she doubted his constancy.

"Francoise! You here! Then I have at last a welcome visitor, and it is the first one to-day."

"Sire, I fear that you have been troubled."

"I have indeed, Francoise."

"But I have a remedy for it."

"And what is that?"

"I shall leave the court, sire, and you shall think no more of what has passed between us. I have brought discord where I meant to bring peace. Let me retire to St. Cyr, or to the Abbey of Fontevrault, and you will no longer be called upon to make such sacrifices for my sake."

The king turned deathly pale, and clutched at her shawl with a trembling hand, as though he feared that she was about to put her resolution into effect that very instant. For years his mind had accustomed itself to lean upon hers. He had turned to her whenever he needed support, and even when, as in the last week, he had broken away from her for a time, it was still all-important to him to know that she was there, the faithful friend, ever forgiving, ever soothing, waiting for him with her ready counsel and sympathy. But that she should leave him now, leave him altogether, such a thought had never occurred to him, and it struck him with a chill of surprised alarm.

"You cannot mean it, Francoise," he cried, in a trembling voice. "No, no, it is impossible that you are in earnest."

"It would break my heart to leave you, sire, but it breaks it also to think that for my sake you are estranged from your own family and ministers."

"Tut! Am I not the king? Shall I not take my own course without heed to them? No, no, Francoise, you must not leave me! You must stay with me and be my wife." He could hardly speak for agitation, and he still grasped at her dress to detain her. She had been precious to him before, but was far more so now that there seemed to be a possibility of his losing her. She felt the strength of her position, and used it to the utmost.

"Some time must elapse before our wedding, sire. Yet during all that interval you will be exposed to these annoyances. How can I be happy when I feel that I have brought upon you so long a period of discomfort?"

"And why should it be so long, Francoise?"

"A day would be too long, sire, for you to be unhappy through my fault. It is a misery to me to think of it. Believe me, it would be better that I should leave you."

"Never! You shall not! Why should we even wait a day, Francoise? I am ready. You are ready. Why should we not be married now?"

"At once! Oh, sire!"

"We shall. It is my wish. It is my order. That is my answer to those who would drive me. They shall know nothing of it until it is done, and then let us see which of them will dare to treat my wife with anything but respect. Let it be done secretly, Francoise. I will send in a trusty messenger this very night for the Archbishop of Paris, and I swear that, if all France stand in the way, he shall make us man and wife before he departs."

"Is it your will, sire?"

"It is; and ah, I can see by your eyes that it is yours also! We shall not lose a moment, Francoise. What a blessed thought of mine, which will silence their tongues forever! When it is ready they may know, but not before. To your room, then, dearest of friends and truest of women! When we meet again, it will be to form a bond which all this court and all this kingdom shall not be able to loose."

The king was all on fire with the excitement of this new resolution. He had lost his air of doubt and discontent, and he paced swiftly about the room with a smiling face and shining eyes. Then he touched a small gold bell, which summoned Bontems, his private body-servant.

"What o'clock is it, Bontems?"

"It is nearly six, sire."

"Hum!" The king considered for some moments. "Do you know where Captain de Catinat is, Bontems?"

"He was in the grounds, sire, but I heard that he would ride back to Paris to-night."

"Does he ride alone?"

"He has one friend with him."

"Who is this friend? An officer of the guards?"

"No, sire; it is a stranger from over the seas, from America, as I understand, who has stayed with him of late, and to whom Monsieur de Catinat has been showing the wonders of your Majesty's palace."

"A stranger! So much the better. Go, Bontems, and bring them both to me."

"I trust that they have not started, sire. I will see." He hurried off, and was back in ten minutes in the cabinet once more.

"Well?"

"I have been fortunate, sire. Their horses had been led out and their feet were in the stirrups when I reached them."

"Where are they, then?"

"They await your Majesty's orders in the ante-room."

"Show them in, Bontems, and give admission to none, not even to the minister, until they have left me."

To De Catinat an audience with the monarch was a common incident of his duties, but it was with profound astonishment that he learned from Bontems that his friend and companion was included in the order. He was eagerly endeavouring to whisper into the young American's ear some precepts and warnings as to what to do and what to avoid, when Bontems reappeared and ushered them into the presence.

It was with a feeling of curiosity, not unmixed with awe, that Amos Green, to whom Governor Dongan, of New York, had been the highest embodiment of human power, entered the private chamber of the greatest monarch in Christendom. The magnificence of the ante-chamber in which he had waited, the velvets, the paintings, the gildings, with the throng of gaily dressed officials and of magnificent guardsmen, had all impressed his imagination, and had prepared him for some wondrous figure robed and crowned, a fit centre for such a scene. As his eyes fell upon a quietly dressed, bright-eyed man, half a head shorter than himself, with a trim dapper figure, and an erect carriage, he could not help glancing round the room to see if this were indeed the monarch, or if it were some other of those endless officials who interposed themselves between him and the other world. The reverent salute of his companion, however, showed him that this must indeed be the king, so he bowed and then drew himself erect with the simple dignity of a man who has been trained in Nature's school.

"Good-evening, Captain de Catinat," said the king, with a pleasant smile. "Your friend, as I understand, is a stranger to this country. I trust, sir, that you have found something here to interest and to amuse you?"

"Yes, your Majesty. I have seen your great city, and it is a wonderful one. And my friend has shown me this palace, with its woods and its grounds. When I go back to my own country I will have much to say of what I have seen in your beautiful land."

"You speak French, and yet you are not a Canadian."

"No, sire; I am from the English provinces."

The king looked with interest at the powerful figure, the bold features, and the free bearing of the young foreigner, and his mind flashed back to the dangers which the Comte de Frontenac had foretold from these same colonies. If this were indeed a type of his race, they must in truth be a people whom it would be better to have as friends than as enemies. His mind, however, ran at present on other things than statecraft, and he hastened to give De Catinat his orders for the night.

"You will ride into Paris on my service. Your friend can go with you. Two are safer than one when they bear a message of state. I wish you, however, to wait until nightfall before you start."

"Yes, sire."

"Let none know your errand, and see that none follow you. You know the house of Archbishop Harlay, prelate of Paris?"

"Yes, sire."

"You will bid him drive out hither and be at the north-west side postern by midnight. Let nothing hold him back. Storm or fine, he must he here to-night. It is of the first importance."

"He shall have your order, sire."

"Very good. Adieu, captain. Adieu, monsieur. I trust that your stay in France may be a pleasant one." He waved his hand, smiling with the fascinating grace which had won so many hearts, and so dismissed the two friends to their new mission.

CHAPTER XIV.
THE LAST CARD.

Madame de Montespan still kept to her rooms, uneasy in mind at the king's disappearance, but unwilling to show her anxiety to the court by appearing among them or by making any inquiry as to what had occurred. While she thus remained in ignorance of the sudden and complete collapse of her fortunes, she had one active and energetic agent who had lost no incident of what had occurred, and who watched her interests with as much zeal as if they were his own. And indeed they were his own; for her brother, Monsieur de Vivonne, had gained everything for which he yearned, money, lands, and preferment, through his sister's notoriety, and he well knew that the fall of her fortunes must be very rapidly followed by that of his own. By nature bold, unscrupulous, and resourceful, he was not a man to lose the game without playing it out to the very end with all the energy and cunning of which he was capable. Keenly alert to all that passed, he had, from the time that he first heard the rumour of the king's intention, haunted the antechamber and drawn his own conclusions from what he had seen. Nothing had escaped him—the disconsolate faces of monsieur and of the dauphin, the visit of Pere la Chaise and Bossuet to the lady's room, her return, the triumph which shone in her eyes as she came away from the interview. He had seen Bontems hurry off and summon the guardsman and his friend. He had heard them order their horses to be brought out in a couple of hours' time, and finally, from a spy whom he employed among the servants, he learned that an unwonted bustle was going forward in Madame de Maintenon's room, that Mademoiselle Nanon was half wild with excitement, and that two court milliners had been hastily summoned to madame's apartment. It was only, however, when he heard from the same servant that a chamber was to be prepared for the reception that night of the Archbishop of Paris that he understood how urgent was the danger.

Madame de Montespan had spent the evening stretched upon a sofa, in the worst possible humour with everyone around her. She had read, but had tossed aside the book. She had written, but had torn up the paper. A thousand fears and suspicions chased each other through her head. What had become of the king, then? He had seemed cold yesterday, and his eyes had been for ever sliding round to the clock. And to-day he had not come at all. Was it his gout, perhaps? Or was it possible that she was again losing her hold upon him? Surely it could not be that! She turned upon her couch and faced the mirror which flanked the door. The candles had just been lit in her chamber, two score of them, each with silver backs which reflected their light until the room was as bright as day. There in the mirror was the brilliant chamber, the deep red ottoman, and the single figure in its gauzy dress of white and silver. She leaned upon her elbow, admiring the deep tint of her own eyes with their long dark lashes, the white curve of her throat, and the perfect oval of her face. She examined it all carefully, keenly, as though it were her rival that lay before her, but nowhere could she see a scratch of Time's malicious nails. She still had her beauty, then. And if it had once won the king, why should it not suffice to hold him? Of course it would do so. She reproached herself for her fears. Doubtless he was indisposed, or perhaps he would come still. Ha! there was the sound of an opening door and of a quick step in her ante-room. Was it he, or at least his messenger with a note from him?

But no, it was her brother, with the haggard eyes and drawn face of a man who is weighed down with his own evil tidings. He turned as he entered, fastened the door, and then striding across the room, locked the other one which led to her boudoir.

"We are safe from interruption," he panted. "I have hastened here, for every second may be invaluable. Have you heard anything from the king?"

"Nothing." She had sprung to her feet, and was gazing at him with a face which was as pale as his own.

"The hour has come for action, Francoise. It is the hour at which the Mortemarts have always shown at their best. Do not yield to the blow, then, but gather yourself to meet it."

"What is it?" She tried to speak in her natural tone, but only a whisper came to her dry lips.

"The king is about to marry Madame de Maintenon."

"The *gouvernante*! The widow Scarron! It is impossible!"

"It is certain."

"To marry? Did you say to marry?"

"Yes, he will marry her."

The woman flung out her hands in a gesture of contempt, and laughed loud and bitterly.

"You are easily frightened, brother," said she. "Ah, you do not know your little sister. Perchance if you were not my brother you might rate my powers more highly. Give me a day, only one little day, and you will see Louis, the proud Louis, down at the hem of my dress to ask my pardon for this slight. I tell you that he cannot break the bonds that hold him. One day is all I ask to bring him back."

"But you cannot have it."

"What?"

"The marriage is to-night."

"You are mad, Charles."

"I am certain of it." In a few broken sentences he shot out all that he had seen and heard. She listened with a grim face, and hands which closed ever tighter and tighter as he proceeded. But he had said the truth about the Mortemarts. They came of a contentious blood, and were ever at their best at a moment of action. Hate rather than dismay filled her heart as she listened, and the whole energy of her nature gathered and quickened to meet the crisis.

"I shall go and see him," she cried, sweeping towards the door.

"No, no, Francoise. Believe me, you will ruin everything if you do. Strict orders have been given to the guard to admit no one to the king."

"But I shall insist upon passing them."

"Believe me, sister, it is worse than useless. I have spoken with the officer of the guard, and the command is a stringent one."

"Ah, I shall manage."

"No, you shall not." He put his back against the door. "I know that it is useless, and I will not have my sister make herself the laughing-stock of the court, trying to force her way into the room of a man who repulses her."

His sister's cheeks flushed at the words, and she paused irresolute.

"Had I only a day, Charles, I am sure that I could bring him back to me. There has been some other influence here, that meddlesome Jesuit or the pompous Bossuet, perhaps. Only one day to counteract their wiles! Can I not see them waving hell-fire before his foolish eyes, as one swings a torch before a bull to turn it? Oh, if I could but baulk them to-night! That woman! that cursed woman! The foul viper which I nursed in my bosom! Oh, I had rather see Louis in his grave than married to her! Charles, Charles, it must be stopped; I say it must be stopped! I will give anything, everything, to prevent it!"

"What will you give, my sister?"

She looked at him aghast. "What! you do not wish me to buy you?" she said.

"No; but I wish to buy others."

"Ha! You see a chance, then?"

"One, and one only. But time presses. I want money."

"How much?"

"I cannot have too much. All that you can spare."

With hands which trembled with eagerness she unlocked a secret cupboard in the wall in which she concealed her valuables. A blaze of jewellery met her brother's eyes as he peered over her shoulder. Great rubies, costly emeralds, deep ruddy beryls, glimmering diamonds, were scattered there in one brilliant shimmering many-coloured heap, the harvest which she had reaped from the king's generosity during more than fifteen years. At one side were three drawers, the one over the other. She drew out the lowest one. It was full to the brim of glittering *louis d'ors*.

"Take what you will!" she said. "And now your plan! Quick!"

He stuffed the money in handfuls into the side pockets of his coat. Coins slipped between his fingers and tinkled and wheeled over the floor, but neither cast a glance at them.

"Your plan?" she repeated.

"We must prevent the Archbishop from arriving here. Then the marriage would be postponed until to-morrow night, and you would have time to act."

"But how prevent it?"

"There are a dozen good rapiers about the court which are to be bought for less than I carry in one pocket. There is De la Touche, young Turberville, old Major Despard, Raymond de Carnac, and the four Latours. I will gather them together, and wait on the road."

"And waylay the archbishop?"

"No; the messengers."

"Oh, excellent! You are a prince of brothers! If no message reaches Paris, we are saved. Go; go; do not lose a moment, my dear Charles."

"It is very well, Francoise; but what are we to do with them when we get them? We may lose our heads over the matter, it seems to me. After all, they are the king's messengers, and we can scarce pass our swords through them."

"No?"

"There would be no forgiveness for that."

"But consider that before the matter is looked into I shall have regained my influence with the king."

"All very fine, my little sister, but how long is your influence to last? A pleasant life for us if at every change of favour we have to fly the country! No, no, Francoise; the most that we can do is to detain the messengers."

"Where can you detain them?"

"I have an idea. There is the castle of the Marquis de Montespan at Portillac."

"Of my husband!"

"Precisely."

"Of my most bitter enemy! Oh, Charles, you are not serious."

"On the contrary, I was never more so. The marquis was away in Paris yesterday, and has not yet returned. Where is the ring with his arms?"

She hunted among her jewels and picked out a gold ring with a broad engraved face.

"This will be our key. When good Marceau, the steward, sees it, every dungeon in the castle will be at our disposal. It is that or nothing. There is no other place where we can hold them safe."

"But when my husband returns?"

"Ah, he may be a little puzzled as to his captives. And the complaisant Marceau may have an evil quarter of an hour. But that may not be for a week, and by that time, my little sister, I have confidence enough in you to think that you really may have finished the campaign. Not another word, for every moment is of value. Adieu, Francoise! We shall not be conquered without a struggle. I will send a message to you to-night to let you know how fortune uses us." He took her fondly in his arms, kissed her, and then hurried from the room.

For hours after his departure she paced up and down with noiseless steps upon the deep soft carpet, her hand still clenched, her eyes flaming, her whole soul wrapped and consumed with jealousy and hatred of her rival. Ten struck, and eleven, and midnight, but still she waited, fierce and eager, straining her ears for every foot-fall which might be the herald of news. At last it came. She heard the quick step in the passage, the tap at the ante-room door, and the whispering of her black page. Quivering with impatience, she rushed in and took the note herself from the dusty cavalier who had brought it. It was but six words scrawled roughly upon a wisp of dirty paper, but it brought the colour back to her cheeks and the smile to her lips. It was her brother's writing, and it ran: "The archbishop will not come to-night."

CHAPTER XV.
THE MIDNIGHT MISSION.

De Catinat in the meanwhile was perfectly aware of the importance of the mission which had been assigned to him. The secrecy which had been enjoined by the king, his evident excitement, and the nature of his orders, all confirmed the rumours which were already beginning to buzz round the court. He knew enough of the intrigues and antagonisms with which the court was full to understand that every precaution was necessary in carrying out his instructions. He waited, therefore, until night had fallen before ordering his soldier-servant to bring round the two horses to one of the less public gates of the grounds. As he and his friend walked together to the spot, he gave the young American a rapid sketch of the situation at the court, and of the chance that this nocturnal ride might be an event which would affect the future history of France.

"I like your king," said Amos Green, "and I am glad to ride in his service. He is a slip of a man to be the head of a great nation, but he has the eye of a chief. If one met him alone in a Maine forest, one would know him as a man who was different to his fellows. Well, I am glad that he is going to marry again, though it's a great house for any woman to have to look after."

De Catinat smiled at his comrade's idea of a queen's duties.

"Are you armed?" he asked. "You have no sword or pistols?"

"No; if I may not carry my gun, I had rather not be troubled by tools that I have never learned to use. I have my knife. But why do you ask?"

"Because there may be danger."

"And how?"

"Many have an interest in stopping this marriage. All the first men of the kingdom are bitterly against it. If they could stop *us*, they would stop *it*, for to-night at least."

"But I thought it was a secret?"

"There is no such thing at a court. There is the dauphin, or the king's brother, either of them, or any of their friends, would be right glad that we should be in the Seine before we reach the archbishop's house this night. But who is this?"

A burly figure had loomed up through the gloom on the path upon which they were going. As it approached, a coloured lamp dangling from one of the trees shone upon the blue and silver of an officer of the guards. It was Major de Brissac, of De Catinat's own regiment.

"Hullo! Whither away?" he asked.

"To Paris, major."

"I go there myself within an hour. Will you not wait, that we may go together?"

"I am sorry, but I ride on a matter of urgency. I must not lose a minute."

"Very good. Good-night, and a pleasant ride."

"Is he a trusty man, our friend the major?" asked Amos Green, glancing back.

"True as steel."

"Then I would have a word with him." The American hurried back along the way they had come, while De Catinat stood chafing at this unnecessary delay. It was a full five minutes before his companion joined him, and the fiery blood of the French soldier was hot with impatience and anger.

"I think that perhaps you had best ride into Paris at your leisure, my friend," said he. "If I go upon the king's service I cannot be delayed whenever the whim takes you."

"I am sorry," answered the other quietly. "I had something to say to your major, and I thought that maybe I might not see him again."

"Well, here are the horses," said the guardsman as he pushed open the postern-gate. "Have you fed an watered them, Jacques?"

"Yes, my captain," answered the man who stood at their head.

"Boot and saddle, then, friend Green, and we shall not draw rein again until we see the lights of Paris in front of us."

The soldier-groom peered through the darkness after them with a sardonic smile upon his face. "You won't draw rein, won't you?" he muttered as he turned away. "Well, we shall see about that, my captain; we shall see about that."

For a mile or more the comrades galloped along, neck to neck and knee to knee. A wind had sprung up from the westward, and the heavens were covered with heavy gray clouds, which drifted swiftly across, a crescent moon peeping fitfully from time to time between the rifts. Even during these moments of brightness the road, shadowed as it was by heavy trees, was very dark, but when the light was shut off it was hard, but for the loom upon either side, to tell where it lay. De Catinat at least found it so, and he peered anxiously over his horse's ears, and stooped his face to the mane in his efforts to see his way.

"What do you make of the road?" he asked at last.

"It looks as if a good many carriage wheels had passed over it to-day."

"What! *Mon Dieu!* Do you mean to say that you can see carriage wheels there?"

"Certainly. Why not?"

"Why, man, I cannot see the road at all."

Amos Green laughed heartily. "When you have travelled in the woods by night as often as I have," said he, "when to show a light may mean to lose your hair, one comes to learn to use one's eyes."

"Then you had best ride on, and I shall keep just behind you. So! *Hola!* What is the matter now?"

There had been the sudden sharp snap of something breaking, and the American had reeled for an instant in the saddle.

"It's one of my stirrup leathers. It has fallen."

"Can you find it?"

"Yes; but I can ride as well without it. Let us push on."

"Very good. I can just see you now."

They had galloped for about five minutes in this fashion, De Catinat's horse's head within a few feet of the other's tail, when there was a second snap, and the guardsman rolled out of the saddle on to the ground. He kept his grip of the reins, however, and was up in an instant at his horse's head, sputtering out oaths as only an angry Frenchman can.

"A thousand thunders of heaven!" he cried. "What was it that happened then?"

"Your leather has gone too."

"Two stirrup leathers in five minutes? It is not possible."

"It is not possible that it should be chance," said the American gravely, swinging himself off his horse. "Why, what is this? My other leather is cut, and hangs only by a thread."

"And so does mine. I can feel it when I pass my hand along. Have you a tinder-box? Let us strike a light."

"No, no; the man who is in the dark is in safety. I let the other folk strike lights. We can see all that is needful to us."

"My rein is cut also."

"And so is mine."

"And the girth of my saddle."

"It is a wonder that we came so far with whole bones. Now, who has played us this little trick?"

"Who could it be but that rogue Jacques! He has had the horses in his charge. By my faith, he shall know what the strappado means when I see Versailles again."

"But why should he do it?"

"Ah, he has been set on to it. He has been a tool in the hands of those who wished to hinder our journey."

"Very like. But they must have had some reason behind. They knew well that to cut our straps would not prevent us from reaching Paris, since we could ride bareback, or, for that matter, could run it if need be."

"They hoped to break our necks."

"One neck they might break, but scarce those of two, since the fate of the one would warn the other."

"Well, then, what do you think that they meant?" cried De Catinat impatiently. "For heaven's sake, let us come to some conclusion, for every minute is of importance."

But the other was not to be hurried out of his cool, methodical fashion of speech and of thought.

"They could not have thought to stop us," said he.

"What did they mean, then? They could only have meant to delay us. And why should they wish to delay us? What could it matter to them if we gave our message an hour or two sooner or an hour or two later? It could not matter."

"For heaven's sake—" broke in De Catinat impetuously.

But Amos Green went on hammering the matter slowly out.

"Why should they wish to delay us, then? There's only one reason that I can see. In order to give other folk time to get in front of us and stop us. That is it, captain. I'd lay you a beaver-skin to a rabbit-pelt that I'm on the track. There's been a party of a dozen horsemen along this ground since the dew began to fall. If they were delayed, they would have time to form their plans before we came."

"By my faith, you may be right," said De Catinat thoughtfully. "What would you propose?"

"That we ride back, and go by some less direct way."

"It is impossible. We should have to ride back to Meudon cross-roads, and then it would add ten miles to our journey."

"It is better to get there an hour later than not to get there at all."

"Pshaw! we are surely not to be turned from our path by a mere guess. There is the St. Germain cross-road about a mile below. When we reach it we can strike to the right along the south side of the river, and so change our course."

"But we may not reach it."

"If anyone bars our way we shall know how to treat with them."

"You would fight, then?"

"Yes."

"What! with a dozen of them?"

"A hundred, if we are on the king's errand."

Amos Green shrugged his shoulders.

"You are surely not afraid?"

"Yes, I am, mighty afraid. Fighting's good enough when there's no help for it. But I call it a fool's plan to ride straight into a trap when you might go round it."

"You may do what you like," said De Catinat angrily.

"My father was a gentleman, the owner of a thousand arpents of land, and his son is not going to flinch in the king's service."

"My father," answered Amos Green, "was a merchant, the owner of a thousand skunk-skins, and his son knows a fool when he sees one."

"You are insolent, sir," cried the guardsman. "We can settle this matter at some more fitting opportunity. At present I continue my mission, and you are very welcome to turn back to Versailles if you are so inclined." He raised his hat with punctilious politeness, sprang on to his horse, and rode on down the road.

Amos Green hesitated a little, and then mounting, he soon overtook his companion. The latter, however, was still in no very sweet temper, and rode with a rigid neck, without a glance or a word for his comrade. Suddenly his eyes caught something in the gloom which brought a smile back to his face. Away in front of them, between two dark tree clumps, lay a vast number of shimmering, glittering yellow points, as thick as flowers in a garden. They were the lights of Paris.

"See!" he cried, pointing. "There is the city, and close here must be the St. Germain road. We shall take it, so as to avoid any danger."

"Very good! But you should not ride too fast, when your girth may break at any moment."

"Nay, come on; we are close to our journey's end. The St. Germain road opens just round this corner, and then we shall see our way, for the lights will guide us."

He cut his horse with his whip, and they galloped together round the curve. Next instant they were both down in one wild heap of tossing heads and struggling hoofs, De Catinat partly covered by his horse, and his comrade hurled twenty paces, where he lay silent and motionless in the centre of the road.

CHAPTER XVI.
"WHEN THE DEVIL DRIVES."

Monsieur de Vivonne had laid his ambuscade with discretion. With a closed carriage and a band of chosen ruffians he had left the palace a good half-hour before the king's messengers, and by the aid of his sister's gold he had managed that their journey should not be a very rapid one. On reaching the branch road he had ordered the coachman to drive some little distance along it, and had tethered all the horses to a fence under his charge. He had then stationed one of the band as a sentinel some distance up the main highway to flash a light when the two courtiers were approaching. A stout cord had been fastened eighteen inches from the ground to the trunk of a wayside sapling, and on receiving the signal the other end was tied to a gate-post upon the further side. The two cavaliers could not possibly see it, coming as it did at the very curve of the road, and as a consequence their horses fell heavily to the ground, and brought them down with them. In an instant the dozen ruffians who had lurked in the shadow of the trees sprang out upon them, sword in hand; but there was no movement from either of their victims. De Catinat lay breathing heavily, one leg under his horse's neck, and the blood trickling in a thin stream down his pale face, and falling, drop by drop, on to his silver shoulder-straps. Amos Green was unwounded, but his injured girth had given way in the fall, and he had been hurled from his horse on to the hard road with a violence which had driven every particle of breath from his body.

Monsieur de Vivonne lit a lantern, and flashed it upon the faces of the two unconscious men. "This is a bad business, Major Despard," said he to the man next him. "I believe that they are both gone."

"Tut! tut! By my soul, men did not die like that when I was young!" answered the other, leaning forward his fierce grizzled face into the light of the lantern. "I've been cast from my horse as often as there are tags to my doublet, but, save for the snap of a bone or two, I never had any harm from it. Pass your rapier under the third rib of the horses, De la Touche; they will never be fit to set hoof to ground again." Two sobbing gasps and the thud of their straining necks falling back to earth told that the two steeds had come to the end of their troubles.

"Where is Latour?" asked Monsieur de Vivonne. "Achille Latour has studied medicine at Montpellier. Where is he?"

"Here I am, your excellency. It is not for me to boast, but I am as handy a man with a lancet as with a rapier, and it was an evil day for some sick folk when I first took to buff and bandolier. Which would you have me look to?"

"This one in the road."

The trooper bent over Amos Green. "He is not long for this world," said he. "I can tell it by the catch of his breath."

"And what is his injury?"

"A subluxation of the epigastrium. Ah, the words of learning will still come to my tongue, but it is hard to put into common terms. Methinks that it were well for me to pass my dagger through his throat, for his end is very near."

"Not for your life!" cried the leader. "If he die without wound, they cannot lay it to our charge. Turn now to the other."

The man bent over De Catinat, and placed his hand upon his heart. As he did so the soldier heaved a long sigh, opened his eyes, and gazed about him with the face of one who knows neither where he is nor how he came there. De Vivonne, who had drawn his hat down over his eyes, and muffled the lower part of his face in his mantle, took out his flask, and poured a little of the contents down the injured man's throat. In an instant a dash of colour had come back into the guardsman's bloodless cheeks, and the light of memory into his eyes. He struggled up on to his feet, and strove furiously to push away those who held him. But his head still swam, and he could scarce hold himself erect.

"I must to Paris!" he gasped; "I must to Paris! It is the king's mission. You stop me at your peril!"

"He has no hurt save a scratch," said the ex-doctor.

"Then hold him fast. And first carry the dying man to the carriage."

The lantern threw but a small ring of yellow light, so that when it had been carried over to De Catinat, Amos Green was left lying in the shadow. Now they brought the light back to where the young man lay. But there was no sign of him. He was gone.

For a moment the little group of ruffians stood staring, the light of their lantern streaming up upon their plumed hats, their fierce eyes, and savage faces. Then a burst of oaths broke from them, and De Vivonne caught the false doctor by the throat, and hurling him down, would have choked him upon the spot, had the others not dragged them apart.

"You lying dog!" he cried. "Is this your skill? The man has fled, and we are ruined!"

"He has done it in his death-struggle," gasped the other hoarsely, sitting up and rubbing his throat. "I tell you that he was *in extremis*. He cannot be far off."

"That is true. He cannot be far off," cried De Vivonne. "He has neither horse nor arms. You, Despard and Raymond de Carnac, guard the other, that he play us no trick. Do you, Latour, and you, Turberville, ride down the road, and wait by the south gate. If he enter Paris at all, he must come in that way. If you get him, tie him before you on your horse, and bring him to the rendezvous. In any case, it matters little, for he is a stranger, this fellow, and only here by chance. Now lead the other to the carriage, and we shall get away before an alarm is given."

The two horsemen rode off in pursuit of the fugitive, and De Catinat, still struggling desperately to escape, was dragged down the St. Germain road and thrust into the carriage, which had waited at some distance while these incidents were being enacted. Three of the horsemen rode ahead, the coachman was curtly ordered to follow them, and De Vivonne, having despatched one of the band with a note to his sister, followed after the coach with the remainder of his desperadoes.

The unfortunate guardsman had now entirely recovered his senses, and found himself with a strap round his ankles, and another round his wrists, a captive inside a moving prison which lumbered heavily along the country road. He had been stunned by the shock of his fall, and his leg was badly bruised by the weight of his horse; but the cut on his forehead was a mere trifle, and the bleeding had already ceased. His mind, however, pained him more than his body. He sank his head into his pinioned hands, and stamped madly with his feet, rocking himself to and fro in his despair. What a fool, a treble fool, he had been! He, an old soldier, who had seen something of war, to walk with open eyes into such a trap! The king had chosen him of all men, as a trusty messenger, and yet he had failed him—and failed him so ignominiously, without shot fired or sword drawn. He was warned, too, warned by a young man who knew nothing of court intrigue, and who was guided only by the wits which Nature had given him. De Catinat dashed himself down upon the leather cushion in the agony of his thoughts.

But then came a return of that common-sense which lies so very closely beneath the impetuosity of the Celt. The matter was done now, and he must see if it could not be mended. Amos Green had escaped. That was one grand point in his favour. And Amos Green had heard the king's message, and realised its importance. It was true that he knew nothing of Paris, but surely a man who could pick his way at night through the forests of Maine would not be baulked in finding so well-known a house as that of the Archbishop of Paris. But then there came a sudden thought which turned De Catinat's heart to lead. The city gates were locked at eight o'clock in the evening. It was now nearly nine. It would have been easy for him, whose uniform was a voucher for his message, to gain his way through. But how could Amos Green, a foreigner and a civilian, hope to pass? It was impossible, clearly impossible. And yet, somehow, in spite of the impossibility, he still clung to a vague hope that a man so full of energy and resource might find some way out of the difficulty.

And then the thought of escape occurred to his mind. Might he not even now be in time, perhaps, to carry his own message? Who were these men who had seized him? They had said nothing to give him a hint as to whose tools they were. Monsieur and the dauphin occurred to his mind. Probably one or the other. He had only recognised one of them, old Major Despard, a man who frequented the low wine-shops of Versailles, and whose sword was ever at the disposal of the longest purse. And where were these people taking him to? It might be to his death. But if they wished to do away with him, why should they have brought him back to consciousness? and why this carriage and drive? Full of curiosity, he peered out of the windows.

A horseman was riding close up on either side; but there was glass in front of the carriage, and through this he could gain some idea as to his whereabouts. The clouds had cleared now, and the moon was shining brightly, bathing the whole wide landscape in its shimmering light. To the right lay the open country, broad plains with clumps of woodland, and the towers of castles pricking out from above the groves. A heavy bell was ringing in some monastery, and its dull booming came and went with the breeze. On the left, but far away, lay the glimmer of Paris. They were leaving it rapidly behind. Whatever his destination, it was neither the capital nor Versailles. Then he began to count the chances of escape. His sword had been removed, and his pistols were still in the holsters beside his unfortunate horse. He was unarmed, then, even if he could free himself, and his captors were at least a dozen in number. There were three on ahead, riding abreast along the white, moonlit road. Then there was one on each side, and he should judge by the clatter of hoofs that there could not be fewer than half a dozen behind. That would make exactly twelve, including the coachman, too many, surely, for an unarmed man to hope to baffle. At the thought of the coachman he had glanced through the glass front at the broad back of the man, and he had suddenly, in the glimmer of the carriage lamp, observed something which struck him with horror.

The man was evidently desperately wounded. It was strange indeed that he could still sit there and flick his whip with so terrible an injury. In the back of his great red coat, just under the left shoulder-blade, was a gash in the cloth, where some weapon had passed, and all round was a wide patch of dark scarlet which told its own tale. Nor was this all. As he raised his whip, the moonlight shone upon his hand, and De Catinat saw with a shudder that it also was splashed and clogged with blood. The guardsman craned his neck to catch a glimpse of the man's face; but his broad-brimmed hat was drawn low, and the high collar of his driving-coat was raised, so that his features were in the shadow. This silent man in front of him, with the horrible marks upon his person, sent a chill to De Catinat's valiant heart, and he muttered over one of Marot's Huguenot psalms; for who but the foul fiend himself would drive a coach with those crimsoned hands and with a sword driven through his body?

And now they had come to a spot where the main road ran onwards, but a smaller side track wound away down the steep slope of a hill, and so in the direction of the Seine. The advance-guard had kept to the main road, and the two horsemen on either side were trotting in the same direction, when, to De Catinat's amazement, the carriage suddenly swerved to one side, and in an instant plunged down the steep incline, the two stout horses galloping at their topmost speed, the coachman standing up and lashing furiously at them, and the clumsy old vehicle bounding along in a way which threw him backwards and forwards from one seat to the other. Behind him he could hear a shout of consternation from the escort, and then the rush of galloping hoofs. Away they flew, the roadside poplars dancing past at either window, the horses thundering along with their stomachs to the earth, and that demon driver still waving those horrible red hands in the moonlight and screaming out to the maddened steeds. Sometimes the carriage jolted one way, sometimes another, swaying furiously, and running on two side wheels as though it must every instant go over. And yet, fast as they went, their pursuers went faster still. The rattle of their hoofs was at their very backs, and suddenly at one of the windows there came into view the red, distended nostrils of a horse. Slowly it drew forward, the muzzle, the eye, the ears, the mane, coming into sight as the rider still gained upon them, and then above them the fierce face of Despard and the gleam of a brass pistol barrel.

"At the horse, Despard, at the horse!" cried an authoritative voice from behind.

The pistol flashed, and the coach lurched over as one of the horses gave a convulsive spring. But the driver still shrieked and lashed with his whip, while the carriage bounded onwards.

But now the road turned a sudden curve, and there, right in front of them, not a hundred paces away, was the Seine, running cold and still in the moonshine. The bank on either side of the highway ran straight down without any break to the water's edge. There was no sign of a bridge, and a black shadow in the centre of the stream showed where the ferry-boat was returning after conveying some belated travellers across. The driver never hesitated, but gathering up the reins, he urged the frightened creatures into the river. They hesitated, however, when they first felt the cold water about their hocks, and even as they did so one of them, with a low moan, fell over upon her side. Despard's bullet had found its mark. Like a flash the coachman hurled himself from the box and plunged into the stream; but the pursuing horsemen were all round him before this, and half-a-dozen hands had seized him ere he could reach deep water, and had dragged him to the bank. His broad hat had been struck off in the struggle, and De Catinat saw his face in the moonshine. Great heavens! It was Amos Green.

CHAPTER XVII.
THE DUNGEON OF PORTILLAC.

The desperadoes were as much astonished as was De Catinat when they found that they had recaptured in this extraordinary manner the messenger whom they had given up for lost. A volley of oaths and exclamations broke from them, as, on tearing off the huge red coat of the coachman, they disclosed the sombre dress of the young American.

"A thousand thunders!" cried one. "And this is the man whom that devil's brat Latour would make out to be dead!"

"And how came he here?"

"And where is Etienne Arnaud?"

"He has stabbed Etienne. See the great cut in the coat!"

"Ay; and see the colour of his hand! He has stabbed him, and taken his coat and hat."

"What! while we were all within stone's cast!"

"Ay; there is no other way out of it."

"By my soul!" cried old Despard, "I had never much love for old Etienne, but I have emptied a cup of wine with him before now, and I shall see that he has justice. Let us cast these reins round the fellow's neck and hang him upon this tree."

Several pairs of hands were already unbuckling the harness of the dead horse, when De Vivonne pushed his way into the little group, and with a few curt words checked their intended violence.

"It is as much as your lives are worth to touch him," said he.

"But he has slain Etienne Arnaud."

"That score may be settled afterwards. To-night he is the king's messenger. Is the other all safe?"

"Yes, he is here."

"Tie this man, and put him in beside him. Unbuckle the traces of the dead horse. So! Now, De Carnac, put your own into the harness. You can mount the box and drive, for we have not very far to go."

The changes were rapidly made; Amos Green was thrust in beside De Catinat, and the carriage was soon toiling up the steep incline which it had come down so precipitately. The American had said not a word since his capture, and had remained absolutely stolid, with his hands crossed over his chest whilst his fate was under discussion. Now that he was alone once more with his comrade, however, he frowned and muttered like a man who feels that fortune has used him badly.

"Those infernal horses!" he grumbled. "Why, an American horse would have taken to the water like a duck. Many a time have I swum my old stallion Sagamore across the Hudson. Once over the river, we should have had a clear lead to Paris."

"My dear friend," cried De Catinat, laying his manacled hands upon those of his comrade, "can you forgive me for speaking as I did upon the way from Versailles?"

"Tut, man! I never gave it a thought."

"You were right a thousand times, and I was, as you said, a fool—a blind, obstinate fool. How nobly you have stood by me! But how came you there? Never in my life have I been so astonished as when I saw your face."

Amos Green chuckled to himself. "I thought that maybe it would be a surprise to you if you knew who was driving you," said he. "When I was thrown from my horse I lay quiet, partly because I wanted to get a grip of my breath, and partly because it seemed to me to be more healthy to lie than to stand with all those swords clinking in my ears. Then they all got round you, and I rolled into the ditch, crept along it, got on the cross-road in the shadow of the trees, and was beside the carriage before ever they knew that I was gone. I saw in a flash that there was only one way by which I could be of use to you. The coachman was leaning round with his head turned to see what was going on behind him. I out with my knife, sprang up on the front wheel, and stopped his tongue forever."

"What! without a sound!"

"I have not lived among the Indians for nothing."

"And then?"

"I pulled him down into the ditch, and I got into his coat and his hat. I did not scalp him."

"Scalp him? Great heavens! Such things are only done among savages."

"Ah! I thought that maybe it was not the custom of the country. I am glad now that I did not do it. I had hardly got the reins before they were all back and bundled you into the coach. I was not afraid of their seeing me, but I was scared lest I should not know which road to take, and so set them on the trail. But they made it easy to me by sending some of their riders in front, so I did well until I saw that by-track and made a run for it. We'd have got away, too, if that rogue hadn't shot the horse, and if the beasts had faced the water."

The guardsman again pressed his comrade's hands. "You have been as true to me as hilt to blade," said he. "It was a bold thought and a bold deed."

"And what now?" asked the American.

"I do not know who these men are, and I do not know whither they are taking us."

"To their villages, likely, to burn us."

De Catinat laughed in spite of his anxiety. "You will have it that we are back in America again," said he. "They don't do things in that way in France."

"They seem free enough with hanging in France. I tell you, I felt like a smoked-out 'coon when that trace was round my neck."

"I fancy that they are taking us to some place where they can shut us up until this business blows over."

"Well, they'll need to be smart about it."

"Why?"

"Else maybe they won't find us when they want us."

"What do you mean?"

For answer, the American, with a twist and a wriggle, drew his two hands apart, and held them in front of his comrade's face.

"Bless you, it is the first thing they teach the papooses in an Indian wigwam. I've got out of a Huron's thongs of raw hide before now, and it ain't very likely that a stiff stirrup leather will hold me. Put your hands out." With a few dexterous twists he loosened De Catinat's bonds, until he also was able to slip his hands free. "Now for your feet, if you'll put them up. They'll find that we are easier to catch than to hold."

But at that moment the carriage began to slow down, and the clank of the hoofs of the riders in front of them died suddenly away. Peeping through the windows, the prisoners saw a huge dark building stretching in front of them, so high and so broad that the night shrouded it in upon every side. A great archway hung above them, and the lamps shone on the rude wooden gate, studded with ponderous clamps and nails. In the upper part of the door was a small square iron grating, and through this they could catch a glimpse of the gleam of a lantern and of a bearded face which looked out at them. De Vivonne, standing in his stirrups, craned his neck up towards the grating, so that the two men most interested could hear little of the conversation which followed. They saw only that the horseman held a gold ring up in the air, and that the face above, which had begun by shaking and frowning, was now nodding and smiling. An instant later the head disappeared, the door swung open upon screaming hinges, and the carriage drove on into the courtyard beyond, leaving the escort, with the exception of De Vivonne, outside. As the horses pulled up, a knot of rough fellows clustered round, and the two prisoners were dragged roughly out. In the light of the torches which flared around them they could see that they were hemmed in by high turreted walls upon every side. A bulky man with a bearded face, the same whom they had seen at the grating, was standing in the centre of the group of armed men issuing his orders.

"To the upper dungeon, Simon!" he cried. "And see that they have two bundles of straw and a loaf of bread until we learn our master's will."

"I know not who your master may be," said De Catinat, "but I would ask you by what warrant he dares to stop two messengers of the king while travelling in his service?"

"By St. Denis, if my master play the king a trick, it will be but tie and tie," the stout man answered, with a grin. "But no more talk! Away with them, Simon, and you answer to me for their safe-keeping."

It was in vain that De Catinat raved and threatened, invoking the most terrible menaces upon all who were concerned in detaining him. Two stout knaves thrusting him from behind and one dragging in front forced him through a narrow gate and along a stone-flagged passage, a small man in black buckram with a bunch of keys in one hand and a swinging lantern in the other leading the way. Their ankles had been so tied that they could but take steps of a foot in length. Shuffling along, they made their way down three successive corridors and through three doors, each of which was locked and barred behind them. Then they ascended a winding stone stair, hollowed out in the centre by the feet of generations of prisoners and of jailers, and finally they were thrust into a small square dungeon, and two trusses of straw were thrown in after them. An instant later a heavy key turned in the lock, and they were left to their own meditations.

Very grim and dark those meditations were in the case of De Catinat. A stroke of good luck had made him at court, and now this other of ill fortune had destroyed him. It would be in vain that he should plead his own powerlessness. He knew his royal master well. He was a man who was munificent when his orders were obeyed, and inexorable when they miscarried. No excuse availed with him. An unlucky man was as abhorrent to him as a negligent one. In this great crisis the king had trusted him with an all-important message, and that message had not been delivered. What could save him now from disgrace and from ruin? He cared nothing for the dim dungeon in which he found himself, nor for the uncertain fate which hung over his head, but his heart turned to lead when he thought of his blasted career, and of the triumph of those whose jealousy had been aroused by his rapid promotion. There were his people in Paris, too—his sweet Adele, his old uncle, who had been as good as a father to him. What protector would they have in their troubles now that he had lost the power that might have shielded them? How long would it be before they were exposed once more to the brutalities of Dalbert and his dragoons? He clenched his teeth at the thought, and threw himself down with a groan upon the litter of straw dimly visible in the faint light which streamed through the single window.

But his energetic comrade had yielded to no feeling of despondency. The instant that the clang of the prison door had assured him that he was safe from interruption he had slipped off the bonds which held him and had felt all round the walls and flooring to see what manner of place this might be. His search had ended in the discovery of a small fireplace at one corner, and of two great clumsy billets of wood, which seemed to have been left there to serve as pillows for the prisoners. Having satisfied himself that the chimney was so small that it was utterly impossible to pass even his head up it, he drew the two blocks of wood over to the window, and was able, by placing one above the other and standing on tiptoe on the highest, to reach the bars which guarded it. Drawing himself up, and fixing one toe in an inequality of the wall, he managed to look out on to the courtyard which they had just quitted. The carriage and De Vivonne were passing out through the gate as he looked, and he heard a moment later the slam of the heavy door and the clatter of hoofs from the troop of horsemen outside. The seneschal and his retainers had disappeared; the torches, too, were gone, and, save for the measured tread of a pair of sentinels in the yard twenty feet beneath him, all was silent throughout the great castle.

And a very great castle it was. Even as he hung there with straining hands his eyes were running in admiration and amazement over the huge wall in front of him, with its fringe of turrets and pinnacles and battlements all lying so still and cold in the moonlight. Strange thoughts will slip into a man's head at the most unlikely moments. He remembered suddenly a bright summer day over the water when first he had come down from Albany, and how his father had met him on the wharf by the Hudson, and had taken him through the water-gate to see Peter Stuyvesant's house, as a sign of how great this city was which had passed from the Dutch to the English. Why, Peter Stuyvesant's house and Peter Stuyvesant's Bowery villa put together would not make one wing of this huge pile, which was itself a mere dog-kennel beside the mighty palace at Versailles. He would that his father were here now; and then, on second thoughts, he would not, for it came back to him that he was a prisoner in a far land, and that his sight-seeing was being done through the bars of a dungeon window.

The window was large enough to pass his body through if it were not for those bars. He shook them and hung his weight upon them, but they were as thick as his thumb and firmly welded. Then, getting some strong hold for his other foot, he supported himself by one hand while he picked with his knife at the setting of the iron. It was cement, as smooth as glass and as hard as marble. His knife turned when he tried to loosen it. But there was still the stone. It was sandstone, not so very hard. If he could cut grooves in it, he might be able to draw out bars, cement, and all. He sprang down to the floor again, and was thinking how he should best set to work, when a groan drew his attention to his companion.

"You seem sick, friend," said he.

"Sick in mind," moaned the other. "Oh, the cursed fool that I have been! It maddens me!"

"Something on your mind?" said Amos Green, sitting down upon his billets of wood. "What was it, then?"

The guardsman made a movement of impatience. "What was it? How can you ask me, when you know as well as I do the wretched failure of my mission. It was the king's wish that the archbishop should marry them. The king's wish is the law. It must be the archbishop or none. He should have been at the palace by now. Ah, my God! I can see the king's cabinet, I can see him waiting, I can see madame waiting, I can hear them speak of the unhappy De Catinat—" He buried his face in his hands once more.

"I see all that," said the American stolidly, "and I see something more."

"What then?"

"I see the archbishop tying them up together."

"The archbishop! You are raving."

"Maybe. But I see him."

"He could not be at the palace."

"On the contrary, he reached the palace about half an hour ago."

De Catinat sprang to his feet. "At the palace!" he screamed. "Then who gave him the message?"

"I did," said Amos Green.

CHAPTER XVIII.
A NIGHT OF SURPRISES.

If the American had expected to surprise or delight his companion by this curt announcement he was woefully disappointed, for De Catinat approached him with a face which was full of sympathy and trouble, and laid his hand caressingly upon his shoulder.

"My dear friend," said he, "I have been selfish and thoughtless. I have made too much of my own little troubles and too little of what you have gone through for me. That fall from your horse has shaken you more than you think. Lie down upon this straw, and see if a little sleep may not—"

"I tell you that the bishop is there!" cried Amos Green impatiently.

"Quite so. There is water in this jug, and if I dip my scarf into it and tie it round your brow—"

"Man alive! Don't you hear me! The bishop is there."

"He is, he is," said De Catinat soothingly. "He is most certainly there. I trust that you have no pain?"

The American waved in the air with his knotted fists. "You think that I am crazed," he cried, "and, by the eternal, you are enough to make me so! When I say that I sent the bishop, I mean that I saw to the job. You remember when I stepped back to your friend the major?"

It was the soldier's turn to grow excited now. "Well?" he cried, gripping the other's arm.

"Well, when we send a scout into the woods, if the matter is worth it, we send a second one at another hour, and so one or other comes back with his hair on. That's the Iroquois fashion, and a good fashion too."

"My God! I believe that you have saved me!"

"You needn't grip on to my arm like a fish-eagle on a trout! I went back to the major, then, and I asked him when he was in Paris to pass by the archbishop's door."

"Well? Well?"

"I showed him this lump of chalk. 'If we've been there,' said I, 'you'll see a great cross on the left side of the door-post. If there's no cross, then pull the latch and ask the bishop if he'll come up to the palace as quick as his horses can bring him.' The major started an hour after us; he would be in Paris by half-past ten; the bishop would be in his carriage by eleven, and he would reach Versailles half an hour ago, that is to say, about half-past twelve. By the Lord, I think I've driven him off his head!"

It was no wonder that the young woodsman was alarmed at the effect of his own announcement. His slow and steady nature was incapable of the quick, violent variations of the fiery Frenchman. De Catinat, who had thrown off his bonds before he had lain down, spun round the cell now, waving his arms and his legs, with his shadow capering up the wall behind him, all distorted in the moonlight. Finally he threw himself into his comrade's arms with a torrent of thanks and ejaculations and praises and promises, patting him with his hands and hugging him to his breast.

"Oh, if I could but do something for you!" he exclaimed. "If I could do something for you!"

"You can, then. Lie down on that straw and go to sleep."

"And to think that I sneered at you! I! Oh, you have had your revenge!"

"For the Lord's sake, lie down and go to sleep!" By persuasions and a little pushing he got his delighted companion on to his couch again, and heaped the straw over him to serve as a blanket. De Catinat was wearied out by the excitements of the day, and this last great reaction seemed to have absorbed all his remaining strength. His lids drooped heavily over his eyes, his head sank deeper into the soft straw, and his last remembrance was that the tireless American was seated cross-legged in the moonlight, working furiously with his long knife upon one of the billets of wood.

So weary was the young guardsman that it was long past noon, and the sun was shining out of a cloudless blue sky, before he awoke. For a moment, enveloped as he was in straw, and with the rude arch of the dungeon meeting in four rough-hewn groinings above his head, he stared about him in bewilderment. Then in an instant the doings of the day before, his mission, the ambuscade, his imprisonment, all flashed back to him, and he sprang to his feet. His comrade, who had been dozing in the corner, jumped up also at the first movement, with his hand on his knife, and a sinister glance directed towards the door.

"Oh, it's you, is it?" said he, "I thought it was the man."

"Has some one been in, then?"

"Yes; they brought those two loaves and a jug of water, just about dawn, when I was settling down for a rest."

"And did he say anything?"

"No; it was the little black one."

"Simon, they called him."

"The same. He laid the things down and was gone. I thought that maybe if he came again we might get him to stop."

"How, then?"

"Maybe if we got these stirrup leathers round his ankles he would not get them off quite as easy as we have done."

"And what then?"

"Well, he would tell us where we are, and what is to be done with us."

"Pshaw! what does it matter since our mission is done?"

"It may not matter to you—there's no accounting for tastes—but it matters a good deal to me. I'm not used to sitting in a hole, like a bear in a trap, waiting for what other folks choose to do with me. It's new to me. I found Paris a pretty close sort of place, but it's a prairie compared to this. It don't suit a man of my habits, and I am going to come out of it."

"There's no help but patience, my friend."

"I don't know that. I'd get more help out of a bar and a few pegs." He opened his coat, and took out a short piece of rusted iron, and three small thick pieces of wood, sharpened at one end.

"Where did you get those, then?"

"These are my night's work. The bar is the top one of the grate. I had a job to loosen it, but there it is. The pegs I whittled out of that log."

"And what are they for?"

"Well, you see, peg number one goes in here, where I have picked a hole between the stones. Then I've made this other log into a mallet, and with two cracks there it is firm fixed, so that you can put your weight on it. Now these two go in the same way into the holes above here. So! Now, you see, you can stand up there and look out of that window without asking too much of your toe joint. Try it."

De Catinat sprang up and looked eagerly out between the bars.

"I do not know the place," said he, shaking his head.

"It may be any one of thirty castles which lie upon the south side of Paris, and within six or seven leagues of it. Which can it be? And who has any interest in treating us so? I would that I could see a coat of arms, which might help us. Ah! there is one yonder in the centre of the mullion of the window. But I can scarce read it at the distance. I warrant that your eyes are better than mine, Amos, and that you can read what is on yonder escutcheon."

"On what?"

"On the stone slab in the centre window."

"Yes, I see it plain enough. It looks to me like three turkey-buzzards sitting on a barrel of molasses."

"Three allurions in chief over a tower proper, maybe. Those are the arms of the Provence De Hautevilles. But it cannot be that. They have no chateau within a hundred leagues. No, I cannot tell where we are."

He was dropping back to the floor, and put his weight upon the bar. To his amazement, it came away in his hand.

"Look, Amos, look!" he cried.

"Ah, you've found it out! Well, I did that during the night."

"And how? With your knife?"

"No; I could make no way with my knife; but when I got the bar out of the grate, I managed faster. I'll put this one back now, or some of those folks down below may notice that we have got it loose."

"Are they all loose?"

"Only the one at present, but we'll get the other two out during the night. You can take that bar out and work with it, while I use my own picker at the other. You see, the stone is soft, and by grinding it you soon make a groove along which you can slip the bar. It will be mighty queer if we can't clear a road for ourselves before morning."

"Well, but even if we could get out into the courtyard, where could we turn to then?"

"One thing at a time, friend. You might as well stick at the Kennebec because you could not see how you would cross the Penobscot. Anyway, there is more air in the yard than in here, and when the window is clear we shall soon plan out the rest."

The two comrades did not dare to do any work during the day, for fear they should be surprised by the jailer, or observed from without. No one came near them, but they ate their loaves and drank their water with the appetite of men who had often known what it was to be without even such simple food as that. The instant that night fell they were both up upon the pegs, grinding away at the hard stone and tugging at the bars. It was a rainy night, and there was a sharp thunder-storm, but they could see very well, while the shadow of the arched window prevented their being seen. Before midnight they had loosened one bar, and the other was just beginning to give, when some slight noise made them turn their heads, and there was their jailer standing, open-mouthed in the middle of the cell, staring up at them.

It was De Catinat who observed him first, and he sprang down at him in an instant with his bar; but at his movement the man rushed for the door, and drew it after him just as the American's tool whizzed past his ear and down the passage. As the door slammed, the two comrades looked at each other. The guardsman shrugged his shoulders and the other whistled.

"It is scarce worth while to go on," said De Catinat.

"We may as well be doing that as anything else. If my picker had been an inch lower I'd have had him. Well, maybe he'll get a stroke, or break his neck down those stairs. I've nothing to work with now, but a few rubs with your bar will finish the job. Ah, dear! You are right, and we are fairly treed!"

A great bell had begun to ring in the chateau, and there was a loud buzz of voices and a clatter of feet upon the stones. Hoarse orders were shouted, and there was the sound of turning keys. All this coming suddenly in the midst of the stillness of the night showed only too certainly that the alarm had been given. Amos Green threw himself down in the straw, with his hands in his pockets, and De Catinat leaned sulkily against the wall, waiting for whatever might come to him. Five minutes passed, however, and yet another five minutes, without anyone appearing. The hubbub in the courtyard continued, but there was no sound in the corridor which led to their cell.

"Well, I'll have that bar out, after all," said the American at last, rising and stepping over to the window. "Anyhow, we'll see what all this caterwauling is about." He climbed up on his pegs as he spoke, and peeped out.

"Come up!" he cried excitedly to his comrade. "They've got some other game going on here, and they are all a deal too busy to bother their heads about us."

De Catinat clambered up beside him, and the two stood staring down into the courtyard. A brazier had been lit at each corner, and the place was thronged with men, many of whom carried torches. The yellow glare played fitfully over the grim gray walls, flickering up sometimes until the highest turrets shone golden against the black sky, and then, as the wind caught them, dying away until they scarce threw a glow upon the cheek of their bearer. The main gate was open, and a carriage, which had apparently just driven in, was standing at a small door immediately in front of their window. The wheels and sides were brown with mud, and the two horses were reeking and heavy-headed, as though their journey had been both swift and long. A man wearing a plumed hat and enveloped in a riding-coat had stepped from the carriage, and then, turning round, had dragged a second person out after him. There was a scuffle, a cry, a push, and the two figures had vanished through the door. As it closed, the carriage drove away, the torches and braziers were extinguished, the main gate was closed once more, and all was as quiet as before this sudden interruption.

"Well!" gasped De Catinat. "Is this another king's messenger they've got?"

"There will be lodgings for two more here in a short time," said Amos Green. "If they only leave us alone, this cell won't hold us long."

"I wonder where that jailer has gone?"

"He may go where he likes, as long as he keeps away from here. Give me your bar again. This thing is giving. It won't take us long to have it out." He set to work furiously, trying to deepen the groove in the stone, through which he hoped to drag the staple. Suddenly he ceased, and strained his ears.

"By thunder!" said he, "there's some one working on the other side."

They both stood listening. There were the thud of hammers, the rasping of a saw, and the clatter of wood from the other side of the wall.

"What can they be doing?"

"I can't think."

"Can you see them?"

"They are too near the wall."

"I think I can manage," said De Catinat. "I am slighter than you." He pushed his head and neck and half of one shoulder through the gap between the bars, and there he remained until his friend thought that perhaps he had stuck, and pulled at his legs to extricate him. He writhed back, however, without any difficulty.

"They are building something," he whispered.

"Building!"

"Yes; there are four of them, with a lantern."

"What can they be building, then?"

"It's a shed, I think. I can see four sockets in the ground, and they are fixing four uprights into them."

"Well, we can't get away as long as there are four men just under our window."

"Impossible."

"But we may as well finish our work, for all that." The gentle scrapings of his iron were drowned amid the noise which swelled ever louder from without. The bar loosened at the end, and he drew it slowly towards him. At that instant, however, just as he was disengaging it, a round head appeared between him and the moonlight, a head with a great shock of tangled hair and a woollen cap upon the top of it. So astonished was Amos Green at the sudden apparition that he let go his grip upon the bar, which, falling outwards, toppled over the edge of the window-sill.

"You great fool!" shrieked a voice from below, "are your fingers ever to be thumbs, then, that you should fumble your tools so? A thousand thunders of heaven! You have broken my shoulder."

"What is it, then?" cried the other. "My faith, Pierre, if your fingers went as fast as your tongue, you would be the first joiner in France."

"What is it, you ape! You have dropped your tool upon me."

"I! I have dropped nothing."

"Idiot! Would you have me believe that iron falls from the sky? I say that you have struck me, you foolish, clumsy-fingered lout."

"I have not struck you yet," cried the other, "but, by the Virgin, if I have more of this I will come down the ladder to you!"

"Silence, you good-for-naughts!" said a third voice sternly. "If the work be not done by daybreak, there will be a heavy reckoning for somebody."

And again the steady hammering and sawing went forward. The head still passed and repassed, its owner walking apparently upon some platform which they had constructed beneath their window, but never giving a glance or a thought to the black square opening beside him. It was early morning, and the first cold light was beginning to steal over the courtyard, before the work was at last finished and the workmen had left. Then at last the prisoners dared to climb up and to see what it was which had been constructed during the night. It gave them a catch of the breath as they looked at it. It was a scaffold.

There it lay, the ill-omened platform of dark greasy boards newly fastened together, but evidently used often before for the same purpose. It was buttressed up against their wall, and extended a clear twenty feet out, with a broad wooden stair leading down from the further side. In the centre stood a headsman's block, all haggled at the top, and smeared with rust-coloured stains.

"I think it is time that we left," said Amos Green.

"Our work is all in vain, Amos," said De Catinat sadly.

"Whatever our fate may be—and this looks ill enough—we can but submit to it like brave men."

"Tut, man; the window is clear! Let us make a rush for it."

"It is useless. I can see a line of armed men along the further side of the yard."

"A line! At this hour!"

"Yes; and here come more. See, at the centre gate! Now what in the name of heaven is this?"

As he spoke the door which faced them opened and a singular procession filed out. First came two dozen footmen, walking in pairs, all carrying halberds, and clad in the same maroon-coloured liveries. After them a huge bearded man, with his tunic off, and the sleeves of his coarse shirt rolled up over his elbows, strode along with a great axe over his left shoulder. Behind him, a priest with an open missal pattered forth prayers, and in his shadow was a woman, clad in black, her neck bared, and a black shawl cast over her head and drooping in front of her bowed face. Within grip of her walked a tall, thin, fierce-faced man, with harsh red features, and a great jutting nose. He wore a flat velvet cap with a single eagle feather fastened into it by a diamond clasp, which gleamed in the morning light. But bright as was his gem, his dark eyes were brighter still, and sparkled from under his bushy brows with a mad brilliancy which bore with it something of menace and of terror. His limbs jerked as he walked, his features twisted, and he carried himself like a man who strives hard to hold himself in when his whole soul is aflame with exultation. Behind him again twelve more maroon-clad retainers brought up the rear of this singular procession.

The woman had faltered at the foot of the scaffold, but the man behind her had thrust her forward with such force that she stumbled over the lower step, and would have fallen had she not clutched at the arm of the priest. At the top of the ladder her eyes met the dreadful block, and she burst into a scream, and shrunk backwards. But again the man thrust her on, and two of the followers caught her by either wrist and dragged her forwards.

"Oh, Maurice! Maurice!" she screamed. "I am not fit to die! Oh, forgive me, Maurice, as you hope for forgiveness yourself! Maurice! Maurice!" She strove to get towards him, to clutch at his wrist, at his sleeve, but he stood with his hand on his sword, gazing at her with a face which was all wreathed and contorted with merriment. At the sight of that dreadful mocking face the prayers froze upon her lips. As well pray for mercy to the dropping stone or to the rushing stream. She turned away, and threw back the mantle which had shrouded her features.

"Ah, sire!" she cried. "Sire! If you could see me now!"

And at the cry and at the sight of that fair pale face, De Catinat, looking down from the window, was stricken as though by a dagger; for there, standing beside the headsman's block, was she who had been the most powerful, as well as the wittiest and the fairest, of the women of France—none other than Francoise de Montespan, so lately the favourite of the king.

CHAPTER XIX.
IN THE KING'S CABINET.

On the night upon which such strange chances had befallen his messengers, the king sat alone in his cabinet. Over his head a perfumed lamp, held up by four little flying Cupids of crystal, who dangled by golden chains from the painted ceiling, cast a brilliant light upon the chamber, which was flashed back twenty-fold by the mirrors upon the wall. The ebony and silver furniture, the dainty carpet of La Savonniere, the silks of Tours, the tapestries of the Gobelins, the gold-work and the delicate chinaware of Sevres—the best of all that France could produce was centred between these four walls. Nothing had ever passed through that door which was not a masterpiece of its kind. And amid all this brilliance the master of it sat, his chin resting upon his hands, his elbows upon the table, with eyes which stared vacantly at the wall, a moody and a solemn man.

But though his dark eyes were fixed upon the wall, they saw nothing of it. They looked rather down the long vista of his own life, away to those early years when what we dream and what we do shade so mistily into one another. Was it a dream or was it a fact, those two men who used to stoop over his baby crib, the one with the dark coat and the star upon his breast, whom he had been taught to call father, and the other one with the long red gown and the little twinkling eyes? Even now, after more than forty years, that wicked, astute, powerful face flashed up, and he saw once more old Richelieu, the great unanointed king of France. And then the other cardinal, the long lean one who had taken his pocket-money, and had grudged him his food, and had dressed him in old clothes. How well he could recall the day when Mazarin had rouged himself for the last time, and how the court had danced with joy at the news that he was no more! And his mother, too, how beautiful she was, and how masterful! Could he not remember how bravely she had borne herself during that war in which the power of the great nobles had been broken, and how she had at last lain down to die, imploring the priests not to stain her cap-strings with their holy oils! And then he thought of what he had done himself, how he had shorn down his great subjects until, instead of being like a tree among saplings, he had been alone, far above all others, with his shadow covering the whole land. Then there were his wars and his laws and his treaties. Under his care France had overflowed her frontiers both on the north and on the east, and yet had been so welded together internally that she had but one voice, with which she spoke through him. And then there was that line of beautiful faces which wavered up in front of him. There was Olympe de Mancini, whose Italian eyes had first taught him that there is a power which can rule over a king; her sister, too, Marie de Mancini; his wife, with her dark little sun-browned face; Henrietta of England, whose death had first shown him the horrors which lie in life; La Valliere, Montespan, Fontanges. Some were dead; some were in convents. Some who had been wicked and beautiful were now only wicked. And what had been the outcome of all this troubled, striving life of his? He was already at the outer verge of his middle years; he had lost his taste for the pleasures of his youth; gout and vertigo were ever at his foot and at his head to remind him that between them lay a kingdom which he could not hope to govern. And after all these years he had not won a single true friend, not one, in his family, in his court, in his country, save only this woman whom he was to wed that night. And she, how patient she was, how good, how lofty! With her he might hope to wipe off by the true glory of his remaining years all the sin and the folly of the past. Would that the archbishop might come, that he might feel that she was indeed his, that he held her with hooks of steel which would bind them as long as life should last!

There came a tap at the door. He sprang up eagerly, thinking that the ecclesiastic might have arrived. It was, however, only his personal attendant, to say that Louvois would crave an interview. Close at his heels came the minister himself, high-nosed and heavy-chinned. Two leather bags were dangling from his hand.

"Sire," said he, when Bontems had retired, "I trust that I do not intrude upon you."

"No, no, Louvois. My thoughts were in truth beginning to be very indifferent company, and I am glad to be rid of them."

"Your Majesty's thoughts can never, I am sure, be anything but pleasant," said the courtier. "But I have brought you here something which I trust may make them even more so."

"Ah! What is that?"

"When so many of our young nobles went into Germany and Hungary, you were pleased in your wisdom to say that you would like well to see what reports they sent home to their friends; also what news was sent out from the court to them."

"Yes."

"I have them here—all that the courier has brought in, and all that are gathered to go out, each in its own bag. The wax has been softened in spirit, the fastenings have been steamed, and they are now open."

The king took out a handful of the letters and glanced at the addresses.

"I should indeed like to read the hearts of these people," said he. "Thus only can I tell the true thoughts of those who bow and simper before my face. I suppose," with a sudden flash of suspicion from his eyes, "that you have not yourself looked into these?"

"Oh, sire, I had rather die!"

"You swear it?"

"As I hope for salvation!"

"Hum! There is one among these which I see is from your own son."

Louvois changed colour, and stammered as he looked at the envelope. "Your Majesty will find that he is as loyal out of your presence as in it, else he is no son of mine," said he.

"Then we shall begin with his. Ha! it is but ten lines long. 'Dearest Achille, how I long for you to come back! The court is as dull as a cloister now that you are gone. My ridiculous father still struts about like a turkey-cock, as if all his medals and crosses could cover the fact that he is but a head lackey, with no more real power than I have. He wheedles a good deal out of the king, but what he does with it I cannot imagine, for little comes my way. I still owe those ten thousand livres to the man in the Rue Orfevre. Unless I have some luck at lansquenet, I shall have to come out soon and join you.' Hem! I did you an injustice, Louvois. I see that you have *not* looked over these letters."

The minister had sat with a face which was the colour of beetroot, and eyes which projected from his head, while this epistle was being read. It was with relief that he came to the end of it, for at least there was nothing which compromised him seriously with the king; but every nerve in his great body tingled with rage as he thought of the way in which his young scape-grace had alluded to him. "The viper!" he cried. "Oh, the foul snake in the grass! I will make him curse the day that he was born."

"Tut, tut, Louvois!" said the king. "You are a man who has seen much of life, and you should be a philosopher. Hot-headed youth says ever more than it means. Think no more of the matter. But what have we here? A letter from my dearest girl to her husband, the Prince de Conti. I would pick her writing out of a thousand. Ah, dear soul, she little thought that my eyes would see her artless prattle! Why should I read it, since I already know every thought of her innocent heart?" He unfolded the sheet of pink scented paper with a fond smile upon his face, but it faded away as his eyes glanced down the page, and he sprang to his feet with a snarl of anger, his hand over his heart and his eyes still glued to the paper. "Minx!" he cried, in a choking voice. "Impertinent, heartless minx! Louvois, you know what I have done for the princess. You know she has been the apple of my eye. What have I ever grudged her? What have I ever denied her?"

"You have been goodness itself, sire," said Louvois, whose own wounds smarted less now that he saw his master writhing.

"Hear what she says of me: 'Old Father Grumpy is much as usual, save that he gives a little at the knees. You remember how we used to laugh at his airs and graces! Well, he has given up all that, and though he still struts about on great high heels, like a Landes peasant on his stilts, he has no brightness at all in his clothes. Of course, all the court follow his example, so you can imagine what a nightmare place this is. Then this woman still keeps in favour, and her frocks are as dismal as Grumpy's coats; so when you come back we shall go into the country together, and you shall dress in red velvet, and I shall wear blue silk, and we shall have a little coloured court of our own in spite of my majestic papa.'"

Louis sank his face in his hands.

"You hear how she speaks of me, Louvois."

"It is infamous, sire; infamous!"

"She calls me names—*me*, Louvois!"

"Atrocious, sire."

"And my knees! one would think that I was an old man!"

"Scandalous. But, sire, I would beg to say that it is a case in which your Majesty's philosophy may well soften your anger. Youth is ever hot-headed, and says more than it means. Think no more of the matter."

"You speak like a fool, Louvois. The child that I have loved turns upon me, and you ask me to think no more of it. Ah, it is one more lesson that a king can trust least of all those who have his own blood in their veins. What writing is this? It is the good Cardinal de Bouillon. One may not have faith in one's own kin, but this sainted man loves me, not only because I have placed him where he is, but because it is his nature to look up to and love those whom God has placed above him. I will read you his letter, Louvois, to show you that there is still such a thing as loyalty and gratitude in France. 'My dear Prince de la Roche-sur-Yon.' Ah, it is to him he writes. 'I promised when you left that I would let you know from time to time how things were going at court, as you consulted me about bringing your daughter up from Anjou, in the hope that she might catch the king's fancy.' What! What! Louvois! What villainy is this? 'The sultan goes from bad to worse. The Fontanges was at least the prettiest woman in France, though between ourselves there was just a shade too much of the red in her hair—an excellent colour in a cardinal's gown, my dear duke, but nothing brighter than chestnut is permissible in a lady. The Montespan, too, was a fine woman in her day, but fancy his picking up now with a widow who is older than himself, a woman, too, who does not even try to make herself attractive, but kneels at her *prie-dieu* or works at her tapestry from morning to night. They say that December and May make a bad match, but my own opinion is that two Novembers make an even worse one.' Louvois! Louvois! I can read no more! Have you a *lettre de cachet*?"

"There is one here, sire."

"For the Bastille?"

"No; for Vincennes."

"That will do very well. Fill it up, Louvois! Put this villain's name in it! Let him be arrested to-night, and taken there in his own caleche. The shameless, ungrateful, foul-mouthed villain! Why did you bring me these letters, Louvois? Oh, why did you yield to my foolish whim? My God, is there no truth, or honour, or loyalty in the world?" He stamped his feet, and shook his clenched hands in the air in the frenzy of his anger and disappointment.

"Shall I, then, put back the others?" asked Louvois eagerly. He had been on thorns since the king had begun to read them, not knowing what disclosures might come next.

"Put them back, but keep the bag."

"Both bags?"

"Ah! I had forgot the other one. Perhaps if I have hypocrites around me, I have at least some honest subjects at a distance. Let us take one haphazard. Who is this from? Ah! it is from the Duc de la Rochefoucauld. He has ever seemed to be a modest and dutiful young man. What has he to say? The Danube—Belgrade—the grand vizier—Ah!" He gave a cry as if he had been stabbed.

"What, then, sire?" The minister had taken a step forward, for he was frightened by the expression upon the king's face.

"Take them away, Louvois! Take them away!" he cried, pushing the pile of papers away from him. "I would that I had never seen them! I will look at them no more! He gibes even at my courage, I who was in the trenches when he was in his cradle! 'This war would not suit the king,' he says. 'For there are battles, and none of the nice little safe sieges which are so dear to him.' By God, he shall pay to me with his head for that jest! Ay, Louvois, it will be a dear gibe to him. But take them away. I have seen as much as I can bear."

The minister was thrusting them back into the bag when suddenly his eye caught the bold, clear writing of Madame de Maintenon upon one of the letters. Some demon whispered to him that here was a weapon which had been placed in his hands, with which he might strike one whose very name filled him with jealousy and hatred. Had she been guilty of some indiscretion in this note, then he might even now, at this last hour, turn the king's heart against her. He was an astute man, and in an instant he had seen his chance and grasped it.

"Ha!" said he, "it was hardly necessary to open this one."

"Which, Louvois? Whose is it?"

The minister pushed forward the letter, and Louis started as his eyes fell upon it.

"Madame's writing!" he gasped.

"Yes; it is to her nephew in Germany."

Louis took it in his hand. Then, with a sudden motion, he threw it down among the others, and then yet again his hand stole towards it. His face was gray and haggard, and beads of moisture had broken out upon his brow. If this too were to prove to be as the others! He was shaken to the soul at the very thought. Twice he tried to pluck it out, and twice his trembling fingers fumbled with the paper. Then he tossed it over to Louvois. "Read it to me," said he.

The minister opened the letter out and flattened it upon the table, with a malicious light dancing in his eyes, which might have cost him his position had the king but read it aright.

"'My dear nephew,'" he read, "'what you ask me in your last is absolutely impossible. I have never abused the king's favour so far as to ask for any profit for myself, and I should be equally sorry to solicit any advance for my relatives. No one would rejoice more than I to see you rise to be major in your regiment, but your valour and your loyalty must be the cause, and you must not hope to do it through any word of mine. To serve such a man as the king is its own reward, and I am sure that whether you remain a cornet or rise to some higher rank, you will be equally zealous in his cause. He is surrounded, unhappily, by many base parasites. Some of these are mere fools, like Lauzun; others are knaves, like the late Fouquet; and some seem to be both fools and knaves, like Louvois, the minister of war.'" Here the reader choked with rage, and sat gurgling and drumming his fingers upon the table.

"Go on, Louvois, go on," said Louis, smiling up at the ceiling.

"'These are the clouds which surround the sun, my dear nephew; but the sun is, believe me, shining brightly behind them. For years I have known that noble nature as few others can know it, and I can tell you that his virtues are his own, but that if ever his glory is for an instant dimmed over, it is because his kindness of heart has allowed him to be swayed by those who are about him. We hope soon to see you back at Versailles, staggering under the weight of your laurels. Meanwhile accept my love and every wish for your speedy promotion, although it cannot be obtained in the way which you suggest.'"

"Ah," cried the king, his love shining in his eyes, "how could I for an instant doubt her! And yet I had been so shaken by the others! Francoise is as true as steel. Was it not a beautiful letter, Louvois?"

"Madame is a very clever woman," said the minister evasively.

"And such a reader of hearts! Has she not seen my character aright?"

"At least she has not read mine, sire."

There was a tap at the door, and Bontems peeped in. "The archbishop has arrived, sire."

"Very well, Bontems. Ask madame to be so good as to step this way. And order the witnesses to assemble in the ante-room."

As the valet hastened away, Louis turned to his minister: "I wish you to be one of the witnesses, Louvois."

"To what, sire?"

"To my marriage."

The minister started. "What, sire! Already?"

"Now, Louvois; within five minutes."

"Very good, sire." The unhappy courtier strove hard to assume a more festive manner; but the night had been full of vexation to him, and to be condemned to assist in making this woman the king's wife was the most bitter drop of all.

"Put these letters away, Louvois. The last one has made up for all the rest. But these rascals shall smart for it, all the same. By-the-way, there is that young nephew to whom madame wrote. Gerard d'Aubigny is his name, is it not?"

"Yes, sire."

"Make him out a colonel's commission, and give him the next vacancy, Louvois."

"A colonel, sire! Why, he is not yet twenty."

"Ay, Louvois. Pray, am I the chief of the army, or are you? Take care, Louvois! I have warned you once before. I tell you, man, that if I choose to promote one of my jack-boots to be the head of a brigade, you shall not hesitate to make out the papers. Now go into the ante-room, and wait with the other witnesses until you are wanted."

There had meanwhile been busy goings-on in the small room where the red lamp burned in front of the Virgin. Francoise de Maintenon stood in the centre, a little flush of excitement on her cheeks, and an unwonted light in her placid gray eyes. She was clad in a dress of shining white brocade, trimmed and slashed with silver serge, and fringed at the throat and arms with costly point lace. Three women, grouped around her, rose and stooped and swayed, putting a touch here and a touch there, gathering in, looping up, and altering until all was to their taste.

"There!" said the head dressmaker, giving a final pat to a rosette of gray silk; "I think that will do, your Majes—that is to say, madame."

The lady smiled at the adroit slip of the courtier dressmaker.

"My tastes lean little towards dress," said she, "yet I would fain look as he would wish me to look."

"Ah, it is easy to dress madame. Madame has a figure. Madame has a carriage. What costume would not look well with such a neck and waist and arm to set it off? But, ah, madame, what are we to do when we have to make the figure as well as the dress? There was the Princess Charlotte Elizabeth. It was but yesterday that we cut her gown. She was short, madame, but thick. Oh, it is incredible how thick she was! She uses more cloth than madame, though she is two hand-breadths shorter. Ah, I am sure that the good God never meant people to be as thick as that. But then, of course, she is Bavarian and not French."

But madame was paying little heed to the gossip of the dressmaker. Her eyes were fixed upon the statue in the corner, and her lips were moving in prayer—prayer that she might be worthy of this great destiny which had come so suddenly upon her, a poor governess; that she might walk straight among the pitfalls which surrounded her upon every side; that this night's work might bring a blessing upon France and upon the man whom she loved. There came a discreet tap at the door to break in upon her prayer.

"It is Bontems, madame," said Mademoiselle Nanon. "He says that the king is ready."

"Then we shall not keep him waiting. Come, mademoiselle, and may God shed His blessing upon what we are about to do!"

The little party assembled in the king's ante-room, and started from there to the private chapel. In front walked the portly bishop, clad in a green vestment, puffed out with the importance of the function, his missal in his hand, and his fingers between the pages at the service *de matrimoniis*. Beside him strode his almoner, and two little servitors of the court in crimson cassocks bearing lighted torches. The king and Madame de Maintenon walked side by side, she quiet and composed, with gentle bearing and downcast eyes, he with a flush on his dark cheeks, and a nervous, furtive look in his eyes, like a man who knows that he is in the midst of one of the great crises of his life. Behind them, in solemn silence, followed a little group of chosen witnesses, the lean, silent Pere la Chaise, Louvois, scowling heavily at the bride, the Marquis de Charmarante, Bontems, and Mademoiselle Nanon.

The torches shed a strong yellow light upon this small band as they advanced slowly through the corridors and *salons* which led to the chapel, and they threw a garish glare upon the painted walls and ceilings, flashing back from gold-work and from mirror, but leaving long trailing shadows in the corners. The king glanced nervously at these black recesses, and at the portraits of his ancestors and relations which lined the walls. As he passed that of his late queen, Maria Theresa, he started and gasped with horror.

"My God!" he whispered; "she frowned and spat at me!"

Madame laid her cool hand upon his wrist. "It is nothing, sire," she murmured, in her soothing voice. "It was but the light flickering over the picture."

Her words had their usual effect upon him. The startled look died away from his eyes, and taking her hand in his he walked resolutely forwards. A minute later they were before the altar, and the words were being read which should bind them forever together. As they turned away again, her new ring blazing upon her finger, there was a buzz of congratulation around her. The king only said nothing, but he looked at her, and she had no wish that he should say more. She was still calm and pale, but the blood throbbed in her temples. "You are Queen of France now," it seemed to be humming—"queen, queen, queen!"

But a sudden shadow had fallen across her, and a low voice was in her ear. "Remember your promise to the Church," it whispered. She started, and turned to see the pale, eager face of the Jesuit beside her.

"Your hand has turned cold, Francoise," said Louis. "Let us go, dearest. We have been too long in this dismal church."

CHAPTER XX.
THE TWO FRANCOISES.

Madame de Montespan had retired to rest, easy in her mind, after receiving the message from her brother. She knew Louis as few others knew him, and she was well aware of that obstinacy in trifles which was one of his characteristics. If he had said that he would be married by the archbishop, then the archbishop it must be; to-night, at least, there should be no marriage. To-morrow was a new day, and if it did not shake the king's plans, then indeed she must have lost her wit as well as her beauty.

She dressed herself with care in the morning, putting on her powder, her little touch of rouge, her one patch near the dimple of her cheek, her loose robe of violet velvet, and her casconet of pearls with all the solicitude of a warrior, who is bracing on his arms for a life and death contest. No news had come to her of the great event of the previous night, although the court already rang with it, for her haughtiness and her bitter tongue had left her without a friend or intimate. She rose, therefore, in the best of spirits, with her mind set on the one question as to how best she could gain an audience with the king.

She was still in her boudoir putting the last touches to her toilet when her page announced to her that the king was waiting in her *salon*. Madame de Montespan could hardly believe in such good fortune. She had racked her brain all morning as to how she should win her way to him, and here he was waiting for her. With a last glance at the mirror, she hastened to meet him.

He was standing with his back turned, looking up at one of Snyders's paintings, when she entered; but as she closed the door, he turned and took two steps towards her. She had run forward with a pretty little cry of joy, her white arms outstretched, and love shining on her face; but he put out his hand, gently and yet with decision, with a gesture which checked her approach. Her hands dropped to her side, her lip trembled, and she stood looking at him with her grief and her fears all speaking loudly from her eyes. There was a look upon his features which she had never seen before, and already something was whispering at the back of her soul that to-day at least his spirit was stronger than her own.

"You are angry with me again," she cried.

He had come with every intention of beginning the interview by telling her bluntly of his marriage; but now, as he looked upon her beauty and her love, he felt that it would have been less brutal to strike her down at his feet. Let some one else tell her, then. She would know soon enough. Besides, there would be less chance then of a scene, which was a thing abhorrent to his soul. His task was, in any case, quite difficult enough. All this ran swiftly through his mind, and she as swiftly read it off in the brown eyes which gazed at her.

"You have something you came to say, and now you have not the heart to say it. God bless the kindly heart which checks the cruel tongue."

"No, no, madame," said Louis; "I would not be cruel. I cannot forget that my life has been brightened and my court made brilliant during all these years by your wit and your beauty. But times change, madame, and I owe a duty to the world which overrides my own personal inclinations. For every reason I think that it is best that we should arrange in the way which we discussed the other day, and that you should withdraw yourself from the court."

"Withdraw, sire! For how long?"

"It must be a permanent withdrawal, madame."

She stood with clenched hands and a pale face staring at him.

"I need not say that I shall make your retirement a happy one as far as in me lies. Your allowance shall be fixed by yourself; a palace shall be erected for you in whatever part of France you may prefer, provided that it is twenty miles from Paris. An estate also—"

"Oh, sire, how can you think that such things as these would compensate me for the loss of your love?" Her heart had turned to lead within her breast. Had he spoken hotly and angrily she might have hoped to turn him as she had done before; but this gentle and yet firm bearing was new to him, and she felt that all her arts were vain against it. His coolness enraged her, and yet she strove to choke down her passion and to preserve the humble attitude which was least natural to her haughty and vehement spirit; but soon the effort became too much for her.

"Madame," said he, "I have thought well over this matter, and it must be as I say. There is no other way at all. Since we must part, the parting had best be short and sharp. Believe me, it is no pleasant matter for me either. I have ordered your brother to have his carriage at the postern at nine o'clock, for I thought that perhaps you would wish to retire after nightfall."

"To hide my shame from a laughing court! It was thoughtful of you, sire. And yet, perhaps, this too was a duty, since we hear so much of duties nowadays, for who was it but you—"

"I know, madame, I know. I confess it. I have wronged you deeply. Believe me that every atonement which is in my power shall be made. Nay, do not look so angrily at me, I beg. Let our last sight of each other be one which may leave a pleasant memory behind it."

"A pleasant memory!" All the gentleness and humility had fallen from her now, and her voice had the hard ring of contempt and of anger. "A pleasant memory! It may well be pleasant to you, who are released from the woman whom you ruined, who can turn now to another without any pale face to be seen within the *salons* of your court to remind you of your perfidy. But to me, pining in some lonely country house, spurned by my husband, despised by my family, the scorn and jest of France, far from all which gave a charm to life, far from the man for whose love I have sacrificed everything—this will be a very pleasant memory to me, you may be sure!"

The king's eyes had caught the angry gleam which shot from hers, and yet he strove hard to set a curb upon his temper. When such a matter had to be discussed between the proudest man and the haughtiest woman in all France, one or the other must yield a point. He felt that it was for him to do so, and yet it did not come kindly to his imperious nature.

"There is nothing to be gained, madame," said he, "by using words which are neither seemly for your tongue nor for my ears. You will do me the justice to confess that where I might command I am now entreating, and that instead of ordering you as my subject, I am persuading you as my friend."

"Oh, you show too much consideration, sire! Our relations of twenty years or so can scarce suffice to explain such forbearance from you. I should indeed be grateful that you have not set your archers of the guard upon me, or marched me from the palace between a file of your musketeers. Sire, how can I thank you for this forbearance?" She curtsied low, with her face set in a mocking smile.

"Your words are bitter, madame."

"My heart is bitter, sire."

"Nay, Francoise, be reasonable, I implore you. We have both left our youth behind."

"The allusion to my years comes gratefully from your lips."

"Ah, you distort my words. Then I shall say no more. You may not see me again, madame. Is there no question which you would wish to ask me before I go?"

"Good God!" she cried; "is this a man? Has it a heart? Are these the lips which have told me so often that he loved me? Are these the eyes which have looked so fondly into mine? Can you then thrust away a woman whose life has been yours as you put away the St. Germain palace when a more showy one was ready for you? And this is the end of all those vows, those sweet whispers, those persuasions, those promises—This!"

"Nay, madame, this is painful to both of us."

"Pain! Where is the pain in your face? I see anger in it because I have dared to speak truth; I see joy in it because you feel that your vile task is done. But where is the pain? Ah, when I am gone all will be so easy to you—will it not? You can go back then to your governess—"

"Madame!"

"Yes, yes, you cannot frighten me! What do I care for all that you can do! But I know all. Do not think that I am blind. And so you would even have married her! You, the descendant of St. Louis, and she the Scarron widow, the poor drudge whom in charity I took into my household! Ah, how your courtiers will smile! how the little poets will scribble! how the wits will whisper! You do not hear of these things, of course, but they are a little painful for your friends."

"My patience can bear no more," cried the king furiously. "I leave you, madame, and forever."

But her fury had swept all fear and discretion from her mind. She stepped between the door and him, her face flushed, her eyes blazing, her face thrust a little forward, one small white satin slipper tapping upon the carpet.

"You are in haste, sire! She is waiting for you, doubtless."

"Let me pass, madame."

"But it was a disappointment last night, was it not, my poor sire? Ah, and for the governess, what a blow! Great heaven, what a blow! No archbishop! No marriage! All the pretty plan gone wrong! Was it not cruel?"

Louis gazed at the beautiful furious face in bewilderment, and it flashed across his mind that perhaps her grief had turned her brain. What else could be the meaning of this wild talk of the archbishop and the disappointment? It would be unworthy of him to speak harshly to one who was so afflicted. He must soothe her, and, above all, he must get away from her.

"You have had the keeping of a good many of my family jewels," said he. "I beg that you will still retain them as a small sign of my regard."

He had hoped to please her and to calm her, but in an instant she was over at her treasure-cupboard hurling double handfuls of precious stones down at his feet. They clinked and rattled, the little pellets of red and yellow and green, rolling, glinting over the floor and rapping up against the oak panels at the base of the walls.

"They will do for the governess if the archbishop comes at last," she cried.

He was more convinced than ever that she had lost her wits. A thought struck him by which he might appeal to all that was softer and more gentle in her nature. He stepped swiftly to the door, pushed it half open, and gave a whispered order. A youth with long golden hair waving down over his black velvet doublet entered the room. It was her youngest son, the Count of Toulouse.

"I thought that you would wish to bid him farewell," said Louis.

She stood staring as though unable to realise the significance of his words. Then it was borne suddenly in upon her that her children as well as her lover were to be taken from her, that this other woman should see them and speak with them and win their love while she was far away. All that was evil and bitter in the woman flashed suddenly up in her, until for the instant she was what the king had thought her. If her son was not for her, then he should be for none. A jewelled knife lay among her treasures, ready to her hand. She caught it up and rushed at the cowering lad. Louis screamed and ran forward to stop her; but another had been swifter than he. A woman had darted through the open door, and had caught the upraised wrist. There was a moment's struggle, two queenly figures swayed and strained, and the knife dropped between their feet. The frightened Louis caught it up, and seizing his little son by the wrist, he rushed from the apartment. Francoise de Montespan staggered back against the ottoman to find herself confronted by the steady eyes and set face of that other Francoise, the woman whose presence fell like a shadow at every turn of her life.

"I have saved you, madame, from doing that which you would have been the first to bewail."

"Saved me! It is you who have driven me to this!"

The fallen favourite leaned against the high back of the ottoman, her hands resting behind her upon the curve of the velvet. Her lids were half closed on her flashing eyes, and her lips just parted to show a gleam of her white teeth. Here was the true Francoise de Montespan, a feline creature crouching for a spring, very far from that humble and soft-spoken Francoise who had won the king back by her gentle words. Madame de Maintenon's hand had been cut in the struggle, and the blood was dripping down from the end of her fingers, but neither woman had time to spare a thought upon that. Her firm gray eyes were fixed upon her former rival as one fixes them upon some weak and treacherous creature who may be dominated by a stronger will.

"Yes, it is you who have driven me to this—you, whom I picked up when you were hard pressed for a crust of bread or a cup of sour wine. What had you? You had nothing—nothing except a name which was a laughing-stock.

And what did I give you? I gave you everything. You know that I gave you everything. Money, position, the entrance to the court. You had them all from me. And now you mock me!"

"Madame, I do not mock you. I pity you from the bottom of my heart."

"Pity? Ha! ha! A Mortemart is pitied by the widow Scarron! Your pity may go where your gratitude is, and where your character is. We shall be troubled with it no longer then."

"Your words do not pain me."

"I can believe that you are not sensitive."

"Not when my conscience is at ease."

"Ah! it has not troubled you, then?"

"Not upon this point, madame."

"My God! How terrible must those other points have been!"

"I have never had an evil thought towards you."

"None towards me? Oh, woman, woman!"

"What have I done, then? The king came to my room to see the children taught. He stayed. He talked. He asked my opinion on this and that. Could I be silent? or could I say other than what I thought?"

"You turned him against me!"

"I should be proud indeed if I thought that I had turned him to virtue."

"The word comes well from your lips."

"I would that I heard it upon yours."

"And so, by your own confession, you stole the king's love from me, most virtuous of widows!"

"I had all gratitude and kindly thought for you. You have, as you have so often reminded me, been my benefactress. It was not necessary for you to say it, for I had never for an instant forgotten it. Yet if the king has asked me what I thought, I will not deny to you that I have said that sin is sin, and that he would be a worthier man if he shook off the guilty bonds which held him."

"Or exchanged them for others."

"For those of duty."

"Pah! Your hypocrisy sickens me! If you pretend to be a nun, why are you not where the nuns are? You would have the best of two worlds— would you not?—have all that the court can give, and yet ape the manners of the cloister. But you need not do it with me! I know you as your inmost heart knows you. I was honest, and what I did, I did before the world. You, behind your priests and your directors and your *prie-dieus* and your missals—do you think that you deceive me, as you deceive others?"

Her antagonist's gray eyes sparkled for the first time, and she took a quick step forward, with one white hand half lifted in rebuke.

"You may speak as you will of me," said she. "To me it is no more than the foolish paroquet that chatters in your ante-room. But do not touch upon things which are sacred. Ah, if you would but raise your own thoughts to such things—if you would but turn them inwards, and see, before it is too late, how vile and foul is this life which you have led! What might you not have done? His soul was in your hands like clay for the potter. If you had raised him up, if you had led him on the higher path, if you had brought out all that was noble and good within him, how your name would have been loved and blessed, from the chateau to the cottage! But no; you dragged him down; you wasted his youth; you drew him from his wife; you marred his manhood. A crime in one so high begets a thousand others in those who look to him for an example; and all, all are upon your soul. Take heed, madame, for God's sake take heed ere it be too late! For all your beauty, there can be for you, as for me, a few short years of life. Then, when that brown hair is white, when that white cheek is sunken, when that bright eye is dimmed—ah, then God pity the sin-stained soul of Francoise de Montespan!"

Her rival had sunk her head for the moment before the solemn words and the beautiful eyes. For an instant she stood silent, cowed for the first time in all her life; but then the mocking, defiant spirit came back to her, and she glanced up with a curling lip.

"I am already provided with a spiritual director, thank you," said she. "Oh, madame, you must not think to throw dust in my eyes! I know you, and know you well!"

"On the contrary, you seem to know less than I had expected. If you know me so well, pray what am I?"

All her rival's bitterness and hatred rang in the tones of her answer. "You are," said she, "the governess of my children, and the secret mistress of the king."

"You are mistaken," answered Madame de Maintenon serenely. "I am the governess of your children, and I am the king's wife."

CHAPTER XXI.
THE MAN IN THE CALECHE.

Often had De Montespan feigned a faint in the days when she wished to disarm the anger of the king. So she had drawn his arms round her, and won the pity which is the twin sister of love. But now she knew what it was to have the senses struck out of her by a word. She could not doubt the truth of what she heard. There was that in her rival's face, in her steady eye, in her quiet voice, which carried absolute conviction with it. She stood stunned for an instant, panting, her outstretched hands feeling at the air, her defiant eyes dulling and glazing. Then, with a short sharp cry, the wail of one who has fought hard and yet knows that she can fight no more, her proud head drooped, and she fell forward senseless at the feet of her rival. Madame de Maintenon stooped and raised her up in her strong white arms. There was true grief and pity in her eyes as she looked down at the snow-pale face which lay against her bosom, all the bitterness and pride gone out of it, and nothing left save the tear which sparkled under the dark lashes, and the petulant droop of the lip, like that of a child which had wept itself to sleep. She laid her on the ottoman and placed a silken cushion under her head. Then she gathered together and put back into the open cupboard all the jewels which were scattered about the carpet. Having locked it, and placed the key on the table where its owner's eye would readily fall upon it, she struck a gong, which summoned the little black page.

"Your mistress is indisposed," said she. "Go and bring her maids to her." And so, having done all that lay with her to do, she turned away from the great silent room, where, amid the velvet and the gilding, her beautiful rival lay like a crushed flower, helpless and hopeless.

Helpless enough, for what could she do? and hopeless too, for how could fortune aid her? The instant that her senses had come back to her she had sent away her waiting women, and lay with clasped hands and a drawn face planning out her own weary future. She must go; that was certain. Not merely because it was the king's order, but because only misery and mockery remained for her now in the palace where she had reigned supreme. It was true that she had held her position against the queen before, but all her hatred could not blind her to the fact that her rival was a very different woman to poor meek little Maria Theresa. No; her spirit was broken at last. She must accept defeat, and she must go.

She rose from the couch, feeling that she had aged ten years in an hour. There was much to be done, and little time in which to do it. She had cast down her jewels when the king had spoken as though they would atone for the loss of his love; but now that the love was gone there was no reason why the jewels should be lost too. If she had ceased to be the most powerful, she might still be the richest woman in France. There was her pension, of course. That would be a munificent one, for Louis was always generous. And then there was all the spoil which she had collected during these long years—the jewels the pearls, the gold, the vases, the pictures, the crucifixes, the watches, the trinkets—together they represented many millions of livres. With her own hands she packed away the more precious and portable of them, while she arranged with her brother for the safe-keeping of the others. All day she was at work in a mood of feverish energy, doing anything and everything which might distract her thoughts from her own defeat and her rival's victory. By evening all was ready, and she had arranged that her property should be sent after her to Petit Bourg, to which castle she intended to retire.

It wanted half an hour of the time fixed for her departure, when a young cavalier, whose face was strange to her, was ushered into the room.

He came with a message from her brother.

"Monsieur de Vivonne regrets, madame, that the rumour of your departure has got abroad among the court."

"What do I care for that, monsieur?" she retorted, with all her old spirit.

"He says, madame, that the courtiers may assemble at the west gate to see you go; that Madame de Neuilly will be there, and the Duchesse de Chambord, and Mademoiselle de Rohan, and—"

The lady shrank with horror at the thought of such an ordeal. To drive away from the palace, where she had been more than queen, under the scornful eyes and bitter gibes of so many personal enemies! After all the humiliations of the day, that would be the crowning cup of sorrow. Her nerve was broken. She could not face it.

"Tell my brother, monsieur, that I should be much obliged if he would make fresh arrangements, by which my departure might be private."

"He bade me say that he had done so, madame."

"Ah! at what hour then?"

"Now. As soon as possible."

"I am ready. At the west gate then?"

"No; at the east. The carriage waits."

"And where is my brother?"

"We are to pick him up at the park gate."

"And why that?"

"Because he is watched; and were he seen beside the carriage, all would be known."

"Very good. Then, monsieur, if you will take my cloak and this casket we may start at once."

They made their way by a circuitous route through the less-used corridors, she hurrying on like a guilty creature, a hood drawn over her face, and her heart in a flutter at every stray footfall. But fortune stood her friend. She met no one, and soon found herself at the eastern postern gate. A couple of phlegmatic Swiss guardsmen leaned upon their muskets upon either side, and the lamp above shone upon the carriage which awaited her. The door was open, and a tall cavalier swathed in a black cloak handed her into it. He then took the seat opposite to her, slammed the door, and the caleche rattled away down the main drive.

It had not surprised her that this man should join her inside the coach, for it was usual to have a guard there, and he was doubtless taking the place which her brother would afterwards occupy. That was all natural enough. But when ten minutes passed by, and he had neither moved nor spoken, she peered at him through the gloom with some curiosity. In the glance which she had of him, as he handed her in, she had seen that he was dressed like a gentleman, and there was that in his bow and wave as he did it which told her experienced senses that he was a man of courtly manners. But courtiers, as she had known them, were gallant and garrulous, and this man was so very quiet and still. Again she strained her eyes through the gloom. His hat was pulled down and his cloak was still drawn across his mouth, but from out of the shadow she seemed to get a glimpse of two eyes which peered at her even as she did at him.

At last the silence impressed her with a vague uneasiness. It was time to bring it to an end.

"Surely, monsieur, we have passed the park gate where we were to pick up my brother."

Her companion neither answered nor moved. She thought that perhaps the rumble of the heavy caleche had drowned her voice.

"I say, monsieur," she repeated, leaning forwards, "that we have passed the place where we were to meet Monsieur de Vivonne."

He took no notice.

"Monsieur," she cried, "I again remark that we have passed the gates."
There was no answer.

A thrill ran through her nerves. Who or what could he be, this silent man? Then suddenly it struck her that he might be dumb.

"Perhaps monsieur is afflicted," she said. "Perhaps monsieur cannot speak. If that be the cause of your silence, will you raise your hand, and I shall understand." He sat rigid and silent.

Then a sudden mad fear came upon her, shut up in the dark with this dreadful voiceless thing. She screamed in her terror, and strove to pull down the window and open the door. But a grip of steel closed suddenly round her wrist and forced her back into her seat. And yet the man's body had not moved, and there was no sound save the lurching and rasping of the carriage and the clatter of the flying horses. They were already out on the country roads far beyond Versailles. It was darker than before, heavy clouds had banked over the heavens, and the rumbling of thunder was heard low down on the horizon.

The lady lay back panting upon the leather cushions of the carriage. She was a brave woman, and yet this sudden strange horror coming upon her at the moment when she was weakest had shaken her to the soul. She crouched in the corner, staring across with eyes which were dilated with terror at the figure on the other side. If he would but say something! Any revelation, any menace, was better than this silence. It was so dark now that she could hardly see his vague outline, and every instant, as the storm gathered, it became still darker. The wind was blowing in little short angry puffs, and still there was that far-off rattle and rumble. Again the strain of the silence was unbearable. She must break it at any cost.

"Sir," said she, "there is some mistake here. I do not know by what right you prevent me from pulling down the window and giving my directions to the coachman."

He said nothing.

"I repeat, sir, that there is some mistake. This is the carriage of my brother, Monsieur de Vivonne, and he is not a man who will allow his sister to be treated uncourteously."

A few heavy drops of rain splashed against one window. The clouds were lower and denser. She had quite lost sight of that motionless figure, but it was all the more terrible to her now that it was unseen. She screamed with sheer terror, but her scream availed no more than her words.

"Sir," she cried, clutching forward with her hands and grasping his sleeve, "you frighten me. You terrify me. I have never harmed you. Why should you wish to hurt an unfortunate woman? Oh, speak to me; for God's sake, speak!"

Still the patter of rain upon the window, and no other sound save her own sharp breathing.

"Perhaps you do not know who I am!" she continued, endeavouring to assume her usual tone of command, and talking now to an absolute and impenetrable darkness. "You may learn when it is too late that you have chosen the wrong person for this pleasantry. I am the Marquise de Montespan, and I am not one who forgets a slight. If you know anything of the court, you must know that my word has some weight with the king. You may carry me away in this carriage, but I am not a person who can disappear without speedy inquiry, and speedy vengeance if I have been wronged. If you would—Oh, Jesus! Have mercy!"

A livid flash of lightning had burst from the heart of the cloud, and, for an instant, the whole country-side and the interior of the caleche were as light as day. The man's face was within a hand's breadth of her own, his mouth wide open, his eyes mere shining slits, convulsed with silent merriment. Every detail flashed out clear in that vivid light— his red quivering tongue, the lighter pink beneath it, the broad white teeth, the short brown beard cut into a peak and bristling forward.

But it was not the sudden flash, it was not the laughing, cruel face, which shot an ice-cold shudder through Francoise de Montespan. It was that, of all men upon earth, this was he whom she most dreaded, and whom she had least thought to see.

"Maurice!" she screamed. "Maurice! it is you!"

"Yes, little wifie, it is I. We are restored to each other's arms, you see, after this interval."

"Oh, Maurice, how you have frightened me! How could you be so cruel? Why would you not speak to me?"

"Because it was so sweet to sit in silence and to think that I really had you to myself after all these years, with none to come between. Ah, little wifie, I have often longed for this hour."

"I have wronged you, Maurice; I have wronged you! Forgive me!"

"We do not forgive in our family, my darling Francoise. Is it not like old days to find ourselves driving together? And in this carriage, too. It is the very one which bore us back from the cathedral where you made your vows so prettily. I sat as I sit now, and you sat there, and I took your hand like this, and I pressed it, and—"

"Oh, villain, you have twisted my wrist! You have broken my arm!"

"Oh, surely not, my little wifie! And then you remember that, as you told me how truly you would love me, I leaned forward to your lips, and—"

"Oh, help! Brute, you have cut my mouth! You have struck me with your ring."

"Struck you! Now who would have thought that spring day when we planned out our future, that this also was in the future waiting for me and you? And this! and this!"

He struck savagely at her face in the darkness. She threw herself down, her head pressed against the cushions. With the strength and fury of a maniac he showered his blows above her, thudding upon the leather or crashing upon the woodwork, heedless of his own splintered hands.

"So I have silenced you," said he at last. "I have stopped your words with my kisses before now. But the world goes on, Francoise, and times change, and women grow false, and men grow stern."

"You may kill me if you will," she moaned.

"I will," he said simply.

Still the carriage flew along, jolting and staggering in the deeply-rutted country roads. The storm had passed, but the growl of the thunder and the far-off glint of a lightning-flash were to be heard and seen on the other side of the heavens. The moon shone out with its clear cold light, silvering the broad, hedgeless, poplar-fringed plains, and shining through the window of the carriage upon the crouching figure and her terrible companion. He leaned back now, his arms folded upon his chest, his eyes gloating upon the abject misery of the woman who had wronged him.

"Where are you taking me?" she asked at last.

"To Portillac, my little wifie."

"And why there? What would you do to me?"

"I would silence that little lying tongue forever. It shall deceive no more men."

"You would murder me?"

"If you call it that."

"You have a stone for a heart."

"My other was given to a woman."

"Oh, my sins are indeed punished."

"Rest assured that they will be."

"Can I do nothing to atone?"

"I will see that you atone."

"You have a sword by your side, Maurice. Why do you not kill me, then, if you are so bitter against me? Why do you not pass it through my heart?"

"Rest assured that I would have done so had I not an excellent reason."

"Why, then?"

"I will tell you. At Portillac I have the right of the high justice, the middle, and the low. I am seigneur there, and can try, condemn, and execute. It is my lawful privilege. This pitiful king will not even know how to avenge you, for the right is mine, and he cannot gainsay it without making an enemy of every seigneur in France."

He opened his mouth again and laughed at his own device, while she, shivering in every limb, turned away from his cruel face and glowing eyes, and buried her face in her hands. Once more she prayed God to forgive her for her poor sinful life. So they whirled through the night behind the clattering horses, the husband and the wife, saying nothing, but with hatred and fear raging in their hearts, until a brazier fire shone down upon them from the angle of a keep, and the shadow of the huge pile loomed vaguely up in front of them in the darkness. It was the Castle of Portillac.

CHAPTER XXII.
THE SCAFFOLD OF PORTILLAC.

And thus it was that Amory de Catinat and Amos Green saw from their dungeon window the midnight carriage which discharged its prisoner before their eyes. Hence, too, came that ominous planking and that strange procession in the early morning. And thus it also happened that they found themselves looking down upon Francoise de Montespan as she was led to her death, and that they heard that last piteous cry for aid at the instant when the heavy hand of the ruffian with the axe fell upon her shoulder, and she was forced down upon her knees beside the block. She shrank screaming from the dreadful, red-stained, greasy billet of wood, but the butcher heaved up his weapon, and the seigneur had taken a step forward with hand outstretched to seize the long auburn hair and to drag the dainty head down with it when suddenly he was struck motionless with astonishment, and stood with his foot advanced and his hand still out, his mouth half open, and his eyes fixed in front of him.

And, indeed, what he had seen was enough to fill any man with amazement. Out of the small square window which faced him a man had suddenly shot head-foremost, pitching on to his outstretched hands and then bounding to his feet. Within a foot of his heels came the head of a second one, who fell more heavily than the first, and yet recovered himself as quickly. The one wore the blue coat with silver facings of the king's guard; the second had the dark coat and clean-shaven face of a man of peace; but each carried a short rusty iron bar in his hand. Not a word did either of them say, but the soldier took two quick steps forward and struck at the headsman while he was still poising himself for a blow at the victim. There was a thud, with a crackle like a breaking egg, and the bar flew into pieces. The heads-man gave a dreadful cry, and dropped his axe, clapped his two hands to his head, and running zigzag across the scaffold, fell over, a dead man, into the courtyard beneath.

Quick as a flash De Catinat had caught up the axe, and faced De Montespan with the heavy weapon slung over his shoulder and a challenge in his eyes.

"Now!" said he.

The seigneur had for the instant been too astounded to speak. Now he understood at least that these strangers had come between him and his prey.

"Seize these men!" he shrieked, turning to his followers.

"One moment!" cried De Catinat, with a voice and manner which commanded attention. "You see by my coat what I am. I am the body-servant of the king. Who touches me touches him. Have a care for yourselves. It is a dangerous game!"

"On, you cowards!" roared De Montespan.

But the men-at-arms hesitated, for the fear of the king was as a great shadow which hung over all France. De Catinat saw their indecision, and he followed up his advantage.

"This woman," he cried, "is the king's own favourite, and if any harm come to a lock of her hair, I tell you that there is not a living soul within this portcullis who will not die a death of torture. Fools, will you gasp out your lives upon the rack, or writhe in boiling oil, at the bidding of this madman?"

"Who are these men, Marceau?" cried the seigneur furiously.

"They are prisoners, your excellency."

"Prisoners! Whose prisoners?"

"Yours, your excellency."

"Who ordered you to detain them?"

"You did. The escort brought your signet-ring."

"I never saw the men. There is devilry in this. But they shall not beard me in my own castle, nor stand between me and my own wife. No, *par dieu!* they shall not and live! You men, Marceau, Etienne, Gilbert, Jean, Pierre, all you who have eaten my bread, on to them, I say!"

He glanced round with furious eyes, but they fell only upon hung heads and averted faces. With a hideous curse he flashed out his sword and rushed at his wife, who knelt half insensible beside the block. De Catinat sprang between them to protect her; but Marceau, the bearded seneschal, had already seized his master round the waist. With the strength of a maniac, his teeth clenched and the foam churning from the corners of his lips, De Montespan writhed round in the man's grasp, and shortening his sword, he thrust it through the brown beard and deep into the throat behind it. Marceau fell back with a choking cry, the blood bubbling from his mouth and his wound; but before his murderer could disengage his weapon, De Catinat and the American, aided by a dozen of the retainers, had dragged him down on to the scaffold, and Amos Green had pinioned him so securely that he could but move his eyes and his lips, with which he lay glaring and spitting at them. So savage were his own followers against him—for Marceau was well loved amongst them— that, with axe and block so ready, justice might very swiftly have had her way, had not a long clear bugle-call, rising and falling in a thousand little twirls and flourishes, clanged out suddenly in the still morning air. De Catinat pricked up his ears at the sound of it like a hound at the huntsman's call.

"Did you hear, Amos?"

"It was a trumpet."

"It was the guards' bugle-call. You, there, hasten to the gate! Throw up the portcullis and drop the drawbridge! Stir yourselves, or even now you may suffer for your master's sins! It has been a narrow escape, Amos!"

"You may say so, friend. I saw him put out his hand to her hair, even as you sprang from the window. Another instant and he would have had her scalped. But she is a fair woman, the fairest that ever my eyes rested upon, and it is not fit that she should kneel here upon these boards." He dragged her husband's long black cloak from him, and made a pillow for the senseless woman with a tenderness and delicacy which came strangely from a man of his build and bearing.

He was still stooping over her when there came the clang of the falling bridge, and an instant later the clatter of the hoofs of a troop of cavalry, who swept with wave of plumes, toss of manes, and jingle of steel into the courtyard. At the head was a tall horseman in the full dress of the guards, with a curling feather in his hat, high buff gloves, and his sword gleaming in the sunlight. He cantered forward towards the scaffold, his keen dark eyes taking in every detail of the group which awaited him there. De Catinat's face brightened at the sight of him, and he was down in an instant beside his stirrup.

"De Brissac!"

"De Catinat! Now where in the name of wonder did you come from?"

"I have been a prisoner. Tell me, De Brissac, did you leave the message in Paris?"

"Certainly I did."

"And the archbishop came?"

"He did."

"And the marriage?"

"Took place as arranged. That is why this poor woman whom I see yonder has had to leave the palace."

"I thought as much."

"I trust that no harm has come to her?"

"My friend and I were just in time to save her. Her husband lies there. He is a fiend, De Brissac."

"Very likely; but an angel might have grown bitter had he had the same treatment."

"We have him pinioned here. He has slain a man, and I have slain another."

"On my word, you have been busy."

"How did you know that we were here?"

"Nay, that is an unexpected pleasure."

"You did not come for us, then?"

"No; we came for the lady."

"And how did this fellow get hold of her?"

"Her brother was to have taken her in his carriage. Her husband learned it, and by a lying message he coaxed her into his own, which was at another door. When De Vivonne found that she did not come, and that her rooms were empty, he made inquiries, and soon learned how she had gone. De Montespan's arms had been seen on the panel, and so the king sent me here with my troop as fast as we could gallop."

"Ah, and you would have come too late had a strange chance not brought us here. I know not who it was who waylaid us, for this man seemed to know nothing of the matter. However, all that will be clearer afterwards. What is to be done now?"

"I have my own orders. Madame is to be sent to Petit Bourg, and any who are concerned in offering her violence are to be kept until the king's pleasure is known. The castle, too, must be held for the king. But you, De Catinat, you have nothing to do now?"

"Nothing, save that I would like well to ride into Paris to see that all is right with my uncle and his daughter."

"Ah, that sweet little cousin of thine! By my soul, I do not wonder that the folk know you well in the Rue St. Martin. Well, I have carried a message for you once, and you shall do as much for me now."

"With all my heart. And whither?"

"To Versailles. The king will be on fire to know how we have fared. You have the best right to tell him, since without you and your friend yonder it would have been but a sorry tale."

"I will be there in two hours."

"Have you horses?"

"Ours were slain."

"You will find some in the stables here. Pick the best, since you have lost your own in the king's service."

The advice was too good to be overlooked. De Catinat, beckoning to Amos Green, hurried away with him to the stables, while De Brissac, with a few short sharp orders, disarmed the retainers, stationed his guardsmen all over the castle, and arranged for the removal of the lady, and for the custody of her husband. An hour later the two friends were riding swiftly down the country road, inhaling the sweet air, which seemed the fresher for their late experience of the dank, foul vapours of their dungeon. Far behind them a little dark pinnacle jutting over a grove of trees marked the chateau which they had left, while on the extreme horizon to the west there came a quick shimmer and sparkle where the level rays of the early sun gleamed upon the magnificent palace which was their goal.

CHAPTER XXIII.
THE FALL OF THE CATINATS.

Two days after Madame de Maintenon's marriage to the king there was held within the humble walls of her little room a meeting which was destined to cause untold misery to many hundreds of thousands of people, and yet, in the wisdom of Providence, to be an instrument in carrying French arts and French ingenuity and French sprightliness among those heavier Teutonic peoples who have been the stronger and the better ever since for the leaven which they then received. For in history great evils have sometimes arisen from a virtue, and most beneficent results have often followed hard upon a crime.

The time had come when the Church was to claim her promise from madame, and her pale cheek and sad eyes showed how vain it had been for her to try and drown the pleadings of her tender heart by the arguments of the bigots around her. She knew the Huguenots of France. Who could know them better, seeing that she was herself from their stock, and had been brought up in their faith? She knew their patience, their nobility, their independence, their tenacity. What chance was there that they would conform to the king's wish? A few great nobles might, but the others would laugh at the galleys, the jail, or even the gallows when the faith of their fathers was at stake. If their creed were no longer tolerated, then, and if they remained true to it, they must either fly from the country or spend a living death tugging at an oar or working in a chain-gang upon the roads. It was a dreadful alternative to present to a people who were so numerous that they made a small nation in themselves. And most dreadful of all, that she who was of their own blood should cast her voice against them. And yet her promise had been given, and now the time had come when it must be redeemed.

The eloquent Bishop Bossuet was there, with Louvois, the minister of war, and the famous Jesuit, Father la Chaise, each piling argument upon argument to overcome the reluctance of the king. Beside them stood another priest, so thin and so pale that he might have risen from his bed of death, but with a fierce light burning in his large dark eyes, and with a terrible resolution in his drawn brows and in the set of his grim, lanky jaw. Madame bent over her tapestry and weaved her coloured silks in silence, while the king leaned upon his hand and listened with the face of a man who knows that he is driven, and yet can hardly turn against the goads. On the low table lay a paper, with pen and ink beside it. It was the order for the revocation, and it only needed the king's signature to make it the law of the land.

"And so, father, you are of opinion that if I stamp out heresy in this fashion I shall assure my own salvation in the next world?" he asked.

"You will have merited a reward."

"And you think so too, Monsieur Bishop?"

"Assuredly, sire."

"And you. Abbe du Chayla?"

The emaciated priest spoke for the first time, a tinge of colour creeping into his corpse-like cheeks, and a more lurid light in his deep-set eyes.

"I know not about assuring your salvation, sire. I think it would take very much more to do that. But there cannot be a doubt as to your damnation if you do not do it."

The king started angrily, and frowned at the speaker.

"Your words are somewhat more curt than I am accustomed to," he remarked.

"In such a matter it were cruel indeed to leave you in doubt. I say again that your soul's fate hangs upon the balance. Heresy is a mortal sin. Thousands of heretics would turn to the Church if you did but give the word. Therefore these thousands of mortal sins are all upon your soul. What hope for it then, if you do not amend?"

"My father and my grandfather tolerated them."

"Then, without some special extension of the grace of God, your father and your grandfather are burning in hell."

"Insolent!" The king sprang from his seat.

"Sire, I will say what I hold to be the truth were you fifty times a king. What care I for any man when I know that I speak for the King of kings? See; are these the limbs of one who would shrink from testifying to truth?" With a sudden movement he threw back the long sleeves of his gown and shot·out his white fleshless arms. The bones were all knotted and bent and screwed into the most fantastic shapes. Even Louvois, the hardened man of the court, and his two brother priests, shuddered at the sight of those dreadful limbs. He raised them above his head and turned his burning eyes upwards.

"Heaven has chosen me to testify for the faith before now," said he. "I heard that blood was wanted to nourish the young Church of Siam, and so to Siam I journeyed. They tore me open; they crucified me; they wrenched and split my bones. I was left as a dead man, yet God has breathed the breath of life back into me that I may help in this great work of the regeneration of France."

"Your sufferings, father," said Louis, resuming his seat, "give you every claim, both upon the Church and upon me, who am its special champion and protector. What would you counsel, then, father, in the case of those Huguenots who refuse to change?"

"They would change," cried Du Chayla, with a drawn smile upon his ghastly face. "They must bend or they must break. What matter if they be ground to powder, if we can but build up a complete Church in the land?" His deep-set eyes glowed with ferocity, and be shook one bony hand in savage wrath above his head.

"The cruelty with which you have been used, then, has not taught you to be more tender to others."

"Tender! To heretics! No, sire, my own pains have taught me that the world and the flesh are as nothing, and that the truest charity to another is to capture his soul at all risks to his vile body. I should have these Huguenot souls, sire, though I turned France into a shambles to gain them."

Louis was evidently deeply impressed by the fearless words and the wild earnestness of the speaker. He leaned his head upon his hand for a little time, and remained sunk in the deepest thought.

"Besides, sire," said Pere la Chaise softly, "there would be little need for these stronger measures of which the good abbe speaks. As I have already remarked to you, you are so beloved in your kingdom that the mere assurance that you had expressed your will upon the subject would be enough to turn them all to the true faith."

"I wish that I could think so, father; I wish that I could think so. But what is this?"

It was his valet who had half opened the door.

"Captain de Catinat is here, who desires to see you at once, sire."

"Ask the captain to enter. Ah!" A happy thought seemed to have struck him. "We shall see what love for me will do in such a matter, for if it is anywhere to be found it must be among my own body-servants."

The guardsman had arrived that instant from his long ride, and leaving Amos Green with the horses, he had come on at once, all dusty and travel-stained, to carry his message to the king. He entered now, and stood with the quiet ease of a man who is used to such scenes, his hand raised in a salute.

"What news, captain?"

"Major de Brissac bade me tell you, sire, that he held the Castle of Portillac, that the lady is safe, and that her husband is a prisoner."

Louis and his wife exchanged a quick glance of relief.

"That is well," said he. "By the way, captain, you have served me in many ways of late, and always with success. I hear, Louvois, that De la Salle is dead of the small-pox."

"He died yesterday, sire."

"Then I desire that you make out the vacant commission of major to Monsieur de Catinat. Let me be the first to congratulate you, major, upon your promotion, though you will need to exchange the blue coat for the pearl and gray of the mousquetaires. We cannot spare you from the household, you see."

De Catinat kissed the hand which the monarch held out to him.

"May I be worthy of your kindness, sire!"

"You would do what you could to serve me, would you not?"

"My life is yours, sire."

"Very good. Then I shall put your fidelity to the proof."

"I am ready for any proof."

"It is not a very severe one. You see this paper upon the table. It is an order that all the Huguenots in my dominions shall give up their errors, under pain of banishment or captivity. Now I have hopes that there are many of my faithful subjects who are at fault in this matter, but who will abjure it when they learn that it is my clearly expressed wish that they should do so. It would be a great joy to me to find that it was so, for it would be a pain to me to use force against any man who bears the name of Frenchman. Do you follow me?"

"Yes, sire." The young man had turned deadly pale, and he shifted his feet, and opened and clasped his hands. He had faced death a dozen times and under many different forms, but never had he felt such a sinking of the heart as came over him now.

"You are yourself a Huguenot, I understand. I would gladly have you, then, as the first-fruit of this great measure. Let us hear from your own lips that you, for one, are ready to follow the lead of your king in this as in other things."

The young guardsman still hesitated, though his doubts were rather as to how he should frame his reply than as to what its substance should be. He felt that in an instant Fortune had wiped out all the good turns which she had done him during his past life, and that now, far from being in her debt, he held a heavy score against her. The king arched his eyebrows and drummed his fingers impatiently as he glanced at the downcast face and dejected bearing.

"Why all this thought?" he cried. "You are a man whom I have raised and whom I will raise. He who has a major's epaulettes at thirty may carry a marshal's baton at fifty. Your past is mine, and your future shall be no less so. What other hopes have you?"

"I have none, sire, outside your service."

"Why this silence, then? Why do you not give the assurance which I demand?"

"I cannot do it, sire."

"You cannot do it!"

"It is impossible. I should have no more peace in my mind, or respect for myself, if I knew that for the sake of position or wealth I had given up the faith of my fathers."

"Man, you are surely mad! There is all that a man could covet upon one side, and what is there upon the other?"

"There is my honour."

"And is it, then, a dishonour to embrace my religion?"

"It would be a dishonour to me to embrace it for the sake of gain without believing in it."

"Then believe it."

"Alas, sire, a man cannot force himself to believe. Belief is a thing which must come to him, not he to it."

"On my word, father," said Louis, glancing with a bitter smile at his Jesuit confessor, "I shall have to pick the cadets of the household from your seminary, since my officers have turned casuists and theologians. So, for the last time, you refuse to obey my request?"

"Oh, sire—" De Catinat took a step forward with outstretched hands and tears in his eyes.

But the king checked him with a gesture. "I desire no protestations," said he. "I judge a man by his acts. Do you abjure or not?"

"I cannot, sire."

"You see," said Louis, turning again to the Jesuit, "it will not be as easy as you think."

"This man is obstinate, it is true, but many others will be more yielding."

The king shook his head. "I would that I knew what to do," said he. "Madame, I know that you, at least, will ever give me the best advice. You have heard all that has been said. What do you recommend?"

She kept her eyes still fixed upon her tapestry, but her voice was firm and clear as she answered:—

"You have yourself said that you are the eldest son of the Church. If the eldest son desert her, then who will do her bidding? And there is truth, too, in what the holy abbe has said. You may imperil your own soul by condoning this sin of heresy. It grows and flourishes, and if it be not rooted out now, it may choke the truth as weeds and briers choke the wheat."

"There are districts in France now," said Bossuet, "where a church is not to be seen in a day's journey, and where all the folk, from the nobles to the peasants, are of the same accursed faith. So it is in the Cevennes, where the people are as fierce and rugged as their own mountains. Heaven guard the priests who have to bring them back from their errors."

"Whom should I send on so perilous a task?" asked Louis.

The Abbe du Chayla was down in a instant upon his knees with his gaunt hands outstretched. "Send me, sire! Me!" he cried. "I have never asked a favour of you, and never will again. But I am the man who could break this people. Send me with your message to the people of the Cevennes."

"God help the people of the Cevennes!" muttered Louis, as he looked with mingled respect and loathing at the emaciated face and fiery eyes of the fanatic. "Very well, abbe," he added aloud; "you shall go to the Cevennes."

Perhaps for an instant there came upon the stern priest some premonition of that dreadful morning when, as he crouched in a corner of 'his burning home, fifty daggers were to rasp against each other in his body. He sunk his face in his hands, and a shudder passed over his gaunt frame. Then he rose, and folding his arms, he resumed his impassive attitude. Louis took up the pen from the table, and drew the paper towards him.

"I have the same counsel, then, from all of you," said he,—"from you, bishop; from you, father; from you, madame; from you, abbe; and from you, Louvois. Well, if ill come from it, may it not be visited upon me! But what is this?"

De Catinat had taken a step forward with his hand outstretched. His ardent, impetuous nature had suddenly broken down all the barriers of caution, and he seemed for the instant to see that countless throng of men, women, and children of his own faith, all unable to say a word for themselves, and all looking to him as their champion and spokesman. He had thought little of such matters when all was well, but now, when danger threatened, the deeper side of his nature was moved, and he felt how light a thing is life and fortune when weighed against a great abiding cause and principle.

"Do not sign it, sire," he cried. "You will live to wish that your hand had withered ere it grasped that pen. I know it, sire. I am sure of it. Consider all these helpless folk—the little children, the young girls, the old and the feeble. Their creed is themselves. As well ask the leaves to change the twigs on which they grow. They could not change. At most you could but hope to turn them from honest folk into hypocrites. And why should you do it? They honour you. They love you. They harm none. They are proud to serve in your armies, to fight for you, to work for you, to build up the greatness of your kingdom. I implore you, sire, to think again before you sign an order which will bring misery and desolation to so many."

For a moment the king had hesitated as he listened to the short abrupt sentences in which the soldier pleaded for his fellows, but his face hardened again as he remembered how even his own personal entreaty had been unable to prevail with this young dandy of the court.

"France's religion should be that of France's king," said he, "and if my own guardsmen thwart me in such a matter, I must find others who will be more faithful. That major's commission in the mousquetaires must go to Captain de Belmont, Louvois."

"Very good, sire."

"And De Catinat's commission may be transferred to Lieutenant Labadoyere."

"Very good, sire."

"And I am to serve you no longer?"

"You are too dainty for my service."

De Catinat's arms fell listlessly to his side, and his head sunk forward upon his breast. Then, as he realised the ruin of all the hopes of his life, and the cruel injustice with which he had been treated, he broke into a cry of despair, and rushed from the room with the hot tears of impotent anger running down his face. So, sobbing, gesticulating, with coat unbuttoned and hat awry, he burst into the stable where placid Amos Green was smoking his pipe and watching with critical eyes the grooming of the horses.

"What in thunder is the matter now?" he asked, holding his pipe by the bowl, while the blue wreaths curled up from his lips.

"This sword," cried the Frenchman—"I have no right to wear it! I shall break it!"

"Well, and I'll break my knife too if it will hearten you up."

"And these," cried De Catinat, tugging at his silver shoulder-straps, "they must go."

"Ah, you draw ahead of me there, for I never had any. But come, friend, let me know the trouble, that I may see if it may not be mended."

"To Paris! to Paris!" shouted the guardsman frantically. "If I am ruined, I may yet be in time to save them. The horses, quick!"

It was clear to the American that some sudden calamity had befallen, so he aided his comrade and the grooms to saddle and bridle.

Five minutes later they were flying on their way, and in little more than an hour their steeds, all reeking and foam-flecked, were pulled up outside the high house in the Rue St. Martin. De Catinat sprang from his saddle and rushed upstairs, while Amos followed in his own leisurely fashion.

The old Huguenot and his beautiful daughter were seated at one side of the great fireplace, her hand in his, and they sprang up together, she to throw herself with a glad cry into the arms of her lover, and he to grasp the hand which his nephew held out to him.

At the other side of the fireplace, with a very long pipe in his mouth and a cup of wine upon a settle beside him, sat a strange-looking man, with grizzled hair and beard, a fleshy red projecting nose, and two little gray eyes, which twinkled out from under huge brindled brows. His long thin face was laced and seamed with wrinkles, crossing and recrossing everywhere, but fanning out in hundreds from the corners of his eyes. It was set in an unchanging expression, and as it was of the same colour all over, as dark as the darkest walnut, it might have been some quaint figure-head cut out of a coarse-grained wood. He was clad in a blue serge jacket, a pair of red breeches smeared at the knees with tar, clean gray worsted stockings, large steel buckles over his coarse square-toed shoes, and beside him, balanced upon the top of a thick oaken cudgel, was a weather-stained silver-laced hat. His gray-shot hair was gathered up behind into a short stiff tail, and a seaman's hanger, with a brass handle, was girded to his waist by a tarnished leather belt.

De Catinat had been too occupied to take notice of this singular individual, but Amos Green gave a shout of delight at the sight of him, and ran forward to greet him. The other's wooden face relaxed so far as to show two tobacco-stained fangs, and, without rising, he held out a great red hand, of the size and shape of a moderate spade.

"Why, Captain Ephraim," cried Amos in English, "who ever would have thought of finding you here? De Catinat, this is my old friend Ephraim Savage, under whose charge I came here."

"Anchor's apeak, lad, and the hatches down," said the stranger, in the peculiar drawling voice which the New Englanders had retained from their ancestors, the English Puritans.

"And when do you sail?"

"As soon as your foot is on her deck, if Providence serve us with wind and tide. And how has all gone with thee, Amos?"

"Right well. I have much to tell you of."

"I trust that you have held yourself apart from all their popish devilry."

"Yes, yes, Ephraim."

"And have had no truck with the scarlet woman."

"No, no; but what is it now?"

The grizzled hair was bristling with rage, and the little gray eyes were gleaming from under the heavy tufts. Amos, following their gaze, saw that De Catinat was seated with his arm round Adele, while her head rested upon his shoulder.

"Ah, if I but knew their snip-snap, lippetty-chippetty lingo! Saw one ever such a sight! Amos, lad, what is the French for 'a shameless hussy'?"

"Nay, nay, Ephraim. Surely one may see such a sight, and think no harm of it, on our side of the water.

"Never, Amos. In no godly country."

"Tut! I have seen folks courting in New York."

"Ah, New York! I said in no godly country. I cannot answer for New York or Virginia. South of Cape Cod, or of New Haven at the furthest, there is no saying what folk will do. Very sure I am that in Boston or Salem or Plymouth she would see the bridewell and he the stocks for half as much. Ah!" He shook his head and bent his brows at the guilty couple.

But they and their old relative were far too engrossed with their own affairs to give a thought to the Puritan seaman. De Catinat had told his tale in a few short, bitter sentences, the injustice that had been done to him, his dismissal from the king's service, and the ruin which had come upon the Huguenots of France. Adele, as is the angel instinct of woman, thought only of her lover and his misfortunes as she listened to his story, but the old merchant tottered to his feet when he heard of the revocation of the Edict, and stood with shaking limbs, staring about him in bewilderment.

"What am I to do?" he cried. "What am I to do? I am too old to begin my life again."

"Never fear, uncle," said De Catinat heartily. "There are other lands beyond France."

"But not for me. No, no; I am too old. Lord, but Thy hand is heavy upon Thy servants. Now is the vial opened, and the carved work of the sanctuary thrown down. Ah, what shall I do, and whither shall I turn?" He wrung his hands in his perplexity.

"What is amiss with him, then, Amos?" asked the seaman. "Though I know nothing of what he says, yet I can see that he flies a distress signal."

"He and his must leave the country, Ephraim."

"And why?"

"Because they are Protestants, and the king will not abide their creed."

Ephraim Savage was across the room in an instant, and had enclosed the old merchant's thin hand in his own great knotted fist. There was a brotherly sympathy in his strong grip and rugged weather-stained face which held up the other's courage as no words could have done.

"What is the French for 'the scarlet woman,' Amos?" he asked, glancing over his shoulder. "Tell this man that we shall see him through. Tell him that we've got a country where he'll just fit in like a bung in a barrel. Tell him that religion is free to all there, and not a papist nearer than Baltimore or the Capuchins of the Penobscot. Tell him that if he wants to come, the *Golden Rod* is waiting with her anchor apeak and her cargo aboard. Tell him what you like, so long as you make him come."

"Then we must come at once," said De Catinat, as he listened to the cordial message which was conveyed to his uncle. "To-night the orders will be out, and to-morrow it may be too late."

"But my business!" cried the merchant.

"Take what valuables you can, and leave the rest. Better that than lose all, and liberty into the bargain."

And so at last it was arranged. That very night, within five minutes of the closing of the gates, there passed out of Paris a small party of five, three upon horseback, and two in a closed carriage which bore several weighty boxes upon the top. They were the first leaves flying before the hurricane, the earliest of that great multitude who were within the next few months to stream along every road which led from France, finding their journey's end too often in galley, dungeon and torture chamber, and yet flooding over the frontiers in numbers sufficient to change the industries and modify the characters of all the neighbouring peoples. Like the Israelites of old, they had been driven from their homes at the bidding of an angry king, who, even while he exiled them, threw every difficulty in the way of their departure. Like them, too, there were none of them who could hope to reach their promised land without grievous wanderings, penniless, friendless, and destitute. What passages befell these pilgrims in their travels, what dangers they met, and overcame in the land of the Swiss, on the Rhine, among the Walloons, in England, in Ireland, in Berlin, and even in far-off Russia, has still to be written. This one little group, however, whom we know, we may follow in their venturesome journey, and see the chances which befell them upon that great continent which had lain fallow for so long, sown only with the weeds of humanity, but which was now at last about to quicken into such glorious life.

PART II.
IN THE NEW WORLD.

CHAPTER XXIV.
THE START OF THE "GOLDEN ROD."

Thanks to the early tidings which the guardsman had brought with him, his little party was now ahead of the news. As they passed through the village of Louvier in the early morning they caught a glimpse of a naked corpse upon a dunghill, and were told by a grinning watchman that it was that of a Huguenot who had died impenitent, but that was a common enough occurrence already, and did not mean that there had been any change in the law. At Rouen all was quiet, and Captain Ephraim Savage before evening had brought both them and such property as they had saved aboard of his brigantine, the Golden Rod. It was but a little craft, some seventy tons burden, but at a time when so many were putting out to sea in open boats, preferring the wrath of Nature to that of the king, it was a refuge indeed. The same night the seaman drew up his anchor and began to slowly make his way down the winding river.

And very slow work it was. There was half a moon shining and a breeze from the east, but the stream writhed and twisted and turned until sometimes they seemed to be sailing up rather than down. In the long reaches they set the yard square and ran, but often they had to lower their two boats and warp her painfully along, Tomlinson of Salem, the mate, and six grave, tobacco-chewing, New England seamen with their broad palmetto hats, tugging and straining at the oars. Amos Green, De Catinat, and even the old merchant had to take their spell ere morning, when the sailors were needed aboard for the handling of the canvas. At last, however, with the early dawn the river broadened out and each bank trended away, leaving a long funnel-shaped estuary between. Ephraim Savage snuffed the air and paced the deck briskly with a twinkle in his keen gray eyes. The wind had fallen away, but there was still enough to drive them slowly upon their course.

"Where's the gal?" he asked.

"She is in my cabin," said Amos Green. "I thought that maybe she could manage there until we got across."

"Where will you sleep yourself, then?"

"Tut, a litter of spruce boughs and a sheet of birch bark over me have been enough all these years. What would I ask better than this deck of soft white pine and my blanket?"

"Very good. The old man and his nephew, him with the blue coat, can have the two empty bunks. But you must speak to that man, Amos. I'll have no philandering aboard my ship, lad—no whispering or cuddling or any such foolishness. Tell him that this ship is just a bit broke off from Boston, and he'll have to put up with Boston ways until he gets off her. They've been good enough for better men than him. You give me the French for 'no philandering,' and I'll bring him up with a round turn when he drifts."

"It's a pity we left so quick or they might have been married before we started. She's a good girl, Ephraim, and he is a fine man, for all that their ways are not the same as ours. They don't seem to take life so hard as we, and maybe they get more pleasure out of it."

"I never heard tell that we were put here to get pleasure out of it," said the old Puritan, shaking his head. "The valley of the shadow of death don't seem to me to be the kind o' name one would give to a play-ground. It is a trial and a chastening, that's what it is, the gall of bitterness and the bond of iniquity. We're bad from the beginning, like a stream that runs from a tamarack swamp, and we've enough to do to get ourselves to rights without any fool's talk about pleasure."

"It seems to me to be all mixed up," said Amos. "like the fat and the lean in a bag of pemmican. Look at that sun just pushing its edge over the trees, and see the pink flush on the clouds and the river like a rosy ribbon behind us. It's mighty pretty to our eyes, and very pleasing to us, and it wouldn't be so to my mind if the Creator hadn't wanted it to be. Many a time when I have lain in the woods in the fall and smoked my pipe, and felt how good the tobacco was, and how bright the yellow maples were, and the purple ash, and the red tupelo blazing among the bushwood, I've felt that the real fool's talk was with the man who could doubt that all this was meant to make the world happier for us."

"You've been thinking too much in them woods," said Ephraim Savage, gazing at him uneasily. "Don't let your sail be too great for your boat, lad, nor trust to your own wisdom. Your father was from the Bay, and you were raised from a stock that cast the dust of England from their feet rather than bow down to Baal. Keep a grip on the word and don't think beyond it. But what is the matter with the old man? He don't seem easy in his mind."

The old merchant had been leaning over the bulwarks, looking back with a drawn face and weary eyes at the red curving track behind them which marked the path to Paris. Adele had come up now, with not a thought to spare upon the dangers and troubles which lay in front of her as she chafed the old man's thin cold hands, and whispered words of love and comfort into his ears. But they had come to the point where the gentle still-flowing river began for the first time to throb to the beat of the sea. The old man gazed forward with horror at the bowsprit as he saw it rise slowly upwards into the air, and clung frantically at the rail as it seemed to slip away from beneath him.

"We are always in the hollow of God's hand," he whispered, "but oh, Adele, it is a dreadful thing to feel His fingers moving under us."

"Come with me, uncle," said De Catinat, passing his arm under that of the old man. "It is long since you have rested. And you, Adele, I pray that you will go and sleep, my poor darling, for it has been a weary journey. Go now, to please me, and when you wake, both France and your troubles will lie behind you."

When father and daughter had left the deck, De Catinat made his way aft again to where Amos Green and the captain were standing.

"I am glad to get them below, Amos," said he, "for I fear that we may have trouble yet."

"And how?"

"You see the white road which runs by the southern bank of the river. Twice within the last half-hour I have seen horsemen spurring for dear life along it. Where the spires and smoke are yonder is Honfleur, and thither it was that these men went. I know not who could ride so madly at such an hour unless they were the messengers of the king. Oh, see, there is a third one!"

On the white band which wound among the green meadows a black dot could be seen which moved along with great rapidity, vanished behind a clump of trees, and then reappeared again, making for the distant city. Captain Savage drew out his glass and gazed at the rider.

"Ay, ay," said he, as he snapped it up again. "It is a soldier, sure enough. I can see the glint of the scabbard which he carries on his larboard side. I think we shall have more wind soon. With a breeze we can show our heels to anything in French waters, but a galley or an armed boat would overhaul us now."

De Catinat, who, though he could speak little English, had learned in America to understand it pretty well, looked anxiously at Amos Green. "I fear that we shall bring trouble on this good captain," said he, "and that the loss of his cargo and ship may be his reward for having befriended us. Ask him whether he would not prefer to land us on the north bank. With our money we might make our way into the Lowlands."

Ephraim Savage looked at his passenger with eyes which had lost something of their sternness. "Young man," said he, "I see that you can understand something of my talk."

De Catinat nodded.

"I tell you then that I am a bad man to beat. Any man that was ever shipmates with me would tell you as much. I just jam my helm and keep my course as long as God will let me. D'ye see?"

De Catinat again nodded, though in truth the seaman's metaphors left him with but a very general sense of his meaning.

"We're comin' abreast of that there town, and in ten minutes we shall know if there is any trouble waiting for us. But I'll tell you a story as we go that'll show you what kind o' man you've shipped with. It was ten years ago that I speak of, when I was in the *Speedwell*, sixty-ton brig, tradin' betwixt Boston and Jamestown, goin' south with lumber and skins and fixin's, d'ye see, and north again with tobacco and molasses. One night, blowin' half a gale from the south'ard, we ran on a reef two miles to the east of Cape May, and down we went with a hole in our bottom like as if she'd been spitted on the steeple o' one o' them Honfleur churches. Well, in the morning there I was washin' about, nigh out of sight of land, clingin' on to half the foreyard, without a sign either of my mates or of wreckage. I wasn't so cold, for it was early fall, and I could get three parts of my body on to the spar, but I was hungry and thirsty and bruised, so I just took in two holes of my waist-belt, and put up a hymn, and had a look round for what I could see. Well, I saw more than I cared for. Within five paces of me there was a great fish, as long pretty nigh as the spar that I was grippin'. It's a mighty pleasant thing to have your legs in the water and a beast like that all ready for a nibble at your toes."

"*Mon Dieu!*" cried the French soldier. "And he have not eat you?"

Ephraim Savage's little eyes twinkled at the reminiscence.

"I ate him," said he.

"What!" cried Amos.

"It's a mortal fact. I'd a jack-knife in my pocket, Same as this one, and I kicked my legs to keep the brute off, and I whittled away at the spar until I'd got a good jagged bit off, sharp at each end, same as a nigger told me once down Delaware way. Then I waited for him, and stopped kicking, so he came at me like a hawk on a chick-a-dee. When he turned up his belly I jammed my left hand with the wood right into his great grinnin' mouth, and I let him have it with my knife between the gills. He tried to break away then, but I held on, d'ye see, though he took me so deep I thought I'd never come up again. I was nigh gone when we got to the surface, but he was floatin' with the white up, and twenty holes in his shirt front. Then I got back to my spar, for we'd gone a long fifty fathoms under water, and when I reached it I fainted dead away."

"And then?"

"Well, when I came to, it was calm, and there was the dead shark floatin' beside me. I paddled my spar over to him and I got loose a few yards of halliard that were hangin' from one end of it. I made a clove-hitch round his tail, d'ye see, and got the end of it slung over the spar and fastened, so as I couldn't lose him. Then I set to work and I ate him in a week right up to his back fin, and I drank the rain that fell on my coat, and when I was picked up by the *Gracie* of Gloucester, I was that fat that I could scarce climb aboard. That's what Ephraim Savage means, my lad, when he says that he is a baddish man to beat."

Whilst the Puritan seaman had been detailing his reminiscence, his eyes had kept wandering from the clouds to the flapping sails and back. Such wind as there was came in little short puffs, and the canvas either drew full or was absolutely slack. The fleecy shreds of cloud above, however, travelled swiftly across the blue sky. It was on these that the captain fixed his gaze, and he watched them like a man who is working out a problem in his mind. They were abreast of Honfleur now, and about half a mile out from it. Several sloops and brigs were lying there in a cluster, and a whole fleet of brown-sailed fishing-boats were tacking slowly in. Yet all was quiet on the curving quay and on the half-moon fort over which floated the white flag with the golden *fleur-de-lis*. The port lay on their quarter now and they were drawing away more quickly as the breeze freshened. De Catinat glancing back had almost made up his mind that their fears were quite groundless when they were brought back in an instant and more urgently than ever.

Round the corner of the mole a great dark boat had dashed into view, ringed round with foam from her flying prow, and from the ten pairs of oars which swung from either side of her. A dainty white ensign drooped over her stern, and in her bows the sun's light was caught by a heavy brass carronade. She was packed with men, and the gleam which twinkled every now and again from amongst them told that they were armed to the teeth. The captain brought his glass to bear upon them and whistled. Then he glanced up at the clouds once more.

"Thirty men," said he, "and they go three paces to our two. You, sir, take your blue coat off this deck or you'll bring trouble upon us. The Lord will look after His own if they'll only keep from foolishness. Get these hatches off, Tomlinson. So! Where's Jim Sturt and Hiram Jefferson? Let them stand by to clap them on again when I whistle. Starboard! Starboard! Keep her as full as she'll draw. Now, Amos, and you, Tomlinson, come here until I have a word with you."

The three stood in consultation upon the poop, glancing back at their pursuers. There could be no doubt that the wind was freshening; it blew briskly in their faces as they looked back, but it was not steady yet, and the boat was rapidly overhauling them. Already they could see the faces of the marines who sat in the stern, and the gleam of the lighted linstock which the gunner held in his hand.

"*Hola!*" cried an officer in excellent English. "Lay her to or we fire"

"Who are you, and what do you want?" shouted Ephraim Savage, in a voice that might have been heard from the bank.

"We come in the king's name, and we want a party of Huguenots from Paris who came on board of your vessel at Rouen."

"Brace back the foreyard and lay her to," shouted the captain. "Drop a ladder over the side there and look smart! So! Now we are ready for them."

The yard was swung round and the vessel lay quietly rising and falling on the waves. The boat dashed alongside, her brass cannon trained upon the brigantine, and her squad of marines with their fingers upon their triggers ready to open fire. They grinned and shrugged their shoulders when they saw that their sole opponents were three unarmed men upon the poop. The officer, a young active fellow with a bristling moustache, like the whiskers of a cat, was on deck in an instant with his drawn sword in his hand.

"Come up, two of you!" he cried. "You stand here at the head of the ladder, sergeant. Throw up a rope and you can fix it to this stanchion. Keep awake down there and be all ready to fire! You come with me, Corporal Lemoine. Who is captain of this ship?"

"I am, sir," said Ephraim Savage submissively.

"You have three Huguenots aboard?"

"Tut! tut! Huguenots, are they? I thought they were very anxious to get away, but as long as they paid their passage it was no business of mine. An old man, his daughter, and a young fellow about your age in some sort of livery."

"In uniform, sir! The uniform of the king's guard. Those are the folk I have come for."

"And you wish to take them back?"

"Most certainly."

"Poor folk! I am sorry for them."

"And so am I, but orders are orders and must be done."

"Quite so. Well, the old man is in his bunk asleep. The maid is in a cabin below. And the other is sleeping down the hold there where we had to put him, for there is no room elsewhere."

"Sleeping, you say? We had best surprise him."

"But think you that you dare do it alone! He has no arms, it is true, but he is a well-grown young fellow. Will you not have twenty men up from the boat?"

Some such thought had passed through the officer's head, but the captain's remark put him upon his mettle.

"Come with me, corporal," said he. "Down this ladder, you say?"

"Yes, down the ladder and straight on. He lies between those two cloth bales." Ephraim Savage looked up with a smile playing about the corners of his grim mouth. The wind was whistling now in the rigging, and the stays of the mast were humming like two harp strings. Amos Green lounged beside the French sergeant who guarded the end of the rope ladder, while Tomlinson, the mate, stood with a bucket of water in his hand exchanging remarks in very bad French with the crew of the boat beneath him.

The officer made his way slowly down the ladder which led into the hold, and the corporal followed him, and had his chest level with the deck when the other had reached the bottom. It may have been something in Ephraim Savage's face, or it may have been the gloom around him which startled the young Frenchman, but a sudden suspicion flashed into his mind.

"Up again, corporal!" he shouted, "I think that you are best at the top."

"And I think that you are best down below, my friend," said the Puritan, who gathered the officer's meaning from his gesture. Putting the sole of his boot against the man's chest he gave a shove which sent both him and the ladder crashing down on to the officer beneath him. As he did so he blew his whistle, and in a moment the hatch was back in its place and clamped down on each side with iron bars.

The sergeant had swung round at the sound of the crash, but Amos Green, who had waited for the movement, threw his arms about him and hurled him overboard into the sea. At the same instant the connecting rope was severed, the foreyard creaked back into position again, and the bucketful of salt water soused down over the gunner and his gun, putting out his linstock and wetting his priming. A shower of balls from the marines piped through the air or rapped up against the planks, but the boat was tossing and jerking in the short choppy waves and to aim was impossible. In vain the men tugged and strained at their oars while the gunner worked like a maniac to relight his linstock and to replace his priming. The boat had lost its weigh, while the brigantine was flying along now with every sail bulging and swelling to bursting-point. Crack! went the carronade at last, and five little slits in the mainsail showed that her charge of grape had flown high. Her second shot left no trace behind it, and at the third she was at the limit of her range. Half an hour afterwards a little dark dot upon the horizon with a golden speck at one end of it was all that could be seen of the Honfleur guard-boat. Wider and wider grew the low-lying shores, broader and broader was the vast spread of blue waters ahead, the smoke of Havre lay like a little cloud upon the northern horizon, and Captain Ephraim Savage paced his deck with his face as grim as ever, but with a dancing light in his gray eyes.

"I knew that the Lord would look after His own," said he complacently. "We've got her beak straight now, and there's not as much as a dab of mud betwixt this and the three hills of Boston. You've had too much of these French wines of late, Amos, lad. Come down and try a real Boston brewing with a double stroke of malt in the mash tub."

CHAPTER XXV.
A BOAT OF THE DEAD.

For two days the *Golden Rod* lay becalmed close to the Cape La Hague, with the Breton coast extending along the whole of the southern horizon. On the third morning, however, came a sharp breeze, and they drew rapidly away from land, until it was but a vague dim line which blended with the cloud banks. Out there on the wide free ocean, with the wind on their cheeks and the salt spray pringling upon their lips, these hunted folk might well throw off their sorrows and believe that they had left for ever behind them all tokens of those strenuous men whose earnest piety had done more harm than frivolity and wickedness could have accomplished. And yet even now they could not shake off their traces, for the sin of the cottage is bounded by the cottage door, but that of the palace spreads its evil over land and sea.

"I am frightened about my father, Amory," said Adele, as they stood together by the shrouds and looked back at the dim cloud upon the horizon which marked the position of that France which they were never to see again.

"But he is out of danger now."

"Out of danger from cruel laws, but I fear that he will never see the promised land."

"What do you mean, Adele? My uncle is hale and hearty."

"Ah, Amory, his very heart-roots were fastened in the Rue St. Martin, and when they were torn his life was torn also. Paris and his business, they were the world to him."

"But he will accustom himself to this new life."

"If it only could be so! But I fear, I fear, that he is over old for such a change. He says not a word of complaint. But I read upon his face that he is stricken to the heart. For hours together he will gaze back at France, with the tears running silently down his cheeks. And his hair has turned from gray to white within the week."

De Catinat also had noticed that the gaunt old Huguenot had grown gaunter, that the lines upon his stern face were deeper, and that his head fell forward upon his breast as he walked. He was about, however, to suggest that the voyage might restore the merchant's health, when Adele gave a cry of surprise and pointed out over the port quarter. So beautiful was she at the instant with her raven hair blown back by the wind, a glow of colour struck into her pale cheeks by the driving spray, her lips parted in her excitement, and one white hand shading her eyes, that he stood beside her with all his thoughts bent upon her grace and her sweetness.

"Look!" she cried. "There is something floating upon the sea. I saw it upon the crest of a wave."

He looked in the direction in which she pointed, but at first he saw nothing. The wind was still behind them, and a brisk sea was running of a deep rich green colour, with long creamy curling caps to the larger waves. The breeze would catch these foam-crests from time to time, and then there would be a sharp spatter upon the decks, with a salt smack upon the lips, and a pringling in the eyes. Suddenly as he gazed, however, something black was tilted up upon the sharp summit of one of the seas, and swooped out of view again upon the further side. It was so far from him that he could make nothing of it, but sharper eyes than his had caught a glance of it. Amos Green had seen the girl point and observed what it was which had attracted her attention.

"Captain Ephraim," cried he, "there's a boat on the starboard quarter."

The New England seaman whipped up his glass and steadied it upon the bulwark.

"Ay, it's a boat," said he, "but an empty one. Maybe it's been washed off from some ship, or gone adrift from shore. Put her hard down, Mr. Tomlinson, for it just so happens that I am in need of a boat at present."

Half a minute later the *Golden Rod* had swung round and was running swiftly down towards the black spot which still bobbed and danced upon the waves. As they neared her they could see that something was projecting over her side.

"It's a man's head!" cried Amos Green.

But Ephraim Savage's grim face grew grimmer. "It's a man's foot," said he. "I think that you had best take the gal below to the cabin."

Amid a solemn hush they ran alongside this lonely craft which hung out so sinister a signal. Within ten yards of her the foreyard was hauled aback and they gazed down upon her terrible crew.

She was a little thirteen-foot cockle-shell, very broad for her length and so flat in the bottom that she had been meant evidently for river or lake work. Huddled together beneath the seats were three folk, a man in the dress of a respectable artisan, a woman of the same class, and a little child about a year old. The boat was half full of water and the woman and child were stretched with their faces downwards, the fair curls of the infant and the dark locks of the mother washing to and fro like water-weeds upon the surface. The man lay with a slate-coloured face, his chin cocking up towards the sky, his eyes turned upwards to the whites, and his mouth wide open showing a leathern crinkled tongue like a rotting leaf. In the bows, all huddled in a heap, and with a single paddle still grasped in his hand, there crouched a very small man clad in black, an open book lying across his face, and one stiff leg jutting upwards with the heel of the foot resting between the rowlocks. So this strange company swooped and tossed upon the long green Atlantic rollers.

A boat had been lowered by the *Golden Rod*, and the unfortunates were soon conveyed upon deck. No particle of either food or drink was to be found, nor anything save the single paddle and the open Bible which lay across the small man's face. Man, woman, and child had all been dead a day at the least, and so with the short prayers used upon the seas they were buried from the vessel's side. The small man had at first seemed also to be lifeless, but Amos had detected some slight flutter of his heart, and the faintest haze was left upon the watch glass which was held before his mouth. Wrapped in a dry blanket he was laid beside the mast, and the mate forced a few drops of rum every few minutes between his lips until the little spark of life which still lingered in him might be fanned to a flame. Meanwhile Ephraim Savage had ordered up the two prisoners whom he had entrapped at Honfleur. Very foolish they looked as they stood blinking and winking in the daylight from which they had been so long cut off.

"Very sorry, captain," said the seaman, "but either you had to come with us, d'ye see, or we had to stay with you. They're waiting for me over at Boston, and in truth I really couldn't tarry."

The French soldier shrugged his shoulders and looked around him with a lengthening face. He and his corporal were limp with sea-sickness, and as miserable as a Frenchman is when first he finds that France has vanished from his view.

"Which would you prefer, to go on with us to America, or go back to France?"

"Back to France, if I can find my way. Oh, I must get to France again if only to have a word with that fool of a gunner."

"Well, we emptied a bucket of water over his linstock and priming, d'ye see, so maybe he did all he could. But there's France, where that thickening is over yonder."

"I see it! I see it! Ah, if my feet were only upon it once more."

"There is a boat beside us, and you may take it."

"My God, what happiness! Corporal Lemoine, the boat! Let us push off at once."

"But you need a few things first. Good Lord, who ever heard of a man pushing off like that! Mr. Tomlinson, just sling a keg of water and a barrel of meat and of biscuit into this boat. Hiram Jefferson, bring two oars aft. It's a long pull with the wind in your teeth, but you'll be there by to-morrow night, and the weather is set fair."

The two Frenchmen were soon provided with all that they were likely to require, and pushed off with a waving of hats and a shouting of *bon voyage*. The foreyard was swung round again and the *Golden Rod* turned her bowsprit for the west. For hours a glimpse could be caught of the boat, dwindling away on the wave-tops, until at last it vanished into the haze, and with it vanished the very last link which connected them with the great world which they were leaving behind them.

But whilst these things had been done, the senseless man beneath the mast had twitched his eyelids, had drawn a little gasping breath, and then finally had opened his eyes. His skin was like gray parchment drawn tightly over his bones, and the limbs which thrust out from his clothes were those of a sickly child. Yet, weak as he was, the large black eyes with which he looked about him were full of dignity and power. Old Catinat had come upon deck, and at the sight of the man and of his dress he had run forward, and had raised his head reverently and rested it in his own arms.

"He is one of the faithful," he cried, "he is one of our pastors. Ah, now indeed a blessing will be upon our journey!"

But the man smiled gently and shook his head. "I fear that I may not come this journey with you," said he, "for the Lord has called me upon a further journey of my own. I have had my summons and I am ready. I am indeed the pastor of the temple at Isigny, and when we heard the orders of the wicked king, I and two of the faithful with their little one put forth in the hope that we might come to England. But on the first day there came a wave which swept away one of our oars and all that was in the boat, our bread, our keg, and we were left with no hope save in Him. And then He began to call us to Him one at a time, first the child, and then the woman, and then the man, until I only am left, though I feel that my own time is not long. But since ye are also of the faithful, may I not serve you in any way before I go?"

The merchant shook his head, and then suddenly a thought flashed upon him, and he ran with joy upon his face and whispered eagerly to Amos Green. Amos laughed, and strode across to the captain.

"It's time," said Ephraim Savage grimly.

Then the whisperers went to De Catinat. He sprang in the air and his eyes shone with delight. And then they went down to Adele in her cabin, and she started and blushed, and turned her sweet face away, and patted her hair with her hands as woman will when a sudden call is made upon her. And so, since haste was needful, and since even there upon the lonely sea there was one coming who might at any moment snap their purpose, they found themselves in a few minutes, this gallant man and this pure woman, kneeling hand in hand before the dying pastor, who raised his thin arm feebly in benediction as he muttered the words which should make them forever one.

Adele had often pictured her wedding to herself, as what young girl has not? Often in her dreams she had knelt before the altar with Amory in the temple of the Rue St. Martin. Or sometimes her fancy had taken her to some of those smaller churches in the provinces, those little refuges where a handful of believers gathered together, and it was there that her thoughts had placed the crowning act of a woman's life. But when had she thought of such a marriage as this, with the white deck swaying beneath them, the ropes humming above, their only choristers the gulls which screamed around them, and their wedding hymn the world-old anthem which is struck from the waves by the wind? And when could she forget the scene? The yellow masts and the bellying sails, the gray drawn face and the cracked lips of the castaway, her father's gaunt earnest features as he knelt to support the dying minister, De Catinat in his blue coat, already faded and weather-stained. Captain Savage with his wooden face turned towards the clouds, and Amos Green with his hands in his pockets and a quiet twinkle in his blue eyes! Then behind all the lanky mate and the little group of New England seamen with their palmetto hats and their serious faces!

And so it was done amid kindly words in a harsh foreign tongue, and the shaking of rude hands hardened by the rope and the oar. De Catinat and his wife leaned together by the shrouds when all was over and watched the black side as it rose and fell, and the green water which raced past them.

"It is all so strange and so new," she said. "Our future seems as vague and dark as yonder cloud-banks which gather in front of us."

"If it rest with me," he answered, "your future will be as merry and bright as the sunlight that glints on the crest of these waves. The country that drove us forth lies far behind us, but out there is another and a fairer country, and every breath of wind wafts us nearer to it. Freedom awaits us there, and we bear with us youth and love, and what could man or woman ask for more?"

So they stood and talked while the shadows deepened into twilight and the first faint gleam of the stars broke out in the darkening heavens above them. But ere those stars had waned again one more toiler had found rest aboard the *Golden Rod*, and the scattered flock from Isigny had found their little pastor once more.

CHAPTER XXVI.
THE LAST PORT.

For three weeks the wind kept at east or north-east, always at a brisk breeze and freshening sometimes into half a gale. The *Golden Rod* sped merrily upon her way with every sail drawing, alow and aloft, so that by the end of the third week Amos and Ephraim Savage were reckoning out the hours before they would look upon their native land once more. To the old seaman who was used to meeting and to parting it was a small matter, but Amos, who had never been away before, was on fire with impatience, and would sit smoking for hours with his legs astride the shank of the bowsprit, staring ahead at the skyline, in the hope that his friend's reckoning had been wrong, and that at any moment he might see the beloved coast line looming up in front of him.

"It's no use, lad," said Captain Ephraim, laying his great red hand upon his shoulder. "They that go down to the sea in ships need a power of patience, and there's no good eatin' your heart out for what you can't get."

"There's a feel of home about the air, though," Amos answered. "It seems to whistle through your teeth with a bite to it that I never felt over yonder. Ah, it will take three months of the Mohawk Valley before I feel myself to rights."

"Well," said his friend, thrusting a plug of Trinidado tobacco into the corner of his cheek, "I've been on the sea since I had hair to my face, mostly in the coast trade, d'ye see, but over the water as well, as far as those navigation laws would let me. Except the two years that I came ashore for the King Philip business, when every man that could carry a gun was needed on the border, I've never been three casts of a biscuit from salt water, and I tell you that I never knew a better crossing than the one we have just made."

"Ay, we have come along like a buck before a forest fire. But it is strange to me how you find your way so clearly out here with never track nor trail to guide you. It would puzzle me, Ephraim, to find America, to say nought of the Narrows of New York."

"I am somewhat too far to the north, Amos. We have been on or about the fiftieth since we sighted Cape La Hague. To-morrow we should make land, by my reckonin'."

"Ah, to-morrow! And what will it be? Mount Desert? Cape Cod? Long Island?"

"Nay, lad, we are in the latitude of the St. Lawrence, and are more like to see the Arcadia coast. Then with this wind a day should carry us south, or two at the most. A few more such voyages and I shall buy myself a fair brick house in Green Lane of North Boston, where I can look down on the bay, or on the Charles or the Mystic, and see the ships comin' and goin'. So I would end my life in peace and quiet."

All day Amos Green, in spite of his friend's assurance, strained his eyes in the fruitless search for land, and when at last the darkness fell he went below and laid out his fringed hunting tunic, his leather gaiters, and his raccoon-skin cap, which were very much more to his taste than the broadcloth coat in which the Dutch mercer of New York had clad him. De Catinat had also put on the dark coat of civil life, and he and Adele were busy preparing all things for the old man, who had fallen so weak that there was little which he could do for himself. A fiddle was screaming in the forecastle, and half the night through hoarse bursts of homely song mingled with the dash of the waves and the whistle of the wind, as the New England men in their own grave and stolid fashion made merry over their home-coming.

The mate's watch that night was from twelve to four, and the moon was shining brightly for the first hour of it. In the early morning, however, it clouded over, and the *Golden Rod* plunged into one of those dim clammy mists which lie on all that tract of ocean. So thick was it that from the poop one could just make out the loom of the foresail, but could see nothing of the fore-topmast-stay sail or the jib. The wind was north-east with a very keen edge to it, and the dainty brigantine lay over, scudding along with her lee rails within hand's touch of the water. It had suddenly turned very cold—so cold that the mate stamped up and down the poop, and his four seamen shivered together under the shelter of the bulwarks. And then in a moment one of them was up, thrusting with his forefinger into the air and screaming, while a huge white wall sprang out of the darkness at the very end of the bowsprit, and the ship struck with a force which snapped her two masts like dried reeds in a wind, and changed her in an instant to a crushed and shapeless heap of spars and wreckage.

The mate had shot the length of the poop at the shock, and had narrowly escaped from the falling mast, while of his four men two had been hurled through the huge gap which yawned in the bows, while a third had dashed his head to pieces against the stock of the anchor. Tomlinson staggered forwards to find the whole front part of the vessel driven inwards, and a single seaman sitting dazed amid splintered spars, flapping sails, and writhing, lashing cordage. It was still as dark as pitch, and save the white crest of a leaping wave nothing was to be seen beyond the side of the vessel. The mate was peering round him in despair at the ruin which had come so suddenly upon them when he found Captain Ephraim at his elbow, half clad, but as wooden and as serene as ever.

"An iceberg," said he, sniffing at the chill air. "Did you not smell it, friend Tomlinson?"

"Truly I found it cold, Captain Savage, but I set it down to the mist."

"There is a mist ever set around them, though the Lord in His wisdom knows best why, for it is a sore trial to poor sailor men. She makes water fast, Mr. Tomlinson. She is down by the bows already."

The other watch had swarmed upon deck and one of them was measuring the well. "There is three feet of water," he cried, "and the pumps sucked dry yesterday at sundown."

"Hiram Jefferson and John Moreton to the pumps!" cried the captain. "Mr. Tomlinson, clear away the long-boat and let us see if we may set her right, though I fear that she is past mending."

"The long-boat has stove two planks," cried a seaman.

"The jolly-boat, then?"

"She is in three pieces."

The mate tore his hair, but Ephraim Savage smiled like a man who is gently tickled by some coincidence.

"Where is Amos Green?"

"Here, Captain Ephraim. What can I do?"

"And I?" asked De Catinat eagerly. Adele and her father had been wrapped in mantles and placed for shelter in the lee of the round house.

"Tell him he can take his spell at the pumps," said the Captain to Amos. "And you, Amos, you are a handy man with a tool. Get into yonder long-boat with a lantern and see if you cannot patch her up."

For half an hour Amos Green hammered and trimmed and caulked, while the sharp measured clanking of the pumps sounded above the dash of the seas. Slowly, very slowly, the bows of the brigantine were settling down, and her stern cocking up.

"You've not much time, Amos, lad," said the captain quietly.

"She'll float now, though she's not quite water-tight."

"Very good. Lower away! Keep up the pump in there! Mr. Tomlinson, see that provisions and water are ready, as much as she will hold. Come with me, Hiram Jefferson."

The seaman and the captain swung themselves down into the tossing boat, the latter with a lantern strapped to his waist. Together they made their way until they were under her mangled bows. The captain shook his head when he saw the extent of the damage.

"Cut away the foresail and pass it over," said he.

Tomlinson and Amos Green cut away the lashings with their knives and lowered the corner of the sail. Captain Ephraim and the seaman seized it, and dragged it across the mouth of the huge gaping leak. As he stooped to do it, however, the ship heaved up upon a swell, and the captain saw in the yellow light of his lantern sinuous black cracks which radiated away backwards from the central hole.

"How much in the well?" he asked.

"Five and a half feet."

"Then the ship is lost. I could put my finger between her planks as far as I can see back. Keep the pumps going there! Have you the food and water, Mr. Tomlinson?"

"Here, sir."

"Lower them over the bows. This boat cannot live more than an hour or two. Can you see anything of the berg?"

"The fog is lifting on the starboard quarter," cried one of the men. "Yes, there is the berg, quarter of a mile to leeward!"

The mist had thinned away suddenly, and the moon glimmered through once more upon the great lonely sea and the stricken ship. There, like a huge sail, was the monster piece of ice upon which they had shattered themselves, rocking slowly to and fro with the wash of the waves.

"You must make for her," said Captain Ephraim. "There is no other chance. Lower the gal over the bows! Well, then, her father first, if she likes it better. Tell them to sit still, Amos, and that the Lord will bear us up if we keep clear of foolishness. So! You're a brave lass for all your niminy-piminy lingo. Now the keg and the barrel, and all the wraps and cloaks you can find. Now the other man, the Frenchman. Ay, ay, passengers first, and you have got to come. Now, Amos! Now the seamen, and you last, friend Tomlinson."

It was well that they had not very far to go, for the boat was weighed down almost to the edge, and it took the baling of two men to keep in check the water which leaked in between the shattered planks. When all were safely in their places. Captain Ephraim Savage swung himself aboard again, which was but too easy now that every minute brought the bows nearer to the water. He came back with a bundle of clothing which he threw into the boat.

"Push off!" he cried.

"Jump in, then."

"Ephraim Savage goes down with his ship," said he quietly. "Friend Tomlinson, it is not my way to give my orders more than once. Push off, I say!"

The mate thrust her out with a boat-hook. Amos and De Catinat gave a cry of dismay, but the stolid New Englanders settled down to their oars and pulled off for the iceberg.

"Amos! Amos! Will you suffer it?" cried the guardsman in French. "My honour will not permit me to leave him thus. I should feel it a stain for ever."

"Tomlinson, you would not leave him! Go on board and force him to come."

"The man is not living who could force him to do what he had no mind for."

"He may change his purpose."

"He never changes his purpose."

"But you cannot leave him, man! You must at least lie by and pick him up."

"The boat leaks like a sieve," said the mate. "I will take her to the berg, leave you all there, if we can find footing, and go back for the captain. Put your heart into it, my lads, for the sooner we are there the sooner we shall get back."

But they had not taken fifty strokes before Adele gave a sudden scream.

"My God!" she cried, "the ship is going down!"

She had settled lower and lower in the water, and suddenly with a sound of rending planks she thrust down her bows like a diving water-fowl, her stern flew up into the air, and with a long sucking noise she shot down swifter and swifter until the leaping waves closed over her high poop lantern. With one impulse the boat swept round again and made backwards as fast as willing arms could pull it. But all was quiet at the scene of the disaster. Not even a fragment of wreckage was left upon the surface to show where the *Golden Rod* had found her last harbour. For a long quarter of an hour they pulled round and round in the moonlight, but not a glimpse could they see of the Puritan seaman, and at last, when in spite of the balers the water was washing round their ankles, they put her head about once more, and made their way in silence and with heavy hearts to their dreary island of refuge.

Desolate as it was, it was their only hope now, for the leak was increasing and it was evident that the boat could not be kept afloat long. As they drew nearer they saw with dismay that the side which faced them was a solid wall of ice sixty feet high without a flaw or crevice in its whole extent. The berg was a large one, fifty paces at least each way, and there was a hope that the other side might be more favourable. Baling hard, they paddled round the corner, but only to find themselves faced by another gloomy ice-crag. Again they went round, and again they found that the berg increased rather than diminished in height. There remained only one other side, and they knew as they rowed round to it that their lives hung upon the result, for the boat was almost settling down beneath them. They shot out from the shadow into the full moonlight and looked upon a sight which none of them would forget until their dying day.

The cliff which faced them was as precipitous as any of the others, and it glimmered and sparkled all over where the silver light fell upon the thousand facets of ice. Right in the centre, however, on a level with the water's edge, there was what appeared to be a huge hollowed-out cave which marked the spot where the Golden Rod had, in shattering herself, dislodged a huge boulder, and so amid her own ruin prepared a refuge for those who had trusted themselves to her. This cavern was of the richest emerald green, light and clear at the edges, but toning away into the deepest purples and blues at the back. But it was not the beauty of this grotto, nor was it the assurance of rescue which brought a cry of joy and of wonder from every lip, but it was that, seated upon an ice boulder and placidly smoking a long corn-cob pipe, there was perched in front of them no less a person than Captain Ephraim Savage of Boston. For a moment the castaways could almost have believed that it was his wraith, were wraiths ever seen in so homely an attitude, but the tones of his voice very soon showed that it was indeed he, and in no very Christian temper either.

"Friend Tomlinson," said he, "when I tell you to row for an iceberg I mean you to row right away there, d'ye see, and not to go philandering about over the ocean. It's not your fault that I'm not froze, and so I would have been if I hadn't some dry tobacco and my tinder-box to keep myself warm."

Without stopping to answer his commander's reproaches, the mate headed for the ledge, which had been cut into a slope by the bows of the brigantine, so that the boat was run up easily on to the ice. Captain Savage seized his dry clothes and vanished into the back of the cave, to return presently warmer in body, and more contented in mind. The long-boat had been turned upside down for a seat, the gratings and thwarts taken out and covered with wraps to make a couch for the lady, and the head knocked out of the keg of biscuits.

"We were frightened for you, Ephraim," said Amos Green. "I had a heavy heart this night when I thought that I should never see you more."

"Tut, Amos, you should have known me better."

"But how came you here, captain?" asked Tomlinson. "I thought that maybe you had been taken down by the suck of the ship."

"And so I was. It is the third ship in which I have gone down, but they have never kept me down yet. I went deeper to-night than when the *Speedwell* sank, but not so deep as in the *Governor Winthrop*. When I came up I swam to the berg, found this nook, and crawled in. Glad I was to see you, for I feared that you had foundered."

"We put back to pick you up and we passed you in the darkness. And what should we do now?"

"Rig up that boat-sail and make quarters for the gal. Then get our supper and such rest as we can, for there is nothing to be done to-night, and there may be much in the morning."

CHAPTER XXVII.
A DWINDLING ISLAND.

Amos Green was aroused in the morning by a hand upon his shoulder, and springing to his feet, found De Catinat standing beside him. The survivors of the crew were grouped about the upturned boat, slumbering heavily after their labours of the night. The red rim of the sun had just pushed itself above the water-line, and sky and sea were one blaze of scarlet and orange from the dazzling gold of the horizon to the lightest pink at the zenith. The first rays flashed directly into their cave, sparkling and glimmering upon the ice crystals and tingeing the whole grotto with a rich warm light. Never was a fairy's palace more lovely than this floating refuge which Nature had provided for them.

But neither the American nor the Frenchman had time now to give a thought to the novelty and beauty of their situation. The latter's face was grave, and his friend read danger in his eyes.

"What is it, then?"

"The berg. It is coming to pieces."

"Tut, man, it is as solid as an island."

"I have been watching it. You see that crack which extends backwards from the end of our grotto. Two hours ago I could scarce put my hand into it. Now I can slip through it with ease. I tell you that she is splitting across."

Amos Green walked to the end of the funnel-shaped recess and found, as his friend had said, that a green sinuous crack extended away backwards into the iceberg, caused either by the tossing of the waves, or by the terrific impact of their vessel. He roused Captain Ephraim and pointed out the danger to him.

"Well, if she springs a leak we are gone," said he. "She's been thawing pretty fast as it is."

They could see now that what had seemed in the moonlight to be smooth walls of ice were really furrowed and wrinkled like an old man's face by the streams of melted water which were continually running down them.

The whole huge mass was brittle and honeycombed and rotten. Already they could hear all round them the ominous drip, drip, and the splash and tinkle of the little rivulets as they fell into the ocean.

"Hullo!" cried Amos Green, "what's that?"

"What then?"

"Did you hear nothing?"

"No."

"I could have sworn that I heard a voice."

"Impossible. We are all here."

"It must have been my fancy then."

Captain Ephraim walked to the seaward face of the cave and swept the ocean with his eyes. The wind had quite fallen away now, and the sea stretched away to the eastward, smooth and unbroken save for a single great black spar which floated near the spot where the *Golden Rod* had foundered.

"We should lie in the track of some ships," said the captain thoughtfully. "There's the codders and the herring-busses. We're over far south for them, I reckon. But we can't be more'n two hundred mile from Port Royal in Arcadia, and we're in the line of the St. Lawrence trade. If I had three white mountain pines, Amos, and a hundred yards of stout canvas I'd get up on the top of this thing, d'ye see, and I'd rig such a jury-mast as would send her humming into Boston Bay. Then I'd break her up and sell her for what she was worth, and turn a few pieces over the business. But she's a heavy old craft, and that's a fact, though even now she might do a knot or two an hour if she had a hurricane behind her. But what is it, Amos?"

The young hunter was standing with his ear slanting, his head bent forwards, and his eyes glancing sideways like a man who listens intently. He was about to answer when De Catinat gave a cry and pointed to the back of the cave.

"Look at the crack now."

It had widened by a foot since they had noticed it last, until it was now no longer a crack. It was a pass.

"Let us go through," said the captain.

"It can but come out on the other side."

"Then let us see the other side."

He led the way and the other two followed him. It was very dark as they advanced, with high dripping ice walls on either side and one little zigzagging slit of blue sky above their heads. Tripping and groping their way, they stumbled along until suddenly the passage grew wider and opened out into a large square of flat ice. The berg was level in the centre and sloped upwards from that point to the high cliffs which bounded it on each side. In three directions this slope was very steep, but in one it slanted up quite gradually, and the constant thawing had grooved the surface with a thousand irregularities by which an active man could ascend. With one impulse they began all three to clamber up until a minute later they were standing not far from the edge of the summit, seventy feet above the sea, with a view which took in a good fifty miles of water. In all that fifty miles there was no sign of life, nothing but the endless glint of the sun upon the waves.

Captain Ephraim whistled. "We are out of luck," said he.

Amos Green looked about him with startled eyes. "I cannot understand it," said he. "I could have sworn—By the eternal, listen to that!" The clear call of a military bugle rang out in the morning air. With a cry of amazement they all three craned forward and peered over the edge.

A large ship was lying under the very shadow of the iceberg. They looked straight down upon her snow-white decks, fringed with shining brass cannon, and dotted with seamen. A little clump of soldiers stood upon the poop going through the manual exercise, and it was from them that the call had come which had sounded so unexpectedly in the ears of the castaways. Standing back from the edge, they had not only looked over the top-masts of this welcome neighbour, but they had themselves been invisible from her decks. Now the discovery was mutual, as was shown by a chorus of shouts and cries from beneath them.

But the three did not wait an instant. Sliding and scrambling down the wet, slippery incline, they rushed shouting through the crack and into the cave where their comrades had just been startled by the bugle-call while in the middle of their cheerless breakfast. A few hurried words and the leaky long-boat had been launched, their possessions had been bundled in, and they were afloat once more. Pulling round a promontory of the berg, they found themselves under the stern of a fine corvette, the sides of which were lined with friendly faces, while from the peak there drooped a huge white banner mottled over with the golden lilies of France. In a very few minutes their boat had been hauled up and they found themselves on board the *St. Christophe* man-of-war, conveying Marquis de Denonville, the new Governor-General of Canada, to take over his duties.

CHAPTER XXVIII.
IN THE POOL OF QUEBEC.

A singular colony it was of which the shipwrecked party found themselves now to be members. The *St. Christophe* had left Rochelle three weeks before with four small consorts conveying five hundred soldiers to help the struggling colony on the St. Lawrence. The squadron had become separated, however, and the governor was pursuing his way alone in the hope of picking up the others in the river. Aboard he had a company of the regiment of Quercy, the staff of his own household, Saint Vallier, the new Bishop of Canada, with several of his attendants, three Recollet friars, and five Jesuits bound for the fatal Iroquois mission, half-a-dozen ladies on their way out to join their husbands, two Ursuline nuns, ten or twelve gallants whom love of adventure and the hope of bettering their fortunes had drawn across the seas, and lastly some twenty peasant maidens of Anjou who were secure of finding husbands waiting for them upon the beach, if only for the sake of the sheets, the pot, the tin plates and the kettle which the king would provide for each of his humble wards.

To add a handful of New England Independents, a Puritan of Boston, and three Huguenots to such a gathering, was indeed to bring fire-brand and powder-barrel together. And yet all aboard were so busy with their own concerns that the castaways were left very much to themselves. Thirty of the soldiers were down with fever and scurvy, and both priests and nuns were fully taken up in nursing them. Denonville, the governor, a pious-minded dragoon, walked the deck all day reading the Psalms of David, and sat up half the night with maps and charts laid out before him, planning out the destruction of the Iroquois who were ravaging his dominions. The gallants and the ladies flirted, the maidens of Anjou made eyes at the soldiers of Quercy, and the bishop Saint Vallier read his offices and lectured his clergy. Ephraim Savage used to stand all day glaring at the good man as he paced the deck with his red-edged missal in his hand, and muttering about the "abomination of desolation," but his little ways were put down to his exposure upon the iceberg, and to the fixed idea in the French mind that men of the Anglo-Saxon stock are not to be held accountable for their actions.

There was peace between England and France at present, though feeling ran high between Canada and New York, the French believing, and with some justice, that the English colonists were whooping on the demons who attacked them. Ephraim and his men were therefore received hospitably on board, though the ship was so crowded that they had to sleep wherever they could find cover and space for their bodies. The Catinats, too, had been treated in an even more kindly fashion, the weak old man and the beauty of his daughter arousing the interest of the governor himself. De Catinat had, during the voyage, exchanged his uniform for a plain sombre suit, so that, except for his military bearing, there was nothing to show that he was a fugitive from the army. Old Catinat was now so weak that he was past the answering of questions, his daughter was forever at his side, and the soldier was diplomatist enough, after a training at Versailles, to say much without saying anything, and so their secret was still preserved. De Catinat had known what it was to be a Huguenot in Canada before the law was altered. He had no wish to try it after.

On the day after the rescue they sighted Cape Breton in the south, and soon running swiftly before an easterly wind, saw the loom of the east end of Anticosti. Then they sailed up the mighty river, though from mid-channel the banks upon either side were hardly to be seen. As the shores narrowed in, they saw the wild gorge of the Saguenay River upon the right, with the smoke from the little fishing and trading station of Tadousac streaming up above the pine trees. Naked Indians with their faces daubed with red clay, Algonquins and Abenakis, clustered round the ship in their birchen canoes with fruit and vegetables from the land, which brought fresh life to the scurvy-stricken soldiers. Thence the ship tacked on up the river past Mal Bay, the Ravine of the Eboulements and the Bay of St. Paul with its broad valley and wooded mountains all in a blaze with their beautiful autumn dress, their scarlets, their purples, and their golds, from the maple, the ash, the young oak, and the saplings of the birch. Amos Green, leaning on the bulwarks, stared with longing eyes at these vast expanses of virgin woodland, hardly traversed save by an occasional wandering savage or hardy *coureur-de-bois*. Then the bold outline of Cape Tourmente loomed up in front of them; they passed the rich placid meadows of Laval's seigneury of Beaupre, and, skirting the settlements of the Island of Orleans, they saw the broad pool stretch out in front of them, the falls of Montmorenci, the high palisades of Cape Levi, the cluster of vessels, and upon the right that wonderful rock with its diadem of towers and its township huddled round its base, the centre and stronghold of French power in America. Cannon thundered from the bastions above, and were echoed back by the warship, while ensigns dipped, hats waved, and a swarm of boats and canoes shot out to welcome the new governor, and to convey the soldiers and passengers to shore.

The old merchant had pined away since he had left French soil, like a plant which has been plucked from its roots. The shock of the shipwreck and the night spent in their bleak refuge upon the iceberg had been too much for his years and strength. Since they had been picked up he had lain amid the scurvy-stricken soldiers with hardly a sign of life save for his thin breathing and the twitching of his scraggy throat. Now, however, at the sound of the cannon and the shouting he opened his eyes, and raised himself slowly and painfully upon his pillow. "What is it, father? What can we do for you?" cried Adele. "We are in America, and here is Amory and here am I, your children."

But the old man shook his head. "The Lord has brought me to the promised land, but He has not willed that I should enter into it," said he. "May His will be done, and blessed be His name forever! But at least I should wish, like Moses, to gaze upon it, if I cannot set foot upon it. Think you, Amory, that you could lend me your arm and lead me on to the deck?"

"If I have another to help me," said De Catinat, and ascending to the deck, he brought Amos Green back with him. "Now, father, if you will lay a hand upon the shoulder of each, you need scarce put your feet to the boards."

A minute later the old merchant was on the deck, and the two young men had seated him upon a coil of rope with his back against the mast, where he should be away from the crush. The soldiers were already crowding down into the boats, and all were so busy over their own affairs that they paid no heed to the little group of refugees who gathered round the stricken man. He turned his head painfully from side to side, but his eyes brightened as they fell upon the broad blue stretch of water, the flash of the distant falls, the high castle, and the long line of purple mountains away to the north-west.

"It is not like France," said he. "It is not green and peaceful and smiling, but it is grand and strong and stern like Him who made it. As I have weakened, Adele, my soul has been less clogged by my body, and I have seen clearly much that has been dim to me. And it has seemed to me, my children, that all this country of America, not Canada alone, but the land where you were born also, Amos Green, and all that stretches away towards yonder setting sun, will be the best gift of God to man. For this has He held it concealed through all the ages, that now His own high purpose may be wrought upon it. For here is a land which is innocent, which has no past guilt to atone for, no feud, nor ill custom, nor evil of any kind. And as the years roll on all the weary and homeless ones, all who are stricken and landless and wronged, will turn their faces to it, even as we have done. And hence will come a nation which will surely take all that is good and leave all that is bad, moulding and fashioning itself into the highest. Do I not see such a mighty people, a people who will care more to raise their lowest than to exalt their richest—who will understand that there is more bravery in peace than in war, who will see that all men are brothers, and whose hearts will not narrow themselves down to their own frontiers, but will warm in sympathy with every noble cause the whole world through? That is what I see, Adele, as I lie here beside a shore upon which I shall never set my feet, and I say to you that if you and Amory go to the building of such a nation then indeed your lives are not misspent. It will come, and when it comes, may God guard it, may God watch over it and direct it!" His head had sunk gradually lower upon his breast and his lids had fallen slowly over his eyes which had been looking away out past Point Levi at the rolling woods and the far-off mountains. Adele gave a quick cry of despair and threw her arms round the old man's neck.

"He is dying, Amory, he is dying!" she cried.

A stern Franciscan friar, who had been telling his beads within a few paces of them, heard the cry and was beside them in an instant.

"He is indeed dying," he said, as he gazed down at the ashen face. "Has the old man had the sacraments of the Church?"

"I do not think that he needs them," answered De Catinat evasively.

"Which of us do not need them, young man!" said the friar sternly. "And how can a man hope for salvation without them? I shall myself administer them without delay."

But the old Huguenot had opened his eyes, and with a last flicker of strength he pushed away the gray-hooded figure which bent over him.

"I left all that I love rather than yield to you," he cried, "and think you that you can overcome me now?"

The Franciscan started back at the words, and his hard suspicious eyes shot from De Catinat to the weeping girl.

"So!" said he. "You are Huguenots, then!"

"Hush! Do not wrangle before a man who is dying!" cried De Catinat in a voice as fierce as his own.

"Before a man who is dead," said Amos Green solemnly.

As he spoke the old man's face had relaxed, his thousand wrinkles had been smoothed suddenly out, as though an invisible hand had passed over them, and his head fell back against the mast. Adele remained motionless with her arms still clasped round his neck and her cheek pressed against his shoulder. She had fainted.

De Catinat raised his wife and bore her down to the cabin of one of the ladies who had already shown them some kindness. Deaths were no new thing aboard the ship, for they had lost ten soldiers upon the outward passage, so that amid the joy and bustle of the disembarking there were few who had a thought to spare upon the dead pilgrim, and the less so when it was whispered abroad that he had been a Huguenot. A brief order was given that he should be buried in the river that very night, and then, save for a sailmaker who fastened the canvas round him, mankind had done its last for Theophile Catinat. With the survivors, however, it was different, and when the troops were all disembarked, they were mustered in a little group upon the deck, and an officer of the governor's suite decided upon what should be done with them. He was a portly, good-humoured, ruddy-cheeked man, but De Catinat saw with apprehension that the friar walked by his side as he advanced along the deck, and exchanged a few whispered remarks with him. There was a bitter smile upon the monk's dark face which boded little good for the heretics.

"It shall be seen to, good father, it shall be seen to," said the officer impatiently, in answer to one of these whispered injunctions. "I am as zealous a servant of Holy Church as you are."

"I trust that you are, Monsieur de Bonneville. With so devout a governor as Monsieur de Denonville, it might be an ill thing even in this world for the officers of his household to be lax."

The soldier glanced angrily at his companion, for he saw the threat which lurked under the words.

"I would have you remember, father," said he, "that if faith is a virtue, charity is no less so." Then, speaking in English: "Which is Captain Savage?"

"Ephraim Savage of Boston."

"And Master Amos Green?"

"Amos Green of New York."

"And Master Tomlinson?"

"John Tomlinson of Salem."

"And master mariners Hiram Jefferson, Joseph Cooper, Seek-grace Spalding, and Paul Cushing, all of Massachusetts Bay?"

"We are all here."

"It is the governor's order that all whom I have named shall be conveyed at once to the trading brig *Hope*, which is yonder ship with the white paint line. She sails within the hour for the English provinces."

A buzz of joy broke from the castaway mariners at the prospect of being so speedily restored to their homes, and they hurried away to gather together the few possessions which they had saved from the wreck. The officer put his list in his pocket and stepped across to where De Catinat leaned moodily against the bulwarks.

"Surely you remember me," he said. "I could not forget your face, even though you have exchanged a blue coat for a black one."

De Catinat grasped the hand which was held out to him.

"I remember you well, De Bonneville, and the journey that we made together to Fort Frontenac, but it was not for me to claim your friendship, now that things have gone amiss with me."

"Tut, man; once my friend always my friend."

"I feared, too, that my acquaintance would do you little good with yonder dark-cowled friar who is glowering behind you."

"Well, well, you know how it is with us here. Frontenac could keep them in their place, but De la Barre was as clay in their hands, and this new one promises to follow in his steps. What with the Sulpitians at Montreal and the Jesuits here, we poor devils are between the upper and the nether stones. But I am grieved from my heart to give such a welcome as this to an old comrade, and still more to his wife."

"What is to be done, then?"

"You are to be confined to the ship until she sails, which will be in a week at the furthest."

"And then?"

"You are to be carried home in her and handed over to the Governor of Rochelle to be sent back to Paris. Those are Monsieur de Denonville's orders, and if they be not carried out to the letter, then we shall have the whole hornet's nest about our ears."

De Catinat groaned as he listened. After all their strivings and trials and efforts, to return to Paris, the scorn of his enemies, and an object of pity to his friends, was too deep a humiliation. He flushed with shame at the very thought. To be led back like the home-sick peasant who has deserted from his regiment! Better one spring into the broad blue river beneath him, were it not for little pale-faced Adele who had none but him to look to. It was so tame! So ignominious! And yet in this floating prison, with a woman whose fate was linked with his own, what hope was there of escape?

De Bonneville had left him, with a few blunt words of sympathy, but the friar still paced the deck with a furtive glance at him from time to time, and two soldiers who were stationed upon the poop passed and repassed within a few yards of him. They had orders evidently to mark his movements. Heartsick he leaned over the side watching the Indians in their paint and feathers shooting backwards and forwards in their canoes, and staring across at the town where the gaunt gable ends of houses and charred walls marked the effect of the terrible fire which a few years before had completely destroyed the lower part.

As he stood gazing, his attention was drawn away by the swish of oars, and a large boat full of men passed immediately underneath where he stood. It held the New Englanders, who were being conveyed to the ship which was to take them home. There were the four seamen huddled together, and there in the sheets were Captain Ephraim Savage and Amos Green, conversing together and pointing to the shipping. The grizzled face of the old Puritan and the bold features of the woodsman were turned more than once in his direction, but no word of farewell and no kindly wave of the hand came back to the lonely exile. They were so full of their own future and their own happiness, that they had not a thought to spare upon his misery. He could have borne anything from his enemies, but this sudden neglect from his friends came too heavily after his other troubles. He stooped his face to his arms and burst in an instant into a passion of sobs. Before he raised his eyes again the brig had hoisted her anchor, and was tacking under full canvas out of the Quebec basin.

CHAPTER XXIX.
THE VOICE AT THE PORT-HOLE.

That night old Theophile Catinat was buried from the ship's side, his sole mourners the two who bore his own blood in their veins. The next day De Catinat spent upon deck, amid the bustle and confusion of the unlading, endeavouring to cheer Adele by light chatter which came from a heavy heart. He pointed out to her the places which he had known so well, the citadel where he had been quartered, the college of the Jesuits, the cathedral of Bishop Laval, the magazine of the old company, dismantled by the great fire, and the house of Aubert de la Chesnaye, the only private one which had remained standing in the lower part. From where they lay they could see not only the places of interest, but something also of that motley population which made the town so different to all others save only its younger sister, Montreal. Passing and repassing along the steep path with the picket fence which connected the two quarters, they saw the whole panorama of Canadian life moving before their eyes, the soldiers with their slouched hats, their plumes, and their bandoleers, habitants from the river *cotes* in their rude peasant dresses, little changed from their forefathers of Brittany or Normandy, and young rufflers from France or from the seigneuries, who cocked their hats and swaggered in what they thought to be the true Versailles fashion. There, too, might be seen little knots of the men of the woods, *coureurs-de-bois* or *voyageurs*, with leathern hunting tunics, fringed leggings, and fur cap with eagle feather, who came back once a year to the cities, leaving their Indian wives and children in some up-country wigwam. Redskins, too, were there, leather-faced Algonquin fishers and hunters, wild Micmacs from the east, and savage Abenakis from the south, while everywhere were the dark habits of the Franciscans, and the black cassocks and broad hats of the Recollets, and Jesuits, the moving spirits of the whole.

Such were the folk who crowded the streets of the capital of this strange offshoot of France which had been planted along the line of the great river, a thousand leagues from the parent country. And it was a singular settlement, the most singular perhaps that has ever been made. For a long twelve hundred miles it extended, from Tadousac in the east, away to the trading stations upon the borders of the great lakes, limiting itself for the most part to narrow cultivated strips upon the margins of the river, banked in behind by wild forests and unexplored mountains, which forever tempted the peasant from his hoe and his plough to the freer life of the paddle and the musket. Thin scattered clearings, alternating with little palisaded clumps of log-hewn houses, marked the line where civilisation was forcing itself in upon the huge continent, and barely holding its own against the rigour of a northern climate and the ferocity of merciless enemies. The whole white population of this mighty district, including soldiers, priests, and woodmen, with all women and children, was very far short of twenty thousand souls, and yet so great was their energy, and such the advantage of the central government under which they lived, that they had left their trace upon the whole continent. When the prosperous English settlers were content to live upon their acres, and when no axe had rung upon the further side of the Alleghanies, the French had pushed their daring pioneers, some in the black robe of the missionary, and some in the fringed tunic of the hunter, to the uttermost ends of the continent. They had mapped out the lakes and had bartered with the fierce Sioux on the great plains where the wooden wigwam gave place to the hide tee-pee. Marquette had followed the Illinois down to the Mississippi, and had traced the course of the great river until, first of all white men, he looked upon the turbid flood of the rushing Missouri. La Salle had ventured even further, and had passed the Ohio, and had made his way to the Mexican Gulf, raising the French arms where the city of New Orleans was afterwards to stand. Others had pushed on to the Rocky Mountains, and to the huge wilderness of the north-west, preaching, bartering, cheating, baptising, swayed by many motives and holding only in common a courage which never faltered and a fertility of resource which took them in safety past every danger. Frenchmen were to the north of the British settlements, Frenchmen were to the west of them, and Frenchmen were to the south of them, and if all the continent is not now French, the fault assuredly did not rest with that iron race of early Canadians.

All this De Catinat explained to Adele during the autumn day, trying to draw her thoughts away from the troubles of the past, and from the long dreary voyage which lay before her. She, fresh from the staid life of the Parisian street and from the tame scenery of the Seine, gazed with amazement at the river, the woods and the mountains, and clutched her husband's arm in horror when a canoeful of wild skin-clad Algonquins, their faces striped with white and red paint, came flying past with the foam dashing from their paddles. Again the river turned from blue to pink, again the old citadel was bathed in the evening glow, and again the two exiles descended to their cabins with cheering words for each other and heavy thoughts in their own hearts.

De Catinat's bunk was next to a port-hole, and it was his custom to keep this open, as the caboose was close to him in which the cooking was done for the crew, and the air was hot and heavy. That night he found it impossible to sleep, and he lay tossing under his blanket, thinking over every possible means by which they might be able to get away from this cursed ship. But even if they got away, where could they go to then? All Canada was sealed to them. The woods to the south were full of ferocious Indians. The English settlements would, it was true, grant them freedom to use their own religion, but what would his wife and he do, without a friend, strangers among folk who spoke another tongue? Had Amos Green remained true to them, then, indeed, all would have been well. But he had deserted them. Of course there was no reason why he should not. He was no blood relation of theirs. He had already benefited them many times. His own people and the life that he loved were waiting for him at home. Why should he linger here for the sake of folk whom he had known but a few months? It was not to be expected, and yet De Catinat could not realise it, could not understand it.

But what was that? Above the gentle lapping of the river he had suddenly heard a sharp clear "Hist!" Perhaps it was some passing boatman or Indian. Then it came again, that eager, urgent summons. He sat up and stared about him. It certainly must have come from the open port-hole. He looked out, but only to see the broad basin, with the loom of the shipping, and the distant twinkle from the lights on Point Levi. As his head dropped back upon the pillow something fell upon his chest with a little tap, and rolling off, rattled along the boards. He sprang up, caught a lantern from a hook, and flashed it upon the floor. There was the missile which had struck him—a little golden brooch. As he lifted it up and looked closer at it, a thrill passed through him. It had been his own, and he had given it to Amos Green upon the second day that he had met him, when they were starting together for Versailles.

This was a signal then, and Amos Green had not deserted them after all. He dressed himself, all in a tremble with excitement, and went upon deck. It was pitch dark, and he could see no one, but the sound of regular footfalls somewhere in the fore part of the ship showed that the sentinels were still there. The guardsman walked over to the side and peered down into the darkness. He could see the loom of a boat.

"Who is there?" he whispered.

"Is that you, De Catinat?

"Yes."

"We have come for you."

"God bless you, Amos."

"Is your wife there?"

"No, but I can rouse her."

"Good! But first catch this cord. Now pull up the ladder!"

De Catinat gripped the line which was thrown to him, and on drawing it up found that it was attached to a rope ladder furnished at the top with two steel hooks to catch on to the bulwarks. He placed them in position, and then made his way very softly to the cabin amidships in the ladies' quarters which had been allotted to his wife. She was the only woman aboard the ship now, so that he was able to tap at her door in safety, and to explain in a few words the need for haste and for secrecy. In ten minutes Adele had dressed, and with her valuables in a little bundle, had slipped out from her cabin. Together they made their way upon deck once more, and crept aft under the shadow of the bulwarks. They were almost there when De Catinat stopped suddenly and ground out an oath through his clenched teeth. Between them and the rope ladder there was standing in a dim patch of murky light the grim figure of a Franciscan friar. He was peering through the darkness, his heavy cowl shadowing his face, and he advanced slowly as if he had caught a glimpse of them. A lantern hung from the mizzen shrouds above him. He unfastened it and held it up to cast its light upon them.

But De Catinat was not a man with whom it was safe to trifle. His life had been one of quick resolve and prompt action. Was this vindictive friar at the last moment to stand between him and freedom? It was a dangerous position to take. The guardsman pulled Adele into the shadow of the mast, and then, as the monk advanced, he sprang out upon him and seized him by the gown. As he did so the other's cowl was pushed back, and instead of the harsh features of the ecclesiastic, De Catinat saw with amazement in the glimmer of the lantern the shrewd gray eyes and strong tern face of Ephraim Savage. At the same instant another figure appeared over the side, and the warm-hearted Frenchman threw himself into the arms of Amos Green.

"It's all right," said the young hunter, disengaging himself with some embarrassment from the other's embrace.

"We've got him in the boat with a buckskin glove jammed into his gullet!"

"Who then?"

"The man whose cloak Captain Ephraim there has put round him. He came on us when you were away rousing your lady, but we got him to be quiet between us. Is the lady there?"

"Here she is."

"As quick as you can, then, for some one may come along."

Adele was helped over the side, and seated in the stern of a birch-bark canoe. The three men unhooked the ladder, and swung themselves down by a rope, while two Indians, who held the paddles, pushed silently off from the ship's side, and shot swiftly up the stream. A minute later a dim loom behind them, and the glimmer of two yellow lights, was all that they could see of the *St. Christophe.*

"Take a paddle, Amos, and I'll take one," said Captain Savage, stripping off his monk's gown. "I felt safer in this on the deck of yon ship, but it don't help in a boat. I believe we might have fastened the hatches and taken her, brass guns and all, had we been so minded."

"And been hanged as pirates at the yard-arm next morning," said Amos. "I think we have done better to take the honey and leave the tree. I hope, madame, that all is well with you."

"Nay, I can hardly understand what has happened, or where we are."

"Nor can I, Amos."

"Did you not expect us to come back for you, then?"

"I did not know what to expect."

"Well, now, but surely you could not think that we would leave you without a word."

"I confess that I was cut to the heart by it."

"I feared that you were when I looked at you with the tail of my eye, and saw you staring so blackly over the bulwarks at us. But if we had been seen talking or planning they would have been upon our trail at once. As it was they had not a thought of suspicion, save only this fellow whom we have in the bottom of the boat here."

"And what did you do?"

"We left the brig last night, got ashore on the Beaupre side, arranged for this canoe, and lay dark all day. Then to-night we got alongside and I roused you easily, for I knew where you slept. The friar nearly spoiled all when you were below, but we gagged him and passed him over the side. Ephraim popped on his gown so that he might go forward to help you without danger, for we were scared at the delay."

"Ah! it is glorious to be free once more. What do I not owe you, Amos?"

"Well, you looked after me when I was in your country, and I am going to look after you now."

"And where are we going?"

"Ah! there you have me. It is this way or none, for we can't get down to the sea. We must make our way over land as best we can, and we must leave a good stretch between Quebec citadel and us before the day breaks, for from what I hear they would rather have a Huguenot prisoner than an Iroquois sagamore. By the eternal, I cannot see why they should make such a fuss over how a man chooses to save his own soul, though here is old Ephraim just as fierce upon the other side, so all the folly is not one way."

"What are you saying about me?" asked the seaman, pricking up his ears at the mention of his own name.

"Only that you are a good stiff old Protestant."

"Yes, thank God. My motto is freedom to conscience, d'ye see, except just for Quakers, and Papists, and—and I wouldn't stand Anne Hutchinsons and women testifying, and suchlike foolishness."

Amos Green laughed. "The Almighty seems to pass it over, so why should you take it to heart?" said he.

"Ah, you're young and callow yet. You'll live to know better. Why, I shall hear you saying a good word soon even for such unclean spawn as this," prodding the prostrate friar with the handle of his paddle.

"I daresay he's a good man, accordin' to his lights."

"And I daresay a shark is a good fish accordin' to its lights. No, lad, you won't mix up light and dark for me in that sort of fashion. You may talk until you unship your jaw, d'ye see, but you will never talk a foul wind into a fair one. Pass over the pouch and the tinder-box, and maybe our friend here will take a turn at my paddle."

All night they toiled up the great river, straining every nerve to place themselves beyond the reach of pursuit. By keeping well into the southern bank, and so avoiding the force of the current, they sped swiftly along, for both Amos and De Catinat were practised hands with the paddle, and the two Indians worked as though they were wire and whipcord instead of flesh and blood. An utter silence reigned over all the broad stream, broken only by the lap-lap of the water against their curving bow, the whirring of the night hawk above them, and the sharp high barking of foxes away in the woods. When at last morning broke, and the black shaded imperceptibly into gray, they were far out of sight of the citadel and of all trace of man's handiwork. Virgin woods in their wonderful many-coloured autumn dress flowed right down to the river edge on either side, and in the centre was a little island with a rim of yellow sand and an out-flame of scarlet tupelo and sumach in one bright tangle of colour in the centre.

"I've passed here before," said De Catinat. "I remember marking that great maple with the blaze on its trunk, when last I went with the governor to Montreal. That was in Frontenac's day, when the king was first and the bishop second."

The Redskins, who had sat like terra-cotta figures, without a trace of expression upon their set hard faces, pricked up their ears at the sound of that name.

"My brother has spoken of the great Onontio," said one of them, glancing round. "We have listened to the whistling of evil birds who tell us that he will never come back to his children across the seas."

"He is with the great white father," answered De Catinat. "I have myself seen him in his council, and he will assuredly come across the great water if his people have need of him."

The Indian shook his shaven head.

"The rutting month is past, my brother," said he, speaking in broken French, "but ere the month of the bird-laying has come there will be no white man upon this river save only behind stone walls."

"What, then? We have heard little! Have the Iroquois broken out so fiercely?"

"My brother, they said they would eat up the Hurons, and where are the Hurons now? They turned their faces upon the Eries, and where are the Eries now? They went westward against the Illinois, and who can find an Illinois village? They raised the hatchet against the Andastes, and their name is blotted from the earth. And now they have danced a dance and sung a song which will bring little good to my white brothers."

"Where are they, then?"

The Indian waved his hand along the whole southern and western horizon.

"Where are they not? The woods are rustling with them. They are like a fire among dry grass, so swift and so terrible!"

"On my life," said De Catinat, "if these devils are indeed unchained, they will need old Frontenac back if they are not to be swept into the river."

"Ay," said Amos, "I saw him once, when I was brought before him with the others for trading on what he called French ground. His mouth set like a skunk trap and he looked at us as if he would have liked our scalps for his leggings. But I could see that he was a chief and a brave man."

"He was an enemy of the Church, and the right hand of the foul fiend in this country," said a voice from the bottom of the canoe.

It was the friar who had succeeded in getting rid of the buckskin glove and belt with which the two Americans had gagged him. He was lying huddled up now glaring savagely at the party with his fiery dark eyes.

"His jaw-tackle has come adrift," said the seaman. "Let me brace it up again."

"Nay, why should we take him farther?" asked Amos. "He is but weight for us to carry, and I cannot see that we profit by his company. Let us put him out."

"Ay, sink or swim," cried old Ephraim with enthusiasm.

"Nay, upon the bank."

"And have him maybe in front of us warning the black jackets."

"On that island, then."

"Very good. He can hail the first of his folk who pass."

They shot over to the island and landed the friar, who said nothing, but cursed them with his eye. They left with him a small supply of biscuit and of flour to last him until he should be picked up. Then, having passed a bend in the river, they ran their canoe ashore in a little cove where the whortleberry and cranberry bushes grew right down to the water's edge, and the sward was bright with the white euphorbia, the blue gentian, and the purple balm. There they laid out their small stock of provisions, and ate a hearty breakfast while discussing what their plans should be for the future.

CHAPTER XXX.
THE INLAND WATERS.

They were not badly provided for their journey. The captain of the Gloucester brig in which the Americans had started from Quebec knew Ephraim Savage well, as who did not upon the New England coast? He had accepted his bill therefore at three months' date, at as high a rate of interest as he could screw out of him, and he had let him have in return three excellent guns, a good supply of ammunition, and enough money to provide for all his wants. In this way he had hired the canoe and the Indians, and had fitted her with meat and biscuit to last them for ten days at the least.

"It's like the breath of life to me to feel the heft of a gun and to smell the trees round me," said Amos. "Why, it cannot be more than a hundred leagues from here to Albany or Schenectady, right through the forest."

"Ay, lad, but how is the gal to walk a hundred leagues through a forest? No, no, let us keep water under our keel, and lean on the Lord."

"Then there is only one way for it. We must make the Richelieu River, and keep right along to Lake Champlain and Lake St. Sacrament. There we should be close by the headwaters of the Hudson."

"It is a dangerous road," said De Catinat, who understood the conversation of his companions, even when he was unable to join in it. "We should need to skirt the country of the Mohawks."

"It's the only way, I guess. It's that or nothing."

"And I have a friend upon the Richelieu River who, I am sure, would help us on our way," said De Catinat with a smile. "Adele, you have heard me talk of Charles de la Noue, seigneur de Sainte Marie?"

"He whom you used to call the Canadian duke, Amory?"

"Precisely. His seigneury lies on the Richelieu, a little south of Fort St. Louis, and I am sure that he would speed us upon our way."

"Good!" cried Amos. "If we have a friend there we shall do well. That clenches it then, and we shall hold fast by the river. Let's get to our paddles then, for that friar will make mischief for us if he can."

And so for a long week the little party toiled up the great waterway, keeping ever to the southern bank, where there were fewer clearings. On both sides of the stream the woods were thick, but every here and there they would curve away, and a narrow strip of cultivated land would skirt the bank, with the yellow stubble to mark where the wheat had grown. Adele looked with interest at the wooden houses with their jutting stories and quaint gable-ends, at the solid, stone-built manor-houses of the seigneurs, and at the mills in every hamlet, which served the double purpose of grinding flour and of a loop-holed place of retreat in case of attack. Horrible experience had taught the Canadians what the English settlers had yet to learn, that in a land of savages it is a folly to place isolated farmhouses in the centre of their own fields. The clearings then radiated out from the villages, and every cottage was built with an eye to the military necessities of the whole, so that the defence might make a stand at all points, and might finally centre upon the stone manor-house and the mill. Now at every bluff and hill near the villages might be seen the gleam of the muskets of the watchers, for it was known that the scalping parties of the Five Nations were out, and none could tell where the blow would fall, save that it must come where they were least prepared to meet it.

Indeed, at every step in this country, whether the traveller were on the St. Lawrence, or west upon the lakes, or down upon the banks of the Mississippi, or south in the country of the Cherokees and of the Creeks, he would still find the inhabitants in the same state of dreadful expectancy, and from the same cause. The Iroquois, as they were named by the French, or the Five Nations as they called themselves, hung like a cloud over the whole great continent. Their confederation was a natural one, for they were of the same stock and spoke the same language, and all attempts to separate them had been in vain. Mohawks, Cayugas, Onondagas, Oneidas, and Senecas were each proud of their own totems and their own chiefs, but in war they were Iroquois, and the enemy of one was the enemy of all. Their numbers were small, for they were never able to put two thousand warriors in the field, and their country was limited, for their villages were scattered over the tract which lies between Lake Champlain and Lake Ontario. But they were united, they were cunning, they were desperately brave, and they were fiercely aggressive and energetic. Holding a central position, they struck out upon each side in turn, never content with simply defeating an adversary, but absolutely annihilating and destroying him, while holding all the others in check by their diplomacy. War was their business, and cruelty their amusement. One by one they had turned their arms against the various nations, until, for a space of over a thousand square miles, none existed save by sufferance. They had swept away Hurons and Huron missions in one fearful massacre. They had destroyed the tribes of the north-west, until even the distant Sacs and Foxes trembled at their name. They had scoured the whole country to westward until their scalping parties had come into touch with their kinsmen the Sioux, who were lords of the great plains, even as they were of the great forests. The New England Indians in the east, and the Shawnees and Delawares farther south, paid tribute to them, and the terror of their arms had extended over the borders of Maryland and Virginia. Never, perhaps, in the world's history has so small a body of men dominated so large a district and for so long a time.

For half a century these tribes had nursed a grudge wards the French since Champlain and some of his followers had taken part with their enemies against them. During all these years they had brooded in their forest villages, flashing out now and again in some border outrage, but waiting for the most part until their chance should come. And now it seemed to them that it had come. They had destroyed all the tribes who might have allied themselves with the white men. They had isolated them. They had supplied themselves with good guns and plenty of ammunition from the Dutch and English of New York. The long thin line of French settlements lay naked before them. They were gathered in the woods, like hounds in leash, waiting for the orders of their chiefs, which should precipitate them with torch and with tomahawk upon the belt of villages.

Such was the situation as the little party of refugees paddled along the bank of the river, seeking the only path which could lead them to peace and to freedom. Yet it was, as they well knew, a dangerous road to follow. All down the Richelieu River were the outposts and blockhouses of the French, for when the feudal system was grafted upon Canada the various seigneurs or native *noblesse* were assigned their estates in the positions which would be of most benefit to the settlement. Each seigneur with his tenants under him, trained as they were in the use of arms, formed a military force exactly as they had done in the middle ages, the farmer holding his fief upon condition that he mustered when called upon to do so. Hence the old officers of the regiment of Carignan, and the more hardy of the settlers, had been placed along the line of the Richelieu, which runs at right angles to the St. Lawrence towards the Mohawk country. The blockhouses themselves might hold their own, but to the little party who had to travel down from one to the other the situation was full of deadly peril. It was true that the Iroquois were not at war with the English, but they would discriminate little when on the warpath, and the Americans, even had they wished to do so, could not separate their fate from that of their two French companions.

As they ascended the St. Lawrence they met many canoes coming down. Sometimes it was an officer or an official on his way to the capital from Three Rivers or Montreal, sometimes it was a load of skins, with Indians or *coureurs-*

de-bois conveying them down to be shipped to Europe, and sometimes it was a small canoe which bore a sunburned grizzly-haired man, with rusty weather-stained black cassock, who zigzagged from bank to bank, stopping at every Indian hut upon his way. If aught were amiss with the Church in Canada the fault lay not with men like these village priests, who toiled and worked and spent their very lives in bearing comfort and hope, and a little touch of refinement too, through all those wilds. More than once these wayfarers wished to have speech with the fugitives, but they pushed onwards, disregarding their signs and hails. From below nothing overtook them, for they paddled from early morning until late at night, drawing up the canoe when they halted, and building a fire of dry wood, for already the nip of the coming winter was in the air.

It was not only the people and their dwellings which were stretched out before the wondering eyes of the French girl as she sat day after day in the stern of the canoe. Her husband and Amos Green taught her also to take notice of the sights of the woodlands, and as they skirted the bank, they pointed out a thousand things which her own senses would never have discerned. Sometimes it was the furry face of a raccoon peeping out from some tree-cleft, or an otter swimming under the overhanging brushwood with the gleam of a white fish in its mouth. Or, perhaps, it was the wild cat crouching along a branch with its wicked yellow eyes fixed upon the squirrels which played at the farther end, or else with a scuttle and rush the Canadian porcupine would thrust its way among the yellow blossoms of the resin weed and the tangle of the whortleberry bushes. She learned, too, to recognise the pert sharp cry of the tiny chick-a-dee, the call of the blue-bird, and the flash of its wings amid the foliage, the sweet chirpy note of the black and white bobolink, and the long-drawn mewing of the cat-bird. On the breast of the broad blue river, with Nature's sweet concert ever sounding from the bank, and with every colour that artist could devise spread out before her eyes on the foliage of the dying woods, the smile came back to her lips, and her cheeks took a glow of health which France had never been able to give. De Catinat saw the change in her, but her presence weighed him down with fear, for he knew that while Nature had made these woods a heaven, man had changed it into a hell, and that a nameless horror lurked behind all the beauty of the fading leaves and of the woodland flowers. Often as he lay at night beside the smouldering fire upon his couch of spruce, and looked at the little figure muffled in the blanket and slumbering peacefully by his side, he felt that he had no right to expose her to such peril, and that in the morning they should turn the canoe eastward again and take what fate might bring them at Quebec. But ever with the daybreak there came the thought of the humiliation, the dreary homeward voyage, the separation which would await them in galley and dungeon, to turn him from his purpose.

On the seventh day they rested at a point but a few miles from the mouth of the Richelieu River, where a large blockhouse, Fort Richelieu, had been built by M. de Saurel. Once past this they had no great distance to go to reach the seigneury of De Catinat's friend of the *noblesse* who would help them upon their way. They had spent the night upon a little island in midstream, and at early dawn they were about to thrust the canoe out again from the sand-lined cove in which she lay, when Ephraim Savage growled in his throat and pointed Out across the water.

A large canoe was coming up the river, flying along as quick as a dozen arms could drive it. In the stern sat a dark figure which bent forward with every swing of the paddles, as though consumed by eagerness to push onwards. Even at that distance there was no mistaking it. It was the fanatical monk whom they had left behind them.

Concealed among the brushwood, they watched their pursuers fly past and vanish round a curve in the stream. Then they looked at one another in perplexity.

"We'd have done better either to put him overboard or to take him as ballast," said Ephraim. "He's hull down in front of us now, and drawing full."

"Well, we can't take the back track anyhow," remarked Amos.

"And yet how can we go on?" said De Catinat despondently. "This vindictive devil will give word at the fort and at every other point along the river. He has been back to Quebec. It is one of the governor's own canoes, and goes three paces to our two."

"Let me cipher it out." Amos Green sat on a fallen maple with his head sunk upon his hands. "Well," said he presently, "if it's no good going on, and no good going back, there's only one way, and that is to go to one side. That's so, Ephraim, is it not?"

"Ay, ay, lad, if you can't run you must tack, but it seems shoal water on either bow."

"We can't go to the north, so it follows that we must go to the south."

"Leave the canoe?"

"It's our only chance. We can cut through the woods and come out near this friendly house on the Richelieu. The friar will lose our trail then, and we'll have no more trouble with him, if he stays on the St. Lawrence."

"There's nothing else for it," said Captain Ephraim ruefully. "It's not my way to go by land if I can get by water, and I have not been a fathom deep in a wood since King Philip came down on the province, so you must lay the course and keep her straight, Amos."

"It is not far, and it will not take us long. Let us get over to the southern bank and we shall make a start. If madame tires, De Catinat, we shall take turns to carry her."

"Ah, monsieur, you cannot think what a good walker I am. In this splendid air one might go on forever."

"We will cross then."

In a very few minutes they were at the other side and had landed at the edge of the forest. There the guns and ammunition were allotted to each man, and his share of the provisions and of the scanty baggage. Then having paid the Indians, and having instructed them to say nothing of their movements, they turned their backs upon the river and plunged into the silent woods.

CHAPTER XXXI.
THE HAIRLESS MAN.

All day they pushed on through the woodlands, walking in single file, Amos Green first, then the seaman, then the lady, and De Catinat bringing up the rear. The young woodsman advanced cautiously, seeing and hearing much that was lost to his companions, stopping continually and examining the signs of leaf and moss and twig. Their route lay for the most part through open glades amid a huge pine forest, with a green sward beneath their feet, made beautiful by the white euphorbia, the golden rod, and the purple aster. Sometimes, however, the great trunks closed in upon them, and they had to grope their way in a dim twilight, or push a path through the tangled brushwood of green sassafras or scarlet sumach. And then again the woods would shred suddenly away in front of them, and they would skirt marshes, overgrown with wild rice and dotted with little dark clumps of alder bushes, or make their way past silent woodland lakes, all streaked and barred with the tree shadows which threw their crimsons and clarets and bronzes upon the fringe of the deep blue sheet of water. There were streams, too, some clear and rippling where the trout flashed and the king-fisher gleamed, others dark and poisonous from the tamarack swamps, where the wanderers had to wade over their knees and carry Adele in their arms. So all day they journeyed 'mid the great forests, with never a hint or token of their fellow-man.

But if man were absent, there was at least no want of life. It buzzed and chirped and chattered all round them from marsh and stream and brushwood. Sometimes it was the dun coat of a deer which glanced between the distant trunks, sometimes the badger which scuttled for its hole at their approach. Once the long in-toed track of a bear lay marked in the soft earth before them, and once Amos picked a great horn from amid the bushes which some moose had shed the month before. Little red squirrels danced and clattered above their heads, and every oak was a choir with a hundred tiny voices piping from the shadow of its foliage. As they passed the lakes the heavy gray stork flapped up in front of them, and they saw the wild duck whirring off in a long

V against the blue sky, or heard the quavering cry of the loon from amid the reeds.

That night they slept in the woods, Amos Green lighting a dry wood fire in a thick copse where at a dozen paces it was invisible. A few drops of rain had fallen, so with the quick skill of the practised woodsman he made two little sheds of elm and basswood bark, one to shelter the two refugees, and the other for Ephraim and himself. He had shot a wild goose, and this, with the remains of their biscuit, served them both for supper and for breakfast. Next day at noon they passed a little clearing, in the centre of which were the charred embers of a fire. Amos spent half an hour in reading all that sticks and ground could tell him. Then, as they resumed their way, he explained to his companions that the fire had been lit three weeks before, that a white man and two Indians had camped there, that they had been journeying from west to east, and that one of the Indians had been a squaw. No other traces of their fellow-mortals did they come across, until late in the afternoon Amos halted suddenly in the heart of a thick grove, and raised his hand to his ear.

"Listen!" he cried.

"I hear nothing," said Ephraim.

"Nor I," added De Catinat.

"Ah, but I do!" cried Adele gleefully. "It is a bell—and at the very time of day when the bells all sound in Paris!"

"You are right, madame. It is what they call the Angelus bell."

"Ah, yes, I hear it now!" cried De Catinat. "It was drowned by the chirping of the birds. But whence comes a bell in the heart of a Canadian forest?"

"We are near the settlements on the Richelieu. It must be the bell of the chapel at the fort."

"Fort St. Louis! Ah, then, we are no great way from my friend's seigneury."

"Then we may sleep there to-night, if you think that he is indeed to be trusted."

"Yes. He is a strange man, with ways of his own, but I would trust him with my life."

"Very good. We shall keep to the south of the fort and make for his house. But something is putting up the birds over yonder. Ah, I hear the sound of steps! Crouch down here among the sumach, until we see who it is who walks so boldly through the woods."

They stooped all four among the brushwood, peeping out between the tree trunks at a little glade towards which Amos was looking. For a long time the sound which the quick ears of the woodsman had detected was inaudible to the others, but at last they too heard the sharp snapping of twigs as some one forced his passage through the undergrowth. A moment later a man pushed his way into the open, whose appearance was so strange and so ill-suited to the spot, that even Amos gazed upon him with amazement.

He was a very small man, so dark and weather-stained that he might have passed for an Indian were it not that he walked and was clad as no Indian had ever been. He wore a broad-brimmed hat, frayed at the edges, and so discoloured that it was hard to say what its original tint had been. His dress was of skins, rudely cut and dangling loosely from his body, and he wore the high boots of a dragoon, as tattered and stained as the rest of his raiment. On his back he bore a huge bundle of canvas with two long sticks projecting from it, and under each arm he carried what appeared to be a large square painting.

"He's no Injun," whispered Amos, "and he's no Woodsman either. Blessed if I ever saw the match of him!"

"He's neither *voyageur*, nor soldier, nor *coureur-de-bois*," said De Catinat.

"'Pears to me to have a jurymast rigged upon his back, and fore and main staysails set under each of his arms," said Captain Ephraim.

"Well, he seems to have no consorts, so we may hail him without fear."

They rose from their ambush, and as they did so the stranger caught sight of them. Instead of showing the uneasiness which any man might be expected to feel at suddenly finding himself in the presence of strangers in such a country, he promptly altered his course and came towards them. As he crossed the glade, however, the sounds of the distant bell fell upon his ears, and he instantly whipped off his hat and sunk his head in prayer. A cry of horror rose, not only from Adele but from everyone of the party, at the sight which met their eyes.

The top of the man's head was gone. Not a vestige of hair or of white skin remained, but in place of it was a dreadful crinkled discoloured surface with a sharp red line running across his brow and round over his ears.

"By the eternal!" cried Amos, "the man has lost his scalp!"

"My God!" said De Catinat. "Look at his hands!"

He had raised them in prayer. Two or three little stumps projecting upwards showed where the fingers had been.

"I've seen some queer figure-heads in my life, but never one like that," said Captain Ephraim.

It was indeed a most extraordinary face which confronted them as they advanced. It was that of a man who might have been of any age and of any nation, for the features were so distorted that nothing could be learned from them. One eyelid was drooping with a puckering and flatness which showed that the ball was gone. The other, however, shot as bright and merry and kindly a glance as ever came from a chosen favourite of fortune. His face was flecked over with peculiar brown spots which had a most hideous appearance, and his nose had been burst and shattered by some terrific blow. And yet, in spite of this dreadful appearance, there was something so noble in the carriage of the man, in the pose of his head and in the expression which still hung, like the scent from a crushed flower, round his distorted features, that even the blunt Puritan seaman was awed by it.

"Good-evening, my children," said the stranger, picking up his pictures again and advancing towards them. "I presume that you are from the fort, though I may be permitted to observe that the woods are not very safe for ladies at present."

"We are going to the manor-house of Charles de la Noue at Sainte Marie," said De Catinat, "and we hope soon to be in a place of safety. But I grieve, sir, to see how terribly you have been mishandled."

"Ah, you have observed my little injuries, then! They know no better, poor souls. They are but mischievous children—merry-hearted but mischievous. Tut, tut, it is laughable indeed that a man's vile body should ever clog his spirit, and yet here am I full of the will to push forward, and yet I must even seat myself on this log and rest myself, for the rogues have blown the calves of my legs off."

"My God! Blown them off! The devils!"

"Ah, but they are not to be blamed. No, no, it would be uncharitable to blame them. They are ignorant poor folk, and the prince of darkness is behind them to urge them on. They sank little charges of powder into my legs and then they exploded them, which makes me a slower walker than ever, though I was never very brisk. 'The Snail' was what I was called at school in Tours, yes, and afterwards at the seminary I was always 'the Snail.'"

"Who are you then, sir, and who is it who has used you so shamefully?" asked De Catinat.

"Oh, I am a very humble person. I am Ignatius Morat, of the Society of Jesus, and as to the people who have used me a little roughly, why, if you are sent upon the Iroquois mission, of course you know what to expect. I have nothing at all to complain of. Why, they have used me very much better than they did Father Jogues, Father Breboeuf, and a good many others whom I could mention. There were times, it is true, when I was quite hopeful of martyrdom, especially when they thought my tonsure was too small, which was their merry way of putting it. But I suppose I was not worthy of it; indeed I know that I was not, so it only ended in just a little roughness."

"Where are you going then?" asked Amos, who had listened in amazement to the man's words.

"I am going to Quebec. You see I am such a useless person that, until I have seen the bishop, I can really do no good at all."

"You mean that you will resign your mission into the bishop's hands?" said De Catinat.

"Oh, no. That would be quite the sort of thing which I should do if I were left to myself, for it is incredible how cowardly I am. You would not think it possible that a priest of God could be so frightened as I am sometimes. The mere sight of a fire makes me shrink all into myself ever since I went through the ordeal of the lighted pine splinters, which have left all these ugly stains upon my face. But then, of course, there is the Order to be thought of, and members of the Order do not leave their posts for trifling causes. But it is against the rules of Holy Church that a maimed man should perform the rites, and so, until I have seen the bishop and had his dispensation, I shall be even more useless than ever."

"And what will you do then?"

"Oh, then, of course, I will go back to my flock."

"To the Iroquois!"

"That is where I am stationed."

"Amos," said De Catinat, "I have spent my life among brave men, but I think that this is the bravest man that I have ever met!"

"On my word," said Amos, "I have seen some good men, too, but never one that I thought was better than this. You are weary, father. Have some of our cold goose, and there is still a drop of cognac in my flask."

"Tut, tut, my son, if I take anything but the very simplest living it makes me so lazy that I become a snail indeed."

"But you have no gun and no food. How do you live?"

"Oh, the good God has placed plenty of food in these forests for a traveller who dare not eat very much. I have had wild plums, and wild grapes, and nuts and cranberries, and a nice little dish of *tripe-de-mere* from the rocks."

The woodsman made a wry face at the mention of this delicacy.

"I had as soon eat a pot of glue," said he. "But what is this which you carry on your back?"

"It is my church. Ah, I have everything here, tent, altar, surplice, everything. I cannot venture to celebrate service myself without the dispensation, but surely this venerable man is himself in orders and will solemnise the most blessed function."

Amos, with a sly twinkle of the eyes, translated the proposal to Ephraim, who stood with his huge red hands clenched, mumbling about the saltless pottage of papacy. De Catinat replied briefly, however, that they were all of the laity, and that if they were to reach their destination before nightfall, it was necessary that they should push on.

"You are right, my son," said the little Jesuit. "These poor people have already left their villages, and in a few days the woods will be full of them, though I do not think that any have crossed the Richelieu yet. There is one thing, however, which I would have you do for me."

"And what is that?"

"It is but to remember that I have left with Father Lamberville at Onondaga the dictionary which I have made of the Iroquois and French languages. There also is my account of the copper mines of the Great Lakes which I visited two years ago, and also an orrery which I have made to show the northern heavens with the stars of each month as they are seen from this meridian. If aught were to go amiss with Father Lamberville or with me, and we do not live very long on the Iroquois mission, it would be well that some one else should profit from my work."

"I will tell my friend to-night. But what are these great pictures, father, and why do you bear them through the wood?" He turned them over as he spoke, and the whole party gathered round them, staring in amazement.

They were very rough daubs, crudely coloured and gaudy. In the first, a red man was reposing serenely upon what appeared to be a range of mountains, with a musical instrument in his hand, a crown upon his head, and a smile upon his face. In the second, a similar man was screaming at the pitch of his lungs, while half-a-dozen black creatures were battering him with poles and prodding him with lances.

"It is a damned soul and a saved soul," said Father Ignatius Morat, looking at his pictures with some satisfaction. "These are clouds upon which the blessed spirit reclines, basking in all the joys of paradise. It is well done this picture, but it has had no good effect, because there are no beaver in it, and they have not painted in a tobacco-pipe. You see they have little reason, these poor folk, and so we have to teach them as best we can through their eyes and their foolish senses. This other is better. It has converted several squaws and more than one Indian. I shall not bring back the saved soul when I come in the spring, but I shall bring five damned souls, which will be one for each nation. We must fight Satan with such weapons as we can get, you see. And now, my children, if you must go, let me first call down a blessing upon you!"

And then occurred a strange thing, for the beauty of this man's soul shone through all the wretched clouds of sect, and, as he raised his hand to bless them, down went those Protestant knees to earth, and even old Ephraim found himself with a softened heart and a bent head listening to the half-understood words of this crippled, half-blinded, little stranger.

"Farewell, then," said he, when they had risen. "May the sunshine of Saint Eulalie be upon you, and may Saint Anne of Beaupre shield you at the moment of your danger."

And so they left him, a grotesque and yet heroic figure, staggering along through the woods with his tent, his pictures, and his mutilation. If the Church of Rome should ever be wrecked it may come from her weakness in high places, where all Churches are at their weakest, or it may be because with what is very narrow she tries to explain that which is very broad, but assuredly it will never be through the fault of her rank and file, for never upon earth have men and women spent themselves more lavishly and more splendidly than in her service.

CHAPTER XXXII.
THE LORD OF SAINTE MARIE.

Leaving Fort St. Louis, whence the bells had sounded, upon their right, they pushed onwards as swiftly as they could, for the sun was so low in the heavens that the bushes in the clearings threw shadows like trees. Then suddenly, as they peered in front of them between the trunks, the green of the sward turned to the blue of the water, and they saw a broad river running swiftly before them. In France it would have seemed a mighty stream, but, coming fresh from the vastness of the St. Lawrence, their eyes were used to great sheets of water. But Amos and De Catinat had both been upon the bosom of the Richelieu before, and their hearts bounded as they looked upon it, for they knew that this was the straight path which led them, the one to home, and the other to peace and freedom. A few days' journeying down there, a few more along the lovely island-studded lakes of Champlain and Saint Sacrament, under the shadow of the tree-clad Adirondacks, and they would be at the headquarters of the Hudson, and their toils and their dangers be but a thing of gossip for the winter evenings.

Across the river was the terrible Iroquois country, and at two points they could see the smoke of fires curling up into the evening air. They had the Jesuit's word for it that none of the war-parties had crossed yet, so they followed the track which led down the eastern bank. As they pushed onwards, however, a stern military challenge suddenly brought them to a stand, and they saw the gleam of two musket barrels which covered them from a thicket overlooking the path.

"We are friends," cried De Catinat.

"Whence come you, then?" asked an invisible sentinel.

"From Quebec."

"And whither are you going?"

"To visit Monsieur Charles de la Noue, seigneur of Sainte Marie."

"Very good. It is quite safe, Du Lhut. They have a lady with them, too. I greet you, madame, in the name of my father."

Two men had emerged from the bushes, one of whom might have passed as a full-blooded Indian, had it not been for these courteous words which he uttered in excellent French. He was a tall slight young man, very dark, with piercing black eyes, and a grim square relentless mouth which could only have come with Indian descent. His coarse flowing hair was gathered up into a scalp-lock, and the eagle feather which he wore in it was his only headgear. A rude suit of fringed hide with caribou-skin mocassins might have been the fellow to the one which Amos Green was wearing, but the gleam of a gold chain from his belt, the sparkle of a costly ring upon his finger, and the delicate richly-inlaid musket which he carried, all gave a touch of grace to his equipment. A broad band of yellow ochre across his forehead and a tomahawk at his belt added to the strange inconsistency of his appearance.

The other was undoubtedly a pure Frenchman, elderly, dark and wiry, with a bristling black beard and a fierce eager face. He, too, was clad in hunter's dress, but he wore a gaudy striped sash round his waist, into which a brace of long pistols had been thrust. His buckskin tunic had been ornamented over the front with dyed porcupine quills and Indian bead-work, while his leggings were scarlet with a fringe of raccoon tails hanging down from them. Leaning upon his long brown gun he stood watching the party, while his companion advanced towards them.

"You will excuse our precautions," said he. "We never know what device these rascals may adopt to entrap us. I fear, madame, that you have had a long and very tiring journey."

Poor Adele, who had been famed for neatness even among housekeepers of the Rue St. Martin, hardly dared to look down at her own stained and tattered dress. Fatigue and danger she had endured with a smiling face, but her patience almost gave way at the thought of facing strangers in this attire.

"My mother will be very glad to welcome you, and to see to every want," said he quickly, as though he had read her thoughts. "But you, sir, I have surely seen you before."

"And I you," cried the guardsman. "My name is Amory de Catinat, once of the regiment of Picardy. Surely you are Achille de la Noue de Sainte Marie, whom I remember when you came with your father to the government *levees* at Quebec."

"Yes, it is I," the young man answered, holding out his hand and smiling in a somewhat constrained fashion. "I do not wonder that you should hesitate, for when you saw me last I was in a very different dress to this."

De Catinat did indeed remember him as one of the band of the young *noblesse* who used to come up to the capital once a year, where they inquired about the latest modes, chatted over the year-old gossip of Versailles, and for a few weeks at least lived a life which was in keeping with the traditions of their order. Very different was he now, with scalp-lock and war-paint, under the shadow of the great oaks, his musket in his hand and his tomahawk at his belt.

"We have one life for the forest and one for the cities," said he, "though indeed my good father will not have it so, and carries Versailles with him wherever he goes. You know him of old, monsieur, and I need not explain my words. But it is time for our relief, and so we may guide you home."

Two men in the rude dress of Canadian *censitaires* or farmers, but carrying their muskets in a fashion which told De Catinat's trained senses that they were disciplined soldiers, had suddenly appeared upon the scene. Young De la Noue gave them a few curt injunctions, and then accompanied the refugees along the path.

"You may not know my friend here," said he, pointing to the other sentinel, "but I am quite sure that his name is not unfamiliar to you. This is Greysolon du Lhut."

Both Amos and De Catinat looked with the deepest curiosity and interest at the famous leader of *coureurs-de-bois*, a man whose whole life had been spent in pushing westward, ever westward, saying little, writing nothing, but always the first wherever there was danger to meet or difficulty to overcome. It was not religion and it was not hope of gain which led him away into those western wildernesses, but pure love of nature and of adventure, with so little ambition that he had never cared to describe his own travels, and none knew where he had been or where he had stopped. For years he would vanish from the settlements away into the vast plains of the Dacotah, or into the huge wilderness of the north-west, and then at last some day would walk back into Sault La Marie, or any other outpost of civilisation, a little leaner, a little browner, and as taciturn as ever. Indians from the furthest corners of the continent knew him as they knew their own sachem. He could raise tribes and bring a thousand painted cannibals to the help of the French who spoke a tongue which none knew, and came from the shores of rivers which no one else had visited. The most daring French explorers, when, after a thousand dangers, they had reached some country which they believed to be new, were as likely as not to find Du Lhut sitting by his camp fire there, some new squaw by his side, and his pipe between his teeth. Or again, when in doubt and danger, with no friends within a thousand miles, the traveller might suddenly meet this silent man, with one or two tattered wanderers of his own kidney, who would help him from his peril, and then vanish as unexpectedly as he came. Such was the man who now walked by their sides along the bank of the Richelieu, and both Amos and De Catinat knew that his presence there had a sinister meaning, and that the place which Greysolon du Lhut had chosen was the place where the danger threatened.

"What do you think of those fires over yonder, Du Lhut?" asked young De la Noue.

The adventurer was stuffing his pipe with rank Indian tobacco, which he pared from a plug with a scalping knife. He glanced over at the two little plumes of smoke which stood straight up against the red evening sky.

"I don't like them," said he.

"They are Iroquois then?"

"Yes."

"Well, at least it proves that they are on the other side of the river."

"It proves that they are on this side."

"What!"

Du Lhut lit his pipe from a tinder paper. "The Iroquois are on this side," said he. "They crossed to the south of us."

"And you never told us. How do you know that they crossed, and why did you not tell us?"

"I did not know until I saw the fires over yonder."

"And how did they tell you?"

"Tut, an Indian papoose could have told," said Du Lhut impatiently. "Iroquois on the trail do nothing without an object. They have an object then in showing that smoke. If their war-parties were over yonder there would be no object. Therefore their braves must have crossed the river. And they could not get over to the north without being seen from the fort. They have got over on the south then."

Amos nodded with intense appreciation. "That's it!" said he, "that's Injun ways. I'll lay that he is right."

"Then they may be in the woods round us. We may be in danger," cried De la Noue.

Du Lhut nodded and sucked at his pipe.

De Catinat cast a glance round him at the grand tree trunks, the fading foliage, the smooth sward underneath with the long evening shadows barred across it. How difficult it was to realise that behind all this beauty there lurked a danger so deadly and horrible that a man alone might well shrink from it, far less one who had the woman whom he loved walking within hand's touch of him. It was with a long heart-felt sigh of relief that he saw a wall of stockade in the midst of a large clearing in front of him, with the stone manor house rising above it. In a line from the stockade were a dozen cottages with cedar-shingled roofs turned up in the Norman fashion, in which dwelt the habitants under the protection of the seigneur's chateau—a strange little graft of the feudal system in the heart of an American forest. Above the main gate as they approached was a huge shield of wood with a coat of arms painted upon it, a silver ground with a chevron ermine between three coronets gules. At either corner a small brass cannon peeped through an embrasure. As they passed the gate the guard inside closed it and placed the huge wooden bars into position. A little crowd of men, women, and children were gathered round the door of the chateau, and a man appeared to be seated on a high-backed chair upon the threshold.

"You know my father," said the young man with a shrug of his shoulders. "He will have it that he has never left his Norman castle, and that he is still the Seigneur de la Noue, the greatest man within a day's ride of Rouen, and of the richest blood of Normandy. He is now taking his dues and his yearly oaths from his tenants, and he would not think it becoming, if the governor himself were to visit him, to pause in the middle of so august a ceremony. But if it would interest you, you may step this way and wait until he has finished. You, madame, I will take at once to my mother, if you will be so kind as to follow me."

The sight was, to the Americans at least, a novel one. A triple row of men, women, and children were standing round in a semicircle, the men rough and sunburned, the women homely and clean, with white caps upon their heads, the children open-mouthed and round-eyed, awed into an unusual quiet by the reverent bearing of their elders. In the centre, on his high-backed carved chair, there sat an elderly man very stiff and erect, with an exceedingly solemn face. He was a fine figure of a man, tall and broad, with large strong features, clean-shaven and deeply-lined, a huge beak of a nose, and strong shaggy eyebrows which arched right up to the great wig, which he wore full and long as it had been worn in France in his youth. On his wig was placed a white hat cocked jauntily at one side with a red feather streaming round it, and he wore a coat of cinnamon-coloured cloth with silver at the neck and pockets, which was still very handsome, though it bore signs of having been frayed and mended more than once. This, with black velvet knee-breeches and high well-polished boots, made a costume such as De Catinat had never before seen in the wilds of Canada.

As they watched, a rude husbandman walked forwards from the crowd, and kneeling down upon a square of carpet placed his hands between those of the seigneur.

"Monsieur de Sainte Marie, Monsieur de Sainte Marie, Monsieur de Sainte Marie," said he three times, "I bring you the faith and homage which I am bound to bring you on account of my fief Herbert, which I hold as a man of faith of your seigneury."

"Be true, my son. Be valiant and true!" said the old nobleman solemnly, and then with a sudden change of tone: "What in the name of the devil has your daughter got there?"

A girl had advanced from the crowd with a large strip of bark in front of her on which was heaped a pile of dead fish.

"It is your eleventh fish which I am bound by my oath to render to you," said the *censitaire*. "There are seventy-three in the heap, and I have caught eight hundred in the month."

"*Peste!*" cried the nobleman. "Do you think, Andre Dubois, that I will disorder my health by eating three-and-seventy fish in this fashion? Do you think that I and my body-servants and my personal retainers and the other members of my household have nothing to do but to eat your fish? In future, you will pay your tribute not more than five at a time. Where is the major-domo? Theuriet, remove the fish to our central store-house, and be careful that the smell does not penetrate to the blue tapestry chamber or to my lady's suite."

A man in very shabby black livery, all stained and faded, advanced with a large tin platter and carried off the pile of white fish. Then, as each of the tenants stepped forward to pay their old-world homage, they all left some share of their industry for their lord's maintenance. With some it was a bundle of wheat, with some a barrel of potatoes, while others had brought skins of deer or of beaver. All these were carried off by the major-domo, until each had paid his tribute, and the singular ceremony was brought to a conclusion. As the seigneur rose, his son, who had returned, took De Catinat by the sleeve and led him through the throng.

"Father," said he, "this is Monsieur de Catinat, whom you may remember some years ago at Quebec."

The seigneur bowed with much condescension, and shook the guardsman by the hand.

"You are extremely welcome to my estates, both you and your body-servants—"

"They are my friends, monsieur. This is Monsieur Amos Green and Captain Ephraim Savage. My wife is travelling with me, but your courteous son has kindly taken her to your lady."

"I am honoured—honoured indeed!" cried the old man, with a bow and a flourish. "I remember you very well, sir, for it is not so common to meet men of quality in this country. I remember your father also, for he served with me at Rocroy, though he was in the Foot, and I in the Red Dragoons of Grissot. Your arms are a martlet in fess upon a field azure, and now that I think of it, the second daughter of your great-grand-father married the son of one of the La Noues of Andelys, which is one of our cadet branches. Kinsman, you are welcome!" He threw his arms suddenly round De Catinat and slapped him three times on the back.

The young guardsman was only too delighted to find himself admitted to such an intimacy.

"I will not intrude long upon your hospitality," said he. "We are journeying down to Lake Champlain, and we hope in a day or two to be ready to go on."

"A suite of rooms shall be laid at your disposal as long as you do me the honour to remain here. *Peste!* It is not every day that I can open my gates to a man with good blood in his veins! Ah, sir, that is what I feel most in my exile, for who is there with whom I can talk as equal to equal? There is the governor, the intendant, perhaps, one or two priests, three or four officers, but how many of the *noblesse*? Scarcely one. They buy their titles over here as they buy their pelts, and it is better to have a canoe-load of beaver skins than a pedigree from Roland. But I forget my duties. You are weary and hungry, you and your friends. Come up with me to the tapestried *salon*, and we shall see if my stewards can find anything for your refreshment. You play piquet, if I remember right? Ah, my skill is leaving me, and I should be glad to try a hand with you."

The manor-house was high and strong, built of gray stone in a framework of wood. The large iron-clamped door through which they entered was pierced for musketry fire, and led into a succession of cellars and store-houses in which the beets, carrots, potatoes, cabbages, cured meat, dried eels, and other winter supplies were placed. A winding stone staircase led them through a huge kitchen, flagged and lofty, from which branched the rooms of the servants or retainers as the old nobleman preferred to call them. Above this again was the principal suite, centering in the dining-hall with its huge fireplace and rude home-made furniture. Rich rugs formed of bear or deer-skin were littered thickly over the brown-stained floor, and antlered heads bristled out from among the rows of muskets which were arranged along the wall. A broad rough-hewn maple table ran down the centre of this apartment, and on this there was soon set a venison pie, a side of calvered salmon, and a huge cranberry tart, to which the hungry travellers did full justice. The seigneur explained that he had already supped, but having allowed himself to be persuaded into joining them, he ended by eating more than Ephraim Savage, drinking more than Du Lhut, and finally by singing a very amorous little French *chanson* with a tra-le-ra chorus, the words of which, fortunately for the peace of the company, were entirely unintelligible to the Bostonian.

"Madame is taking her refection in my lady's boudoir," he remarked, when the dishes had been removed. "You may bring up a bottle of Frontiniac from bin thirteen, Theuriet. Oh, you will see, gentlemen, that even in the wilds we have a little, a very little, which is perhaps not altogether bad. And so you come from Versailles, De Catinat? It was built since my day, but how I remember the old life of the court at St. Germain, before Louis turned serious! Ah, what innocent happy days they were when Madame de Nevailles had to bar the windows of the maids of honour to keep out the king, and we all turned out eight deep on to the grass plot for our morning duel! By Saint Denis, I have not quite forgotten the trick of the wrist yet, and, old as I am, I should be none the worse for a little breather." He strutted in his stately fashion over to where a rapier and dagger hung upon the wall, and began to make passes at the door, darting in and out, warding off imaginary blows with his poniard, and stamping his feet with little cries of "Punto! reverso! stoccata! dritta! mandritta!" and all the jargon of the fencing schools. Finally he rejoined them, breathing heavily and with his wig awry.

"That was our old exercise," said he. "Doubtless you young bloods have improved upon it, and yet it was good enough for the Spaniards at Rocroy and at one or two other places which I could mention. But they still see life at the court, I understand. There are still love passages and blood lettings. How has Lauzun prospered in his wooing of Mademoiselle de Montpensier? Was it proved that Madame de Clermont had bought a phial from Le Vie, the poison woman, two days before the soup disagreed so violently with monsieur? What did the Due de Biron do when his nephew ran away with the duchess? Is it true that he raised his allowance to fifty thousand livres for having done it?" Such were the two-year-old questions which had not been answered yet upon the banks of the Richelieu River. Long into the hours of the night, when his comrades were already snoring under their blankets, De Catinat, blinking and yawning, was still engaged in trying to satisfy the curiosity of the old courtier, and to bring him up to date in all the most minute gossip of Versailles.

CHAPTER XXXIII.
THE SLAYING OF BROWN MOOSE.

Two days were spent by the travellers at the seigneury of Sainte Marie, and they would very willingly have spent longer, for the quarters were comfortable and the welcome warm, but already the reds of autumn were turning to brown, and they knew how suddenly the ice and snow come in those northern lands, and how impossible it would be to finish their journey if winter were once fairly upon them. The old nobleman had sent his scouts by land and by water, but there were no signs of the Iroquois upon the eastern banks, so that it was clear that De Lhut had been mistaken. Over on the other side, however, the high gray plumes of smoke still streamed up above the trees as a sign that their enemies were not very far off. All day from the manor-house windows and from the stockade they could see those danger signals which reminded them that a horrible death lurked ever at their elbow.

The refugees were rested now and refreshed, and of one mind about pushing on.

"If the snow comes, it will be a thousand times more dangerous," said Amos, "for we shall leave a track then that a papoose could follow."

"And why should we fear?" urged old Ephraim.

"Truly this is a desert of salt, even though it lead to the vale of Hinnom, but we shall be borne up against these sons of Jeroboam. Steer a straight course, lad, and jam your helm, for the pilot will see you safe."

"And I am not frightened, Amory, and I am quite rested now," said Adele. "We shall be so much more happy when we are in the English Provinces, for even now, how do we know that that dreadful monk may not come with orders to drag us back to Quebec and Paris?"

It was indeed very possible that the vindictive Franciscan, when satisfied that they had not ascended to Montreal, or remained at Three Rivers, might seek them on the banks of the Richelieu. When De Catinat thought of how he passed them in his great canoe that morning, his eager face protruded, and his dark body swinging in time to the paddles, he felt that the danger which his wife suggested was not only possible but imminent. The seigneur was his friend, but the seigneur could not disobey the governor's orders. A great hand, stretching all the way from Versailles, seemed to hang over them, even here in the heart of the virgin forest, ready to snatch them up and carry them back into degradation and misery. Better all the perils of the woods than that!

But the seigneur and his son, who knew nothing of their pressing reasons for haste, were strenuous in urging De Catinat the other way, and in this they were supported by the silent Du Lhut, whose few muttered words were always more weighty than the longest speech, for he never spoke save about that of which he was a master.

"You have seen my little place," said the old nobleman, with a wave of his beruffled ring-covered hand. "It is not what I should wish it, but such as it is, it is most heartily yours for the winter, if you and your comrades would honour me by remaining. As to madame, I doubt not that my own dame and she will find plenty to amuse and occupy them, which reminds me, De Catinat, that you have not yet been presented. Theuriet, go to your mistress and inform her that I request her to be so good as to come to us in the hall of the dais."

De Catinat was too seasoned to be easily startled, but he was somewhat taken aback when the lady, to whom the old nobleman always referred in terms of exaggerated respect, proved to be as like a full-blooded Indian squaw as the hall of the dais was to a French barn. She was dressed, it was true, in a bodice of scarlet taffeta with a black skirt, silver-buckled shoes, and a scented pomander ball dangling by a silver chain from her girdle, but her face was of the colour of the bark of the Scotch fir, while her strong nose and harsh mouth, with the two plaits of coarse black hair which dangled down her back, left no possible doubt as to her origin.

"Allow me to present you, Monsieur de Catinat," said the Seigneur de Sainte Marie solemnly, "to my wife, Onega de la Noue de Sainte Marie, chatelaine by right of marriage to this seigneury, and also to the Chateau d'Andelys in Normandy, and to the estate of Varennes in Provence, while retaining in her own right the hereditary chieftainship on the distaff side of the nation of the Onondagas. My angel, I have been endeavouring to persuade our friends to remain with us at Sainte Marie instead of journeying on to Lake Champlain."

"At least leave your White Lily at Sainte Marie," said the dusky princess, speaking in excellent French, and clasping with her ruddy fingers the ivory hand of Adele. "We will hold her safe for you until the ice softens, and the leaves and the partridge berries come once more. I know my people, monsieur, and I tell you that the woods are full of murder, and that it is not for nothing that the leaves are the colour of blood, for death lurks behind every tree."

De Catinat was more moved by the impressive manner of his hostess than by any of the other warnings which he had received. Surely she, if anyone, must be able to read the signs of the times.

"I know not what to do!" he cried in despair. "I must go on, and yet how can I expose her to these perils? I would fain stay the winter, but you must take my word for it, sir, that it is not possible."

"Du Lhut, you know how things should be ordered," said the seigneur. "What should you advise my friend to do, since he is so set upon getting to the English Provinces before the winter comes?"

The dark silent pioneer stroked his beard with his hand as he pondered over the question.

"There is but one way," said he at last, "though even in it there is danger. The woods are safer than the river, for the reeds are full of *cached* canoes. Five leagues from here is the blockhouse of Poitou, and fifteen miles beyond, that of Auvergne. We will go to-morrow to Poitou through the woods and see if all be safe. I will go with you, and I give you my word that if the Iroquois are there, Greysolon du Lhut will know it. The lady we shall leave here, and if we find that all is safe we shall come back for her. Then in the same fashion we shall advance to Auvergne, and there you must wait until you hear where their war-parties are. It is in my mind that it will not be very long before we know."

"What! You would part us!" cried Adele aghast.

"It is best, my sister," said Onega, passing her arm caressingly round her. "You cannot know the danger, but we know it, and we will not let our White Lily run into it. You will stay here to gladden us, while the great chief Du Lhut, and the French soldier, your husband, and the old warrior who seems so wary, and the other chief with limbs like the wild deer, go forward through the woods and see that all is well before you venture."

And so it was at last agreed, and Adele, still protesting, was consigned to the care of the lady of Sainte Marie, while De Catinat swore that without a pause he would return from Poitou to fetch her. The old nobleman and his son would fain have joined them in their adventure, but they had their own charge to watch and the lives of many in their keeping, while a small party were safer in the woods than a larger one would be. The seigneur provided them with a letter for De Lannes, the governor of the Poitou blockhouse, and so in the early dawn the four of them crept like shadows from the stockade-gate, amid the muttered good wishes of the guard within, and were lost in an instant in the blackness of the vast forest.

From La Noue to Poitou was but twelve miles down the river, but by the woodland route where creeks were to be crossed, reed-girt lakes to be avoided, and paths to be picked among swamps where the wild rice grew higher than their heads, and the alder bushes lay in dense clumps before them, the distance was more than doubled. They walked in single file, Du Lhut leading, with the swift silent tread of some wild creature, his body bent forward, his gun ready in the bend of his arm, and his keen dark eyes shooting little glances to right and left, observing everything from the tiniest mark upon the ground or tree trunk to the motion of every beast and bird of the brushwood. De Catinat walked behind, then Ephraim Savage, and then Amos, all with their weapons ready and with every sense upon the alert. By midday they were more than half-way, and halted in a thicket for a scanty meal of bread and cheese, for De Lhut would not permit them to light a fire.

"They have not come as far as this," he whispered, "and yet I am sure that they have crossed the river. Ah, Governor de la Barre did not know what he did when he stirred these men up, and this good dragoon whom the king has sent us now knows even less."

"I have seen them in peace," remarked Amos. "I have traded to Onondaga and to the country of the Senecas. I know them as fine hunters and brave men."

"They are fine hunters, but the game that they hunt best are their fellow-men. I have myself led their scalping parties, and I have fought against them, and I tell you that when a general comes out from France who hardly knows enough to get the sun behind him in a fight, he will find that there is little credit to be gained from them. They talk of burning their villages! It would be as wise to kick over the wasps' nest, and think that you have done with the wasps. You are from New England, monsieur?"

"My comrade is from New England; I am from New York."

"Ah, yes. I could see from your step and your eye that the woods were as a home to you. The New England man goes on the waters and he slays the cod with more pleasure than the caribou. Perhaps that is why his face is so sad. I have been on the great water, and I remember that my face was sad also. There is little wind, and so I think that we may light our pipes without danger. With a good breeze I have known a burning pipe fetch up a scalping party from two miles' distance, but the trees stop scent, and the Iroquois noses are less keen than the Sioux and the Dacotah. God help you, monsieur, if you should ever have an Indian war. It is bad for us, but it would be a thousand times worse for you."

"And why?"

"Because we have fought the Indians from the first, and we have them always in our mind when we build. You see how along this river every house and every hamlet supports its neighbour? But you, by Saint Anne of Beaupre, it made my scalp tingle when I came on your frontiers and saw the lonely farm-houses and little clearings out in the woods with no help for twenty leagues around. An Indian war is a purgatory for Canada, but it would be a hell for the English Provinces!"

"We are good friends with the Indians," said Amos. "We do not wish to conquer."

"Your people have a way of conquering although they say that they do not wish to do it," remarked Du Lhut. "Now, with us, we bang our drums, and wave our flags, and make a stir, but no very big thing has come of it yet. We have never had but two great men in Canada. One was Monsieur de la Salle, who was shot last year by his own men down the great river, and the other, old Frontenac, will have to come back again if New France is not to be turned into a desert by the Five Nations. It would surprise me little if by this time two years the white and gold flag flew only over the rock of Quebec. But I see that you look at me impatiently, Monsieur de Catinat, and I know that you count the hours until we are back at Sainte Marie again. Forward, then, and may the second part of our journey be as peaceful as the first."

For an hour or more they picked their way through the woods, following in the steps of the old French pioneer. It was a lovely day with hardly a cloud in the heavens, and the sun streaming down through the thick foliage covered the shaded sward with a delicate network of gold. Sometimes where the woods opened they came out into the pure sunlight, but only to pass into thick glades beyond, where a single ray, here and there, was all that could break its way through the vast leafy covering. It would have been beautiful, these sudden transitions from light to shade, but with the feeling of impending danger, and of a horror ever lurking in these shadows, the mind was tinged with awe rather than admiration. Silently, lightly, the four men picked their steps among the great tree trunks.

Suddenly Du Lhut dropped upon his knees and stooped his ear to the ground. He rose, shook his head, and walked on with a grave face, casting quick little glances into the shadows in every direction.

"Did you hear something?" whispered Amos.

Du Lhut put his finger to his lips, and then in an instant was down again upon his face with his ear fixed to the ground. He sprang up with the look of a man who has heard what he expected to hear.

"Walk on," said he quietly, "and behave exactly as you have done all day."

"What is it, then?"

"Indians."

"In front of us?"

"No, behind us."

"What are they doing?"

"They are following us."

"How many of them?"

"Two, I think."

The friends glanced back involuntarily over their shoulders into the dense blackness of the forest. At one point a single broad shaft of light slid down between two pines and cast a golden blotch upon their track. Save for this one vivid spot all was sombre and silent.

"Do not look round," whispered Du Lhut sharply. "Walk on as before."

"Are they enemies?"

"They are Iroquois."

"And pursuing us?"

"No, we are now pursuing them."

"Shall we turn, then?"

"No, they would vanish like shadows,"

"How far off are they?"

"About two hundred paces, I think."

"They cannot see us, then?"

"I think not, but I cannot be sure. They are following our trail, I think."

"What shall we do, then?"

"Let us make a circle and get behind them."

Turning sharp to the left he led them in a long curve through the woods, hurrying swiftly and yet silently under the darkest shadows of the trees. Then he turned again, and presently halted.

"This is our own track," said he.

"Ay, and two Redskins have passed over it," cried Amos, bending down, and pointing to marks which were entirely invisible to Ephraim Savage or De Catinat.

"A full-grown warrior and a lad on his first warpath," said Du Lhut. "They were moving fast, you see, for you can hardly see the heel marks of their moccasins. They walked one behind the other. Now let us follow them as they followed us, and see if we have better luck."

He sped swiftly along the trail with his musket cocked in his hand, the others following hard upon his heels, but there was no sound, and no sign of life from the shadowy woods in front of them. Suddenly Du Lhut stopped and grounded his weapon.

"They are still behind us," he said.

"Still behind us?"

"Yes. This is the point where we branched off. They have hesitated a moment, as you can see by their footmarks, and then they have followed on."

"If we go round again and quicken our pace we may overtake them."

"No, they are on their guard now. They must know that it could only be on their account that we went back on our tracks. Lie here behind the fallen log and we shall see if we can catch a glimpse of them."

A great rotten trunk, all green with mould and blotched with pink and purple fungi, lay to one side of where they stood. Behind this the Frenchman crouched, and his three companions followed his example, peering through the brushwood screen in front of them. Still the one broad sheet of sunshine poured down between the two pines, but all else was as dim and as silent as a vast cathedral with pillars of wood and roof of leaf. Not a branch that creaked, nor a twig that snapped, nor any sound at all save the sharp barking of a fox somewhere in the heart of the forest. A thrill of excitement ran through the nerves of De Catinat. It was like one of those games of hide-and-seek which the court used to play, when Louis was in a sportive mood, among the oaks and yew hedges of Versailles. But the forfeit there was a carved fan, or a box of bonbons, and here it was death.

Ten minutes passed and there was no sign of any living thing behind them.

"They are over in yonder thicket," whispered Du Lhut, nodding his head towards a dense clump of brushwood, two hundred paces away.

"Have you seen them?"

"No."

"How do you know, then?"

"I saw a squirrel come from his hole in the great white beech-tree yonder. He scuttled back again as if something had scared him. From his hole he can see down into that brushwood."

"Do you think that they know that we are here?"

"They cannot see us. But they are suspicious. They fear a trap."

"Shall we rush for the brushwood?"

"They would pick two of us off, and be gone like shadows through the woods. No, we had best go on our way."

"But they will follow us."

"I hardly think that they will. We are four and they are only two, and they know now that we are on our guard and that we can pick up a trail as quickly as they can themselves. Get behind these trunks where they cannot see us. So! Now stoop until you are past the belt of alder bushes. We must push on fast now, for where there are two Iroquois there are likely to be two hundred not very far off."

"Thank God that I did not bring Adele!" cried De Catinat.

"Yes, monsieur, it is well for a man to make a comrade of his wife, but not on the borders of the Iroquois country, nor of any other Indian country either."

"You do not take your own wife with you when you travel, then?" asked the soldier.

"Yes, but I do not let her travel from village to village. She remains in the wigwam."

"Then you leave her behind?"

"On the contrary, she is always there to welcome me. By Saint Anne, I should be heavy-hearted if I came to any village between this and the Bluffs of the Illinois, and did not find my wife waiting to greet me."

"Then she must travel before you."

Du Lhut laughed heartily, without, however, emitting a sound.

"A fresh village, a fresh wife," said he. "But I never have more than one in each, for it is a shame for a Frenchman to set an evil example when the good fathers are spending their lives so freely in preaching virtue to them. Ah, here is the Ajidaumo Creek, where the Indians set the sturgeon nets. It is still seven miles to Poitou."

"We shall be there before nightfall, then?"

"I think that we had best wait for nightfall before we make our way in. Since the Iroquois scouts are out as far as this, it is likely that they lie thick round Poitou, and we may find the last step the worst unless we have a care, the more so if these two get in front of us to warn the others." He paused a moment with slanting head and sidelong ear. "By Saint Anne," he muttered, "we have not shaken them off. They are still upon our trail!"

"You hear them?"

"Yes, they are no great way from us. They will find that they have followed us once too often this time. Now, I will show you a little bit of woodcraft which may be new to you. Slip off your moccasins, monsieur."

De Catinat pulled off his shoes as directed, and Du Lhut did the same.

"Put them on as if they were gloves," said the pioneer, and an instant later Ephraim Savage and Amos had their comrades' shoes upon their hands.

"You can sling your muskets over your back. So! Now down on all fours, bending yourselves double, with your hands pressing hard upon the earth. That is excellent. Two men can leave the trail of four! Now come with me, monsieur."

He flitted from tree to tree on a line which was parallel to, but a few yards distant from, that of their comrades. Then suddenly he crouched behind a bush and pulled De Catinat down beside him.

"They must pass us in a few minutes," he whispered. "Do not fire if you can help it." Something gleamed in Du Lhut's hand, and his comrade, glancing down, saw that he had drawn a keen little tomahawk from his belt. Again the mad wild thrill ran through the soldier's blood, as he peered through the tangled branches and waited for whatever might come out of the dim silent aisles of tree-boles.

And suddenly he saw something move. It flitted like a shadow from one trunk to the other so swiftly that De Catinat could not have told whether it were beast or human. And then again he saw it, and yet again, sometimes one shadow, sometimes two shadows, silent, furtive, like the *loup-garou* with which his nurse had scared him in his childhood. Then for a few moments all was still once more, and then in an instant there crept out from among the bushes the most terrible-looking creature that ever walked the earth, an Iroquois chief upon the war-trail.

He was a tall powerful man, and his bristle of scalp-locks and eagle feathers made him look a giant in the dim light, for a good eight feet lay between his beaded moccasin and the topmost plume of his headgear. One side of his face was painted in soot, ochre, and vermilion to resemble a dog, and the other half as a fowl, so that the front view was indescribably grotesque and strange. A belt of wampum was braced round his loin-cloth, and a dozen scalp-locks fluttered out as he moved from the fringe of his leggings. His head was sunk forward, his eyes gleamed with a sinister light, and his nostrils dilated and contracted like those of an excited animal. His gun was thrown forward, and he crept along with bended knees, peering, listening, pausing, hurrying on, a breathing image of caution. Two paces behind him walked a lad of fourteen, clad and armed in the same fashion, but without the painted face and without the horrid dried trophies upon the leggings. It was his first campaign, and already his eyes shone and his nostrils twitched with the same lust for murder which burned within his elder. So they advanced, silent, terrible, creeping out of the shadows of the wood, as their race had come out of the shadows of history, with bodies of iron and tiger souls.

They were just abreast of the bush when something caught the eye of the younger warrior, some displaced twig or fluttering leaf, and he paused with suspicion in every feature. Another instant and he had warned his companion, but Du Lhut sprang out and buried his little hatchet in the skull of the older warrior. De Catinat heard a dull crash, as when an axe splinters its way into a rotten tree, and the man fell like a log, laughing horribly, and kicking and striking with his powerful limbs. The younger warrior sprang like a deer over his fallen comrade and dashed on into the wood, but an instant later there was a gunshot among the trees in front, followed by a faint wailing cry.

"That is his death-whoop," said Du Lhut composedly. "It was a pity to fire, and yet it was better than letting him go."

As he spoke the two others came back, Ephraim ramming a fresh charge into his musket.

"Who was laughing?" asked Amos.

"It was he," said Du Lhut, nodding towards the dying warrior, who lay with his head in a horrible puddle, and his grotesque features contorted into a fixed smile. "It's a custom they have when they get their death-blow. I've known a Seneca chief laugh for six hours on end at the torture-stake. Ah, he's gone!"

As he spoke the Indian gave a last spasm with his hands and feet, and lay rigid, grinning up at the slit of blue sky above him.

"He's a great chief," said Du Lhut. "He is Brown Moose of the Mohawks, and the other is his second son. We have drawn first blood, but I do not think that it will be the last, for the Iroquois do not allow their war-chiefs to die unavenged. He was a mighty fighter, as you may see by looking at his neck."

He wore a peculiar necklace which seemed to De Catinat to consist of blackened bean pods set upon a string. As he stooped over it he saw to his horror that they were not bean pods, but withered human fingers.

"They are all right fore-fingers," said Du Lhut, "so everyone represents a life. There are forty-two in all. Eighteen are of men whom he has slain in battle, and the other twenty-four have been taken and tortured."

"How do you know that?"

"Because only eighteen have their nails on. If the prisoner of an Iroquois be alive, he begins always by biting his nails off. You see that they are missing from four-and-twenty."

De Catinat shuddered. What demons were these amongst whom an evil fate had drifted him? And was it possible that his Adele should fall into the hands of such fiends? No, no, surely the good God, for whose sake they had suffered so much, would not permit such an infamy! And yet as evil a fate had come upon other women as tender as Adele—upon other men as loving as he. What hamlet was there in Canada which had not such stories in their record? A vague horror seized him as he stood there. We know more of the future than we are willing to admit, away down in those dim recesses of the soul where there is no reason, but only instincts and impressions. Now some impending terror cast its cloud over him. The trees around, with their great protruding limbs, were like shadowy demons thrusting out their gaunt arms to seize him. The sweat burst from his forehead, and he leaned heavily upon his musket.

"By Saint Eulalie," said Du Lhut, "for an old soldier you turn very pale, monsieur, at a little bloodshed."

"I am not well. I should be glad of a sup from your cognac bottle."

"Here it is, comrade, and welcome! Well, I may as well have this fine scalp that we may have something to show for our walk." He held the Indian's head between his knees, and in an instant, with a sweep of his knife, had torn off the hideous dripping trophy.

"Let us go!" cried De Catinat, turning away in disgust.

"Yes, we shall go! But I shall also have this wampum belt marked with the totem of the Bear. So! And the gun too. Look at the 'London' printed upon the lock. Ah, Monsieur Green, Monsieur Green, it is not hard to see where the enemies of France get their arms."

So at last they turned away, Du Lhut bearing his spoils, leaving the red grinning figure stretched under the silent trees. As they passed on they caught a glimpse of the lad lying doubled up among the bushes where he had fallen. The pioneer walked very swiftly until he came to a little stream which prattled down to the big river. Here he slipped off his boots and leggings, and waded down it with his companions for half a mile or so.

"They will follow our tracks when they find him," said he, "but this will throw them off, for it is only on running water that an Iroquois can find no trace. And now we shall lie in this clump until nightfall, for we are little over a mile from Port Poitou, and it is dangerous to go forward, for the ground becomes more open."

And so they remained concealed among the alders whilst the shadows turned from short to long, and the white drifting clouds above them were tinged with the pink of the setting sun. Du Lhut coiled himself into a ball with his pipe between his teeth and dropped into a light sleep, pricking up his ears and starting at the slightest sound from the woods around them. The two Americans whispered together for a long time, Ephraim telling some long story about the cruise of the brig *Industry*, bound to Jamestown for sugar and molasses, but at last the soothing hum of a gentle breeze through the branches lulled them off also, and they slept. De Catinat alone remained awake, his nerves still in a tingle from that strange sudden shadow which had fallen upon his soul. What could it mean? Not surely that Adele was in danger? He had heard of such warnings, but had he not left her in safety behind cannons and stockades? By the next evening at latest he would see her again. As he lay looking up through the tangle of copper leaves at the sky beyond, his mind drifted like the clouds above him, and he was back once more in the jutting window in the Rue St. Martin, sitting on the broad *bancal*, with its Spanish leather covering, with the gilt wool-bale creaking outside, and his arm round shrinking, timid Adele, she who had compared herself to a little mouse in an old house, and who yet had courage to stay by his side through all this wild journey. And then again he was back at Versailles. Once more he saw the brown eyes of the king, the fair bold face of De Montespan, the serene features of De Maintenon— once more he rode on his midnight mission, was driven by the demon coachman, and sprang with Amos upon the scaffold to rescue the most beautiful woman in France. So clear it was and so vivid that it was with a start that he came suddenly to himself, and found that the night was creeping on in an American forest, and that Du Lhut had roused himself and was ready for a start.

"Have you been awake?" asked the pioneer.

"Yes."

"Have you heard anything?"

"Nothing but the hooting of the owl."

"It seemed to me that in my sleep I heard a gunshot in the distance."

"In your sleep?"

"Yes, I hear as well asleep as awake and remember what I hear. But now you must follow me close, and we shall be in the fort soon."

"You have wonderful ears, indeed," said De Catinat, as they picked their way through the tangled wood. "How could you hear that these men were following us to-day? I could make out no sound when they were within hand-touch of us."

"I did not hear them at first."

"You saw them?"

"No, nor that either."

"Then how could you know that they were there?"

"I heard a frightened jay flutter among the trees after we were past it. Then ten minutes later I heard the same thing. I knew then that there was some one on our trail, and I listened."

"*Peste!* you are a woodsman indeed!"

"I believe that these woods are swarming with Iroquois, although we have had the good fortune to miss them. So great a chief as Brown Moose would not start on the path with a small following nor for a small object. They must mean mischief upon the Richelieu. You are not sorry now that you did not bring madame?"

"I thank God for it!"

"The woods will not be safe, I fear, until the partridge berries are out once more. You must stay at Sainte Marie until then, unless the seigneur can spare men to guard you."

"I had rather stay there forever than expose my wife to such devils."

"Ay, devils they are, if ever devils walked upon earth. You winced, monsieur, when I took Brown Moose's scalp, but when you have seen as much of the Indians as I have done your heart will be as hardened as mine. And now we are on the very borders of the clearing, and the blockhouse lies yonder among the clump of maples. They do not keep very good watch, for I have been expecting during these last ten minutes to hear the *qui vive*. You did not come as near to Sainte Marie unchallenged, and yet De Lannes is as old a soldier as La Noue. We can scarce see now, but yonder, near the river, is where he exercises his men."

"He does so now," said Amos. "I see a dozen of them drawn up in a line at their drill."

"No sentinels, and all the men at drill!" cried Du Lhut in contempt. "It is as you say, however, for I can see them myself with their ranks open, and each as stiff and straight as a pine stump. One would think to see them stand so still that there was not an Indian nearer than Orange. We shall go across to them, and by Saint Anne, I shall tell their commander what I think of his arrangements."

Du Lhut advanced from the bushes as he spoke, and the four men crossed the open ground in the direction of the line of men who waited silently for them in the dim twilight. They were within fifty paces, and yet none of them had raised hand or voice to challenge their approach. There was something uncanny in the silence, and a change came over Du Lhut's face as he peered in front of him. He craned his head round and looked up the river.

"My God!" he screamed. "Look at the fort!" They had cleared the clump of trees, and the outline of the blockhouse should have shown up in front of them. There was no sign of it. It was gone!

CHAPTER XXXIV.
THE MEN OF BLOOD.

So unexpected was the blow that even De Lhut, hardened from his childhood to every shock and danger, stood shaken and dismayed. Then, with an oath, he ran at the top of his speed towards the line of figures, his companions following at his heels.

As they drew nearer they could see through the dusk that it was not indeed a line. A silent and motionless officer stood out some twenty paces in front of his silent and motionless men. Further, they could see that he wore a very high and singular head-dress. They were still rushing forward, breathless with apprehension, when to their horror this head-dress began to lengthen and broaden, and a great bird flapped heavily up and dropped down again on the nearest tree-trunk. Then they knew that their worst fears were true, and that it was the garrison of Poitou which stood before them.

They were lashed to low posts with willow withies, some twenty of them, naked all, and twisted and screwed into every strange shape which an agonised body could assume. In front where the buzzard had perched was the gray-headed commandant, with two cinders thrust into his sockets and his flesh hanging from him like a beggar's rags. Behind was the line of men, each with his legs charred off to the knees, and his body so haggled and scorched and burst that the willow bands alone seemed to hold it together. For a moment the four comrades stared in silent horror at the dreadful group. Then each acted as his nature bade him. De Catinat staggered up against a tree-trunk and leaned his head upon his arm, deadly sick. Du Lhut fell down upon his knees and said something to heaven, with his two clenched hands shaking up at the darkening sky. Ephraim Savage examined the priming of his gun with a tightened lip and a gleaming eye, while Amos Green, without a word, began to cast round in circles in search of a trail.

But Du Lhut was on his feet again in a moment, and running up and down like a sleuth-hound, noting a hundred things which even Amos would have overlooked. He circled round the bodies again and again. Then he ran a little way towards the edge of the woods, and then came back to the charred ruins of the blockhouse, from some of which a thin reek of smoke was still rising.

"There is no sign of the women and children," said he.

"My God! There were women and children?"

"They are keeping the children to burn at their leisure in their villages. The women they may torture or may adopt as the humour takes them. But what does the old man want?"

"I want you to ask him, Amos," said the seaman, "why we are yawing and tacking here when we should be cracking on all sail to stand after them?"

Du Lhut smiled and shook his head. "Your friend is a brave man," said he, "if he thinks that with four men we can follow a hundred and fifty."

"Tell him, Amos, that the Lord will bear us up," said the other excitedly. "Say that He will be with us against the children of Jeroboam, and we will cut them off utterly, and they shall be destroyed. What is the French for 'slay and spare not'? I had as soon go about with my jaw braced up, as with folk who cannot understand a plain language."

But Du Lhut waved aside the seaman's suggestions. "We must have a care now," said he, "or we shall lose our own scalps, and be the cause of those at Sainte Marie losing theirs as well."

"Sainte Marie!" cried De Catinat. "Is there then danger at Sainte Marie?"

"Ay, they are in the wolf's mouth now. This business was done last night. The place was stormed by a war-party of a hundred and fifty men. This morning they left and went north upon foot. They have been *cached* among the woods all day between Poitou and Sainte Marie."

"Then we have come through them?"

"Yes, we have come through them. They would keep their camp to-day and send out scouts. Brown Moose and his son were among them and struck our trail. To-night—"

"To-night they will attack Sainte Marie?"

"It is possible. And yet with so small a party I should scarce have thought that they would have dared. Well, we can but hasten back as quickly as we can, and give them warning of what is hanging over them."

And so they turned for their weary backward journey, though their minds were too full to spare a thought upon the leagues which lay behind them or those which were before. Old Ephraim, less accustomed to walking than his younger comrades, was already limping and footsore, but, for all his age, he was as tough as hickory, and full of endurance. Du Lhut took the lead again and they turned their faces once more towards the north.

The moon was shining brightly in the sky, but it was little aid to the travellers in the depths of the forest. Where it had been shadowy in the daytime it was now so absolutely dark that De Catinat could not see the tree-trunks against which he brushed. Here and there they came upon an open glade bathed in the moonshine, or perhaps a thin shaft of silver light broke through between the branches, and cast a great white patch upon the ground, but Du Lhut preferred to avoid these more open spaces, and to skirt the glades rather than to cross them. The breeze had freshened a little, and the whole air was filled with the rustle and sough of the leaves. Save for this dull never-ceasing sound all would have been silent had not the owl hooted sometimes from among the tree-tops, and the night-jar whirred above their heads.

Dark as it was, Du Lhut walked as swiftly as during the sunlight, and never hesitated about the track. His comrades could see, however, that he was taking them a different way to that which they had gone in the morning, for twice they caught a sight of the glimmer of the broad river upon their left, while before they had only seen the streams which flowed into it. On the second occasion he pointed to where, on the farther side, they could see dark shadows flitting over the water.

"Iroquois canoes," he whispered. "There are ten of them with eight men in each. They are another party, and they are also going north."

"How do you know that they are another party?"

"Because we have crossed the trail of the first within the hour."

De Catinat was filled with amazement at this marvellous man who could hear in his sleep and could detect a trail when the very tree-trunks were invisible to ordinary eyes. Du Lhut halted a little to watch the canoes, and then turned his back to the river, and plunged into the woods once more. They had gone a mile or two when suddenly he came to a dead stop, snuffing at the air like a hound on a scent.

"I smell burning wood," said he. "There is a fire within a mile of us in that direction."

"I smell it too," said Amos. "Let us creep up that way and see their camp."

"Be careful, then," whispered Du Lhut, "for your lives may hang from a cracking twig."

They advanced very slowly and cautiously until suddenly the red flare of a leaping fire twinkled between the distant trunks. Still slipping through the brushwood, they worked round until they had found a point from which they could see without a risk of being seen.

A great blaze of dry logs crackled and spurtled in the centre of a small clearing. The ruddy flames roared upwards, and the smoke spread out above it until it looked like a strange tree with gray foliage and trunk of fire. But no living being was in sight and the huge fire roared and swayed in absolute solitude in the midst of the silent woodlands. Nearer they crept and nearer, but there was no movement save the rush of the flames, and no sound but the snapping of the sticks.

"Shall we go up to it?" whispered De Catinat. The wary old pioneer shook his head. "It may be a trap," said he.

"Or an abandoned camp?"

"No, it has not been lit more than an hour."

"Besides, it is far too great for a camp fire," said Amos.

"What do you make of it?" asked Du Lhut.

"A signal."

"Yes, I daresay that you are right. This light is not a safe neighbour, so we shall edge away from it and then make a straight line for Sainte Marie."

The flames were soon but a twinkling point behind them, and at last vanished behind the trees. Du Lhut pushed on rapidly until they came to the edge of a moonlit clearing. He was about to skirt this, as he had done others, when suddenly he caught De Catinat by the shoulder and pushed him down behind a clump of sumach, while Amos did the same with Ephraim Savage.

A man was walking down the other side of the open space. He had just emerged, and was crossing it diagonally, making in the direction of the river. His body was bent double, but as he came out from the shadow of the trees they could see that he was an Indian brave in full war-paint, with leggings, loin-cloth, and musket. Close at his heels came a second, and then a third and a fourth, on and on until it seemed as if the wood were full of men, and that the line would never come to an end. They flitted past like shadows in the moonlight, in absolute silence, all crouching and running in the same swift stealthy fashion. Last of all came a man in the fringed tunic of a hunter, with a cap and feather upon his head. He passed across like the others, and they vanished into the shadows as silently as they had appeared. It was five minutes before Du Lhut thought it safe to rise from their shelter.

"By Saint Anne," he whispered, "did you count them?"

"Three hundred and ninety-six," said Amos.

"I made it four hundred and two."

"And you thought that there were only a hundred and fifty of them!" cried De Catinat.

"Ah, you do not understand. This is a fresh band. The others who took the blockhouse must be over there, for their trail lies between us and the river."

"They could not be the same," said Amos, "for there was not a fresh scalp among them."

Du Lhut gave the young hunter a glance of approval. "On my word," said he, "I did not know that your woodsmen are as good as they seem to be. You have eyes, monsieur, and it may please you some day to remember that Greysolon du Lhut told you so."

Amos felt a flush of pride at these words from a man whose name was honoured wherever trader or trapper smoked round a camp fire. He was about to make some answer when a dreadful cry broke suddenly out of the woods, a horrible screech, as from some one who was goaded to the very last pitch of human misery. Again and again, as they stood with blanched cheeks in the darkness, they heard that awful cry swelling up from the night and ringing drearily through the forest.

"They are torturing the women," said Du Lhut.

"Their camp lies over there."

"Can we do nothing to aid them?" cried Amos.

"Ay, ay, lad," said the captain in English. "We can't pass distress signals without going out of our course. Let us put about and run down yonder."

"In that camp," said Du Lhut slowly, "there are now nearly six hundred warriors. We are four. What you say has no sense. Unless we warn them at Sainte Marie, these devils will lay some trap for them. Their parties are assembling by land and by water, and there may be a thousand before daybreak. Our duty is to push on and give our warning."

"He speaks the truth," said Amos to Ephraim. "Nay, but you must not go alone!" He seized the stout old seaman by the arm and held him by main force to prevent him from breaking off through the woods.

"There is one thing which we can do to spoil their night's amusement," said Du Lhut. "The woods are as dry as powder, and there has been no drop of rain for a long three months."

"Yes?"

"And the wind blows straight for their camp, with the river on the other side of it."

"We should fire the woods!"

"We cannot do better."

In an instant Du Lhut had scraped together a little bundle of dry twigs, and had heaped them up against a withered beech tree which was as dry as tinder. A stroke of flint and steel was enough to start a little smoulder of flame, which lengthened and spread until it was leaping along the white strips of hanging bark. A quarter of a mile farther on Du Lhut did the same again, and once more beyond that, until at three different points the forest was in a blaze. As they hurried onwards they could hear the dull roaring of the flames behind them, and at last, as they neared Sainte Marie, they could see, looking back, the long rolling wave of fire travelling ever westward towards the Richelieu, and flashing up into great spouts of flame as it licked up a clump of pines as if it were a bundle of faggots. Du Lhut chuckled in his silent way as he looked back at the long orange glare in the sky.

"They will need to swim for it, some of them," said he. "They have not canoes to take them all off. Ah, if I had but two hundred of my *coureurs-de-bois* on the river at the farther side of them not one would have got away."

"They had one who was dressed like a white man," remarked Amos.

"Ay, and the most deadly of the lot. His father was a Dutch trader, his mother an Iroquois, and he goes by the name of the Flemish Bastard. Ah, I know him well, and I tell you that if they want a king in hell, they will find one all ready in his wigwam. By Saint Anne, I have a score to settle with him, and I may pay it before this business is over. Well, there are the lights of Sainte Marie shining down below there. I can understand that sigh of relief, monsieur, for, on my word, after what we found at Poitou, I was uneasy myself until I should see them."

CHAPTER XXXV.
THE TAPPING OF DEATH.

Day was just breaking as the four comrades entered the gate of the stockade, but early as it was the *censitaires* and their families were all afoot staring at the prodigious fire which raged to the south of them. De Catinat burst through the throng and rushed upstairs to Adele, who had herself flown down to meet him, so that they met in each other's arms half-way up the great stone staircase with a burst of those little inarticulate cries which are the true unwritten language of love. Together, with his arm round her, they ascended to the great hall where old De la Noue with his son were peering out of the window at the wonderful spectacle.

"Ah, monsieur," said the old nobleman, with his courtly bow, "I am indeed rejoiced to see you safe under my roof again, not only for your own sake, but for that of madame's eyes, which, if she will permit an old man to say so, are much too pretty to spoil by straining them all day in the hopes of seeing some one coming out of the forest. You have done forty miles, Monsieur de Catinat, and are doubtless hungry and weary. When you are yourself again I must claim my revenge in piquet, for the cards lay against me the other night."

But Du Lhut had entered at De Catinat's heels with his tidings of disaster.

"You will have another game to play, Monsieur de Sainte-Marie," said he. "There are six hundred Iroquois in the woods and they are preparing to attack."

"Tut, tut, we cannot allow our arrangements to be altered by a handful of savages," said the seigneur. "I must apologise to you, my dear De Catinat, that you should be annoyed by such people while you are upon my estate. As regards the piquet, I cannot but think that your play from king and knave is more brilliant than safe. Now when I played piquet last with De Lannes of Poitou—"

"De Lannes of Poitou is dead, and all his people," said Du Lhut. "The blockhouse is a heap of smoking ashes."

The seigneur raised his eyebrows and took a pinch of snuff, tapping the lid of his little round gold box.

"I always told him that his fort would be taken unless he cleared away those maple trees which grew up to the very walls. They are all dead, you say?"

"Every man."

"And the fort burned?"

"Not a stick was left standing."

"Have you seen these rascals?"

"We saw the trail of a hundred and fifty. Then there were a hundred in canoes, and a war-party of four hundred passed us under the Flemish Bastard. Their camp is five miles down the river, and there cannot be less than six hundred."

"You were fortunate in escaping them."

"But they were not so fortunate in escaping us. We killed Brown Moose and his son, and we fired the woods so as to drive them out of their camp."

"Excellent! Excellent!" said the seigneur, clapping gently with his dainty hands. "You have done very well indeed, Du Lhut! You are, I presume, very tired?"

"I am not often tired. I am quite ready to do the journey again."

"Then perhaps you would pick a few men and go back into the woods to see what these villains are doing?"

"I shall be ready in five minutes."

"Perhaps you would like to go also, Achille?" His son's dark eyes and Indian face lit up with a fierce joy.

"Yes, I shall go also," he answered.

"Very good, and we shall make all ready in your absence. Madame, you will excuse these little annoyances which mar the pleasure of your visit. Next time that you do me the honour to come here I trust that we shall have cleared all these vermin from my estate. We have our advantages. The Richelieu is a better fish pond, and these forests are a finer deer preserve than any of which the king can boast. But on the other hand we have, as you see, our little troubles. You will excuse me now, as there are one or two things which demand my attention. De Catinat, you are a tried soldier and I should be glad of your advice. Onega, give me my lace handkerchief and my cane of clouded amber, and take care of madame until her husband and I return."

It was bright daylight now, and the square enclosure within the stockade was filled with an anxious crowd who had just learned the evil tidings. Most of the *censitaires* were old soldiers and trappers who had served in many Indian wars, and whose swarthy faces and bold bearing told their own story. They were sons of a race which with better fortune or with worse has burned more powder than any other nation upon earth, and as they stood in little groups discussing the situation and examining their arms, a leader could have asked for no more hardy or more war-like following. The women, however, pale and breathless, were hurrying in from the outlying cottages, dragging their children with them, and bearing over their shoulders the more precious of their household goods. The confusion, the hurry, the cries of the children, the throwing down of bundles and the rushing back for more, contrasted sharply with the quiet and the beauty of the woods which encircled them, all bathed in the bright morning sunlight. It was strange to look upon the fairy loveliness of their many-tinted foliage, and to know that the spirit of murder and cruelty was roaming unchained behind that lovely screen.

The scouting party under Du Lhut and Achille de la Noue had already left, and at the order of the seigneur the two gates were now secured with huge bars of oak fitted into iron staples on either side. The children were placed in the lower store-room with a few women to watch them, while the others were told off to attend to the fire buckets, and to reload the muskets. The men had been paraded, fifty-two of them in all, and they were divided into parties now for the defence of each part of the stockade. On one side it had been built up to within a few yards of the river, which not only relieved them from the defence of that face, but enabled them to get fresh water by throwing a bucket at the end of a rope from the stockade. The boats and canoes of Sainte Marie were drawn up on the bank just under the wall, and were precious now as offering a last means of escape should all else fail. The next fort, St. Louis, was but a few leagues up the river, and De la Noue had already sent a swift messenger to them with news of the danger. At least it would be a point on which they might retreat should the worst come to the worst. And that the worst might come to the worst was very evident to so experienced a woodsman as Amos Green. He had left Ephraim Savage snoring in a deep sleep upon the floor, and was now walking round the defences with his pipe in his mouth, examining with a critical eye every detail in connection with them. The stockade was very strong, nine feet high and closely built of oak stakes which were thick enough to turn a bullet. Half-way up it was loop-holed in long narrow slits for the fire of the defenders. But on the other hand the trees grew up to within a hundred yards of it, and formed a screen for the attack, while the garrison was so scanty that it could not spare more than twenty men at the utmost for each face. Amos knew how daring and dashing were the Iroquois warriors, how cunning and fertile of resource, and his face darkened as he thought of the young wife who had come so far in their safe-keeping, and of the women and children whom he had seen crowding into the fort.

"Would it not be better if you could send them up the river?" he suggested to the seigneur.

"I should very gladly do so, monsieur, and perhaps if we are all alive we may manage it to-night if the weather should be cloudy. But I cannot spare the men to guard them, and I cannot send them without a guard when we know that Iroquois canoes are on the river and their scouts are swarming on the banks."

"You are right. It would be madness."

"I have stationed you on this eastern face with your friends and with fifteen men. Monsieur de Catinat, will you command the party?"

"Willingly."

"I will take the south face as it seems to be the point of danger. Du Lhut can take the north, and five men should be enough to watch the river side."

"Have we food and powder?"

"I have flour and smoked eels enough to see this matter through. Poor fare, my dear sir, but I daresay you learned in Holland that a cup of ditch water after a brush may have a better smack than the blue-sealed Frontiniac which you helped me to finish the other night. As to powder, we have all our trading stores to draw upon."

"We have not time to clear any of these trees?" asked the soldier.

"Impossible. They would make better shelter down than up."

"But at least I might clear that patch of brushwood round the birch sapling which lies between the east face and the edge of the forest. It is good cover for their skirmishers."

"Yes, that should be fired without delay."

"Nay, I think that I might do better," said Amos. "We might bait a trap for them there. Where is this powder of which you spoke?"

"Theuriet, the major-domo, is giving out powder in the main store-house."

"Very good." Amos vanished upstairs, and returned with a large linen bag in his hand. This he filled with powder, and then, slinging it over his shoulder, he carried it out to the clump of bushes and placed it at the base of the sapling, cutting a strip out of the bark immediately above the spot. Then with a few leafy branches and fallen leaves he covered the powder bag very carefully over so that it looked like a little hillock of earth. Having arranged all to his satisfaction he returned, clambering over the stockade, and dropping down upon the other side.

"I think that we are all ready for them now," said the seigneur. "I would that the women and children were in a safe place, but we may send them down the river to-night if all goes well. Has anyone heard anything of Du Lhut?"

"Jean has the best ears of any of us, your excellency," said one man from beside the brass corner cannon. "He thought that he heard shots a few minutes ago."

"Then he has come into touch with them. Etienne, take ten men and go to the withered oak to cover them if they are retreating, but do not go another yard on any pretext. I am too short-handed already. Perhaps, De Catinat, you wish to sleep?"

"No, I could not sleep."

"We can do no more down here. What do you say to a round or two of piquet? A little turn of the cards will help us to pass the time."

They ascended to the upper hall, where Adele came and sat by her husband, while the swarthy Onega crouched by the window looking keenly out into the forest. De Catinat had little thought to spare upon the cards, as his mind wandered to the danger which threatened them and to the woman whose hand rested upon his own. The old nobleman, on the other hand, was engrossed by the play, and cursed under his breath, or chuckled and grinned as the luck swayed one way or the other. Suddenly as they played there came two sharp raps from without.

"Some one is tapping," cried Adele.

"It is death that is tapping," said the Indian woman at the window.

"Ay, ay, it was the patter of two spent balls against the woodwork. The wind is against our hearing the report. The cards are shuffled. It is my cut and your deal. The capot, I think, was mine."

"Men are rushing from the woods," cried Onega.

"Tut! It grows serious!" said the nobleman. "We can finish the game later. Remember that the deal lies with you. Let us see what it all means."

De Catinat had already rushed to the window. Du Lhut, young Achille de la Noue, and eight of the covering party were running with their heads bent towards the stockade, the door of which had been opened to admit them. Here and there from behind the trees came little blue puffs of smoke, and one of the fugitives who wore white calico breeches began suddenly to hop instead of running and a red splotch showed upon the white cloth. Two others threw their arms round him and the three rushed in abreast while the gate swung into its place behind them. An instant later the brass cannon at the corner gave a flash and a roar while the whole outline of the wood was traced in a rolling cloud, and the shower of bullets rapped up against the wooden wall like sleet on a window.

CHAPTER XXXVI.
THE TAKING OF THE STOCKADE.

Having left Adele to the care of her Indian hostess, and warned her for her life to keep from the windows, De Catinat seized his musket and rushed downstairs. As he passed a bullet came piping through one of the narrow embrasures and starred itself in a little blotch of lead upon the opposite wall. The seigneur had already descended and was conversing with Du Lhut beside the door.

"A thousand of them, you say?"

"Yes, we came on a fresh trail of a large war-party, three hundred at the least. They are all Mohawks and Cayugas with a sprinkling of Oneidas. We had a running fight for a few miles, and we have lost five men."

"All dead, I trust."

"I hope so, but we were hard pressed to keep from being cut off. Jean Mance is shot through the leg."

"I saw that he was hit."

"We had best have all ready to retire to the house if they carry the stockade. We can scarce hope to hold it when they are twenty to one."

"All is ready."

"And with our cannon we can keep their canoes from passing, so we might send our women away to-night."

"I had intended to do so. Will you take charge of the north side? You might come across to me with ten of your men now, and I shall go back to you if they change their attack."

The firing came in one continuous rattle now from the edges of the wood, and the air was full of bullets. The assailants were all trained shots, men who lived by their guns, and to whom a shaking hand or a dim eye meant poverty and hunger. Every slit and crack and loop-hole was marked, and a cap held above the stockade was blown in an instant from the gun barrel which supported it. On the other hand, the defenders were also skilled in Indian fighting, and wise in every trick and lure which could protect themselves or tempt their enemies to show. They kept well to the sides of the loop-holes, watching through little crevices of the wood, and firing swiftly when a chance offered. A red leg sticking straight up into the air from behind a log showed where one bullet at least had gone home, but there was little to aim at save a puff and flash from among the leaves, or the shadowy figure of a warrior seen for an instant as he darted from one tree-trunk to the other. Seven of the Canadians had already been hit, but only three were mortally wounded, and the other four still kept manfully to their loop-holes, though one who had been struck through the jaw was spitting his teeth with his bullets down into his gun-barrel. The women sat in a line upon the ground, beneath the level of the loop-holes, each with a saucerful of bullets and a canister of powder, passing up the loaded guns to the fighting men at the points where a quick fire was most needful.

At first the attack had been all upon the south face, but as fresh bodies of the Iroquois came up their line spread and lengthened until the whole east face was girt with fire, which gradually enveloped the north also. The fort was ringed in by a great loop of smoke, save only where the broad river flowed past them. Over near the further bank the canoes were lurking, and one, manned by ten warriors, attempted to pass up the stream, but a good shot from the brass gun dashed in her side and sank her, while a second of grape left only four of the swimmers whose high scalp-locks stood out above the water like the back-fins of some strange fish. On the inland side, however, the seigneur had ordered the cannon to be served no more, for the broad embrasures drew the enemy's fire, and of the men who had been struck half were among those who worked the guns.

The old nobleman strutted about with his white ruffles and his clouded cane behind the line of parched smoke-grimed men, tapping his snuff-box, shooting out his little jests, and looking very much less concerned than he had done over his piquet.

"What do you think of it, Du Lhut?" he asked.

"I think very badly of it. We are losing men much too fast."

"Well, my friend, what can you expect? When a thousand muskets are all turned upon a little place like this, some one must suffer for it. Ah, my poor fellow, so you are done for too!"

The man nearest him had suddenly fallen with a crash, lying quite still with his face in a platter of the sagamite which had been brought out by the women. Du Lhut glanced at him and then looked round.

"He is in a line with no loop-hole, and it took him in the shoulder," said he. "Where did it come from then? Ah, by Saint Anne, look there!" He pointed upwards to a little mist of smoke which hung round the summit of a high oak.

"The rascal overlooks the stockade. But the trunk is hardly thick enough to shield him at that height. This poor fellow will not need his musket again, and I see that it is ready primed." De la Noue laid down his cane, turned back his ruffles, picked up the dead man's gun, and fired at the lurking warrior. Two leaves fluttered out from the tree and a grinning vermilion face appeared for an instant with a yell of derision. Quick as a flash Du Lhut brought his musket to his shoulder and pulled the trigger. The man gave a tremendous spring and crashed down through the thick foliage. Some seventy or eighty feet below him a single stout branch shot out, and on to this he fell with the sound of a great stone dropping into a bog, and hung there doubled over it, swinging slowly from side to side like a red rag, his scalp-lock streaming down between his feet. A shout of exultation rose from the Canadians at the sight, which was drowned in the murderous yell of the savages.

"His limbs twitch. He is not dead," cried De la Noue.

"Let him die there," said the old pioneer callously, ramming a fresh charge into his gun. "Ah, there is the gray hat again. It comes ever when I am unloaded."

"I saw a plumed hat among the brushwood."

"It is the Flemish Bastard. I had rather have his scalp than those of his hundred best warriors."

"Is he so brave then?"

"Yes, he is brave enough. There is no denying it, for how else could he be an Iroquois war-chief? But he is clever and cunning, and cruel— Ah, my God, if all the stories told are true, his cruelty is past believing. I should fear that my tongue would wither if I did but name the things which this man has done. Ah, he is there again."

The gray hat with the plume had shown itself once more in a rift of the smoke. De la Noue and Du Lhut both fired together, and the cap fluttered up into the air. At the same instant the bushes parted, and a tall warrior sprang out into full view of the defenders. His face was that of an Indian, but a shade or two lighter, and a pointed black beard hung down over his hunting tunic. He threw out his hands with a gesture of disdain, stood for an instant looking steadfastly at the fort, and then sprang back into cover amid a shower of bullets which chipped away the twigs all round him.

"Yes, he is brave enough," Du Lhut repeated with an oath. "Your *censitaires* have had their hoes in their hands more often than their muskets, I should judge from their shooting. But they seem to be drawing closer upon the east face, and I think that they will make a rush there before long."

The fire had indeed grown very much fiercer upon the side which was defended by De Catinat, and it was plain that the main force of the Iroquois were gathered at that point. From every log, and trunk, and cleft, and bush came the red flash with the gray halo, and the bullets sang in a continuous stream through the loop-holes. Amos had whittled a little hole for himself about a foot above the ground, and lay upon his face loading and firing in his own quiet methodical fashion. Beside him stood Ephraim Savage, his mouth set grimly, his eyes flashing from under his down-drawn brows, and his whole soul absorbed in the smiting of the Amalekites. His hat was gone, his grizzled hair flying in the breeze, great splotches of powder mottled his mahogany face, and a weal across his right cheek showed where an Indian bullet had grazed him. De Catinat was bearing himself like an experienced soldier, walking up and down among his men with short words of praise or of precept, those fire-words rough and blunt which bring a glow to the heart and a flush to the cheek. Seven of his men were down, but as the attack grew fiercer upon his side it slackened upon the others, and the seigneur with his son and Du Lhut brought ten men to reinforce them. De la Noue was holding out his snuff-box to De Catinat when a shrill scream from behind them made them both look round. Onega, the Indian wife, was wringing her hands over the body of her son. A glance showed that the bullet had pierced his heart and that he was dead.

For an instant the old nobleman's thin face grew a shade paler, and the hand which held out the little gold box shook like a branch in the wind. Then he thrust it into his pocket again and mastered the spasm which had convulsed his features.

"The De la Noues always die upon the field of honour," he remarked. "I think that we should have some more men in the angle by the gun."

And now it became clear why it was that the Iroquois had chosen the eastern face for their main attack. It was there that the clump of cover lay midway between the edge of the forest and the stockade. A storming party could creep as far as that and gather there for the final rush. First one crouching warrior, and then a second, and then a third darted across the little belt of open space, and threw themselves down among the bushes. The fourth was hit, and lay with his back broken a few paces out from the edge of the wood, but a stream of warriors continued to venture the passage, until thirty-six had got across, and the little patch of underwood was full of lurking savages. Amos Green's time had come.

From where he lay he could see the white patch where he had cut the bark from the birch sapling, and he knew that immediately underneath it lay the powder bag. He sighted the mark, and then slowly lowered his barrel until he had got to the base of the little trees as nearly as he could guess it among the tangle of bushes. The first shot produced no result, however, and the second was aimed a foot lower. The bullet penetrated the bag, and there was an explosion which shook the manor-house and swayed the whole line of stout stockades as though they were corn-stalks in a breeze. Up to the highest summits of the trees went the huge column of blue smoke, and after the first roar there was a deathly silence which was broken by the patter and thud of falling bodies. Then came a wild cheer from the defenders, and a furious answering whoop from the Indians, while the fire from the woods burst out with greater fury than ever.

But the blow had been a heavy one. Of the thirty-six warriors, all picked for their valour, only four regained the shelter of the woods, and those so torn and shattered that they were spent men. Already the Indians had lost heavily, and this fresh disaster made them reconsider their plan of attack, for the Iroquois were as wary as they were brave, and he was esteemed the best war-chief who was most chary of the lives of his followers. Their fire gradually slackened, and at last, save for a dropping shot here and there, it died away altogether.

"Is it possible that they are going to abandon the attack?" cried De Catinat joyously. "Amos, I believe that you have saved us."

But the wily Du Lhut shook his head. "A wolf would as soon leave a half-gnawed bone as an Iroquois such a prize as this."

"But they have lost heavily."

"Ay, but not so heavily as ourselves in proportion to our numbers. They have fifty out of a thousand, and we twenty out of threescore. No, no, they are holding a council, and we shall soon hear from them again. But it may be some hours first, and if you will take my advice you will have an hour's sleep, for you are not, as I can see by your eyes, as used to doing without it as I am, and there may be little rest for any of us this night."

De Catinat was indeed weary to the last pitch of human endurance. Amos Green and the seaman had already wrapped themselves in their blankets and sunk to sleep under the shelter of the stockade. The soldier rushed upstairs to say a few words of comfort to the trembling Adele, and then throwing himself down upon a couch he slept the dreamless sleep of an exhausted man. When at last he was roused by a fresh sputter of musketry fire from the woods the sun was already low in the heavens, and the mellow light of evening tinged the bare walls of the room. He sprang from his couch, seized his musket, and rushed downstairs. The defenders were gathered at their loop-holes once more, while Du Lhut, the seigneur, and Amos Green were whispering eagerly together. He noticed as he passed that Onega still sat crooning by the body of her son, without having changed her position since morning.

"What is it, then? Are they coming on?" he asked.

"They are up to some devilry," said Du Lhut, peering out at the corner of the embrasure. "They are gathering thickly at the east fringe, and yet the firing comes from the south. It is not the Indian way to attack across the open, and yet if they think help is coming from the fort they might venture it."

"The wood in front of us is alive with them," said Amos. "They are as busy as beavers among the underwood."

"Perhaps they are going to attack from this side, and cover the attack by a fire from the flank."

"That is what I think," cried the seigneur. "Bring the spare guns up here and all the men except five for each side."

The words were hardly out of his mouth when a shrill yell burst from the wood, and in an instant a cloud of warriors dashed out and charged across the open, howling, springing, and waving their guns or tomahawks in the air. With their painted faces, smeared and striped with every vivid colour, their streaming scalp-locks, their waving arms, their open mouths, and their writhings and contortions, no more fiendish crew ever burst into a sleeper's nightmare. Some of those in front bore canoes between them, and as they reached the stockade they planted them against it and swarmed up them as if they had been scaling-ladders. Others fired through the embrasures and loop-holes, the muzzles of their muskets touching those of the defenders, while others again sprang unaided on to the tops of the palisades and jumped fearlessly down upon the inner side. The Canadians, however, made such a resistance as might be expected from men who knew that no mercy awaited them. They fired whilst they had time to load, and then, clubbing their muskets, they smashed furiously at every red head which showed above the rails. The din within the stockade was infernal, the shouts and cries of the French, the whooping of the savages, and the terrified screaming of the frightened women blending into one dreadful uproar, above which could be heard the high shrill voice of the old seigneur imploring his *censitaires* to stand fast. With his rapier in his hand, his hat lost, his wig awry, and his dignity all thrown to the winds, the old nobleman showed them that day how a soldier of Rocroy could carry himself, and with Du Lhut, Amos, De Catinat and Ephraim Savage, was ever in the forefront of the defence. So desperately did they fight, the sword and musket-butt outreaching the tomahawk, that though at one time fifty Iroquois were over the palisades, they had slain or driven back nearly all of them when a fresh wave burst suddenly over the south face which had been stripped of its defenders. Du Lhut saw in an instant that the enclosure was lost and that only one thing could save the house.

"Hold them for an instant," he screamed, and rushing at the brass gun he struck his flint and steel and fired it straight into the thick of the savages. Then as they recoiled for an instant he stuck a nail into the touch-hole and drove it home with a blow from the butt of his gun. Darting across the yard he spiked the gun at the other corner, and was back at the door as the remnants of the garrison were hurled towards it by the rush of the assailants. The Canadians darted in, and swung the ponderous mass of wood into position, breaking the leg of the foremost warrior who had striven to follow them. Then for an instant they had time for breathing and for council.

CHAPTER XXXVII.
THE COMING OF THE FRIAR.

But their case was a very evil one. Had the guns been lost so that they might be turned upon the door, all further resistance would have been vain, but Du Lhut's presence of mind had saved them from that danger. The two guns upon the river face and the canoes were safe, for they were commanded by the windows of the house. But their numbers were terribly reduced, and those who were left were weary and wounded and spent. Nineteen had gained the house, but one had been shot through the body and lay groaning in the hall, while a second had his shoulder cleft by a tomahawk and could no longer raise his musket. Du Lhut, De la Noue, and De Catinat were uninjured, but Ephraim Savage had a bullet-hole in his forearm, and Amos was bleeding from a cut upon the face. Of the others hardly one was without injury, and yet they had no time to think of their hurts for the danger still pressed and they were lost unless they acted. A few shots from the barricaded windows sufficed to clear the enclosure, for it was all exposed to their aim; but on the other hand they had the shelter of the stockade now, and from the further side of it they kept up a fierce fire upon the windows. Half-a-dozen of the *censitaires* returned the fusillade, while the leaders consulted as to what had best be done.

"We have twenty-five women and fourteen children," said the seigneur. "I am sure that you will agree with me, gentlemen, that our first duty is towards them. Some of you, like myself, have lost sons or brothers this day. Let us at least save our wives and sisters."

"No Iroquois canoes have passed up the river," said one of the Canadians. "If the women start in the darkness they can get away to the fort."

"By Saint Anne of Beaupre," exclaimed Du Lhut, "I think it would be well if you could get your men out of this also, for I cannot see how it is to be held until morning."

A murmur of assent broke from the other Canadians, but the old nobleman shook his bewigged head with decision.

"Tut! Tut! What nonsense is this!" he cried. "Are we to abandon the manor-house of Sainte Marie to the first gang of savages who choose to make an attack upon it? No, no, gentlemen, there are still nearly a score of us, and when the garrison learn that we are so pressed, which will be by to-morrow morning at the latest, they will certainly send us relief."

Du Lhut shook his head moodily.

"If you stand by the fort I will not desert you," said he, "and yet it is a pity to sacrifice brave men for nothing."

"The canoes will hardly hold the women and children as it is," cried Theuriet. "There are but two large and four small. There is not space for a single man."

"Then that decides it," said De Catinat. "But who are to row the women?"

"It is but a few leagues with the current in their favour, and there are none of our women who do not know how to handle a paddle."

The Iroquois were very quiet now, and an occasional dropping shot from the trees or the stockade was the only sign of their presence. Their losses had been heavy, and they were either engaged in collecting their dead, or in holding a council as to their next move. The twilight was gathering in, and the sun had already sunk beneath the tree-tops. Leaving a watchman at each window, the leaders went round to the back of the house where the canoes were lying upon the bank. There were no signs of the enemy upon the river to the north of them.

"We are in luck," said Amos. "The clouds are gathering and there will be little light."

"It is luck indeed, since the moon is only three days past the full," answered Du Lhut. "I wonder that the Iroquois have not cut us off upon the water, but it is likely that their canoes have gone south to bring up another war-party. They may be back soon, and we had best not lose a moment."

"In an hour it might be dark enough to start."

"I think that there is rain in those clouds, and that will make it darker still."

The women and children were assembled and their places in each boat were assigned to them. The wives of the censitaires, rough hardy women whose lives had been spent under the shadow of a constant danger, were for the most part quiet and collected, though a few of the younger ones whimpered a little. A woman is always braver when she has a child to draw her thoughts from herself, and each married woman had one now allotted to her as her own special charge until they should reach the fort. To Onega, the

Indian wife of the seigneur, who was as wary and as experienced as a war sachem of her people, the command of the women was entrusted.

"It is not very far, Adele," said De Catinat, as his wife clung to his arm. "You remember how we heard the Angelus bells as we journeyed through the woods. That was Fort St. Louis, and it is but a league or two."

"But I do not wish to leave you, Amory. We have been together in all our troubles. Oh, Amory, why should we be divided now?"

"My dear love, you will tell them at the fort how things are with us, and they will bring us help."

"Let the others do that, and I will stay. I will not be useless, Amory. Onega has taught me to load a gun. I will not be afraid, indeed I will not, if you will only let me stay."

"You must not ask it, Adele. It is impossible, child I could not let you stay."

"But I feel so sure that it would be best."

The coarser reason of man has not yet learned to value those subtle instincts which guide a woman. De Catinat argued and exhorted until he had silenced if he had not convinced her.

"It is for my sake, dear. You do not know what a load it will be from my heart when I know that you are safe. And you need not be afraid for me. We can easily hold the place until morning. Then the people from the fort will come, for I hear that they have plenty of canoes, and we shall all meet again."

Adele was silent, but her hands tightened upon his arm. Her husband was still endeavouring to reassure her when a groan burst from the watcher at the window which overlooked the stream.

"There is a canoe on the river to the north of us," he cried.

The besieged looked at each other in dismay. The Iroquois had then cut off their retreat after all.

"How many warriors are in it?" asked the seigneur.

"I cannot see. The light is not very good, and it is in the shadow of the bank."

"Which way is it coming?"

"It is coming this way. Ah, it shoots out into the open now, and I can see it. May the good Lord be praised! A dozen candles shall burn in Quebec Cathedral if I live till next summer!"

"What is it then?" cried De la Noue impatiently.

"It is not an Iroquois canoe. There is but one man in it. He is a Canadian."

"A Canadian!" cried Du Lhut, springing up to the window. "Who but a madman would venture into such a hornet's nest alone! Ah, yes, I can see him now. He keeps well out from the bank to avoid their fire. Now he is in midstream and he turns towards us. By my faith, it is not the first time that the good father has handled a paddle."

"It is a Jesuit!" said one, craning his neck. "They are ever where there is most danger."

"No, I can see his capote," cried another. "It is a Franciscan friar!"

An instant later there was the sound of a canoe grounding upon the pebbles, the door was unbarred, and a man strode in, attired in the long brown gown of the Franciscans. He cast a rapid glance around, and then, stepping up to De Catinat, laid his hand upon his shoulder.

"So, you have not escaped me!" said he. "We have caught the evil seed before it has had time to root."

"What do you mean, father?" asked the seigneur. "You have made some mistake. This is my good friend Amory de Catinat, of a noble French family."

"This is Amory de Catinat, the heretic and Huguenot," cried the monk. "I have followed him up the St. Lawrence, and I have followed him up the Richelieu, and I would have followed him to the world's end if I could but bring him back with me."

"Tut, father, your zeal carries you too far," said the seigneur. "Whither would you take my friend, then?"

"He shall go back to France with his wife. There is no place in Canada for heretics."

Du Lhut burst out laughing. "By Saint Anne, father," said he, "if you could take us all back to France at present we should be very much your debtors."

"And you will remember," said De la Noue sternly, "that you are under my roof and that you are speaking of my guest."

But the friar was not to be abashed by the frown of the old nobleman.

"Look at this," said he, whipping a paper out of his bosom. "It is signed by the governor, and calls upon you, under pain of the king's displeasure, to return this man to Quebec. Ah, monsieur, when you left me upon the island that morning you little thought that I would return to Quebec for this, and then hunt you down so many hundreds of miles of river. But I have you now, and I shall never leave you until I see you on board the ship which will carry you and your wife back to France."

For all the bitter vindictiveness which gleamed in the monk's eyes, De Catinat could not but admire the energy and tenacity of the man.

"It seems to me, father, that you would have shone more as a soldier than as a follower of Christ," said he; "but, since you have followed us here, and since there is no getting away, we may settle this question at some later time."

But the two Americans were less inclined to take so peaceful a view. Ephraim Savage's beard bristled with anger, and he whispered something into Amos Green's ear.

"The captain and I could easily get rid of him," said the young woodsman, drawing De Catinat aside. "If he *will* cross our path he must pay for it."

"No, no, not for the world, Amos! Let him alone. He does what he thinks to be his duty, though his faith is stronger than his charity, I think. But here comes the rain, and surely it is dark enough now for the boats."

A great brown cloud had overspread the heavens, and the night had fallen so rapidly that they could hardly see the gleam of the river in front of them. The savages in the woods and behind the captured stockade were quiet, save for an occasional shot, but the yells and whoops from the cottages of the *censitaires* showed that they were being plundered by their captors. Suddenly a dull red glow began to show above one of the roofs.

"They have set it on fire," cried Du Lhut. "The canoes must go at once, for the river will soon be as light as day. In! In! There is not an instant to lose!"

There was no time for leave-taking. One impassioned kiss and Adele was torn away and thrust into the smallest canoe, which she shared with Onega, two children, and an unmarried girl. The others rushed into their places, and in a few moments they had pushed off, and had vanished into the drift and the darkness. The great cloud had broken and the rain pattered heavily upon the roof, and splashed upon their faces as they strained their eyes after the vanishing boats.

"Thank God for this storm!" murmured Du Lhut. "It will prevent the cottages from blazing up too quickly."

But he had forgotten that though the roofs might be wet the interior was as dry as tinder. He had hardly spoken before a great yellow tongue of flame licked out of one of the windows, and again and again, until suddenly half of the roof fell in, and the cottage was blazing like a pitch-bucket. The flames hissed and sputtered in the pouring rain, but, fed from below, they grew still higher and fiercer, flashing redly upon the great trees, and turning their trunks to burnished brass. Their light made the enclosure and the manor-house as clear as day, and exposed the whole long stretch of the river. A fearful yell from the woods announced that the savages had seen the canoes, which were plainly visible from the windows not more than a quarter of a mile away.

"They are rushing through the woods. They are making for the water's edge," cried De Catinat.

"They have some canoes down there," said Du Lhut.

"But they must pass us!" cried the Seigneur of Sainte Marie. "Get down to the cannon and see if you cannot stop them."

They had hardly reached the guns when two large canoes filled with warriors shot out from among the reeds below the fort, and steering out into mid-stream began to paddle furiously after the fugitives.

"Jean, you are our best shot," cried De la Noue. "Lay for her as she passes the great pine tree. Lambert, do you take the other gun. The lives of all whom you love may hang upon the shot!"

The two wrinkled old artillerymen glanced along their guns and waited for the canoes to come abreast of them. The fire still blazed higher and higher, and the broad river lay like a sheet of dull metal with two dark lines, which marked the canoes, sweeping swiftly down the centre. One was fifty yards in front of the other, but in each the Indians were bending to their paddles and pulling frantically, while their comrades from the wooded shores whooped them on to fresh exertions. The fugitives had already disappeared round the bend of the river.

As the first canoe came abreast of the lower of the two guns, the Canadian made the sign of the cross over the touch-hole and fired. A cheer and then a groan went up from the eager watchers. The discharge had struck the surface close to the mark, and dashed such a shower of water over it that for an instant it looked as if it had been sunk. The next moment, however, the splash subsided, and the canoe shot away uninjured, save that one of the rowers had dropped his paddle while his head fell forward upon the back of the man in front of him. The second gunner sighted the same canoe as it came abreast of him, but at the very instant when he stretched out his match to fire a bullet came humming from the stockade and he fell forward dead without a groan.

"This is work that I know something of, lad," said old Ephraim, springing suddenly forward. "But when I fire a gun I like to train it myself. Give me a help with the handspike and get her straight for the island. So! A little lower for an even keel! Now we have them!" He clapped down his match and fired.

It was a beautiful shot. The whole charge took the canoe about six feet behind the bow, and doubled her up like an eggshell. Before the smoke had cleared she had foundered, and the second canoe had paused to pick up some of the wounded men. The others, as much at home in the water as in the woods, were already striking out for the shore.

"Quick! Quick!" cried the seigneur. "Load the gun! We may get the second one yet!"

But it was not to be. Long before they could get it ready the Iroquois had picked up their wounded warriors and were pulling madly up-stream once more. As they shot away the fire died suddenly down in the burning cottages and the rain and the darkness closed in upon them.

"My God!" cried De Catinat furiously, "they will be taken. Let us abandon this place, take a boat, and follow them. Come! Come! Not an instant is to be lost!"

"Monsieur, you go too far in your very natural anxiety," said the seigneur coldly. "I am not inclined to leave my post so easily!"

"Ah, what is it? Only wood and stone, which can be built again. But to think of the women in the hands of these devils! Oh, I am going mad! Come! Come! For Christ's sake come!" His face was deadly pale, and he raved with his clenched hands in the air.

"I do not think that they will be caught," said Du Lhut, laying his hand soothingly upon his shoulder. "Do not fear. They had a long start and the women here can paddle as well as the men. Again, the Iroquois canoe was overloaded at the start, and has the wounded men aboard as well now. Besides, these oak canoes of the Mohawks are not as swift as the Algonquin birch barks which we use. In any case it is impossible to follow, for we have no boat."

"There is one lying there."

"Ah, it will but hold a single man. It is that in which the friar came."

"Then I am going in that! My place is with Adele!" He flung open the door, rushed out, and was about to push off the frail skiff, when some one sprang past him, and with a blow from a hatchet stove in the side of the boat.

"It is my boat," said the friar, throwing down the axe and folding his arms. "I can do what I like with it."

"You fiend! You have ruined us!"

"I have found you and you shall not escape me again."

The hot blood flushed to the soldier's head, and picking up the axe, he took a quick step forward. The light from the open door shone upon the grave, harsh face of the friar, but not a muscle twitched nor a feature changed as he saw the axe whirl up in the hands of a furious man. He only signed himself with the cross, and muttered a Latin prayer under his breath. It was that composure which saved his life. De Catinat hurled down the axe again with a bitter curse, and was turning away from the shattered boat, when in an instant, without a warning, the great door of the manor-house crashed inwards, and a flood of whooping savages burst into the house.

CHAPTER XXXVIII.
THE DINING HALL OF SAINTE MARIE.

What had occurred is easily explained. The watchers in the windows at the front found that it was more than flesh and blood could endure to remain waiting at their posts while the fates of their wives and children were being decided at the back. All was quiet at the stockade, and the Indians appeared to be as absorbed as the Canadians in what was passing upon the river. One by one, therefore, the men on guard had crept away and had assembled at the back to cheer the seaman's shot and to groan as the remaining canoe sped like a bloodhound down the river in the wake of the fugitives. But the savages had one at their head who was as full of wiles and resource as Du Lhut himself. The Flemish Bastard had watched the house from behind the stockade as a dog watches a rat-hole, and he had instantly discovered that the defenders had left their post. With a score of other warriors he raised a great log from the edge of the forest, and crossing the open space unchallenged, he and his men rushed it against the door with such violence as to crack the bar across and tear the wood from the hinges. The first intimation which the survivors had of the attack was the crash of the door, and the screams of two of the negligent watchmen who had been seized and scalped in the hall. The whole basement floor was in the hands of the Indians, and De Catinat and his enemy the friar were cut off from the foot of the stairs.

Fortunately, however, the manor-houses of Canada were built with the one idea of defence against Indians, and even now there were hopes for the defenders. A wooden ladder which could be drawn up in case of need hung down from the upper windows to the ground upon the river-side. De Catinat rushed round to this, followed by the friar. He felt about for the ladder in the darkness. It was gone.

Then indeed his heart sank in despair. Where could he fly to? The boat was destroyed. The stockades lay between him and the forest, and they were in the hands of the Iroquois. Their yells were ringing in his ears. They had not seen him yet, but in a few minutes they must come upon him. Suddenly he heard a voice from somewhere in the darkness above him.

"Give me your gun, lad," it said. "I see the loom of some of the heathen down by the wall."

"It is I. It is I, Amos," cried De Catinat. "Down with the ladder or I am a dead man."

"Have a care. It may be a ruse," said the voice of Du Lhut.

"No, no, I'll answer for it," cried Amos, and an instant later down came the ladder. De Catinat and the friar rushed up it, and they hardly had their feet upon the rungs when a swarm of warriors burst out from the door and poured along the river bank. Two muskets flashed from above, something plopped like a salmon in the water, and next instant the two were among their comrades and the ladder had been drawn up once more.

But it was a very small band who now held the last point to which they could retreat. Only nine of them remained, the seigneur, Du Lhut, the two Americans, the friar, De Catinat, Theuriet the major-domo, and two of the *censitaires*. Wounded, parched, and powder-blackened, they were still filled with the mad courage of desperate men who knew that death could come in no more terrible form than through surrender. The stone staircase ran straight up from the kitchen to the main hall, and the door, which had been barricaded across the lower part by two mattresses, commanded the whole flight. Hoarse whisperings and the click of the cocking of guns from below told that the Iroquois were mustering for a rush.

"Put the lantern by the door," said Du Lhut, "so that it may throw the light upon the stair. There is only room for three to fire, but you can all load and pass the guns. Monsieur Green, will you kneel with me, and you, Jean Duval? If one of us is hit let another take his place at once. Now be ready, for they are coming!"

As he spoke there was a shrill whistle from below, and in an instant the stair was filled with rushing red figures and waving weapons. Bang! Bang! Bang! went the three guns, and then again and again Bang! Bang! Bang! The smoke was so thick in the low-roofed room that they could hardly see to pass the muskets to the eager hands which grasped for them. But no Iroquois had reached the barricade, and there was no patter of their feet now upon the stair. Nothing but an angry snarling and an occasional groan from below. The marksmen were uninjured, but they ceased to fire and waited for the smoke to clear.

And when it cleared they saw how deadly their aim had been at those close quarters. Only nine shots had been fired, and seven Indians were littered up and down on the straight stone stair. Five of them lay motionless, but two tried to crawl slowly back to their friends. Du Lhut and the *censitaire* raised their muskets, and the two crippled men lay still.

"By Saint Anne!" said the old pioneer, as he rammed home another bullet. "If they have our scalps we have sold them at a great price. A hundred squaws will be howling in their villages when they hear of this day's work."

"Ay, they will not forget their welcome at Sainte Marie," said the old nobleman. "I must again express my deep regret, my dear De Catinat, that you and your wife should have been put to such inconvenience when you have been good enough to visit me. I trust that she and the others are safe at the fort by this time."

"May God grant that they are! Oh, I shall never have an easy moment until I see her once more."

"If they are safe we may expect help in the morning, if we can hold out so long. Chambly, the commandant, is not a man to leave a comrade at a pinch."

The cards were still laid out at one end of the table, with the tricks overlapping each other, as they had left them on the previous morning. But there was something else there of more interest to them, for the breakfast had not been cleared away, and they had been fighting all day with hardly bite or sup. Even when face to face with death, Nature still cries out for her dues, and the hungry men turned savagely upon the loaf, the ham, and the cold wild duck. A little cluster of wine bottles stood upon the buffet, and these had their necks knocked off, and were emptied down parched throats. Three men still took their turn, however, to hold the barricade, for they were not to be caught napping again. The yells and screeches of the savages came up to them as though all the wolves of the forest were cooped up in the basement, but the stair was deserted save for the seven motionless figures.

"They will not try to rush us again," said Du Lhut with confidence. "We have taught them too severe a lesson."

"They will set fire to the house."

"It will puzzle them to do that," said the major-domo. "It is solid stone, walls and stair, save only for a few beams of wood, very different from those other cottages."

"Hush!" cried Amos Green, and raised his hand. The yells had died away, and they heard the heavy thud of a mallet beating upon wood.

"What can it be?"

"Some fresh devilry, no doubt."

"I regret to say, messieurs," observed the seigneur, with no abatement of his courtly manner, "that it is my belief that they have learned a lesson from our young friend here, and that they are knocking out the heads of the powder-barrels in the store-room."

But Du Lhut shook his head at the suggestion. "It is not in a Redskin to waste powder," said he. "It is a deal too precious for them to do that. Ah, listen to that!"

The yellings and screechings had begun again, but there was a wilder, madder ring in their shrillness, and they were mingled with snatches of song and bursts of laughter.

"Ha! It is the brandy casks which they have opened," cried Du Lhut. "They were bad before, but they will be fiends out of hell now."

As he spoke there came another burst of whoops, and high above them a voice calling for mercy. With horror in their eyes the survivors glanced from one to the other. A heavy smell of burning flesh rose from below, and still that dreadful voice shrieking and pleading. Then slowly it quavered away and was silent forever.

"Who was it?" whispered De Catinat, his blood running cold in his veins.

"It was Jean Corbeil, I think."

"May God rest his soul! His troubles are over. Would that we were as peaceful as he! Ah, shoot him! Shoot!"

A man had suddenly sprung out at the foot of the stair and had swung his arm as though throwing something. It was the Flemish Bastard. Amos Green's musket flashed, but the savage had sprung back again as rapidly as he appeared. Something splashed down amongst them and rolled across the floor in the lamp-light.

"Down! Down! It is a bomb!" cried De Catinat

But it lay at Du Lhut's feet, and he had seen it clearly. He took a cloth from the table and dropped it over it.

"It is not a bomb," said he quietly, "and it *was* Jean Corbeil who died."

For four hours sounds of riot, of dancing and of revelling rose up from the store-house, and the smell of the open brandy casks filled the whole air. More than once the savages quarrelled and fought among themselves, and it seemed as if they had forgotten their enemies above, but the besieged soon found that if they attempted to presume upon this they were as closely watched as ever. The major-domo, Theuriet, passing between a loop-hole and a light, was killed instantly by a bullet from the stockade, and both Amos and the old seigneur had narrow escapes until they blocked all the windows save that which overlooked the river. There was no danger from this one, and, as day was already breaking once more, one or other of the party was forever straining their eyes down the stream in search of the expected succour.

Slowly the light crept up the eastern sky, a little line of pearl, then a band of pink, broadening, stretching, spreading, until it shot its warm colour across the heavens, tinging the edges of the drifting clouds. Over the woodlands lay a thin gray vapour, the tops of the high oaks jutting out like dim islands from the sea of haze. Gradually as the light increased the mist shredded off into little ragged wisps, which thinned and drifted away, until at last, as the sun pushed its glowing edge over the eastern forests, it gleamed upon the reds and oranges and purples of the fading leaves, and upon the broad blue river which curled away to the northward. De Catinat, as he stood at the window looking out, was breathing in the healthy resinous scent of the trees, mingled with the damp heavy odour of the wet earth, when suddenly his eyes fell upon a dark spot upon the river to the north of them. "There is a canoe coming down!" he cried. In an instant they had all rushed to the opening, but Du Lhut sprang after them, and pulled them angrily towards the door.

"Do you wish to die before your time?" he cried.

"Ay, ay!" said Captain Ephraim, who understood the gesture if not the words. "We must leave a watch on deck. Amos, lad, lie here with me and be ready if they show."

The two Americans and the old pioneer held the barricade, while the eyes of all the others were turned upon the approaching boat. A groan broke suddenly from the only surviving *censitaire*.

"It is an Iroquois canoe!" he cried.

"Impossible!"

"Alas, your excellency, it is so, and it is the same one which passed us last night."

"Ah, then the women have escaped them."

"I trust so. But alas, seigneur, I fear that there are more in the canoe now than when they passed us."

The little group of survivors waited in breathless anxiety while the canoe sped swiftly up the river, with a line of foam on either side of her, and a long forked swirl in the waters behind. They could see that she appeared to be very crowded, but they remembered that the wounded of the other boat were aboard her. On she shot and on, until as she came abreast of the fort she swung round, and the rowers raised their paddles and burst into a shrill yell of derision. The stern of the canoe was turned towards them now, and they saw that two women were seated in it. Even at that distance there was no mistaking the sweet pale face or the dark queenly one beside it. The one was Onega and the other was Adele.

CHAPTER XXXIX.
THE TWO SWIMMERS.

Charles de la Noue, Seigneur de Sainte Marie, was a hard and self-contained man, but a groan and a bitter curse burst from him when he saw his Indian wife in the hands of her kinsmen, from whom she could hope for little mercy. Yet even now his old-fashioned courtesy to his guest had made him turn to De Catinat with some words of sympathy, when there was a clatter of wood, something darkened the light of the window, and the young soldier was gone. Without a word he had lowered the ladder and was clambering down it with frantic haste. Then as his feet touched the ground he signalled to his comrades to draw it up again, and dashing into the river he swam towards the canoe. Without arms and without a plan he had but the one thought that his place was by the side of his wife in this, the hour of her danger. Fate should bring him what it brought her, and he swore to himself, as he clove a way with his strong arms, that whether it were life or death they should still share it together.

But there was another whose view of duty led him from safety into the face of danger. All night the Franciscan had watched De Catinat as a miser watches his treasure, filled with the thought that this heretic was the one little seed which might spread and spread until it choked the chosen vineyard of the Church. Now when he saw him rush so suddenly down the ladder, every fear was banished from his mind save the overpowering one that he was about to lose his precious charge. He, too, clambered down at the very heels of his prisoner, and rushed into the stream not ten paces behind him.

And so the watchers at the window saw the strangest of sights. There, in mid-stream, lay the canoe, with a ring of dark warriors clustering in the stern, and the two women crouching in the midst of them. Swimming madly towards them was De Catinat, rising to the shoulders with the strength of every stroke, and behind him again was the tonsured head of the friar, with his brown capote and long trailing gown floating upon the surface of the water behind him. But in his zeal he had thought too little of his own powers. He was a good swimmer, but he was weighted and hampered by his unwieldy clothes. Slower and slower grew his stroke, lower and lower his head, until at last with a great shriek of *In manus tuas, Domine!* he threw up his hands, and vanished in the swirl of the river. A minute later the watchers, hoarse with screaming to him to return, saw De Catinat pulled aboard the Iroquois canoe, which was instantly turned and continued its course up the river.

"My God!" cried Amos hoarsely. "They have taken him. He is lost."

"I have seen some strange things in these forty years, but never the like of that!" said Du Lhut.

The seigneur took a little pinch of snuff from his gold box, and flicked the wandering grains from his shirt-front with his dainty lace handkerchief.

"Monsieur de Catinat has acted like a gentleman of France," said he. "If I could swim now as I did thirty years ago, I should be by his side."

Du Lhut glanced round him and shook his head. "We are only six now," said he. "I fear they are up to some devilry because they are so very still."

"They are leaving the house!" cried the *censitaire*, who was peeping through one of the side windows. "What can it mean? Holy Virgin, is it possible that we are saved? See how they throng through the trees. They are making for the canoe. Now they are waving their arms and pointing."

"There is the gray hat of that mongrel devil amongst them," said the captain. "I would try a shot upon him were it not a waste of powder and lead."

"I have hit the mark at as long a range," said Amos, pushing his long brown gun through a chink in the barricade which they had thrown across the lower half of the window. "I would give my next year's trade to bring him down."

"It is forty paces further than my musket would carry," remarked Du Lhut, "but I have seen the English shoot a great way with those long guns."

Amos took a steady aim, resting his gun upon the window sill, and fired. A shout of delight burst from the little knot of survivors. The Flemish Bastard had fallen. But he was on his feet again in an instant and shook his hand defiantly at the window.

"Curse it!" cried Amos bitterly, in English. "I have hit him with a spent ball. As well strike him with a pebble."

"Nay, curse not, Amos, lad, but try him again with another pinch of powder if your gun will stand it."

The woodsman thrust in a full charge, and chose a well-rounded bullet from his bag, but when he looked again both the Bastard and his warriors had disappeared. On the river the single Iroquois canoe which held the captives was speeding south as swiftly as twenty paddles could drive it, but save this one dark streak upon the blue stream, not a sign was to be seen of their enemies. They had vanished as if they had been an evil dream. There was the bullet-spotted stockade, the litter of dead bodies inside it, the burned and roofless cottages, but the silent woods lay gleaming in the morning sunshine as quiet and peaceful as if no hell-burst of fiends had ever broken out from them.

"By my faith, I believe that they have gone!" cried the seigneur.

"Take care that it is not a ruse," said Du Lhut. "Why should they fly before six men when they have conquered sixty?"

But the *censitaire* had looked out of the other window, and in an instant he was down upon his knees with his hands in the air, and his powder blackened face turned upwards, pattering out prayers and thanksgivings. His five comrades rushed across the room and burst into a shriek of joy. The upper reach of the river was covered with a flotilla of canoes from which the sun struck quick flashes as it shone upon the musket-barrels and trappings of the crews. Already they could see the white coats of the regulars, the brown tunics of the *coureurs-de-bois*, and the gaudy colours of the Hurons and Algonquins. On they swept, dotting the whole breadth of the river, and growing larger every instant, while far away on the southern bend, the Iroquois canoe was a mere moving dot which had shot away to the farther side and lost itself presently under the shadow of the trees. Another minute and the survivors were out upon the bank, waving their caps in the air, while the prows of the first of their rescuers were already grating upon the pebbles. In the stern of the very foremost canoe sat a wizened little man with a large brown wig, and a gilt-headed rapier laid across his knees. He sprang out as the keel touched bottom, splashing through the shallow water with his high leather boots, and rushing up to the seigneur, he flung himself into his arms.

"My dear Charles," he cried, "you have held your house like a hero. What, only six of you! Tut, tut, this has been a bloody business!"

"I knew that you would not desert a comrade, Chambly. We have saved the house, but our losses have been terrible. My son is dead. My wife is in that Iroquois canoe in front of you."

The commandant of Fort St. Louis pressed his friend's hand in silent sympathy.

"The others arrived all safe," he said at last. "Only that one was taken, on account of the breaking of a paddle. Three were drowned and two captured. There was a French lady in it, I understand, as well as madame."

"Yes, and they have taken her husband as well."

"Ah, poor souls! Well, if you are strong enough to join us, you and your friends, we shall follow after them without the loss of an instant. Ten of my men will remain to guard the house, and you can have their canoe. Jump in then, and forward, for life and death may hang upon our speed!"

CHAPTER XL.
THE END.

The Iroquois had not treated De Catinat harshly when they dragged him from the water into their canoe. So incomprehensible was it to them why any man should voluntarily leave a place of safety in order to put himself in their power that they could only set it down to madness, a malady which inspires awe and respect among the Indians. They did not even tie his wrists, for why should he attempt to escape when he had come of his own free will? Two warriors passed their hands over him, to be sure that he was unarmed, and he was then thrust down between the two women, while the canoe darted in towards the bank to tell the others that the St. Louis garrison was coming up the stream. Then it steered out again, and made its way swiftly up the centre of the river. Adele was deadly pale and her hand, as her husband laid his upon it, was as cold as marble.

"My darling," he whispered, "tell me that all is well with you—that you are unhurt!"

"Oh, Amory, why did you come? Why did you come, Amory? Oh, I think I could have borne anything, but if they hurt you I could not bear that."

"How could I stay behind when I knew that you were in their hands? I should have gone mad!"

"Ah, it was my one consolation to think that you were safe."

"No, no, we have gone through so much together that we cannot part now. What is death, Adele? Why should we be afraid of it?"

"I am not afraid of it."

"And I am not afraid of it. Things will come about as God wills it, and what He wills must in the end be the best. If we live, then we have this memory in common. If we die, then we go hand-in-hand into another life. Courage, my own, all will be well with us."

"Tell me, monsieur," said Onega, "is my lord still living?"

"Yes, he is alive and well."

"It is good. He is a great chief, and I have never been sorry, not even now, that I have wedded with one who was not of my own people. But ah, my son! Who shall give my son back to me? He was like the young sapling, so straight and so strong! Who could run with him, or leap with him, or swim with him? Ere that sun shines again we shall all be dead, and my heart is glad, for I shall see my boy once more."

The Iroquois paddles had bent to their work until a good ten miles lay between them and Sainte Marie. Then they ran the canoe into a little creek upon their own side of the river, and sprang out of her, dragging the prisoners after them. The canoe was carried on the shoulders of eight men some distance into the wood, where they concealed it between two fallen trees, heaping a litter of branches over it to screen it from view. Then, after a short council, they started through the forest, walking in single file, with their three prisoners in the middle. There were fifteen warriors in all, eight in front and seven behind, all armed with muskets and as swift-footed as deer, so that escape was out of the question. They could but follow on, and wait in patience for whatever might befall them.

All day they pursued their dreary march, picking their way through vast morasses, skirting the borders of blue woodland lakes where the gray stork flapped heavily up from the reeds at their approach, or plunging into dark belts of woodland where it is always twilight, and where the falling of the wild chestnuts and the chatter of the squirrels a hundred feet above their heads were the only sounds which broke the silence. Onega had the endurance of the Indians themselves, but Adele, in spite of her former journeys, was footsore and weary before evening. It was a relief to De Catinat, therefore, when the red glow of a great fire beat suddenly through the tree-trunks, and they came upon an Indian camp in which was assembled the greater part of the war-party which had been driven from Sainte Marie. Here, too, were a number of the squaws who had come from the Mohawk and Cayuga villages in order to be nearer to the warriors. Wigwams had been erected all round in a circle, and before each of them were the fires with kettles slung upon a tripod of sticks in which the evening meal was being cooked. In the centre of all was a very fierce fire which had been made of brushwood placed in a circle, so as to leave a clear space of twelve feet in the middle. A pole stood up in the centre of this clearing, and something all mottled with red and black was tied up against it. De Catinat stepped swiftly in front of Adele that she might not see the dreadful thing, but he was too late. She shuddered, and drew a quick breath between her pale lips, but no sound escaped her.

"They have begun already, then," said Onega composedly. "Well, it will be our turn next, and we shall show them that we know how to die."

"They have not ill-used us yet," said De Catinat. "Perhaps they will keep us for ransom or exchange."

The Indian woman shook her head. "Do not deceive yourself by any such hope," said she. "When they are as gentle as they have been with you it is ever a sign that you are reserved for the torture. Your wife will be married to one of their chiefs, but you and I must die, for you are a warrior, and I am too old for a squaw."

Married to an Iroquois! Those dreadful words shot a pang through both their hearts which no thought of death could have done. De Catinat's head dropped forward upon his chest, and he staggered and would have fallen had Adele not caught him by the arm.

"Do not fear, dear Amory," she whispered. "Other things may happen but not that, for I swear to you that I shall not survive you. No, it may be sin or it may not, but if death will not come to me, I will go to it."

De Catinat looked down at the gentle face which had set now into the hard lines of an immutable resolve. He knew that it would be as she had said, and that, come what might, that last outrage would not befall them. Could he ever have believed that the time would come when it would send a thrill of joy through his heart to know that his wife would die?

As they entered the Iroquois village the squaws and warriors had rushed towards them, and they passed through a double line of hideous faces which jeered and jibed and howled at them as they passed. Their escort led them through this rabble and conducted them to a hut which stood apart. It was empty, save for some willow fishing-nets hanging at the side, and a heap of pumpkins stored in the corner.

"The chiefs will come and will decide upon what is to be done with us," said Onega. "Here they are coming now, and you will soon see that I am right, for I know the ways of my own people."

An instant later an old war-chief, accompanied by two younger braves and by the bearded half-Dutch Iroquois who had led the attack upon the manor-house, strolled over and stood in the doorway, looking in at the prisoners, and shooting little guttural sentences at each other. The totems of the Hawk, the Wolf, the Bear, and the Snake showed that they each represented one of the great families of the Nation. The Bastard was smoking a stone pipe, and yet it was he who talked the most, arguing apparently with one of the younger savages, who seemed to come round at last to his opinion. Finally the old chief said a few short stern words, and the matter appeared to be settled.

"And you, you beldame," said the Bastard in French to the Iroquois woman, "you will have a lesson this night which will teach you to side against your own people."

"You half-bred mongrel," replied the fearless old woman, "you should take that hat from your head when you speak to one in whose veins runs the best blood of the Onondagas. You a warrior? You who, with a thousand at your back, could not make your way into a little house with a few poor husbandmen within it! It is no wonder that your father's people have cast you out! Go back and work at the beads, or play at the game of plum-stones, for some day in the woods you might meet with a man, and so bring disgrace upon the nation which has taken you in!"

The evil face of the Bastard grew livid as he listened to the scornful words which were hissed at him by the captive. He strode across to her, and taking her hand he thrust her forefinger into the burning bowl of his pipe. She made no effort to remove it, but sat with a perfectly set face for a minute or more, looking out through the open door at the evening sunlight and the little groups of chattering Indians. He had watched her keenly in the hope of hearing a cry, or seeing some spasm of agony upon her face, but at last, with a curse, he dashed down her hand and strode from the hut. She thrust her charred finger into her bosom and laughed.

"He is a good-for-nought!" she cried. "He does not even know how to torture. Now, I could have got a cry out of him. I am sure of it. But you— monsieur, you are very white!"

"It was the sight of such a hellish deed. Ah, if we were but set face to face, I with my sword, he with what weapon he chose, by God, he should pay for it with his heart's blood."

The Indian woman seemed surprised. "It is strange to me," she said, "that you should think of what befalls me when you are yourselves under the same shadow. But our fate will be as I said."

"Ah!"

"You and I are to die at the stake. She is to be given to the dog who has left us."

"Ah!"

"Adele! Adele! What shall I do!" He tore his hair in his helplessness and distraction.

"No, no, fear not, Amory, for my heart will not fail me. What is the pang of death if it binds us together?"

"The younger chief pleaded for you, saying that the *Mitche Manitou* had stricken you with madness, as could be seen by your swimming to their canoe, and that a blight would fall upon the nation if you were led to the stake. But this Bastard said that love came often like madness among the pale-faces, and that it was that alone which had driven you. Then it was agreed that you should die and that she should go to his wigwam, since he had led the war-party. As for me, their hearts were bitter against me, and I also am to die by the pine splinters."

De Catinat breathed a prayer that he might meet his fate like a soldier and a gentleman.

"When is it to be?" he asked.

"Now! At once! They have gone to make all ready! But you have time yet, for I am to go first."

"Amory, Amory, could we not die together now?" cried Adele, throwing her arms round her husband. "If it be sin, it is surely a sin which will be forgiven us. Let us go, dear. Let us leave these dreadful people and this cruel world and turn where we shall find peace."

The Indian woman's eyes flashed with satisfaction.

"You have spoken well, White Lily," said she. "Why should you wait until it is their pleasure to pluck you. See, already the glare of their fire beats upon the tree-trunks, and you can hear the howlings of those who thirst for your blood. If you die by your own hands, they will be robbed of their spectacle, and their chief will have lost his bride. So you will be the victors in the end, and they the vanquished. You have said rightly, White Lily. There lies the only path for you!"

"But how to take it?"

Onega glanced keenly at the two warriors who stood as sentinels at the door of the hut. They had turned away, absorbed in the horrible preparations which were going on. Then she rummaged deeply within the folds of her loose gown and pulled out a small pistol with two brass barrels and double triggers in the form of winged dragons. It was only a toy to look at, all carved and scrolled and graven with the choicest work of the Paris gunsmith. For its beauty the seigneur had bought it at his last visit to Quebec, and yet it might be useful, too, and it was loaded in both barrels.

"I meant to use it on myself," said she, as she slipped it into the hand of De Catinat. "But now I am minded to show them that I can die as an Onondaga should die, and that I am worthy to have the blood of their chiefs in my veins. Take it, for I swear that I will not use it myself, unless it be to fire both bullets into that Bastard's heart."

A flush of joy shot over De Catinat as his fingers closed round the pistol. Here was indeed a key to unlock the gates of peace. Adele laid her cheek against his shoulder and laughed with pleasure.

"You will forgive me, dear," he whispered.

"Forgive you! I bless you, and love you with my whole heart and soul. Clasp me close, darling, and say one prayer before you do it."

They had sunk on their knees together when three warriors entered the hut and said a few abrupt words to their country-woman. She rose with a smile.

"They are waiting for me," said she. "You shall see, White Lily, and you also, monsieur, how well I know what is due to my position. Farewell, and remember Onega!"

She smiled again, and walked from the hut amidst the warriors with the quick firm step of a queen who sweeps to a throne.

"Now, Amory!" whispered Adele, closing her eyes, and nestling still closer to him.

He raised the pistol, and then, with a quick sudden intaking of the breath, he dropped it, and knelt with glaring eyes looking up at a tree which faced the open door of the hut.

It was a beech-tree, exceedingly old and gnarled, with its bark hanging down in strips and its whole trunk spotted with moss and mould. Some ten feet above the ground the main trunk divided into two, and in the fork thus formed a hand had suddenly appeared, a large reddish hand, which shook frantically from side to side in passionate dissuasion. The next instant, as the two captives still stared in amazement, the hand disappeared behind the trunk again and a face appeared in its place, which still shook from side to side as resolutely as its forerunner. It was impossible to mistake that mahogany, wrinkled skin, the huge bristling eyebrows, or the little glistening eyes. It was Captain Ephraim Savage of Boston!

And even as they stared and wondered a sudden shrill whistle burst out from the depths of the forest, and in a moment every bush and thicket and patch of brushwood were spouting fire and smoke, while the snarl of the musketry ran round the whole glade, and the storm of bullets whizzed and pelted among the yelling savages. The Iroquois' sentinels had been drawn in by their bloodthirsty craving to see the prisoners die, and now the Canadians were upon them, and they were hemmed in by a ring of fire. First one way and then another they rushed, to be met always by the same blast of death, until finding at last some gap in the attack they streamed through, like sheep through a broken fence, and rushed madly away through the forest, with the bullets of their pursuers still singing about their ears, until the whistle sounded again to recall the woodsmen from the chase.

But there was one savage who had found work to do before he fled. The Flemish Bastard had preferred his vengeance to his safety! Rushing at Onega, he buried his tomahawk in her brain, and then, yelling his war-cry, he waved the blood-stained weapon above his head, and flew into the hut where the prisoners still knelt. De Catinat saw him coming, and a mad joy glistened in his eyes. He rose to meet him, and as he rushed in he fired both barrels of his pistol into the Bastard's face. An instant later a swarm of Canadians had rushed over the writhing bodies, the captives felt warm friendly hands which grasped their own, and looking upon the smiling, well-known faces of Amos Green, Savage, and Du Lhut, they knew that peace had come to them at last.

And so the refugees came to the end of the toils of their journey, for that winter was spent by them in peace at Fort St. Louis, and in the spring, the Iroquois having carried the war to the Upper St. Lawrence, the travellers were able to descend into the English provinces, and so to make their way down the Hudson to New York, where a warm welcome awaited them from the family of Amos Green. The friendship between the two men was now so cemented together by common memories and common danger that they soon became partners in fur-trading, and the name of the Frenchman came at last to be as familiar in the mountains of Maine and on the slopes of the Alleghanies as it had once been in the *salons* and corridors of Versailles. In time De Catinat built a house on Staten Island, where many of his fellow-refugees had settled, and much of what he won from his fur-trading was spent in the endeavour to help his struggling Huguenot brothers. Amos Green had married a Dutch maiden of Schenectady, and as Adele and she became inseparable friends, the marriage served to draw closer the ties of love which held the two families together.

As to Captain Ephraim Savage, he returned safely to his beloved Boston, where he fulfilled his ambition by building himself a fair brick house upon the rising ground in the northern part of the city, whence he could look down both upon the shipping in the river and the bay. There he lived, much respected by his townsfolk, who made him selectman and alderman, and gave him the command of a goodly ship when Sir William Phips made his attack upon Quebec, and found that the old Lion Frontenac was not to be driven from his lair. So, honoured by all, the old seaman lived to an age which carried him deep into the next century, when he could already see with his dim eyes something of the growing greatness of his country.

The manor-house of Sainte Marie was soon restored to its former prosperity, but its seigneur was from the day that he lost his wife and son a changed man. He grew leaner, fiercer, less human, forever heading parties which made their way into the Iroquois woods and which outrivalled the savages themselves in the terrible nature of their deeds. A day came at last when he sallied out upon one of these expeditions, from which neither he nor any of his men ever returned. Many a terrible secret is hid by those silent woods, and the fate of Charles de la Noue, Seigneur de Sainte Marie, is among them.